Axe Backwards
The Maine Lumberjacks
Book 4

Daphne Elliot

Copyright © 2025 by Daphne Elliot

All rights reserved.

No part of this book may be reproduced in any form or by any electronic or mechanical means, including information storage and retrieval systems, without prior written permission from the publisher. Without in any way limiting the author's exclusive rights under copyright, any use of this publication to "train" generative artificial intelligence ("AI") to generate text is expressly prohibited.

This book is a work of fiction, created without the use of AI technology. The names, characters, places, and events in this book are the product of the author's imagination, and any resemblance to actual events or places or persons, living or dead, is entirely coincidental.

Published by Melody Publishing, LLC

Editing by Beth Lawton at VB Edits

Cover by 50's Vintage Dame

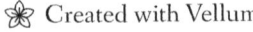 Created with Vellum

To the people who've been told they are "too much." You're not difficult, intimidating, over the top, or unreasonable. You're a fucking supernova. Never dull your shine for lesser people who wish to tear you down. Never lower your standards, and never, ever stop sharing your gifts with the world.

Foreword

This book contains themes that may be difficult for some readers. This book depicts infertility and discusses deaths that occur off-page.

Chapter 1
Victoria

"Did you hear me?"

Pulse quickening, I surveyed the coffee shop, wishing the reclaimed oak floors would open up and swallow me whole.

"Memorial Day."

Panic was settling in. This had to be a hallucination. I didn't sleep much these days, and to make matters worse, the people who'd moved into the apartment above mine had been making an unholy racket last night, making it impossible to get even my usual three or four hours.

I grasped the top of the cute wooden booth, steadying myself. The Caffeinated Moose was a hipster coffee shop that had opened about a year ago. While I'd worried at first that our little logging community might not welcome exposed ductwork and six-dollar lattes, the place had been steadily busy since opening day.

Raeanna had a handful of employees these days, and they almost always sold out of their signature blueberry lemon scones by nine.

I'd stopped here for a good-luck Americano before my meeting, but clearly, it had done me no good.

"I'm pregnant," she repeated, her voice high-pitched and defiant.

"Congrats," I blurted out as tears stung my eyes and my throat tightened.

She was speaking, but I was too intent on remaining conscious to process her words.

This could not be happening. Not today.

My brain flooded with the all-consuming guilt I'd worked so hard to heal from. The constant barrage of questions and concern, friends holding their babies and saying "you're next!" and well-meaning relatives questioning why we hadn't started a family yet.

Alexandra babbled on about her due date. In winter maybe? Then she made a comment about our mother. Another regarding her wedding, which she'd been talking about for months. My mind could not process any of it.

My body was broken. Unable to fulfill its purpose. And now she was pregnant?

Did she really have to tell me this *today* of all days?

"I'm walking into a meeting." My words were curt, but it was all I could muster. "Can I call you back later?"

She continued speaking, but I didn't register anything. Not when my world was collapsing around me. I pushed my way through the busy morning crowd and into the bathroom.

The old dead bolt was brass and heavy, but I managed to get it to turn. Once I was safely ensconced and alone, I cried. I didn't outright sob. No, I'd save that for later. For now, I let the tears flow, knowing that holding them back would only hurt more.

Axe Backwards

Alexandra and Graham were having a baby.

Together.

My baby sister.

And my ex-husband.

I flattened a hand against the wall to brace myself, willing my lungs to take in oxygen.

Breathe. Just breathe.

In my experience, when a day starts out this badly, it'll only get worse. Even a minor inconvenience can quickly spiral into full-blown disaster with the right set of circumstances.

I closed my eyes, focusing on nothing but my breath. There was time to be angry and hurt and betrayed. So much time for that.

Later. Right now, I was in public, and I was scheduled to attend an important meeting in fifteen minutes.

So I took ten cleansing breaths and then rooted around in my purse for the mascara and lip gloss I kept for emergencies.

Fix your face and get on with it.

My eyes were red and my face was blotchy, but I had no choice but to pull myself together.

Business mode. People are depending on you.

I did my best to fix my makeup, then I brushed my hair and smoothed down my skirt. After years in corporate PR, one would think I'd be a master at this.

Pitching, schmoozing, convincing people to open their wallets.

I used to eat up city sidewalks in four-inch heels.

I raked in six figures while using my expense account to

its fullest, dining and drinking and shopping in the finest places.

My confidence rivaled that of ten mediocre men. Nothing and no one stood in my way.

Regardless of the news I had just received, I had to show up and do my damn job. This was my purpose, and it was the only thing I had left.

Yes, meetings like this were the worst part of the job, but they couldn't be avoided. The food pantry had only survived the last year because of the generosity of Owen Hebert, who sent a construction crew to replace our roof pro bono and made a sizable donation on top of that.

As huge as the gesture was, it wasn't enough. There was never enough.

The summer lumberjack fundraiser had helped, but now that it was April, we were running out of those funds. We needed a big infusion of cash before the end of the year.

The food pantry's resources were needed year-round, but the urgency grew during the summer when local kids couldn't get breakfast and lunch at school.

A mobile lunch truck would help tremendously. I'd seen it in Boston and in other bigger towns. The food bank or another organization would park at a playground or community space, giving families access to meals and supplies in multiple locations.

Doing so put less stress on the physical building and went directly to the kids who needed to eat.

It's go time. Get out there and get the money. You can do this.

With a slow breath out, I turned and grasped the door handle with one hand and went for the dead bolt with the other. I would crush this meeting and then go home and feel my feelings.

Only an ancient oak door stood in my way. And it wasn't opening.

I clutched the tarnished brass dead bolt and twisted my wrist.

It didn't budge.

I used both hands next, wrenching it back as hard as I could.

In response, there was a snapping sound, and the turn piece finally moved.

But the dead bolt was stuck in the doorframe.

Fuck.

I wiggled the turn piece back and forth, but the damn dead bolt, which was probably older than electricity, was fully engaged, anchoring the door to the frame.

Tremors racked my body. They were slight at first, just enough to make my hands shake. Fuck, fuck, fuck.

Then my throat went tight. This could not be happening.

Panting now, I checked my smartwatch. I only had eleven minutes to make it across Main Street and get to the meeting.

Think, Vic, think.

I banged on the door, putting my shoulder into it. God help me.

It was no use. I needed help.

I dug my phone out of my purse and googled the number for the Caffeinated Moose. I'd calmly tell them what happened, and someone would help me out.

It rang and rang. No one picked up.

Daphne Elliot

It was morning rush; it was so loud out there. Even if poor Raeanna could hear the phone, she probably didn't have time to pick it up.

I closed my eyes, my mind flipping through the faces of townsfolk who could help.

Loretta's image snagged my attention. Yes. She was sitting by the window with a group of ladies who were knitting and sipping tea.

Clearing my throat, I pulled up her contact information and called.

"Victoria, how are you?" she asked, a buzz of the people in the background.

Loretta had been president of our local bank before she retired and found her true purpose as a town gossip and busybody. Even I had to admit that woman knew how to get shit done.

"I'm here," I said, finding it hard to speak. "I'm at the Caffeinated Moose."

"That's lovely."

"I'm locked in the bathroom."

A small gasp escaped her. "Oh dear."

"Can you tell Raeanna that I need help? The lock on the door broke."

"Of course. Don't panic, sweetie. We'll figure it out. Are you hurt?"

"No."

After I disconnected the call, I waited, once again focusing on my breathing.

I rubbed my temples. I was not canceling this meeting. Aunt Lou was struggling, and I'd promised her that I would keep everyone in this county fed.

Axe Backwards

The woman had been single-handedly running the food pantry for thirty years, and I had a fucking MBA. Surely I could solicit a few donations from the local rich assholes.

Except I had a heavy wooden door standing between me and my objective.

"Vic?" Raeanna called as the door shook a little. "We're working on getting you out. Looks like the lock is broken. I called the fire department, but they're out on a call."

I banged my head gently against the solid wood. Of course they were. This was a tiny town. The entire Lovewell fire department was probably out rescuing a cat from a tree.

I pinched the bridge of my nose, conceding defeat. I'd have to call Charles Huxley's office and reschedule. I got the impression he liked to feel important by toying with the plebs, of which I was one, so I'd had to jump through hoops to meet with him, and it had taken months to get on his calendar.

But he was a powerful guy with a lot of connections. As a former lieutenant governor and owner of a large, successful construction company, he was an important ally in the fight against food insecurity.

Fuck.

Motherfucking door.

After my sister's phone call, I should have expected a ridiculous scenario like this. I should have been prepared to find a stupid, broken dead bolt standing between me and what I hoped was a big donation.

I was pulling up the number to Mr. Huxley's office when a deep, muffled voice called out.

"Ma'am? I'm going to take the door down. You okay in there?"

"Yes," I shouted. Excellent. I guess the fire department had made it after all.

"Stand as far from the door as you can and face the wall. There may be debris."

The room wasn't large, but I went to the far corner, next to the toilet, and turned around. With my luck, I'd end up with wood shards in my ass.

A loud crack startled me.

It was followed by a splintering sound.

Good.

Then another.

"That's a good one," the deep voice said.

The comment was followed by a grunt and then a big thump.

I peered over my shoulder, finding several pieces of wood on the floor between me and the door.

"Please face the wall, ma'am," the voice commanded.

I did as I was told, but not before catching sight of a muscular torso in a tight T-shirt. The voice was familiar, but I couldn't place it.

He didn't sound like Chief Mitchell. Or Matt Graves or Lieutenant Vargas. I thought I knew all the firemen in town.

A loud crash echoed through the room, making me jump, but I forced myself not to turn.

"That was the lock housing," the man on the other side of the door said. "You can come out now."

I turned and took in the damage. He'd cut through the doorframe with an axe, then knocked out the lock. As he pushed what was left of the door open with a gloved hand, several pieces fell away. He pulled back the shards, then a muscled forearm covered with tattoos appeared.

Axe Backwards

A wave of gratitude flooded me. *Who was this guy?*

He, along with a few other people, cleared the rest of the debris. Then he reached out to me.

I took his offered hand, stepping over a pile of splintered wood on the tile floor.

In the hallway, I looked up at my rescuer. He was tall, and his sandy brown hair fell over his bright blue eyes. Where I expected turnout gear, he was wearing a tight black T-shirt and a pair of cargo pants made of Gore-Tex or some other expensive high-tech fabric.

Probably a hiker or adrenaline junky passing through town.

More and more often, tourists had been coming to Lovewell. This town was finally putting itself on the map as a gateway to the Northern Maine wilderness.

On second thought, this guy was familiar. And by the way his blue eyes widened when he took me in, he knew me too.

"You okay, Victoria?" he asked, squeezing my hand.

Only then did it hit me.

Chapter 2
Noah

Victoria Randolph.

Wow. It had been years.

I hadn't thought of her in a while, but in my mind, I pictured her as the smiling captain of the soccer team. She had a bouncy ponytail and was always wearing athletic shorts.

The pretty, sporty girl. The girl everyone liked.

The woman currently scowling at me and clinging to my forearm?

She was different.

Mature. Beautiful. Intimidating.

And furious.

"Who are you? Where is the fire department?"

Before I could respond, Raeanna pushed past me and gripped her by the upper arms.

"Oh my God, Vic. Are you okay?" She pulled her into a hug. "That door is probably a million years old. I'm so sorry."

"I'm okay," Victoria said slowly, staring at me as I took a step back, then another.

Daphne Elliot

Raeanna hummed, unconvinced. "Thank God Noah was here and had an axe in his truck."

"Noah Hebert?" Victoria's eyes widened as if she'd only now realized who I was.

"At your service," I replied with a smirk.

We assessed one another for what seemed like an eternity while my mind spun wildly, cataloging every detail I knew about her.

Her glossy dark hair fell past her shoulders, and she was dressed in black. Dressy black. Businesslike.

Her lips were glossy and a deep red.

She looked completely different and yet somehow the same as she had in high school.

I was still memorizing her features when she looked away, her cheeks going pink.

"I'm so sorry," she said to Rae. "I'll pay for the damage. But I've got to run to this meeting." She checked her watch, ignoring me completely.

"That door has been a pain in my ass since I opened the shop. No need to pay for damages. Where are you headed?"

"Across the square. I have a meeting with Huxley."

I didn't know who Huxley was, but by the way Rae herded her down the hall, it was clear she understood the gravity.

"You better run. We'll clean up here. When your meeting is over, come back for lunch. It's on me, okay?"

With a nod, Victoria shuffled for the exit. Frozen to the spot, I watched her as she weaved her way through the crowd of gawking townsfolk and out the door before taking off at a sprint down the sidewalk.

Rae put a hand on my arm, breaking the spell.

Axe Backwards

"Thank you," she said, her tone sincere. "I can't believe that happened."

I smiled down at her. She was a tiny woman in her forties with curly auburn hair tied back with a bandanna. I'd only met her a few days ago, but Tess and I had been here every day since, so we'd become friendly.

Her kids were school-aged, but she'd already brought over a few toys and board books for Tess. She was one of the most thoughtful people I'd encountered in a long time.

"Let me clean up and help you fix it," I said.

"No, no. I'll do it. I'll call Mark and have him hit the hardware store after the field trip. He's chaperoning the fourth-grade visit to Baxter State Park. It's days like this I'm glad I married someone handy."

She was already picking up scraps of wood, and one of the staff members, a young guy with spiked blue hair and a nose ring, produced a large black trash bag.

I ignored her refusal of help and took the broom the guy brought with him as well.

Once the big pieces had been disposed of and I'd swept up the shards of wood, she blocked off the door.

After we put everything away, I headed back to the bay window where my mother was entertaining my daughter, who was currently mouthing on a chocolate chip cookie the size of her face.

"Seriously? It's nine a.m."

With a casual shrug, my mother brought her maple latte to her lips. "I did what I had to do to keep her calm while you went off to be a hero. Who could resist this face?"

She squeezed Tess's cheek, making her giggle.

"Yeah, yeah." I slid into my seat and sipped my now cold coffee. "You enjoy spoiling her."

Smiling wide, she bounced Tess on her knee. "Of course I do. I did my time parenting you six hooligans. Now I get to spoil the grandbabies and do what I want."

She loved being a grandma, and when I arrived with Tess in tow, she jumped right in to help. My niece Merry had been the only grandchild for more than a decade, but these days there was a Hebert baby boom. Finn's son Thor was only a month older than Tess and Gus's daughter Simone had arrived two weeks ago. Debbie Hebert had definitely found her purpose in spoiling her grandkids.

"Now, I want to—"

"Mom." I held up a hand. "I love you, but no."

"I have so much room." She pleaded.

"Our apartment is great. We've got everything we need. I appreciate all your help, but I'm doing this myself."

Despite what I kept telling her, the apartment wasn't actually all that great. Or particularly spacious. But it was good enough for now. My older brother Finn had lived there for a while after he was discharged from the Navy, so he'd helped connect me with the landlord.

Tess and I were still getting settled, but we'd be comfortable. I loved my mom, but I hadn't lived with her since high school, and being back in this town was hard enough without sleeping in my childhood bedroom.

My world had imploded last year, upending every single part of my life. And while I was scared shitless, I was determined to figure it out.

So space was necessary.

"And you're sure you're okay?"

Axe Backwards

I nodded, patting her hand.

"Please know that you're always welcome. It's still your home. Hell, I only got Cole out six months ago."

My chest pinched at the affection in her teasing tone. In addition to mothering her five sons, my mom had also let my half brother move in after he was injured and his pro hockey career ended.

Cole was the product of an affair between my father and his assistant. When Tammi got pregnant, my dad left us to marry her. Yet my mom had been more of a parent to Cole than either of his biological parents ever were.

That was the essence of Debbie Hebert right there. Total saint.

And one of the many reasons why, after the legal custody stuff was finalized in California, I headed east. For more than a decade, I'd wanted nothing to do with this town, but I was a dad now, and I knew Tess would be surrounded by love here.

Given what she'd been through, all the trauma and the loss of her parents, the least I could do was give her as much love as I could find.

Eager to move on to a topic that did not include our living situation, I cleared my throat.

"Mom, that woman in the bathroom. Victoria Randolph?"

She nodded, her smile bright, while Tess smeared cookie drool on the table. Good thing I never left the house without wipes. It was one of those dad lessons I'd learned the hard way.

I took advantage of her distraction and took the rest of the giant cookie away.

Daphne Elliot

My girl was sharp, though, and immediately shrieked while violently pushing her fingertips together, the sign for "more."

I shook my hands out, responding with a sign of my own. "All done."

"*No*." Her little face went red as she furiously signed "more, more, more."

"One more bite." I broke off a small piece. "Then all done." I waved my hands to add some finality.

She snatched the hunk of cookie from my hand and shoved it into her mouth.

"The baby sign language is adorable," my mom crooned while offering Tess another piece of the cookie I'd just risked my life to remove from her clutches. Great, exactly what I needed: a ten-month-old on a sugar high. "She is such a little smarty pants."

I took the rest of the cookie from her and shoved it into my mouth. It was soggy, but at this point, I might as well stress eat while my mother tried to guilt me into moving back in with her.

"Victoria came back to town..." She tapped her chin. "A couple of years ago." She peered over her shoulder, then angled in close and lowered her voice. "Terrible divorce. So bad she left Boston and came up here."

I nodded, my stomach twisting with shame. I shouldn't have asked. It was none of my business. She'd never seemed like the type to stick around Lovewell.

"She's a superhero. Took over as director of the food pantry from her Aunt Lou, serves on multiple town committees, and is always pitching in to help."

My heart sank. "What happened to Lou?" She'd been a

fixture in this town since my childhood, always organizing canned food drives for the holidays at our school.

"She has MS," my mother said, her lips turned down. "She's healthy, but she can't keep up with it anymore. Victoria is a force of nature. Did some fancy corporate thing in the city, so she's got a good head for business."

I nodded, forearms on the table. As my mother spoke, my brain rapidly integrated this new information. Random memories popped into my head—Jude mentioning that Vic had gotten married, and even visits to the food pantry to volunteer when I was in high school.

"Noah," my mom said, snapping me back to the present.

I disappeared mentally like that from time to time. My brain got going, drawing connections and pulling up memories. When it did, I'd fall into it. Jude had always been patient with me, but many people in my life were not.

"Sorry. Just thinking. Tell me more about Simone."

She pulled out her phone and scrolled through photos. Because she'd been born early, it was not yet safe to visit with Tess, who could bring along lots of germs. So I let my mother delightedly fill me in and chatter while I ruminated over all I'd learned in the last ten minutes.

Victoria Randolph. She'd been a grade above me in school. We hadn't interacted much, but in a small town, everyone knew everyone.

Her parents had moved up in social status after her dad had invented something big, and they moved away. I think, like me, she headed off to college and never looked back.

While my mom chattered on, several townsfolk gawked at me. I couldn't imagine what the rumor mill was saying, not that I had the attention span to care. Others came to say hello and smile at Tess, who was now scrunching up her face.

With her brows raised and her eyes on me, she stacked her hands and separated them. The sign for pooping.

"Oh boy." I took her from her grandma and snagged the diaper bag from the booth. "Something's brewing."

"Come to dinner tonight."

I bent down to kiss my mom on the cheek, then picked up our trash with my free hand.

"We're still getting into a routine," I said, catching a whiff of a very dirty diaper. "I think it's best I try to get her to sleep in her crib."

My mother didn't put up an argument. She gave me a sweet smile and nodded. I couldn't escape her invitations forever, and I wouldn't try, but I needed a minute to catch my breath. Tess wasn't sleeping, and doing anything to make that situation worse was asking for trouble. I wished I could blame the cross-country move, but in reality, she'd never been a good sleeper.

It was entirely my fault. According to a couple of the books I'd read and one pediatrician, I was supposed to sleep train her.

What I discovered as I read was that "sleep train" was the polite way of saying I should leave her in bed to scream.

There was no way I could do it. She was too precious and had been through too much. If my Tessie girl needed snuggles, then I would give them.

I would rock her and hold her until my back gave out. The last thing I'd ever do was leave her feeling scared and alone. And if she was spoiled as a result, so be it. There were a lot worse things in life than having an overprotective dad.

Axe Backwards

At my truck in the parking lot, I opened the back door, pulled my supplies out of the diaper bag, and got to work. Not to brag, but I was fantastic at handling diapers. Treating each blowout like an emergency that should be handled with precision, strategy, and a thorough risk assessment was the key.

After she was clean and buttoned back up, I picked her up.

Immediately, she threw her tiny arms around my neck and buried her face in the crook there.

"Love you, Tessie."

When she'd loosened her hold so she could check out our surroundings, I spun her, holding her close, and surveyed Main Street. This town had changed a lot. In addition to the coffee shop, there was now a salon and a hardware store. Rumor had it a pizzeria was opening in the vacant storefront at the corner too.

The most significant difference had little to do with the new businesses or the newly planted trees lining the sidewalk. For me, the biggest change was in the energy of the place.

As I held my sweet baby girl, I couldn't help but hope that Tess and I could start fresh here. I'd never replace what she'd lost, but hopefully, I could give her a future.

Chapter 3
Victoria

My anxiety was raging, Charles Huxley did not strike me as the type of man who enjoyed the presence of a loud woman, and I was too frazzled and exhausted to do even a decent impression of a quiet, well-mannered person today.

Fuck it.

I pushed open the door to Huxley Industries. The office took up the entire top floor of a pretty brick building near one end of downtown. Despite the frigid temperatures, each window was decorated with window boxes filled with blooming flowers. The interior was spotless, with recessed lighting and dark wood furniture. A large fireplace took up one end of the foyer.

I plastered a smile onto my face as I approached the receptionist. Before I could introduce myself, though, Charles Huxley was striding across the space.

He was tall and slim, with thick white hair. His blue suit,

without a tie, made him look like he should be sailing his yacht rather than meeting with me.

"It's a pleasure to see you."

His teeth were impossibly white and perfectly straight. Being this close to them made me regret not being more vigilant with my retainer in high school.

He shook my hand a little too vigorously, then ushered me into a large office with a bay window and a massive mahogany desk.

As we settled, him behind his desk, and me in the guest seat across from him, I took out my portfolio.

"How is Louise?" He rested his forearms casually on the surface in front of him. "She has always been such a dear friend."

I had to bite back a laugh at that statement. To avoid giving away how ridiculous I thought the statement was, I ducked my head and pretended to hunt in my purse for a pen.

Aunt Louise loathed politicians and hated rich, entitled people like the Huxleys. One of the biggest reasons the food pantry had struggled so much over the years was that she was constitutionally incapable of sucking up to wealthy people.

Thankfully, I was better at it. I'd encountered plenty of self-important pricks in my lifetime. Hell, I'd married one. So I had a long résumé of experience to draw from.

With a forced smile, I finally focused on him. Charles Huxley was harmless, and I needed to get on his good side. He owned several companies and controlled a lot of the local real estate. He had money and access.

He was a former lieutenant governor and knew a lot of important people in Augusta.

Axe Backwards

In the past few years, he'd shifted his business interests to the area and would be a great partner for the food pantry. He could bring in donations and help with grants and political stuff. There were so many opportunities to help build up this community if I could only get my hands on the funds and connections.

Needless to say, this meeting was critical.

"Here is our prospectus." I held out the glossy booklet I'd spent a fortune having printed at the Staples in Orono. "As you can see, the area is facing record food insecurity, and on page seven, we detail the regional assets that have closed or reduced their impact since the pandemic."

With his lips pressed together, he flipped through, skimming the pages.

"We're looking at unprecedented increases in need in the region and state, and locally, we're outpacing them."

He nodded.

"We truly have more clients than we can handle, and those numbers are only growing." I was veering off my prepared script and starting to sweat. I had been hopeful that the stats about childhood hunger were all I'd need to hook him in.

He continued his perusal of the prospectus, casually flipping through the pages.

All my data, costs, and projections were laid out.

And this man was barely glancing at any of it.

"You know," he said. "My son would be the perfect person to help you with this. Give you some great ideas for improvement."

His son? I almost vomited in my mouth.

"Give me one second." He held up an elegant finger and picked up his phone.

Dammit. I didn't need "help" or "ideas" with the food pantry. I needed money. Donations, philanthropy, call it what you want. I was good at this. I attended national calls and trainings. I put in the work to do my best. And we were pushing every single day to help every person in need. I needed money, time, and the ability to clone myself to get all the work done. Not a meeting with failson Denis Huxley.

I shifted uncomfortably. The last thing I wanted was the Huxleys to mansplain nonprofit management to me.

When Denis entered the room, I stood and forced a smile. If I made all this sound mundane, was it possible they would cut me a check and leave me to it?

"Victoria," he said, taking my outstretched hand and pulling me into a hug. I was not a hugger. Physical contact with strangers and even acquaintances was one of the things I avoided most in life. The way my body stiffened didn't deter him, though.

Denis Huxley was the worst. As a kid, he was a little shit, and from what I could tell, not much had changed.

Charles urged us both to sit, and while he talked, I pretended to take notes, hoping I could extract myself sooner rather than later.

When Denis put his hand on my shoulder, it took all my willpower not to shrug him off. "I think Victoria and I could work well together, Dad." He beamed at me. "Establish a true partnership."

I had to contain my revulsion. Instead, I mentally recited statistics, reminding myself of all the good we could do.

I would not fail. I could not fail.

Axe Backwards

The community needed me.

"Yes." My tone was a little too bright, but it was the best I could do. "Though there isn't much to partner on. We're looking for sustained philanthropic commitments. If you look at page ten, there is a list of fundraisers we're considering. We'd love to have the Huxley name on board as a sponsor."

The men gave me identical noncommittal nods. Clearly Charles had worked hard to groom Denis.

This meeting would go one of two ways. Either they'd be willing to donate and tell me now, or they wouldn't. They'd give me the "this is outside the scope of our giving this year" spiel. Or the "we're focusing our charitable portfolio on animal issues this year."

I could usually tell whether I'd walk out with a check within the first few minutes.

But these guys were stringing me along. Batting me around like a cat with a mouse.

Frustrated but holding it in, I stood. "I've already taken up so much of your time." With a fake smile in place once more, I lifted my chin. "Let's put a follow-up on our calendars."

"No need," Denis said. "You and I can meet personally. I'll work up a proposal for you."

Brow raised, I scrutinized him. Proposal? Shit. What I was asking for was fairly straightforward, but I'd heard the rumors. Apparently they were true. When it came to the Huxleys, things were never straightforward.

"Of course," I said, backing out of the office. "And thanks again."

Chapter 4
Noah

Tess was the best baby. Maybe I didn't have any basis for comparison, but in my bones, I knew she was exceptional.

But no one was perfect, and she had one teeny-tiny flaw.

She wanted to be held all the time.

Like twenty-four hours a day.

And here's the thing. I indulged her.

After all she'd been through, the thought of putting her down alone in her crib gutted me. I couldn't ignore her sad little cry when she needed comfort.

I owed her love and safety. So I started babywearing. I picked up a variety of carriers and wraps, and thanks to mom content on YouTube, I got pretty good at tying them up. We had wraps and carriers for every occasion and temperature, and my collection hung neatly on a rack I'd built by the door.

She preferred to nap on me. So I'd wrap her up and let her sleep while I folded laundry or made dinner. I discovered that fresh air soothed her, so we'd go for evening hikes and she'd fall asleep along the way.

Daphne Elliot

When she woke up at night, I'd walk around, rocking and snuggling her, feeding her when she was smaller. She'd nuzzle into my neck and go back to sleep in her crib for a bit.

But the cross-country move had shaken us both up.

The girl had always wanted to be held, but now that desire was constant.

I'd worked hard to make her comfortable and happy in our new apartment. It was technically a two-bedroom, but the second was a glorified closet.

So I took the tiny one for myself, cramming a twin bed I picked up from my mom into it, and gave Tess the big room. I turned it into a nursery, equipped with a glider, humidifier, a sound machine, and the butterfly mobile she loved to stare at as she drifted off—at least while we were in California.

Since the move, it wasn't enough. The crib she'd slept in for months now repulsed her. The only place she wanted to be was in my arms. At ten months old, she could scream her lungs out when she felt like it. So, in the interest of survival, I'd hold her and walk circles around the apartment.

As long as I kept moving and kept her close, she'd sleep.

It wasn't sustainable, but I had no idea what else to do.

I'd put on a podcast and roam around, feeling her little heart beat against my chest. When I thought I might pass out from exhaustion, I'd press my lips to her head and inhale her baby smell and keep going.

It was after one when a knock sounded on the door. I was so caught up in the classical music I was listening to, I wasn't sure I'd actually heard it. But the second time, there was no denying it.

I removed my headphones and unlocked the door. Through a couple of inches I'd pulled it open, I could make out a woman standing in the dark hallway. She was wearing athletic shorts and a thin tank top. Her dark hair was pulled into a ponytail, and her lip was curled in annoyance.

"Victoria?"

She cocked her head, her eyes narrowing. "Noah? You're my obnoxiously loud new neighbor?"

I pointed at Tess, who was starting to stir now that I'd stopped walking.

With a shake of her head, Victoria pushed herself into the apartment. "Give me the baby."

I resumed my pacing, following the path I'd created in my mind. "Nah, we're good."

"Bullshit. If that poor kid isn't wailing, then you're stomping around like an elephant. What's going on? Is she sick?"

With a huff, I glared at her. I was hardly an elephant.

"I can hear everything that happens up here. Damn old buildings and shoddy HVAC." She looked me up and down. "And you're not a small guy, so you make noise when you pace." Shrugging, she shut the door behind her.

Okay, then. I guess this was now a social visit.

"You live downstairs," I murmured, still moving around in the dimly lit living room–slash–dining room. The space was small and open to the kitchen, but the apartment was clean and had a lot of windows.

Maybe it was egocentric of me, but I hadn't considered the person who may live below me. I was flailing, and though Lovewell was a life raft in a storm, I was still trying to steady myself.

I turned to face her. In the dim light, in the middle of the night, and without makeup, the woman was beautiful. At the coffee shop yesterday morning, she'd looked mature and businesslike. But right now, in my living room, she looked like the girl I remembered. Kind and friendly, with a hint of sass.

"I'm sorry we woke you." A wave of exhaustion rolled over me. If she could really hear the hours of pacing I'd done, I could only imagine she was as tired as I was. "We're having some trouble adjusting to our new routine. And I'm so damn tired."

"Can I help?"

The question was a simple one, but the answer was incredibly complex.

"Thanks, but we're good. I'll walk more softly."

Head tilted, she assessed me. "You haven't sleep trained."

"Not that it's any of your business," I gritted out, the words causing Tess to stir, "but no, and I'm not gonna." With that, I turned and padded toward the window.

"Okay." She appeared beside me and stroked Tess's back. "I'm not judging. I couldn't let a baby scream either."

I looked at her kind, concerned face and let out a sigh. "She's not my biological daughter." The last thing I wanted to do was explain all the details. "I'm her guardian. Well, I was appointed her legal guardian, and now I'm midway through the process of adopting her. It's complicated."

She nodded, saying nothing, just rubbing soft circles on Tess's back. She looked up at me. "You're a natural," she said softly.

For reasons unknown, those words were exactly what I needed in that moment.

"Thank you."

Axe Backwards

My body lit up in an unfamiliar way at her proximity, but I pushed the sensation down.

"She's beautiful," she said, her voice soft.

With a whimper, Tess picked her head up off my shoulder. But a second later, she burrowed into me again, never opening her eyes. "How old?"

"Ten months," I said. "She's a peanut."

"May I hold her?" She extended her arms. "I can walk a few laps for you."

A pang of guilt hit me. It was two a.m.

I could barely stand, and I'd known this woman basically all my life. Though not well, admittedly. Either way, she didn't look like a kidnapper or a predator. And I'd be right here if she wanted to hold her. What was the harm?

I unwrapped the long piece of fabric holding Tess to my chest and handed her over gently. She stirred, letting out a small cry. Heart in my throat, I was ready to pull her back in, but before I could, Victoria brought her to her chest, bouncing and swaying like a professional.

She walked slowly, speaking softly, and Tess eased her head onto my neighbor's shoulder and closed her eyes.

My baby girl wasn't used to being held by anyone but me. It had even taken time for her to warm up to my mom, who was an absolute pro. As I watched this easy interaction, I couldn't help but feel slightly betrayed.

That emotion vanished quickly, though, when I took a moment to really look at the two of them.

With Tess in her arms, Vic transformed. Her eyes softened, and so did her tone, as she glided around my apartment. She wasn't angry or impatient, despite how late it was.

"Don't just stare at me," she hissed, keeping her voice low. "Sleep."

"But—"

She shook her head. "Lie on the couch and close your eyes for an hour. I'll keep her asleep. You clearly need rest."

The gnawing guilt was back. "But what about you?"

"I don't sleep much." She waved me off, then resumed gently rubbing Tess's back. "Sleep."

Dubious, I stretched out on the small couch. My legs hung over one of the arms, but I was too tired to care. I'd slept in far more uncomfortable places. This was one of my superpowers. The ability to sleep anywhere and function on nothing more than a power nap.

So I lay there, watching the scene in front of me. Terrified to close my eyes.

But I didn't have a choice. My brain was barely functioning. Would it really do any harm to drift off for a few minutes?

We were in my apartment. Tess was happily asleep. And I knew this woman. I'd just close my eyes for a little bit.

I WOKE TO THE SOUND OF BABY GIGGLES, WONDERING IF I'd dreamed the middle-of-the-night encounter. Surely Victoria Randolph hadn't actually come to my door at one a.m. to hold my baby like a ponytailed superhero.

I cracked one eye open and was instantly blinded by the sunlight streaming through the large window.

My head felt heavy and my back ached. I'd woken up

more comfortably after spending a night sleeping on the ground.

Using more effort than should be necessary, I lifted my arm to check my watch. Seven.

I shot up, my heart plummeting. Tess. *Shit.*

I hadn't managed to make it to my feet before I saw them.

Tess in her highchair, dressed and giggling as Vic made silly faces and fed her from a baby food container.

Tess clapped and signed for more as Vic slowly scooped another spoonful for her.

With a heavy sigh, I slumped back down on the couch.

"Good morning, Sleeping Beauty," Vic said, holding the spoon aloft and moving it like it was an airplane.

Resting my elbows on my knees, I craned forward and rubbed my temples. "I'm so sorry."

God, how could I have been out for so long? And how could I sleep so deeply that I hadn't heard anything while Vic clearly dressed my daughter and then got her set up for breakfast?

"No need to apologize. Obviously, you needed the sleep. I tried to wake you to ask about the feeding schedule early this morning, but you mumbled about *Frozen* and rolled over."

Finally standing, I shuffled to the coffee maker. Blessedly, the carafe was already full.

A wave of gratitude washed over me, but it was quickly replaced with embarrassment. I was supposed to be better at this. I'd been a single dad for months now.

After pouring a generous cup and taking a few sips of the

scalding liquid in hopes of jump-starting my brain, I dropped a kiss to my little girl's head.

"Da. Da," she shouted, giving me a gummy smile.

Nothing had ever sounded better than that. Knowing she saw me, that I made her smile, that she wanted my attention, lifted my heart every damn time.

"Da." With a giggle, she pointed one finger at the corner of her mouth and scrunched it up.

I gave her a smile and kept my tone easy. "What's the magic word?"

Blinking up at me, she rubbed her chest, the sign for "please."

I opened the cabinet and retrieved the Cheerios she'd asked for, then put a handful on the tray of her highchair.

"She signs," I explained to Vic. "This one." I demonstrated the first sign she'd given me. "Is for cereal, or any kind of finger food. She's not picky."

"That's incredible." Vic's whole face was lit up. "Is she some kind of baby genius?"

A chuckle escaped me, and maybe my chest puffed up a little. It was as if this woman knew exactly what to say to me. I turned to her, noticing then that she was wearing a faded blue Lake Tahoe sweatshirt. My sweatshirt.

My chest went from expanded to tight in an instant. Damn, she looked cute in it. It had been a long, long time since a woman had borrowed my clothes.

With a grunt, Tess signed for more.

I scooped another handful from the box and dumped it on her tray. "While I am certain she is a super genius." I gave my little girl a wink. "Baby sign language is relatively common. I watched a few YouTube videos, then a few more, and got pretty into it."

Vic looked from the baby to me and back again, her eyes swimming with wonderment. "But she's telling you what she wants."

"Yup." I put the box away and went back to my coffee. "I started signing to her at three months old, and she was signing back around eight months. I wanted to create a secure bond between us, and I hoped—I still do—that she'd feel confident that I could meet her needs."

Vic stared at me for a long moment, then shook her head. I couldn't tell whether she was impressed or weirded out.

"Thank you," I said. "For feeding her."

She shrugged. "We had a great time together. Didn't we?"

Gurgling, Tess smacked her fists on the tray of her highchair. Obviously, she was delighted by Vic, even though she'd only met her last night.

The whole thing was surreal. After being on our own for many months, this new person was here, doing the things I should be doing.

And I barely knew her.

My hackles rose, my protective dad instincts taking over.

But then my beautiful baby girl babbled, garnering my attention, and I willed myself to relax. I'd spent so much of my life playing defense against an invisible enemy. All because I let myself be controlled by my insecurities.

These days, I was determined to do better. For my girl.

"You must be exhausted," I said.

Vic shook her head. "Nah. I have insomnia. Slept a few hours before I came up here."

My stomach twisted. "Insomnia? That's rough."

She held a spoonful of pears out to Tess, which she gobbled up. "Eh. It's fine. Since my divorce, I can't sleep."

That's right. My mother had mentioned a divorce.

"Do you want to talk about it?"

Her back went ramrod straight, and she turned, giving me a withering look. "No. I definitely do not want to talk about it."

Noted.

"I figured I'd offer, since we're friends now."

She barked out a laugh. "We're not friends. Tess and me? We're friends. You're the guy who snores on the couch."

Ouch.

Though she was still facing Tess, I caught the way her lips quirked. Vic was a little sarcastic. I liked that.

"Tess has never complained."

"Because you never taught her the sign for 'Dad, you snore like a chainsaw.' If you had, I bet she'd be furiously signing it every night. Poor baby would get an elbow injury from all the sign language."

Hands held up in defeat, I laughed. "Okay, okay. Maybe I do snore. Sorry about that. It was the couch. But thank you again. I had no idea how badly I needed to sleep."

"I can stay a bit longer," Vic offered. "If you want to shower, or, I don't know, brush your teeth?"

Face heating, I slapped a hand over my mouth. Gross. I had become the cautionary parent tale, having no time to shower or brush my own damn teeth.

I jumped up. "Good idea. I'll be back in five."

"Make it ten," she shouted over her shoulder.

Chapter 5
Victoria

Dressed in a pair of jeans and a T-shirt and with my hair scraped back in a ponytail, I hopped into the car and headed to the food pantry. Fridays were our busiest day of the week, since we weren't open on weekends. I was weirdly energized, given I'd gotten almost no sleep.

For the most part, I was used to it. Most nights, I couldn't quiet my brain. I'd lie in bed and repeat all my past mistakes until I passed out or had to get ready for work. And when I did sleep, I was plagued by nightmares.

Last night wasn't anywhere close to typical for me. It was weird, yes, but it was fun. Soothing a fussy baby and softly singing Joni Mitchell songs to her all night was gratifying. It was nice feeling useful.

And Noah? God, that poor guy was struggling. Normally I didn't put much stock in town gossip, but the rumors about his reappearance were flying. And last night, he'd given me a tiny glimpse into their situation. His and Tess's.

Daphne Elliot

I barely knew the guy, but we'd crossed a threshold last night. He'd trusted me with his kid, and I'd helped him out. Maybe it did make us friends.

I wasn't sure I knew how to be a friend anymore. For years, Graham had isolated me. If I went out without him, he would get upset, and I'd never hear the end of it. After a while, it was easier to not go out on my own.

He was dismissive of the few friends I did have. The only people he wanted to hang out with were those he cared about.

Now I was free to make my own choices. And if that included making friends with the single dad upstairs, then so be it.

The freedom I'd found since my divorce felt better than I imagined it would.

I could eat what I wanted. Watch TV shows I was interested in. Go out, stay in, take up a silly hobby, plan a weird trip. After two years on my own, I was still wrapping my head around it.

How much I'd given up in order to be Graham's wife.

How I had so happily handed over my autonomy wholesale.

To be a *we* instead of a *me*.

That was now my baby sister's future. She would soon become Mrs. Graham Whitehall. And she would have his child.

I sipped my coffee as I pulled up to the food pantry. Chip, who'd owned the hardware store for decades and had passed it down to his son a few years ago, led the Friday morning volunteer brigade. This group consisted of mostly men in their seventies who wanted to get out of the house.

Axe Backwards

They called themselves the geezer squad and came equipped with back braces and wrist supports.

And they did a damn good job unpacking the trucks.

As I hopped out of my car, Chip gave me a salute. "Produce is coming from Bangor in ten, boss."

"Thank you. I need to send an email, and then I'll be out to unload with you. I cleaned and disinfected the second fridge yesterday."

He nodded, already gesturing to a group of his poker buddies who were lining up the dollies for the crates of apples, potatoes, and the other produce we'd receive today.

Inside, I hoofed it up two flights of stairs. Aunt Lou had renovated this old mansion on the outskirts of town in the eighties. She'd turned the first floor into an open space where clients could shop for groceries. It was equipped with a check-in station, where they had to show IDs before picking out the items they needed, and wheeled shelving we could easily rearrange. The old kitchen at the back of the house was fitted with refrigerators to store the perishable items we'd stocked for distribution each day.

On the second floor, we stored hygiene items and other household goods. There was a community space up here as well, where we held events. Our offices were crammed into the eaves on the top floor. From there, I took calls, paid bills, and applied for every grant I could find.

The jewel in the crown was the cinderblock-style garage. Last year, with an infusion of cash and some free construction labor, we'd renovated it and repaired the roof. Now it housed our commercial-grade refrigerator and freezer walk-ins. More freezer space gave us the ability to accept more meat deliveries, which had been crucial for many of our clients. We now had long-term storage and could parcel our distributions and plan in advance.

Out front, a large truck pulled up, so I dropped my purse and laptop and shed my hoodie. I was about to get a hell of a workout.

I rushed down the stairs and out the door, smiling at our garage as I passed it. Every time I looked at it—with efficient insulation, proper ventilation, and a shiny new metal roof—I said a prayer of thanks for Owen Hebert. He may have taken my best volunteer away when Lila moved to Boston with him, but he'd done so much good for the people of this region.

And now I was developing a strange late-night friendship with his brother.

Fucking small towns.

"You look pale," Lou said, moving her knight.

I shrugged. My brain was foggy. There was no way she wasn't going to spank me. That shouldn't have been a surprise. Lou was an excellent chess player, and despite her tutoring over the years, I was mediocre at best.

"Are you taking care of yourself?"

Ignoring her question, I turned up the volume on the Bluetooth speaker. We started out with checkers when I was a little girl and worked our way up to chess. We also dabbled in card games when we needed a change. Naturally, she was great at cribbage too.

No matter what we were doing, we'd listen to music. Usually Dolly, but sometimes Tina Turner or Cher.

Axe Backwards

Aunt Lou closed her eyes and swayed to "Yellow Roses."

"Such a good fucking song."

My chest pinched at the genuine peace in her expression. No disease would take her spirit. She'd been doing so well for so long, but now, in her sixties, she needed a lot more help.

"If you won't talk to me about your health and happiness, how about work?" She moved again, one step closer to checking me.

"What are you doing about the egg shortage? And have you heard back from Feeding America? That grant application was fucking pristine. You are damn good at this."

Aunt Lou was a true saint. For decades, she'd devoted herself to helping others. She had never met a problem she would not roll up her sleeves and solve, and she loved nothing more than drinking whiskey and swearing like a sailor on shore leave.

I arched a brow. "It's good to see this place isn't dimming your shine."

"You know my favorite word is *fuck*," she said as I contemplated my next move. "I'm going nuts here. Everyone is always smiling and the place is so clean and shiny. What am I supposed to do all day?"

We'd been over this many times since she'd moved in. Here, she could live independently but have support and community. "Join the walking club," I said, like I did every time she asked that question. "Or play bridge. Go to the shopping center. Get your hair done. Isn't there a community garden here?"

She glared at me. "I miss doing important shit."

Daphne Elliot

"You still help me with accounting. You still proofread the grant applications. You haven't been put out to pasture."

Straightening, she harrumphed. I had her there. She could no longer unload the trucks and be on her feet all day helping clients, but that didn't mean she couldn't stay involved.

"Any luck recruiting more volunteers? People around here need to do more. Communities are built on effort and hard work. If we all sat around on our asses, society would crumble."

She'd been giving this lecture my entire life. No one was more energetic and willing to help than Aunt Lou. In her mind, everyone else should be too.

I nodded. "The high school is giving academic credit for volunteer hours. Several rising seniors are set to do a summer internship."

Her expression softened a fraction, but she didn't stop her inquisition. "And diapers? Did the diaper bank in Portland approve our request?"

"Not yet, but I'm optimistic. I'll have to pay for delivery, but we could receive three times as many as we have been. Other items too. Baby shampoo, more formula. I think it'll make a big difference."

Our community needed much more than food. I was grateful for every bruised apple we received, but the need didn't stop there. Diapers were at the top of our list, as were feminine hygiene products.

"I've been thinking about adding a laundry facility," I said as Lou slid her queen into position.

"Check." She zeroed in on my face. "How and where?"

Axe Backwards

"The basement. I'm going hard on larger corporate donors. Hoping I can get some washers and dryers donated."

She hummed. "It's a great idea..."

It was, but it would take a lot of work to make it happen. Especially after my strange and unresolved meeting with the Huxleys yesterday.

My busy nighttime babysitting activities had kept me from fretting over the absolute shitshow the whole day had been. And how devastated I'd been when I'd gotten that phone call.

I picked up Lou's whiskey tumbler and took a long drink. "Alex is pregnant."

She pinched the bridge of her nose. As always, her nails were painted fire-engine red. "You've got to be shitting me."

I shook my head.

She covered my hand with hers, her skin papery soft. "I'm so sorry, sweets. Pregnant? The wedding is only a few months away."

I shook my head. "Mom didn't call you? They're moving it up to Memorial Day weekend. She bought a thirty-thousand-dollar dress for Alex and is demanding they get married while it still fits."

"Jesus."

"Yup. Rather than a few months, we've got a few weeks."

"Gimme my drink back." She took the glass from me and downed its contents in one gulp. "You gonna be okay?"

I shrugged. "I feel like shit right now, but eventually I'll be okay."

Graham had done me a favor. The countless faceless women he'd met on Tinder had done me a favor.

Though I could have done without the chlamydia.

But antibiotics did the trick. Thank you, science.

All of it had given me the strength to leave. I should have done it long before, but I'd been programmed to keep calm and smile and do all I could to preserve the happy façade I hid behind. From a young age, my parents had taught me appearances were all that mattered.

Aunt Lou got up and returned with a container of cookies-and-cream ice cream and two spoons. For as long as I could remember, she had kept a carton in her freezer for me.

It's because of her that I finally got out. Because she'd provided counterprogramming to my parents' toxic messaging, she'd helped me figure out who I was and what I wanted.

Graham was a lawyer and philanthropist. My parents were obsessed with him. He checked every box.

Knew all the right people. Had played lacrosse in prep school.

He was the kind of guy who owned his own tuxedo.

He played golf with the deputy mayor.

He was ambitious and driven, and together, we built what looked like a dream life. High-powered careers, exotic travel, an expensive condo with ocean views, and elite social events.

But day by day, I disappeared.

He didn't like to be inconvenienced, so I learned to be small, to not take up too much space, and not to have too many opinions.

So when he worked late, I didn't question it. If I did, he'd fault me for being controlling or demanding. I forced myself to accept that he was important and successful. I lived in a state of denial, sitting alone in our overpriced condo, reading the boring ass nonfiction books he'd buy for me while he was out fucking half of Boston.

"I love you, kid." Lou chased a bite of ice cream with a sip of whiskey. "I see how strong and generous and amazing you are. Even if those dumb fucks don't."

Tears stung at the backs of my eyes. After all the work I'd done on myself, I had to go watch my baby sister marry my ex-husband while pregnant with his child.

I'd worked so hard to heal, to rebuild my life, to find my passion and make new friends, only to end up being the sad, barren spinster at Perfect Princess Alexandra's wedding.

I put my head in my hands and cried.

Lou draped one thin arm around me and pulled me close. "I know this seems epically shitty, but I promise, the universe has good things waiting for you."

All I could do was sob in response.

"It's okay. Let it out. Cry and rage. Do whatever you need to do. Because you are going to that wedding, and you are going to look beautiful and unbothered. You hear me?"

I nodded. There was no way that was happening, but I didn't have the strength to argue.

"Do you think Chris Evans is free? You need a hot date."

A hiccup of a laugh escaped me. "He just got married."

"Aw, fuck. I was holding out hope he'd drive up from Massachusetts, fall in love with you, and then introduce me to Robert Downey Jr."

Though the tears continued to fall, I couldn't help but grin. God, I loved her.

"I mean it, kid. If you're gonna survive this, you need a killer outfit and a hot date."

Chapter 6
Noah

"I'm worried about you," Jude called from the floor as Tess crawled all over him.

I shook my head and continued to cut the blueberries into microscopic pieces. Jude was always worried about me. It was the natural order of the universe.

Gus was the responsible eldest brother and had been our father's right hand.

Owen was brilliant, ambitious and diligent.

Finn, dedicated and focused, went straight into the Navy and became a pilot.

Jude and I were a matching set. Physically, at least.

We looked alike, but our temperaments couldn't have been more different.

He was cautious and quiet.

I was his opposite.

Yin and yang, as my mother used to call us.

We balanced out well.

All our lives, it felt as though neither of us could exist without the other.

Even during all the years I stayed away, we'd remained close. Although we rarely did more than text, we were always connected, and we always understood one another. Even when we didn't communicate, I could feel him.

"When are you not worried about me?" I quipped.

He picked up Tess and blew on her belly. "You know what I mean. Doing this all yourself? After everything that happened?"

I continued prepping Tess's dinner, trying to ignore the sincerity in his voice. Though I wouldn't admit it, I was screwed. I'd been placed in an impossible situation, but I wouldn't change it for the world. "I've got this down."

I'd come by my confidence naturally.

Failing or falling—part of my daily life—I'd pick myself up and move on to the next adventure or injury.

I didn't sweat much. Being part of a big family had its advantages. My dad was too busy to pay much attention, and my siblings let me be me. My mom never pressured me to change or pursue a different path. She was busy enough trying to keep us all alive and fed.

I spent my childhood in the woods, running free with Jude, without a care in the world. School was challenging, and I struggled to fit in at times. But I had my brothers and a giant forest, and that was enough.

After high school, Lovewell felt too small. When the world called, I left. And I'd been making it work ever since.

"This is a good place to grow up," I said.

He stood and buckled Tess into her highchair. Jude had only met her a week ago, and he had it down already. It was who he was. Thoughtful, thorough. It was why he was so good at what he did for the family timber business. It was why he was such an incredible musician. "The best place."

"I want her to grow up surrounded by people who love her."

"We'll give her that."

"But." I sighed, my heart pinching.

He folded his hands over his T-shirt—today's read "Catalina Wine Mixer"—and waited for me to finish. Jude had never been scared off by a little silence.

"I'm worried that I can't do it. That I'm not built for this. That I'll let her down and fuck it all up."

His face went stony. "You will not."

My gut clenched as I surveyed my little girl. "She's already lost so much. And she's stuck with me."

Tipping to one side, he pressed a kiss to the top of Tess's head. "You are so much more capable than you give yourself credit for."

It was such a Jude thing to say. All wise and shit. But he'd spent the last decade growing and changing and becoming a responsible adult. I'd taken a different path.

"You don't know that." I popped open a jar of sweet potato purée and dug a baby spoon from the drawer. "You don't even know me."

He took a step back, his expression a mask of hurt.

Instantly, I regretted my words.

Lips pursed, he studied me. Behind his glasses, his eyes were the exact shade of blue as mine. We even had the same sandy brown hair. Jude kept his short and his beard full. We weren't identical twins, but we fooled a lot of people when we were kids. Even now, in our thirties, it was sometimes like looking into a more responsible, more mature mirror.

With a grunt, he punched my shoulder.

"No violence in front of the baby," I hissed, rubbing at the spot. Shit, that hurt.

"We shared a placenta, asshole. You can't make statements like that."

I glared at him, but before I could fire back, a loud knock echoed through the space.

"I'll make myself useful," he grumbled.

I sat at the table with the jar of sweet potatoes, smiling at my little girl, who was grinning and signing "more" over and over.

"Hi, Jude," a feminine voice said. "Is Noah here? I wanted to drop this off."

Tess kicked her feet and screeched, and the sound got louder as my neighbor appeared, holding my folded blue sweatshirt.

"Sorry," she said, giving Tess a big wave and a smile. "I accidentally took this with me."

"Thanks."

"I'm headed out to pick up burgers from the Moose," Jude said, sidling up beside her.

It was a blatant lie. We had no such plans. Though I wouldn't turn down a giant burger. Lovewell had minimal takeout options, and cooking meals for myself was not exactly a priority at the moment.

He darted a look my way, then focused on her. "Stay and hang out with us."

"I don't want to intrude."

"You aren't. I promise. I didn't realize the two of you were friends." He arched a brow at me.

Axe Backwards

I could see the cogs moving. Fuck. I had to shut this down quickly.

Vic beat me to it. "He rescued me from a broken bathroom door yesterday morning at the coffee shop. And last night, when his endless pacing kept me awake, I came up to hang out with this cutie so he could get a little sleep."

She waved at Tess again. My daughter waved back with one hand while stuffing blueberry pieces into her mouth with the other.

Jude nodded, his eyes darting from Vic to me and back again. He was a vault, the last person to ever gossip, but that didn't mean he wouldn't give me all kinds of shit.

"She's a good neighbor," I said lamely. "And Tess likes her."

"Tess"—Vic stepped closer and ruffled the baby's hair, giving me the perfect view of her cleavage—"has excellent taste."

"She does," Jude agreed. "I'll pick up the food. Help yourself to a beer. I brought some over, since this guy's fridge is usually empty."

Keeping my attention locked on my neighbor's face rather than her tits, I made a mental note to punch my brother later.

The way Vic smiled at Tess banished the annoyance building inside me. In fact, watching the two of them together made me melt a little.

She looked different today. I'd seen her business-professional look, and I'd seen her in pj's. But tonight, she wore dark jeans that molded to the curve of her hips, red sneakers, and a slouchy black T-shirt.

Fuck, she was pretty. Her eyes were bright and her lips

were full. And fuck if the dimples that appeared when she smiled didn't bowl me over.

Once Jude left, she and I fell into an easy rhythm. She gave me the rundown of the work she was doing at the food pantry and played on the floor with Tess while I cleaned up and marveled at how effortless she made it all sound.

"You're good at what you do."

She lifted one shoulder and let it fall. "I've learned a lot from Aunt Lou. And I have a background in corporate communications, so I'm keeping my head above water, but I wouldn't say I was good."

"Still, taking on the existing needs of the community while growing the offerings and connecting with new potential donors?"

"It's the first time in my life I've had a job I'm passionate about," she admitted. "For so long, I went through the motions, and now, it doesn't feel like work. It feels like a calling."

My heart thumped against my sternum. Her calling. I was familiar with the concept. With being called to serve a greater purpose. For years, I woke up day after day, knowing that it could be my last but that it would be worth it if I could save just one more person.

Until several months ago, I knew who I was and how I wanted to exist in this world.

Now?

Now I was an unemployed single dad without a clue.

"You okay?" Vic was suddenly standing next to me, holding Tess. "You were kind of staring into space."

I shook my head. "Sorry. I do that sometimes. Get stuck in my own head."

Axe Backwards

"I don't mind. You seem upset."

Usually, I would brush off a moment like this with sarcasm or by laughing at myself. But the way she looked at me, like she was genuinely concerned about me, made me think better of it.

She was close, very close, and Tess was comfortable with her. Yesterday, she'd been a stranger, and now she looked like she belonged in my house, holding my child.

There was something about her, something sad and complicated, that made me feel a little less alone.

I opened my mouth, searching for a way to explain what was going on in my head, but my words were cut off by the buzzer for the door downstairs.

"That's Jude," I said, scooping Tess out of her arms.

I expected him to come in with waffle fries and lumberjack stories and provide a necessary distraction from the unease swirling in my gut. Instead, he claimed there was a "work emergency," handed me a bag of delicious-smelling food, and took off.

He was full of shit. It was spring, which meant there was far too much mud to make the roads to any of the logging sites navigable. On top of that, it was eight p.m. on a Friday night.

But Vic didn't seem bothered. She happily pulled plates from the cabinet and beers from the fridge while I put Tess in her jammies and brushed her teeth. She was sleepy, but there was no way in hell she'd miss out on hanging with Vic, so I grabbed a wrap from the dresser in her room and got her situated.

When I walked into the kitchen, Vic froze with a French fry halfway to her mouth.

"You did not wrap up that baby and come out here to eat a burger."

"Sure did." I pressed a kiss to Tess's head.

She wiggled, trying to get a peek at her new friend, but she loved the pressure of the wrap. The research I'd done indicated that it helped regulate a baby's nervous system.

"She loves to sleep snuggled up like this."

Grinning, Vic shook her head. "I should take a photo and post it to Instagram. We'll go viral."

I rolled my eyes. Her attention made me feel slightly shy and embarrassed. And those were not sensations I normally experienced.

We settled on the couch and watched *Schitt's Creek*, which Jude had originally come over to force me to start. We laughed through the first two episodes, and I successfully demonstrated how I could eat a double cheeseburger without dropping so much as a dollop of ketchup on Tess's head.

"So," she said. She loaded the dishwasher while I walked around with an almost asleep Tess. "I propose shifts. I'll take first watch, and you can go downstairs and sleep in my bed. It's a hell of a lot more comfortable than the couch."

"No need. I have a bed."

"An ancient twin with a threadbare blanket." She scoffed. "I saw the closet you call a bedroom while I was here last night. There's no way you can't hold your arms out and touch both walls at the same time. And I bet your feet hang off the end."

She was right, of course, but the apartment was temporary. A place to land while we figured things out.

"I have a king-size bed with a memory foam mattress and

high thread-count sheets," she said. "Did the laundry this morning. I'll give you a few hours before I have to crash."

No. I couldn't impose more than I had. And sleeping in her bed? We were neighbors who really didn't know each other, and that was far too intimate.

Even as I mentally rejected the idea, exhaustion settled deep in my bones. Tess was still acting like her crib was an active volcano, and I wasn't sure when I'd get another offer this good.

"I'll think about it." I bounced gently as I walked. "But first, I want to watch another episode."

With a hum, she looked at her watch. "Okay. One more."

Around eleven, Vic shoved her keys at me. "Don't judge me for the mess, but my bed is really comfortable. And you look like shit."

If I had any energy at all, I'd be offended by the comment. Sure, I missed the person I used to be, but I couldn't imagine my life without my little bean. I wouldn't trade the days I spent caring for her for anything.

It was the paradox of parenthood, I supposed.

The first-floor apartment was warm and inviting and a tiny bit chaotic, just like its inhabitant. One wall was covered in overflowing bookcases and an oversized chair. The kitchen appliances were colorful, and the walls were covered in pretty photographs. Everything had a place. I wasn't sure what she thought she had to apologize for.

I locked the door and placed the keys on the hook beside it, then toed off my shoes. Like my apartment, the main bedroom was off the living room. As she'd promised, when I entered, I was greeted by a king-size bed with an ornate wooden headboard. It took up so much space there was barely room for the two nightstands.

The area rug beneath it was soft, and the duvet looked like a fluffy green cloud.

Okay, maybe this sleep plan would be easier than I'd anticipated.

The moment I made contact with the high-end mattress, I let out a groan. My back still hadn't recovered from sleeping on the couch last night. I stretched out, grateful for the dozen or so pillows, and made a mental note to buy more for myself. Maybe they would make my pathetic twin a little easier to bear.

As I closed my eyes, my mind immediately went to the smile on Vic's face when she saw Tess and how delighted my little girl had been in return. I was falling asleep in her bed while she walked with my baby one floor up. Surely that made us friends. My chest expanded. I liked that. More than ever, I needed a friend.

The easy sensation was quickly replaced by guilt. Emily and Jack were the best friends I'd ever had. They'd been gone for nine months now, and I couldn't imagine having that kind of bond with another person. The ache would never go away, and it only got worse when I looked into Tess's beautiful eyes. More and more, she was looking like her mother. Some days just the sight of her made it hard to breathe.

That was the funny thing about grief. It was always there, in the shadows, waiting to step into the light as a reminder of how bad things could get. A testimony to how much a person had lost.

The day I stood in front of a judge and learned that I

would be caring for this child changed me on the cellular level.

Months later, I was still processing it all. As much as I loved being her dad, the loss she and I both had suffered was an ache that would never go away. Every smile, every giggle lifted me up while breaking my heart, because her real parents weren't here to see it.

And they were dead because of me.

Chapter 7
Victoria

I was engrossed in my newest audiobook purchase and folding laundry when a knocking sound caught my attention. Tapping Pause, I cocked my head and listened. When a second knock sounded on the door, I abandoned the towels on my bed and hustled out of the bedroom.

Noah hovered in the hallway, wearing a tight T-shirt that showed off his tattoos and a backward baseball cap. Tess was propped on his hip, gnawing at Sophie the Giraffe's head, a drop of drool clinging to her chin.

He gave me one of his cocky smiles. "Get changed. We're going hiking."

Even as a thrill shot through me, I lazily leaned on the doorframe. "Really?"

He had mentioned it the other day, but I hadn't thought he was serious. For the last ten days, I had spent most evenings upstairs. We took turns making dinner and playing with Tess, then we slept in shifts between episodes of *Schitt's Creek*. We'd already made it halfway through season two.

"Tess is going stir crazy." He kissed the top of her head, making me melt a little inside. "She requested a waterfall. So we're gonna do the Waterford trail to Moxie falls."

With a huff of a laugh, I straightened. "She requested X falls?"

The girl's signing game was on point, but at ten months old, her conversation mostly revolved around food.

Moxie falls was about forty minutes outside of town. The short hike there was challenging, but the exquisite views and the small wading pools made it worth the effort.

He nodded. "My girl gets itchy if she doesn't get enough forest time. Come on. It's gonna be a beautiful day."

Tess held her free hand out to me and shouted, "Ick-Ick."

In the last couple of days, she'd started calling me "Ick-Ick," and though it wasn't the most flattering moniker, I was shamelessly thrilled she'd given me a name. I felt like the coolest kid in the world when she smiled at me and shouted it at full volume.

"Okay, give me ten minutes."

"Meet us at the Caffeinated Moose. We'll pick up coffee and sandwiches for the road."

I dug my beat-up old daypack out of the bottom of the closet and tossed a hat and gloves into it, then threw on a few layers. May in Maine was far colder than most realized. A water bottle, granola bars, and an extra pair of socks rounded out the extent of my hiking prep. Knowing Noah, he'd have every type of emergency supply ever created in his truck, so my minimalist approach would be fine.

When I stepped into the coffee shop, Tess was beaming. Several locals were cooing at her, and she was basking in the

Axe Backwards

attention. She wasn't the only one being fawned over, either. There were more than a few women cooing at Noah as well.

The hot dad look was really working for him. The tight T-shirts, the backward hat, and the full sleeve of tattoos only made the babywearing look sexier.

With a big smile, he reached past Mrs. Dupont, holding out a large latte.

Before I could take a sip, she was watching me, her focus intense. "I knew it." She stomped her foot. "You two are dating."

"Uh," I said, mouth full of lava-hot coffee.

"Jodie, Steph," she called to a small group of women in the back corner of the shop. "You owe me. They are together."

Jodie, or Miss Wetherbee, as I called her when she was my elementary school PE teacher, gave us a thumbs-up.

"Actually," I said, nudging Noah, who was chuckling. "We are not dating. We're friends."

"And neighbors," he added.

Tess yelled, "Ick-Ick," the sound ear-piercing, and reached for me.

Cheeks heating, I took her from Noah and balanced her on my hip, turning away so I could take another sip of coffee without her getting her hands on it. It was the best I could do to avoid speaking more about this.

Mrs. Dupont frowned and looked from Noah to me and back again. "Sure, you're not."

Noah smiled. "We're neighbors. Victoria came upstairs last week because I was making a lot of noise trying to get Tess to sleep. From there, we became friends."

It sounded so simple when he explained it. It was true.

Daphne Elliot

Though we'd only really gotten to know each other over the last several days, we'd become good friends. And I adored Tess. She was a bright ray of sunshine in my life. Day after day, I looked forward to seeing her.

Noah himself was good company. He was funny and relaxed and so adorably in over his head with an infant to care for.

Our friendship came with no pressure, no expectations. The antithesis of being with Graham. Even being in the same room with my ex would make me anxious and self-conscious. Did I look okay? Was I saying and doing the right things? Talking too much? Too little?

In the little cocoon of Noah's apartment, we played with the baby, shared casual dinners, and laughed at a funny sitcom. I never wore makeup or put effort into sounding intelligent. It was refreshing, being 100 percent myself.

Sure, he was easy on the eyes and a lot of fun to hang out with, but I didn't have it in me to experience attraction or desire. Not anymore. Those sensations had died with Graham's betrayal and my divorce.

And while I was annoyed at the invasive questions and town gossip, it beat the hell out of being asked when I was going to have a baby. Those questions and comments killed me every single time. I was always amazed by how even casual acquaintances felt entitled to information about my fucking uterus.

I gave her a sweet smile. With a little huff, Mrs. Dupont went back to her table. Probably to spread more gossip. Once she'd settled in and peeked over her shoulder at us, we grabbed our snacks and headed to the car.

On the drive to the trail, we played "We Didn't Start the

Axe Backwards

Fire" on repeat. It was Tess's favorite song. She danced in her car seat, babbling along and rocking out. The third time through, I pulled out my phone and started googling the historical references Noah and I didn't understand. Turns out I didn't know all that much about the Cold War.

After zipping Tess into her puffy coat and pulling a hat with pink cat ears over her head, Noah put her in a hiking backpack. The moment she was settled on his back, she kicked her heels and screeched a happy sound.

The forest around us was dense, and the light dappled as it broke through the trees here and there.

I'd never get tired of this. The beauty and grandeur of Maine. The ability to exist in the wilderness. No cars, no noise, no chaos.

The peaceful soundtrack created by the crunching of our boots on the trail, the rushing of the water ahead, and the chirping of the birds.

Though it was technically spring, a sunny forty-degree day like this was about as good as it got this time of year, so I relished every moment I could.

There was no better place to stretch my legs and clear my head. Alexandra's wedding was two weeks away, and the lump in my throat grew every time I thought about it. By now, it was a wonder I hadn't choked to death on it.

At the advice of Aunt Lou, I'd bought a really gorgeous dress. It was deep purple and dipped low in the back. When I tried it on, I'd felt like a tall, glamorous supermodel rather than a thirty-five-year-old pear-shaped woman who was barely five-six.

Despite the gorgeous armor I'd don and the fashion therapy session, suffocating dread filled me each time I imagined watching Alexandra, with her baby bump and white dress, soaking in the attention at her big white wedding while my family made a fuss over Graham.

Tears stung my eyes, but I blinked them away and focused on the path and the little girl who was babbling and clapping as birds flew overhead.

My legs burned already. I relished the sensation. This was good. Nature and exercise. This was part of the reason I'd moved back to Maine.

We stopped for water a couple of times, and within an hour, we had reached the base of the falls. Massive rock formations created a small break and tide pools swirling with icy cold water.

Up ahead, the falls roared, the water raging down the stark granite, all power and fury.

We settled on a large flat rock next to a small pool, far from the danger of the falls. Noah took Tess out of her carrier and set her on the ground, where she immediately picked up a rock and inspected it. She set it down and found another.

Between sips of water, Noah shook his head. "I spent so many years swearing I didn't miss Maine."

"Same. I vowed I'd be a city girl for life, but when my life went sideways, I hustled right back up here. It didn't take long once I was back to realize that's what I am. A Mainer."

A low chuckle rumbled out of him. "It suits you."

We broke out our picnic, Tess delighting in the frosted maple scone Noah set on a camping plate for her. She gummed it with a grin, then broke off pieces for her rock friends, who she had arranged in a circle where she sat.

Axe Backwards

"You gonna tell me why you seem so upset?" he asked gently.

Inhaling deeply, I watched the falls. Could I?

"No pressure."

Normally I would change the subject. I'd been taught at a young age that being ruled by emotions was bad. That I should deflect and deny. Make pleasant small talk and keep my feelings to myself.

But I was tied up in knots, and they were making it impossible to enjoy this beautiful day.

Noah and I had been sharing meals and sleeping in the same bed for the last week. At different times, of course, but still.

We were friends. Good friends.

"My youngest sister is getting married in two weeks."

He sat patiently, head tilted, waiting for me to elaborate.

"She's marrying my ex-husband, and the thought of going to the wedding makes me want to vomit. On top of that, she's pregnant. After experiencing infertility and divorce and a thousand other terrible scenarios, I don't know if I can do it."

He turned his hat around, as if putting it on the right way would help him think, and steepled his fingers.

Shit, he was gorgeous.

"Hold on." He sat up straight. "Your ex-husband is marrying your baby sister? Isn't she a lot younger than you are?"

I nodded. "Nine years. Six years younger than Elizabeth. She was an oopsie baby."

"So she's..." He raised his eyebrows, probably doing the math in his head.

"Twenty-six." I winced.

He shook his head. "You said he cheated…"

"Not with Alex," I corrected, understanding where his train of thought was headed. "She was living in Chicago when that happened. She moved back to Boston last year, and since Graham socializes with my parents at the country club, he and Alexandra got to know one another."

"Are you sure?"

"Yes. He preferred Tinder and one-time hookups with twenty-somethings. Nothing long term."

His jaw went rigid. "Oh fuck."

My eyes stung again. Dammit. I put my head in my hands, too tired to fight the pain. The first clue I had was when a friend from work told me she'd seen a Tinder profile she swore was his. Then I found the photos and texts on his phone.

Red-hot shame flooded my veins like it did every time I remembered those days.

"Sorry." I sniffled. "It's been two years since I found out, and I'm still so ashamed."

"Why?" he asked, his voice soft. "You didn't do anything wrong."

"But maybe I did."

He grabbed my hands and squeezed, staring deep into my eyes. "You. Did. Nothing. Wrong."

I blinked, my eyes filling with tears again.

"You did nothing wrong."

"But." The tears were falling now, rolling straight down my cheeks. God, this was so embarrassing.

"Stop that." The sharpness of his tone startled me. "He

treated you like garbage. That is not your fault. You have nothing to be ashamed of."

I blinked at him, sniffling. If only it were that easy. That simple.

"Say it."

Before I knew what was happening, he was standing and pulling me to my feet. He scooped up Tess and situated her on his hip.

"I'm serious. The way we speak to ourselves matters. If you're walking around thinking you deserved to be treated so badly or that you caused it in some way, then I'll make it my mission to correct you. Because you're dead fucking wrong."

The gesture was thoughtful, but the situation went far beyond the cheating. My parents and their expectations of me complicated matters exponentially. Not to mention my strained relationships with my sisters and the belief I once held that marriage was the be-all and end-all. That I'd found my person and would be happy and loved and accepted forever.

"Say it. Out loud and in your own head. You did nothing wrong."

Logically, I knew I wasn't at fault. Being naïve wasn't a crime. Neither was giving away trust so easily. But the stigma that came with a failed marriage by my early thirties was like a sin I'd carry with me forever. Being cheated on so many times, so brazenly, was like a tattoo on my heart, permanent and painful.

"I did nothing wrong," I said softly.

"You can do better than that."

"Ick-Ick," Tess said, scone crumbs in her eyebrows and down the front of her jacket.

"Shout it," Noah commanded.

"I did nothing wrong," I said louder, though not at full volume. It was too peaceful out here to be so disruptive.

"A little better. Walk up there." He pointed at the path that led to the falls. "Scream it. Scream whatever you want. Let it out. You can't carry all this shit around with you forever."

The lump in my throat grew once more, making it hard to swallow.

With one expectant brow raised, he put his free hand on my shoulder.

He stood so close, his chest almost touched mine when he inhaled. His warmth seeped into me, chasing away the sadness and bringing with it a new sensation.

His proximity awakened my body. His masculine scent lit a low flame deep inside me. The weight of his large hand grounded me.

"Shout," he commanded.

With a deep breath in, I willed my pounding heart not to leap out of my chest. Then I spun and strode toward the rushing water, focusing on the sound and only stopping when I could feel the mist on my face.

"I did nothing wrong!" I shouted as loud as I could. "I didn't deserve it."

The tears fell again, mixing with the mist coating my skin. But it felt good. Therapeutic. The cold air in my lungs, the icy mist on my face. Staring down nature and letting loose.

"I hate the way he made me feel," I yelled. "I hate what he did to me."

I sucked in a harsh breath, energized.

Axe Backwards

"I did nothing wrong," I screamed with all my might, my voice drowned by the pounding of the water against the rocks.

For a long moment, I stood in that place, catching my breath. When the tears had stopped, I carefully made my way back to where Noah was standing with Tess.

He was beaming. "That's my girl," he said softly as I approached.

My heart clenched at the sentiment, but I was too raw to linger on the meaning of that response.

Wiping at my cheeks, I went back to where we'd set up our picnic and picked up a scone for myself. For a while, we ate and played with Tess, supervising her as she crawled around on the rocks. By the time we began the hike back to the car, I felt lighter and exhilarated.

The dread that had plagued me this morning lightened a modicum. It wasn't gone altogether, but for the first time in a long time, a gentle contentedness took up residence inside me.

We were down the steep trail, on the last leg through the forest, when Noah finally spoke again.

"We should work out the details for the wedding."

I turned to him, my mouth agape.

Tess had conked out, her cheek resting on the back of Noah's head, and was snoring softly.

"I'm going with you," he said before I could formulate a single word. "For moral support."

Stunned, I stumbled over a rock in the path.

He grasped my arm, steadying me. "I assume that, as the bride's sister, you get a plus-one."

I nodded.

"So Memorial Day? My mom has been desperate to spend more time with Tess. I'm sure she'd babysit."

My mind raced and my heart pinched. The two of us were only friends. But the possibility of not having to face my family alone was very tempting. "Isn't that a lot to ask?"

"For my mom?" He shook his head. "She raised six kids almost completely on her own. And I don't know if you've noticed, but she's baby crazy. She turned Gus's old room into a nursery for Thor and Simone, so she's got a crib and changing table and highchair. She's itching to get Tess over there. I'll be lucky if she gives her up after the wedding."

I forced a smile even as my stomach soured. I'd give anything for a mom like that. One who was loving and generous, who rolled with the punches. Who loved her kids enough to let them be who they needed to be.

"You don't understand," I pleaded. "My mother, my sisters. They aren't kind people. They'll spend the whole day looking down at you."

I had nothing in common with any of them, and they were about as fond of me as I was of them. Our goals and outlook and priorities couldn't have been more different. For years, I'd kept my feelings about them to myself. It was almost freeing to admit it out loud to Noah instead of pretending we were too busy to get together regularly.

"You think your family can scare me off? Please. I've battled two-thousand-degree flames many, many times. Your mother's glares have nothing on a wall of fire burning off all the available oxygen."

Huh. I'd forgotten about his heroic firefighting career. The Noah I knew was a loving dad who was desperate for a few hours of sleep each night.

Axe Backwards

But the man was undeniably gorgeous. Though I was incapable of feeling attraction, he could absolutely make a splash as my date.

With his height, muscles, and thick hair, he would make Graham so jealous. My ex was incredibly vain.

As we continued down the trail, I had to push myself to keep pace with him.

"It may seem weird," he admitted, his long legs eating up the distance back to the parking lot. "But it's only a wedding. I'll be a gentleman. You don't have to worry about that."

I kept my focus fixed on the ground ahead of me, ensuring I didn't trip over exposed tree roots or another rock, but in my periphery, I could swear his cheeks went a bit pink under his stubble.

"You've done so much for me and for Tess. You're an incredible friend."

My heart swelled. I was thankful for the unlikely friendship we'd struck up. I was pretty sure I needed the connection even more than he needed the extra set of hands.

"The entire town already thinks we're dating," he said.

True enough, and it was annoying as hell.

"So if I came as your date, we wouldn't have to worry that they'd question the status."

"Doesn't matter anyway. My parents would never deign to invite anyone from Lovewell. They think this town is beneath them."

The moment they climbed that society ladder, they got the hell out of rural Maine and ditched the entire community.

As we rounded the bend and the parking lot came into sight, the sun shone brightly, warming my face.

It felt incredible. Not only the heat but being here with Noah and Tess. The fresh air in my lungs and good friends by my side. Would taking him to the wedding really be so bad? It was unlikely anyone would question it, and having a trusted friend at my side would make the entire weekend much more tolerable.

"Aunt Lou is going. I promised I'd give her a ride."

"Great. I can help her get around."

The ease with which he offered made my heart thump. Of course he'd go out of his way not just for me, but for my beloved aunt. "The wedding is in Kennebunkport."

He whistled.

"At a fancy yacht club." I cringed. "And it's black-tie."

Lips pressed together, he nodded. "I can manage."

"And it will be ridiculous and over-the-top. Alexandra is my parents' favorite. The entire thing will be nauseating."

"You're not talking me out of this. I'll get to be there with you, so I'll have a great time. Plus, it's been years since I've had a lobster roll."

I tossed my head back and laughed. "I'll buy you ten. We'll call it compensation for the pain and suffering my mother will cause."

He stopped walking abruptly, a smile splitting his face. "Deal."

He held his hand out, and I took it. Ignoring the way my heart sped up when his skin made contact with mine.

Chapter 8
Victoria

"I made so much. Take more."

"Okay, okay. You don't have to force me." I added another hunk of eggplant parm to my plate. It smelled so damn good. There was no way I wouldn't come back for seconds.

Alice was always feeding us, which made her one of my favorite people. The woman was an excellent cook. I was not, so I rarely ate as well as I did when she was the one putting on a meal.

Her home was a big timber-style lodge up on the mountain. Her husband, Henri, had built it years ago as some kind of man cave fortress, but Alice had added small touches here and there, making it feel like the inside of a magazine.

The house was almost as beautiful as the love the two of them had for one another.

No one deserved that kind of devotion more than she did.

Her two children were incredible, rounding out the most inspiring kind of family unit.

Daphne Elliot

Being here strengthened my resolve. When I had my own home, when I'd figured myself out career-wise and financially, I would follow her example. For so long, I'd wanted to foster, and each time I was with Alice, that longing only grew.

Graham had scoffed at the idea. But every day I became more convinced that it was the right path for me. Maybe my journey to parenthood wouldn't be conventional, but I was ready to explore the possibilities. Finances were a consideration and my primary stressor right now. But I'd deal with that eventually.

Making friends in one's thirties wasn't for the faint of heart. By this time in their lives, most people were entrenched and settled. In the city, I'd never found my people.

But within weeks of returning to Lovewell, I had been adopted by Alice and Becca. It had started with an appointment for a haircut. I walked in needing a trim and left with dinner plans.

Now the three of us got together regularly—usually at Alice's house—to check in, have dinner, and decompress.

We were an unlikely trio. The newlywed, the widow, and the divorcée. All of whom had come to Lovewell for different reasons.

Alice had come to help revive a failing school and make some big changes in her life.

After her husband died, Becca had moved to his hometown, looking to provide stability and healing for her young daughter.

I'd returned because I had nowhere else to go. Aunt Lou

Axe Backwards

was here, and Lovewell was the only place that had ever truly felt like home.

"When are you coming in? Your roots are making me twitchy," Becca groused, slicing a loaf of bread at the kitchen island.

I shrugged.

"Hair that gorgeous needs care."

Head tipped to one side, I ran my fingers through the end of my ponytail.

Graham thought long hair was juvenile. While we were married, I maintained a sharp, angular bob. With blond highlights, of course, because, according to him, the color was sophisticated and sexy.

But now, I'd let my hair grow wild and free. It was more wavy than curly, and a little frizzy. It did what it wanted when it wanted.

Most days, it wanted a ponytail.

Alice was curvy with blond hair and deep green eyes. She had the kind of all-American apple-cheeked beauty that stopped people in their tracks.

Becca was tall and lean with an edgy vibe. Her hair was cut in a trendy short style and she had several tattoos. She was part soccer mom and part badass.

And then there was me. Medium height, medium build, frizzy hair, and a can-do attitude.

See? Quite a trio.

Alice leaned back against the couch cushion, smiling. "I think the *I don't give a fuck* look suits you."

The bark of a laugh that escaped me echoed off the tall wood-paneled ceiling.

"That is true," Becca said, scooping up a bite of eggplant

parm. "After you had that stick up your ass surgically removed, your complexion has improved. Your skin has never looked better."

Alice sipped from her glass of water, then carefully set it on a coaster on the end table. "You're glowing. Are you finally sleeping again?"

I shook my head. "No. I'm getting less sleep than usual, actually. I'm helping out my neighbor. His baby won't sleep, so I'm walking circles with her in the middle of the night."

"So the rumors are true?" Becca clapped, her face lighting up. "You're boning the hot single dad?"

Alice wiggled in her seat. "I heard it from Steph, who heard it from Cole at knitting club, so I know the intel is good."

"Guys. No." My stomach sank. Damn Lovewell and its rumor mill. "Not at all."

As if choreographed, their faces fell simultaneously.

"We've become friends. He recently moved cross-country with a baby, and I've been all messed up about Alexandra's pregnancy and the wedding."

Alice gasped, her eyes widening. "Alex is pregnant?"

I nodded.

Becca stood and paced to one side of the room, then stomped back. "Your ex is a motherfucker. Your sister too. I hate them both, and I've never even met them."

Alice shimmied off the couch and wandered into the kitchen. A moment later, she returned with another bottle of wine. "How did they even end up together?"

The answer to that question was more than a little complex. So I went with the simplest explanation I could. "Alexandra is the princess of the family. She's a lot younger than Elizabeth and me, and what she wants, she gets."

Becca cocked a brow. "Including your shitty ex."

I shrugged and held out my empty wineglass to Alice. "I guess so."

She obliged, using a heavy hand as she poured. "Is Elizabeth okay with this?"

"I guess. She lives in her own world. She's got her own problems. Two homes, three kids, and one semi-public cheating scandal. A few years ago, Ralph slept with my niece's kindergarten teacher."

"Jesus."

"They moved and pretended it never happened. Now she's addicted to Pilates and Adderall."

"God, your family sounds like the definition of dysfunctional." The second the words left her mouth, Becca grimaced. "Sorry. That was harsh."

I shrugged. Therapy had given me some perspective. I wanted to love them, and I wanted relationships with them all, but I had grown to accept we were too different.

"How did they take it when you got divorced?" Alice asked.

"My mom was furious. Screamed at me and then gave me the silent treatment for weeks. She doesn't believe chronic cheating and infecting one's spouse with an STI should be grounds for divorce."

"Oh fuck."

"Yup." My stomach twisted painfully. "So much fucking fun. I was the family disgrace, especially after my sister stayed with her husband when he cheated. My mother said to me, 'You think you deserve better, but you don't.'"

In unison, my friends screamed.

Alice leaned forward, bottle held out to top off my wine again.

"I can't." I cupped a hand over the rim. "I have to drive."

She shook her head. "After a confession like that, we have to open another bottle. I'll have Henri drive you home."

"Or you could call Noah," Becca teased.

I stared at her. "We're just friends."

Unfazed, she grinned.

"He's good-looking," I admitted. "And one of the best people I know. But that part of me is broken."

It's as if the anger and betrayal that overtook me during my divorce festered and bubbled violently enough that it killed any ability to be attracted to men.

"You'll recover." Becca tipped her glass my way, confident.

"Did you?" I countered.

With a deep sigh, she shook her head. "It's different. I can feel physical attraction, trust me. I've had a couple of flings since I moved here."

I didn't know much about her not-quite-love life, but she did, at one time, have a friends-with-benefits arrangement with Noah's oldest brother Gus. That ended on good terms, and the two of them were still friends. He'd reconnected with his ex-wife, and they'd recently welcomed a baby.

"But love another person?" She lowered her chin and gave her head a shake. "No. I still love Dan. I could never give my heart to someone else, especially while Kali is young. Together, she and I—my in-laws too—keep his memory alive. We celebrate his birthdays and talk about him all the time. He's a presence in all of our lives."

Axe Backwards

"But it makes it impossible for you to move on," Alice said.

"I don't want to move on." She straightened, shoulders back, certain. It broke my heart a little, knowing she'd loved Dan so deeply, only to lose him in such a traumatic way. "When he passed, I wasn't sure I could function. I could barely get out of bed, let alone go through the motions. But moving here helped. Now my business is thriving, and my little girl and I are doing well."

"This town gave me my life back," Alice said.

Becca raised her glass. "Same. It's allowed me to figure out how to live again. How to be happy. But falling in love? Can't do it."

"Then you know where I'm coming from," I said, wine sloshing over the rim of my glass.

Alice patiently handed me a napkin.

"No. The opposite, in fact. I had the real deal, and I'll never have it again. You, though? You may have been married, but you've never had that real, true, perfect love. It's out there. You're afraid of getting hurt again. Eventually, the fear will subside, and you'll feel things again."

If only it were as easy as waiting for the bad feelings to pass. The primary substance of my cellular makeup was a jumbled mess of those terrible emotions.

When we were married, I would lie in bed while Graham answered emails on his phone. The frame was a weird slab of wood that had cost a ridiculous amount of money, and our sheets were a bright starched white. Our housekeeper came every Tuesday and was always sure to iron them.

Our bedroom was stark and lonely. All the lighting was

recessed and our bed faced massive windows that looked out at the harbor and Logan Airport.

I'd lie there, wearing fancy silk pajamas with a weird waistband that dug into my skin, watching planes fly in.

The runway was a tiny strip that abutted the ocean.

But the lights and signals always did the trick.

Even in the dark, those pilots trusted themselves enough to land, to keep their passengers safe.

I'd stare at the blinking lights of the air traffic control tower, aching from the inside out. Because of the man sitting a foot away from me. The man who would roll over any minute and expect me to fuck him didn't know a damn thing about me. Nothing that mattered, anyway. And he didn't want to know me. Or see me.

He ignored me unless I could be of use to him. Sometimes, he'd go entire days without really looking at me or speaking to me.

And the agony of the loneliness that ate at me left me hollowed out.

When he betrayed me, when he cheated, lied, and blamed me for it all, I swore I'd never put myself in that position again. I killed off that lonely, sad, vulnerable woman. I'd never be her again.

"I mean it. My lady parts are offline. It's not happening for me."

"Sure." Alice waved me off. "But you get horny, don't you?"

My chest opened up like an empty crevasse. "Nope." And it was the truth. I was practically dead inside.

Becca angled forward, elbows on her knees, cradling her wineglass. "Do you have a vibrator?"

Axe Backwards

"Four." I sighed. "I tried them all, hoping one would do the trick so I could, you know, finish. But no luck."

"So you have no orgasms?"

"Nope. No desire, no attraction. No orgasms. It's not surprising, really. My husband cheated on me, which led to a nasty divorce, and just as I thought the end of the dark tunnel was in sight, he knocked up my baby sister."

Alice sat back on the couch, massaging her temples. "I'm so sorry. No orgasms? How do you function?"

Becca rolled her eyes. "Don't listen to her. She's getting railed by her hot lumberjack husband all the time."

Alice's cheeks went pink. She was such a blusher, and the wine didn't help. "Not all the time." She smirked. "We have kids and jobs, so it's hard to make it happen more than two to three times a week."

Groaning, Becca dropped her head back. "Kill the bitch."

She set her wineglass down, then picked up a throw pillow and chucked it at our friend. I followed suit, and soon we were all giggling uncontrollably on the floor of the living room.

I loved these women. I hadn't expected to find true friendship and support in rural Maine. When I returned, I figured Aunt Lou would be my one and only confidant. But the universe knew I needed badass women in my life and sent them my way.

We were still catching our breath when Henri and the kids walked in. He was a beast of a man, always in a flannel shirt and work boots, but his grumpy exterior softened the minute he laid eyes on his wife.

Alice popped up and kissed the kids' heads. Her son

Tucker, a lanky preteen with dark hair that obscured his eyes, was now taller than her.

"Did you have fun at Auntie Adele's house?"

"I got to play with Thor," Goldie, a little blond firecracker in human form, gushed. "He's so funny and cute."

"Auntie taught me to use a soldering iron," Tucker boasted.

Alice frowned, but Henri laughed. Tucker was always building and fixing things. He'd even helped me figure out the broadband at the food pantry.

"Good. It's time for showers and bed," Alice said. "I'll be up in a bit."

Henri put his arm around his wife's waist and kissed her cheek. "Everything okay here, ladies?"

"All good. Brawny." His wife beamed up at him. "But my friends could use rides home in a bit."

Though he wasn't much for smiling, his lips quirked beneath his beard, and he gave us a small bow. "At your service."

Becca nudged me with a pointy elbow. "See? You, too, could have a lumberjack to attend to all your needs. First, you have to get your head out of your ass, then you jump Noah."

Hands flat on the plush rug on either side of me, I rolled my eyes. "We're just friends. Also, he's a firefighter, not a lumberjack."

Alice dropped to the floor next to me. "Lumberjack is not a vocation." She giggled. "It's a state of being."

Chapter 9
Noah

Calling the Lovewell Fire Department small would be a gross exaggeration. It consisted of a four-man crew, one dispatcher on shift at a time, and a handful of volunteers. The firehouse sat next to the police station off Main Street, and its façade was a deep red brick. When I pulled up, a few guys in blue work pants were milling around in front of the bay doors, washing the engine.

For a moment, I sat in the truck, giving myself a pep talk and digging deep for a little excitement. I was lucky I'd even scored a meeting, so I needed to make the most of it.

Chief Mitchell greeted me with a big smile. He was in his late forties with a thick mustache and stern dad energy that reminded me of my brother Gus.

"You've got quite the résumé." He leaned back, making his desk chair creak. "A hotshot. Bureau of Land Management special operations, national forest certifications, squad leader of the Northern Tahoe region, specialized training in hot spotting, tree felling, and structure protection?"

I took a deep breath. I wasn't the kind of guy who sat at a

desk or did a lot of work using a computer. It had taken me all weekend and a lot of help from Jude to double-check my certifications and get it all typed up. It was strange, to distill all my experiences and hard work into typed words on a page.

He stood and reached out. "I want to shake your hand again. This is quite a record of service."

I got to my feet. "Thank you, sir."

"While I'm thrilled to meet you and would love to hear your war stories over a beer, I'm not sure I've got a job for you."

Lips pressed into a line, I nodded. It had been a long shot at such a small department, but I wasn't qualified for much else.

"We've got a limited budget and no open positions at the moment, but if something opens up." He removed his hat and ran his fingers through his hair. "It would also be quite different for you. We're first responders. We don't fight overly complex fires or craft strategy here. What we handle is far more basic."

"I understand," I said, keeping my tone even. A routine, boring gig was precisely why I wanted it. "I'm a father now." I shoved my hands into my pockets. "I can't deploy to fires for weeks at a time. I can't take the kind of risks I used to."

"I get it. Wish I could help."

Though I was disappointed, Tess and I would be okay if I didn't find a job immediately. I had been living off the payout I received last year when Owen had sold the family timber company, and I wasn't at risk of using it up anytime soon. It wasn't a ton, but it was enough to keep us comfortable for now. Career-wise, I wasn't sure where I'd land. I was

Axe Backwards

proud of the specialized skills I'd obtained over the years. Unfortunately, they didn't seem to be in demand up here, and I couldn't go back to the West Coast.

Being a dad was my first priority. But I wasn't used to not working. I preferred to be useful. To be of service in some way.

With a nod, I pulled my keys from my pocket. "Thank you for your time."

"You know." He scratched his chin. "My cousin runs the Katahdin search and rescue team. They're always recruiting qualified talent."

The Appalachian Trail ran through Maine, culminating at Mt. Katahdin, so this region attracted a great number of hikers, campers, backcountry skiers, and those looking for remote fly-fishing. Which was great for Finn, who had recently started a flight tourism company. It was booming, which meant the forests of Maine were seeing plenty of traffic. It made sense that the search and rescue team would be active and hiring.

I couldn't be out in the wilderness away from Tess, and despite the résumé he'd complimented me on, few of my skills would translate.

"I'd love to learn more." I might as well get the information, though I imagined emergency medical certifications would be a must, and I'd only had basic EMS training.

"Good man." He slapped my back and walked me out.

I fought back a forlorn sigh. I'd made it another day, yet I was no closer to figuring out what I was doing.

From the firehouse, I turned left and headed for the diner. My mom had taken Tess to the playground and was planning to drop her off later, so while I had a little time to myself, I'd drown my sorrows in a slice of blueberry pie. Or maybe two.

I patted my stomach. Fitness used to define me. It was the first and most important requirement of my job. We trained relentlessly, hiking while wearing sixty-pound packs and having pull-up competitions in our spare time.

Anymore, hauling boxes of diapers was the closest thing I got to a workout. But I was feeling less like myself with each passing day. I needed a job, a routine, and to set a path for the future for Tess and me.

At the moment, it looked like that path would involve a dad bod, and I'd have to deal with that.

When I slid into a booth, Bernice greeted with her usual snarky charm.

"Where's the cute baby?"

"With grandma," I said, lacing my fingers on the tabletop. "Coffee, please. And pie."

"Your girlfriend prefers apple." Her tone was one of disbelief.

Apple pie was objectively delicious, but up here, it was heresy to acknowledge the deliciousness of any pie that wasn't blueberry. Any pie that wasn't Bernice's blueberry, really.

"I don't have a girlfriend." I kept my tone polite. With the way gossip grew and spread around here when I was a kid, I figured there wasn't much more I could do.

"Sure you do. Lou's niece. Trust me, take her a slice of apple. She'll be grateful."

Eyes squeezed shut, I pinched the bridge of my nose. "Not my girlfriend. We're just friends."

Axe Backwards

Bernice clicked her tongue. "This isn't a situationship, is it? You young people. Jesus."

God, was it too much to ask to sit here and eat my feelings in peace?

"No." Mrs. Dupont craned her neck from where she sat two tables over. Erica and Loraine were with her, each with a steaming mug. "That's what the kids do now, on TikTok. They don't date."

And then, just as I thought this couldn't get more embarrassing, Father Renee, the ancient priest who'd given me my first communion, stood and approached.

"Now, son, I know you've only just returned to town, but poor Victoria went through a very bad divorce. She's a kind, helpful woman. And while I'd like it if she came to mass more often, I hope you do right by her."

With a long exhale, I closed my eyes. In theory, moving back here with Tess was a wonderful idea. She'd grow up in the Maine wilderness, surrounded by family, running wild with her cousins, ensconced in the supportive embrace of an idyllic small town.

Despite how halcyon my misguided fantasy was, I'd conveniently forgotten how nosy and overbearing the locals could be. I barely opened up about my life to my siblings. I surely wouldn't be broadcasting my relationship status to Father Renee and the local busybodies.

Even so, I smiled. I'd be Vic's boyfriend this weekend.

Oh no. My stomach sank. *The wedding.* I had to find nice clothes. It was black-tie, whatever the hell that meant.

I picked up my phone. Though there were six of us, I only had one brother who knew anything about this.

Daphne Elliot

> **NOAH**
> I need a favor.

> **OWEN**
> ?

I APPRECIATED MY SECOND-OLDEST BROTHER. HE NEVER guilted me or interrogated me. He didn't hound me about the reasoning behind my choices. He was a busy man, so I could count on him to get right to the point.

> **NOAH**
> I'm going to a black-tie wedding at the Kennebunkport Yacht Club this weekend. What the hell do I wear?

> **OWEN**
> A Tux

> **NOAH**
> Thank you, Captain Obvious. How do I get one?

> **OWEN**
> Hang on. I've got a guy.
>
> Who invited you to a society wedding at the yacht club?

> **NOAH**
> I'm going with Victoria. It's her sister's wedding.

> **OWEN**
> Can you drive to Bangor?

Axe Backwards

I checked my watch. I was in and out of the fire station in under thirty minutes, and Tess was due to nap soon. An hour's drive would be fine.

> NOAH
> Yes.

Within minutes, my brother had texted an address.

> OWEN
> Tell him I sent you. My assistant is sending over a list of things you'll need for the weekend.

> NOAH
> Thank you. I owe you.

> OWEN
> Victoria's a wonderful person. Don't fuck up.

My instinct was to respond, to tell him we were friends, that I was doing her a favor, that she helped me with Tess. But I was too damn tired to try to convince yet another person.

I could only push the "just friends" rock up the hill so

many times in one day.

I didn't have time anyway. I had to haul ass to Bangor if I wanted to get what I needed and be back before Mom showed up with Tess.

"Bernice," I said with a smile. "Can I grab that pie to go?"

Chapter 10
Noah

The inn was beautiful. The historic structure sat on a peninsula overlooking the ocean. I stood at the end of the dock, surveying the vast rocky coastline. I'd missed this.

I was an inland guy. We usually rolled our eyes at anything related to Downeast, as it was called, but the hoity-toity lobster and lighthouse part of Maine was breathtaking.

I hadn't been here since I was a kid. Mom would rent a beach house in Wells every summer, and we'd run wild for a week, tide pooling and competing to see who could catch the coolest ocean creatures.

Where Jude carefully caught his crabs with a net, I used my hands. Naturally, that involved getting pinched many times. I probably still had a few faint scars from those adventures.

I smiled at the memory, deciding then that I'd carry on the tradition. I'd bring Tess down here in the summer to enjoy the ocean. To feel the sand between her toes and experience the joy of finding a starfish at low tide. Maine was large and diverse and consistently underestimated. The natural beauty was incredible, and the salty ocean air had already helped clear my mind.

Living in survival mode made it difficult to stop and enjoy the small moments. And becoming a parent had taught me that life was full of small moments that needed to be savored.

Currently, I was missing those small moments. I missed my baby girl. Mom had already texted me dozens of photos and videos, but my chest ached with longing to snuggle her, to press a kiss to her head, to sing her to sleep.

I didn't regret coming, though. Vic hadn't been herself for the past couple of days. Not that I could blame her. I could only imagine how difficult this weekend would be for her.

As I waited for her to come down from our room so we could head to the rehearsal and cocktail reception, I vowed to give her my all. I'd make sure she had fun and I'd distract her from the pain and bad memories. I'd kidnap her if I had to and take off in search of the best lobster roll in town.

She'd barely spoken on the ride down. Aunt Lou didn't allow for silence, though. She spent the trip filling us in on all the gossip going around at her assisted living facility. She had always been a live wire, that lady. I could see why Vic loved her so much.

Dressed and ready for the evening in clothing Owen's guy insisted on, I hung out by the dock for a while, taking in the scenery, and FaceTimed with Mom and Tess. Eventually, Vic joined me.

I'd left the hotel room so she could do her hair and

makeup in peace. There were two beds, thank God, but it was still tight quarters and I didn't want to make her uncomfortable.

Her simple black dress was short and flowy and showed a lot of leg. The way she'd styled her hair, down and all shiny and wavy, took a moment to get used to. I hadn't seen her without her hair in a ponytail since I'd come back to Lovewell. The heels she wore were sexy as hell, only accentuating her toned legs.

Staggering a little, I put my hand over my heart. "Damn, I have the hottest date."

She swatted at me. "Don't flirt with me."

"Can't help it. I've got a hot date and we gotta make it look like I'm head over heels for you."

"I know." She huffed a laugh. "I'm sure it's a great hardship."

I took her hand and spun her around, making her swishy skirt flare out and giving me a glimpse of her thighs. "Not at all. This weekend will be a piece of cake."

Vic was kind and funny. She was also very, very pretty. I'd been keeping her firmly in the friend zone in my head. But I was a red-blooded man, so it was impossible to ignore her shiny hair, her chocolate brown eyes, and her very round ass.

So I compartmentalized. Vic was a friend; I couldn't look at her like that.

I was good at keeping all my thoughts where they belonged. When I went into fire mode, I was all business. If someone asked for my birthday while I was directing a disaster response, I doubt I could recall it.

"Are you ready?" I asked, offering her my arm.

Daphne Elliot

The long, boring rehearsal was on the beach. Within minutes, it was clear the bride was a bit of a diva, but I smiled, chatted, and held Vic's hand. Playing the supportive boyfriend was not difficult. The gratitude shining in my date's eyes every time she looked at me only made it easier.

After the rehearsal, we were ushered to an oceanfront patio area where a string quartet was playing and waiters were at the ready, bearing silver trays of champagne and small, complicated foods.

I still couldn't square it with my childhood memories. The Randolphs hadn't always been rich. Mr. Randolph was a plumber and Mrs. Randolph ran a dance studio in town. Our paths didn't cross much, but everyone in town knew their success story. It was practically part of the town folklore by now.

"Hard to believe plumbing supplies paid for all this," Vic mused, sipping her champagne and watching her parents double air-kiss guests.

"What was it again?" I asked, marveling at our surroundings.

"It's a tool to clear vent stacks," she explained. "When I was in high school, Dad came up with an idea for how to make it easier. It had come to him while he was on a roof. He came home, built a prototype, tested it a few times, and then called his cousin, who's a patent lawyer."

She shrugged and blew out a breath, making her cheeks puff out.

"The rest is history. With it, plumbers don't have to get on roofs as much, which makes the job safer, faster, and easier. Once Dad found investors, Randolph Plumbing

Axe Backwards

Supply was born. Plumbers use Dad's tools every day, and my parents get a portion of the sales."

"Impressive," I said. "I've seen the trucks all over the US."

"It was bizarre. One day we were a normal family, and the next we were rich. And not like *let's go to Disney World and buy new cars instead of used* rich, but live in a mansion and vacation on the French Riviera rich."

I hadn't known Vic for long. Not really. We'd run in different circles as kids. But one of the things that struck me about her was how down-to-earth she was. How she loved hiking and good coffee and greeted everyone in town with a smile. It was hard to square this person I knew to the people surrounding us.

"I don't belong here," she said as if reading my mind. "My parents and sisters changed after we left Maine. While I went to college, they moved to an expensive Boston suburb and bought a big house. My sisters went to private school, and my parents joined the country club."

"And that's not you."

She gave me a glare. "Of course not. I'm the last person who belongs at a country club. Trust me, my ex-husband reminded me of that frequently."

I looked over to where the happy couple was greeting guests. Graham was exactly as Vic had described. A tanned, Botoxed, capped-teeth Ken doll. His suit probably cost more than my car and he had a shiny watch on his wrist, but his pompous attitude was doing most of the work.

"Let's go find more of those scallop things," I said, pulling Vic away from where she was staring at them.

For the first hour, we made pleasant chit-chat with out-of-town guests and checked in with Aunt Lou often to make sure was comfortable.

Vic was finally loosening up, and for a while, I hoped that things would not be as tense as she feared.

But then her mother descended.

I'd only heard tidbits of information about Miranda Randolph from gossip in town and from Vic herself. None of it did her justice. She had a harsh dark bob and she wore a lot of jewelry and a sneer. She cornered us by the bar, forcing introductions and interrogating her eldest daughter about her job, her friends, and how she'd met me.

"You're looking a bit hippy," she said through gritted teeth. "I suppose there are no Pilates classes up there in the sticks."

Deflating beside me, Vic smoothed down the skirt of her dress.

It wasn't my place, but I was having trouble keeping my mouth shut while Miranda listed all the things she believed to be wrong with her daughter.

I almost lost it when she leaned in, running her fingers along Vic's cheek, and said, "Surely there's a decent dermatologist in Bangor. You should make an appointment. You won't be young forever. A few laser treatments could go a long way."

God, this woman was a fucking delight. As Mrs. Randolph's face was pulled so tight she resembled a rabid dog, I had to bite back the urge to comment.

Thankfully she moved on from judging her daughter to grilling us about our relationship and my job. So I shifted gears and focused on being a supportive, friendly plus-one as

Axe Backwards

Vic went with the story we'd settled on. That we were neighbors who started as friends and eventually became more.

"A Hebert?" Her mother scoffed.

Her derision wasn't a shock. My family didn't have the best reputation. My dad was doing time in federal prison, after all.

As Miranda yammered on, several people came over to say hello. The bride, who wore a serene expression, rubbed at her stomach, which looked pretty flat to me, continuously. Then a tall and painfully thin woman I assumed that was Vic's other sister appeared.

"What do you do?" Alexandra asked me, still unnecessarily cradling the nonexistent bump. The tone of her voice indicated that anything less than investment banker or CEO would be insufficient.

"Firefighter." It wasn't technically true, but something told me that mentioning my state of unemployment would not have gone over well.

The moment the word came out of my mouth, all three of their faces fell. It was apparent that I was no longer worth speaking to. It was for the best, really. This interaction needed to end.

I put my arm around Vic. My protective instincts were screaming at me to throw her over my shoulder and make a run for the nearest lobster shack for beer, real food, and a break from this bullshit.

Before I could put my foolproof plan into action, though, another woman came barreling through the crowd.

"You said you weren't dating," Mrs. Dupont insisted, fluffing her teased blond hair. Her late husband had been mayor when I was a kid. She was one of those mean, insular types who thought she was better than the rest of us.

Though she wasn't too good for gossip. That was her main stock-in-trade.

Vic's mother and sisters exchanged looks, their expressions all narrowing. Several conversations nearby quieted, as if everyone within earshot was listening in.

Next to me, Vic stiffened. "We were keeping it quiet," she said, her tone soft and her cheeks going pink.

"This one doesn't date much," Mrs. Dupont announced loud enough for the entire room to hear. "Probably still in love with the groom."

In response, Vic gasped. Alexandra rubbed her baby bump, wearing a smug smirk.

Fuck. This had to be Vic's worst nightmare come to life. People were staring and whispering, their judgment and gleeful looks impossible to ignore.

"Of course they're dating," Aunt Lou said, batting at ankles with her cane as she pushed her way into the group. She threw Mrs. Dupont an absolutely murderous look, then eyed me up and down. "Look at him. If she didn't lock him down, I would have. You know I have a weakness for firefighters."

I pulled Vic closer, rubbing a hand down her upper arm.

"He looks like that." Lou gestured to me, almost hitting Alexandra with her cane—likely on purpose. "*And* he's a hero?" She put her hand over her heart. "Swoon. My Victoria's taste has improved so much since she moved north." She shot a glare in Graham's direction.

Alexandra glowered, and beside her, Miranda rolled her

eyes. I was pretty sure that was the only facial expression she was capable of making.

Mrs. Dupont's nostrils flared. "They're always together," she said, "but we all know they're only friends. His own mother confirmed it at knitting group last Tuesday."

Anger ignited in my chest. Why this vile woman was so concerned with my personal life was infuriating. But the heartbreak I felt for Vic, who was shrinking little by little beside me, was far more acute.

I had to remedy this situation. Make her feel better. No, Vic wasn't my girlfriend. Though I wouldn't admit it to this old biddy or the snobs surrounding us. But she was my friend. I cared deeply for her. And just being here was traumatic. There was no way I'd let her be humiliated like this.

"I'm sorry, Mrs. Dupont," I said, keeping my tone disgustingly polite. "But I take offense. There's no way on earth I could spend even a small amount of time with this woman and not fall wildly in love with her."

Aunt Lou smiled at me. I was smiling back when movement behind her caught my eye. It was Graham. The bastard ex-husband himself was sauntering our way, wearing a smug smile and one of those preppy sport coats, looking like he'd come in from fox hunting.

Blood boiling, I clenched my fists.

He was at least a few years older than Vic, maybe over forty, and brimming with the kind of unearned confidence his daddy's money had probably bought him.

I was several inches taller and, from the look of things, could snap him in half if I needed to. And it was beginning to look like that may be the only way to escape this nightmare.

Daphne Elliot

Holding a glass of what I imagined was expensive scotch, his sneer fully in place, he ambled over. He had the absolute audacity to blatantly look Vic up and down.

My heart pounded in my ears. There were two options here: grab Vic and make a run for it or stand our ground and shut these snobby jerks up for good.

I did what I'd been trained to do. Assess, strategize, and find a way to minimize the damage. I chose the second option.

Turning to Vic, I tucked a strand of hair behind her ear.

She peered up at me, her eyes swimming with discomfort. Fuck. More than anything, I wished I had the power to fix it all.

Since I couldn't take away the hurt, I did the next best thing. I stared into those chocolate brown eyes and said, "I'm crazy about you. Please, no more secrets."

Then, cupping her chin, I angled in and gently brushed my lips against hers.

She rose up on her tiptoes to meet me, and what should have been a quick peck evolved quickly.

With a groan, I pulled her closer. Instantly, her fingers were in my hair, her arms around my neck.

Fuck. This was a mistake.

It felt too easy. Too natural and too damn hot.

Very hot.

Weirdly hot.

My brain switched off, and instead of being the affectionate peck I'd envisioned, we lingered.

The world around us faded into the background. No one else mattered.

When I pulled away, she blinked up at me, her pupils

blown wide and her lips parted. We stared at each other for a moment before I turned to her family and grabbed her hand.

"If you'll excuse us, my girl needs a drink."

Without a second of hesitation, I pulled her toward the bar, leaving the crowd gaping.

Behind us, a whistle rang out. I didn't have to turn around to know it was Aunt Lou.

Chapter 11
Victoria

The wedding went off without a hitch. Every detail was tasteful and perfect. A federal judge who golfed with my dad performed the oceanfront ceremony, and the guest list included all the Boston business and social elite, just as my mom had always dreamed.

At the reception, Graham and Alexandra barely interacted, each working the crowd and soaking up the attention.

My baby sister looked beautiful. All willowy limbs and wide blue eyes. She'd changed into the dress she'd purchased to wear to the reception only. There were easily over two hundred people here, so thankfully, my family mostly ignored my presence.

Sadly, Graham's was everywhere. As were his colleagues, friends, and fraternity brothers. So far, they'd generally treated me in one of two ways: either they totally ignored me or they went out of their way to chat, pretending to be interested in my life. The second type of interaction was epically worse.

At least Noah was here. He was an incredible fake date

and hype man, constantly talking up my achievements at the food pantry or telling funny stories about Lovewell.

Then there was the kiss.

We had not spoken of it.

But it had happened. And I'd been thinking about it nonstop since last night.

Noah, the gentleman that he was, had spent the entire day attempting to rescue me from my shitty family.

Last night, before his lips had touched mine, I'd been spiraling into a panic. The contact had grounded me. Pulled me out of the shame vortex that consumed me every time my mother and sisters were near.

It wouldn't happen again. Obviously. We were pretending until after the wedding. Nothing more. We'd stepped up our act since the interrogation yesterday, but that mostly entailed holding hands and hanging out. Which, given this crowd, was not a hardship at all.

In Lovewell, he fit in easily with his outdoorsy, lumberjack vibe.

But he looked dangerously good in a tux. Today, he was working an *Ivy League banker who climbs mountains on the weekends* vibe. Though I was wearing heels, he still towered over me, and each time he touched me, his rough calluses rasping against my skin, I had to fight the shiver that worked its way through me.

As a server passed by, he snagged two champagne flutes, then tapped his against mine.

"To the happy couple," I said with an eye roll.

"Oh, yes." He gagged. "Best wishes."

We sipped our drinks, chatting and laughing on the outskirts of the dance floor, hoping we could avoid any more scrutiny. We'd made it through the ceremony and dinner. We only had to hold out a little longer, and then we could get out of here.

He hovered close, the stubble on his cheek grazing my earlobe, and a slight zing zipped through me. Nothing major, just a tiny electrical current running under my skin.

It was strange and yet not unwelcome.

"May I have this dance?"

My parents had spared no expense, and the twelve-piece band was fantastic.

I peered up at him, those piercing blue eyes doing a number on me. They were always arresting, but with champagne in my system, the effect was more powerful. My feet hurt, but there was no way I'd say no.

Because a tiny part of me, so tiny I'd never admit it out loud, enjoyed pretending to be Noah's girlfriend. He was an incredible friend, but being on the receiving end of his attentiveness and all the small but meaningful gestures he would, presumably, bestow upon a woman he was seeing? If I wasn't careful, I could get far too comfortable with this. For the first time, I saw him as a romantic, sexy guy, not just an exhausted single dad.

He took my glass, and as the band played "My Best Friend" by Tim McGraw, he led me onto the dance floor.

"You look beautiful," he said as I wrapped my arms around his neck.

I leaned back so I could see his face. "Thanks. You look pretty good too."

With a shrug, he angled in close again. "This old thing?"

At his proximity, I shivered in anticipation. His lips near my skin lit me up from the inside out. Maybe it was the alcohol, or maybe it was because I was wearing a very expensive and very revealing gown, but my body was on high alert.

"This dress." He ran his fingers down the deep V in the back. "Is so sexy."

I swallowed. Those electric currents? They were zapping the shit out of me now.

"You sure you're okay? You looked shaken up after photos."

My mother had pulled me aside to remind me of what a disappointment I was. But with his fingertips grazing my bare skin, I barely remembered what she said.

"My mother," I said, her words coming back to me. "She said it was such a shame I couldn't, in her words, 'hold on' to Graham."

He scoffed. "No way."

My stomach roiled, at odds with the gentle way we moved on the dance floor. "Yes. And then she told me that it was for the best because my failure—again, her words—was Alex's triumph."

He laughed. Full-on laughed.

"Fuck. That is the most ridiculous shit I've ever heard. Who talks like that, especially to their own daughter? Is your mother a real human, or is she a cartoon villain?"

Before I knew what was happening, I was laughing too. He was right. The entire thing was preposterous. My mother was vile. This was a happy day. She had no reason to cut me down. Yet she took every opportunity she got.

And I'd allowed it. Why wouldn't I? It was all I knew. Day after day, year after year, she'd treated me this way.

"Thank you." I wiped at a stray tear. "I needed to laugh. This whole weekend..."

Axe Backwards

His blue eyes darkened to the color of stormy waters, and his fingers flexed on my waist.

He was thinking about the kiss.

Shit, now I was thinking about the kiss.

"When do you think we can leave?" He craned his neck and scanned our surroundings, breaking the spell.

"After they cut the cake," I replied. "Then we can bounce."

He gave me a sly smile. To say our hotel room was luxurious was an understatement. Last night, we'd watched *Schitt's Creek* before falling asleep in our respective king size beds. It was a lot like being home in Lovewell, except without Tess and with a little more sleep for us both.

I missed that little bugger, and by the way he kept checking his phone and how he smiled at the photos Debbie sent every hour, he was too. Tess was having the time of her life with her grandma, who had undoubtedly been letting her mainline sugar and *Bluey* all weekend.

We planned to leave first thing tomorrow morning, skipping the post-wedding brunch and dropping Aunt Lou off on the way back. The geezer squad had handled all of yesterday's deliveries, but summer was coming, which was our busiest time, so I had lots of work to catch up on at the food pantry.

This weekend had been surreal. Part nightmare, part daydream. I couldn't wait to plant my feet on the ground and get back to reality.

A reality in which Noah and I were friends.

Friends who did not kiss.

We snuck slices of cake and were heading for the exit when my mother hurried over with Elizabeth on her heels.

My stomach sank. I'd had more than enough of both of them this weekend.

"Thank you for coming," she said formally, as though, instead of sharing DNA, we were mere acquaintances.

Noah's strong arm was instantly around me, pulling me close. He did this every time my hackles rose. As if he could sense it. I shouldn't have been surprised that he'd create a physical shield of protection around me this way. Given his career, he obviously had a hero complex.

I wasn't complaining. It was strangely comforting.

"We'll see so much more of one another soon." She gave me a sly smile.

Ice filled my veins. "What do you mean?"

She sipped her champagne, nose in the air. "Oh, I didn't tell you? Dad and I purchased a lake house."

The slow smile that spread across her face was so wide I worried her facelift stitches had come loose.

Relief hit me. Okay, so they bought another house. I wasn't sure why it mattered to me. I had no intention of visiting.

"In Lovewell."

My eye twitched.

"We'll be there in two weeks. Alexandra will join us for the summer so she can rest, poor thing."

"But you don't like Lovewell," I blurted out.

"It's more of a compound, really," she said, as if she hadn't heard me. "But we need a place to spend summers with our grandchild." She beamed at Alex, who was posing for photos while cupping her still flat stomach. Graham hovered next to her, his face ruddy from the abundance of alcohol he'd already consumed.

Axe Backwards

"You have two grandchildren already." I glanced at Elizabeth.

She was too busy staring at the bar where Ralph was flirting with one of Alex's sorority sisters. Bastard.

My mother smiled wider, her gaze shifting to Noah. "Of course. All the grandkids are welcome. It's a beautiful property. With a lot of privacy. You know we deeply value our privacy."

My mother in Lovewell? And my sisters? A wave of dread washed over me, threatening to pull me under. This couldn't be happening.

Life had finally taken a turn for the better, and here my family was, on standby to crush the joy from it.

"This will give us a chance to get to know you better, Noah," my mom said, her tone lacking even a hint of enthusiasm. "And your... *family*." The way she emphasized the word made it sound like she'd rather spend time with a pack of feral raccoons.

No matter that Noah's family was lovely and generous. In her mind, they were nowhere near acceptable.

"Summers up north are so beautiful," she trilled. "Dad is having our boat transported to the lake there, and our property has a cottage for Marnie too." Marnie was my parents' long-time housekeeper. Of course my mother wouldn't deign to make her own bed or brew her own coffee, even on vacation.

"We'll see each other all the time. Won't that be lovely? We get so little time with you, Victoria." Despite her words, her tone was pure threat.

"Vic is very busy. I'm not sure how often she'll have time to come out to your new place," Noah said, jumping to my defense. "She's got a lot of fundraising planned. The work she's done with the food pantry has been incredible, and she's bringing in even more resources."

My mother ignored him. She did not give a shit about the food pantry. Her idea of charitable work involved gowns and diamonds, not actually helping those in need.

The lump in my throat grew, threatening to suffocate me. Lovewell had become my sanctuary, my happy place. It was free from the drama and toxicity that came with my family. I had friends and I had a job I was passionate about. Now they were coming back?

Onto my turf?

For months?

I wanted to cry. And scream and stomp my feet.

Before the urge could overtake me, Noah pulled me close and kissed the top of my head.

And with that simple gesture, my mind cleared.

I was done. With this conversation and this wedding.

Seeming to sense how close I was to shutting down, Noah cupped my cheek gently. "Looks like I need to get my girl home." His voice was little more than a whisper.

It was for me, not for our audience. But it did the trick.

Turning to my mother, he forced a smile. "It's getting late." He craned his neck, peering around her. "Is that Senator Blakely? Looks like he may be leaving."

"Oh no." She whipped around and stomped away, prepared to continue her social climbing and leaving me to catch my breath. Elizabeth dutifully followed her, looking morose as usual.

Blowing out a breath, I looked up at Noah. "I'm fucked."

He pulled my body flush against his. The heat of him

was a comfort in the cool night air. I buried my head in my chest, willing all thoughts of this wedding and my family away.

"It's gonna be okay," he said into my hair. "Let's get you home."

Chapter 12
Noah

Until yesterday, I was sure Vic was exaggerating when she talked about how awful her family was. I had expected them to be snobbish, but nothing had prepared me for just how cruel they'd been to her.

Her father, who was far too busy talking to his golf cronies to do more than acknowledge her, wasn't much better. The man seemed content to stand idly by while her mother terrorized his oldest daughter.

I'd seen a very different side of her this weekend. Back in Lovewell, she was one of the most confident, level-headed people I knew. But for the last forty-five minutes, she'd been shaking her head and muttering to herself. This weekend had left her all out of sorts. While I didn't have the first clue how to make things better, I wanted to at least offer my support.

"You don't have to argue with yourself," I said softly as we passed Augusta on 95. "You can talk to me."

"Or me," Lou said from the back seat where she was playing *Words with Friends* on her phone.

Vic stared out the window. "Sorry. I talk to myself a lot."

"It's a sign of genius."

That garnered a hint of a smile. "More like I'm losing my mind, but I appreciate the positive spin on it."

"For what it's worth," Aunt Lou said, "you handled the weekend beautifully. You're a good kid. You showed up for your sister and kept your chin up."

I couldn't help but think there was more to this story than I knew. It all weighed so heavily on Vic, and it killed me to know how painful it was.

I was the guy who ran away, the brother who was AWOL for family gatherings and holidays.

For so long I thought it was for the best. Now, witnessing the strength she mustered to show up, despite how difficult it was, I was rethinking all of it. Maybe staying away hadn't been brave. Maybe, all this time, I'd been a coward.

"I think you were brave."

In response, she scoffed and curled up in the passenger seat. She was dressed in sweats, with her hair back in its usual ponytail. She looked beautiful.

At the wedding, she was glamorous and sexy. But right now, looking vulnerable in the front seat of my truck, she looked like my best friend.

After a long stretch of silence, she finally spoke again. "My family is coming to Lovewell. For the entire summer."

The words hung in the air between us for a solid half mile.

"And I'm spiraling." One fat tear rolled down her cheek, quickly followed by another and another.

I almost drove off the road. The sight gutted me and sent

my mind spinning. What could I do to make it better? How could I make her laugh and smile again?

"That was so painful." Her voice was smaller than I'd ever heard it.

Aunt Lou reached over the seatback and handed her a tissue.

I kept my eyes on the road. *Fuck. Crying. Tears. How do I fix this?*

"What if—" Vic bit her lip and shifted in her seat. "What if we kept pretending?"

Oh fuck. Of all the possibilities I'd come up with to help her during the drive—ice cream, a Britney Spears singalong, maybe a quick soft shoe routine on the side of the road—being her fake boyfriend beyond today had not entered my consciousness.

"I know it's a lot to ask."

Vic's slumped shoulders and the pain in her eyes killed me. The way those people spoke to her made me want to fell a tree and make sure it landed on their car. A dozen times this weekend, she'd faded away into a distant, beautiful person I didn't recognize.

It was fun pretending to be in love with her, and it was too goddamn easy. I'd never been in love, and I'd never had a long-term girlfriend. Most of my relationships ended after a few months. Usually, I'd work nonstop during fire season, which wasn't conducive to maintaining relationships.

But I'd also never met a woman who made me want to give my all to a relationship. Not the way Jack had with Emily. Living with them, having a front-row seat to their love story, made it impossible to deny that they'd found in one another something they could not live without.

Maybe it was the way I was wired. I'd always lived to chase the next adventure, and my whole life, I'd feared boredom.

These days, my brothers were finding their people and building adult lives.

I had Tess now. She was my person. And I'd spend my whole life loving her and caring for her.

What woman would want to come in second place to my daughter?

If the women at the wedding this weekend were any indication, not many.

Every single one of my hero instincts was screaming at me to put on my cape and fix this for her.

"It's not," I said, racking my brain for words that would help. "I can understand why you want to."

"He's an excellent boyfriend," Lou added from the back seat.

Vic cracked a teary smile. "Yes. You performed perfectly. Polite, smart, and sexy as hell in a tux."

My heart stumbled. Oh shit.

That was new information.

In my periphery, she turned to look out the windshield, her cheeks flushing.

She thought I was sexy? *Interesting.* Irrelevant, but interesting, nonetheless.

My knee-jerk reaction was to say yes. To say *I'll pretend to be your fake boyfriend forever. Please keep smiling and never cry again.*

But I hated lying. And I'd come back to Lovewell to rebuild trust with my family.

Axe Backwards

It was a miracle they hadn't disowned me when I showed up with a secret baby last month.

I'd fled as soon as I could, and I didn't keep in touch. I'd been too busy living a life of adventure. All the while, they'd worried about me.

The last thing I wanted was to hurt them again. Especially Jude. We were two halves of a whole. I'd already lost Jack. I couldn't lose my twin too.

Behind me, Lou cleared her throat. "Here's a wild idea. What if the two of you actually dated? You'd fall in love and live happily ever after. That would be a real fuck-you to your mother."

I didn't dare look at Vic. My heart raced and my sweaty palms stuck to the steering wheel. That would be ridiculous. Impossible. We were both busy. And I had a lot to accomplish before I could even consider being in a committed relationship.

I clung to those logical, reasonable thoughts. Or I tried. My brain, the traitor, circled round and round, back to the sensation of her lips on mine, the way she gasped slightly when we'd broken apart, the warmth of her beneath my palm when I gripped her hips and pulled her body flush against mine.

I could live a thousand years and not forget a single detail of the kiss I shared with Victoria Randolph. It was unlike anything I'd ever experienced before.

"You're both grown, but if you want to act like children and pretend, that's your choice."

"We're just friends, Aunt Lou." Vic's tone was defiant, her posture rigid.

Okay, then. My heart sank a little, but I pushed away the niggle of disappointment.

"You keep saying that—"

"Because it's true."

I kept my attention fixed firmly on the road rather than on the beautiful, sad woman in my passenger seat. If I looked at her, I was worried I'd give in to the urge to pull over, drop to one knee, and propose just for the prospect of another kiss and to make her forget about Graham. What kind of name was that anyway? He was a pair of pleated khakis in human form.

"My sweet Vic, listen to me," Lou said. "That shithead treated you terribly. I'd love nothing more than to shove a nine iron up his ass. And your parents? The idiots have their priorities all screwed up. I hate how much they've hurt you."

I knew what was at stake. I'd seen her face as Alexandra smugly rubbed her belly. The way Graham had looked her up and down like she wasn't good enough.

The way they treated her, dismissed her, made me stupid. Stupid with loyalty for my friend, and maybe the tiniest bit stupid with lust.

"Maybe," Aunt Lou started, squeezing Vic's shoulder, "the best way to heal is to date a wonderful man who makes you happy. Not Noah, of course. Since you two aren't interested in one another." She eyed me in the rearview mirror and gave me a wink. "But we can find someone else. You're wonderful. Once the town knows you're on the market, there will be hotties lining up for a chance with you."

I gripped the steering wheel, making the leather creak beneath my hands. I didn't want Vic to date anyone else. Lou wasn't wrong about how incredible she was. Smart, beautiful, and funny. Plus, she cared deeply and worked hard for the people and things she loved.

The thought of losing her created a pit in my gut. And the idea of some other bozo getting a chance with her sent anger coursing through my veins.

"I can't date for real," Vic said. "I don't feel attraction anymore. I'm not interested in anyone."

My stomach clenched. She couldn't feel attraction? I guess I was the only one who'd gotten my ass kicked by that kiss, then.

Lou threw up her hands. "Jesus H. Christ. Shit-For-Brains really did a number on you."

Turning in her seat, Vic glared at her aunt. "Stop talking like I'm a helpless victim. I don't have the capacity for romantic relationships anymore. That's it. It's not the end of the world. And the last thing I want to do is explain such a personal, delicate issue to my mother and sisters. Especially the one carrying my ex-husband's baby."

Suddenly, she was crying again. Big, fat sobs this time.

"I'm sorry, sweetie," Lou said, rubbing a soothing hand down her niece's arm. "The last thing I want is to make you feel worse."

Vic covered her face with her hands. "I don't want to have to explain to the world that I'm broken. I don't want scorn. Or worse, pity. For once, I'd like my family to think I have my shit together. That my life is great. Is that so much to ask?"

As I peered over at her beautiful, tearstained face, I knew I couldn't possibly say no to her.

A literal damsel in distress sat in the front seat of my car, asking me to pretend to be her boyfriend. To touch her and kiss her and take her out on dates.

In what universe would I ever say no?

I still couldn't shake the feel of her lips, the scent of her hair.

The minute she kissed me, I was a goner.

Eventually, I'd have to deal with the shit my family would give me, but for Vic, I'd endure anything. I'd never have a chance for anything real with her, so I might as well enjoy faking it for a summer.

"I'll be your fake boyfriend," I said, keeping my eyes on the road. "We can do what we did this weekend. It'll be easy. We already spend a lot of time together, and the town thinks we're dating."

Straightening, she examined me, the hope emanating from her breaking my heart. "I promise I won't ask too much of you."

That was the thing. She could ask whatever she wanted of me. She should ask more of others. Demand more and better.

She didn't have to make herself small or minimize her needs.

She could be who she needed to be. She should be.

"You can ask whatever you want. I owe you. Not only for Tess, but for being my friend when I needed one. It would be my great honor to be your fake boyfriend."

As she wiped her tears with the sleeve of her sweatshirt, she squeezed my biceps firmly.

I may have flexed a bit. Who could blame me? I'd landed my dream fake girlfriend.

"Thank you."

Axe Backwards

"I'd like the record to reflect that I think this is a terrible idea," Lou chimed in.

"I'm ignoring you." Vic finally cracked a smile.

"Mark my words: by the end of the summer, you'll either fall madly in love or hate each other's guts."

My new fake girlfriend scoffed. "You watch too many movies."

"Kid, when you've lived as long as I have, you learn things. And this"—she pointed from Vic to me, then rubbed her hands together—"has the makings of an epic story."

"Don't be so dramatic," Vic chastised. "You won't tell anyone, will you?"

"Me?" Lou's tone was one of disbelief. "Of course not. I love you and respect your choices. Even if those choices are baffling and misguided."

"Thank you," Vic and I said in unison.

"I'm gonna get ordained and officiate your wedding." The comment sounded less like a prediction and more like a threat.

Vic laughed to herself as I took the exit that led to Lou's assisted living facility.

I'd just put the truck in park when a doorman stepped out of the building. He took Lou's bag from me while Vic gave her aunt a big hug.

"Thanks for a fun weekend," the older woman said to me. "And take good care of my girl."

"I will."

She patted Vic's cheek. "Use protection!"

With a gasp, Vic reared back. "*Aunt Lou.*"

"I mean it. Don't do anything I wouldn't do." She gave us a saucy wink and headed into the building.

Chapter 13
Victoria

I was suffering from a major hangover. Not from alcohol, but from the stress of the past weekend. I had an outrageous amount of work to catch up on and the volunteers had done a great job, but there were always a dozen more tasks waiting for my attention. Now that we were past Memorial Day, the clock was ticking, and I had to get reoriented before the kids were out of school for the summer and families needed more support than ever.

The weird dance I'd been doing with the Huxleys had not paid off yet, so the mobile food truck I'd dreamed of was off the table for the season.

I'd had visions of pickups at local parks and bag lunches for kids and families. But there were capital and operational costs to consider, and so far, none of my grant applications had borne fruit.

I wasn't giving up. I was pivoting. Denis had invited me to lunch today, and as much as it turned my stomach, I was determined to win him over. I'd spent my entire sleepless night obsessing about it. Though the man was not a topic I particularly liked to dwell on, thoughts of our upcoming meeting were a welcome distraction from the wedding insanity and my new fake relationship with Noah.

I leaned closer to the bathroom mirror, examining the dark circles under my eyes. I'd sleep eventually. Someday. Maybe when I'd figured all my shit out? A girl could hope...

I was inspecting the pores on my nose when I heard a knock.

With an annoyed huff, I padded to the door. But when I swung it open and saw who was waiting for me on the other side, my mood changed instantly.

"*Ick.*" My favorite kid dove for me, almost flying out of her dad's arms.

I hugged her and spun in a circle. "Did you have fun with your grandma?"

In response, she gave me a sloppy kiss on the cheek.

I was still grinning at her when I caught sight of Noah. He stood in the doorway, dressed in mesh shorts and a T-shirt with the sleeves cut off. The simple piece of clothing highlighted the miles of muscle and ink of his arms. His body was strong and hard, but his face was lit with a big grin that caused the dimples just visible underneath the heavy scruff to pop.

"It's early. Where are you going?"

"For a run." He took off his hat and settled it on his head again. "We were hoping you'd come along."

When I'd clawed my way out of bed this morning, I'd felt like I'd been hit by a bus, but Tess's smile and Noah's arms had perked me up.

"I'm slow."

Axe Backwards

He shrugged. "I'll be pushing the jogging stroller, so I don't intend on breaking any records. It's a beautiful day."

He wasn't wrong, and I was full of nervous energy that needed an outlet. Seeing my gorgeous sisters and mother this weekend definitely hadn't helped my body confidence.

I passed Tess to him and took a step back. "Okay, I'll get changed."

When I stepped out onto the sidewalk, they were waiting for me. Tess was bundled up in a fancy-looking jogging stroller with a sippy cup in her hand and a handful of Cheerios on the tray.

"Let's walk to the end of Main Street first. Then we can jog."

With a nod, I followed his lead. "What are you wearing?"

He patted the dark green vest he'd strapped on over his T-shirt. "Weight vest."

I picked up my pace. I was practically jogging already to keep up with his long strides. "So you plan to run up a mountain while pushing a stroller and wearing a weight vest?"

He nodded. "Fitness is a big part of my job. Was, I guess." His face fell. Clearly he missed his old life. "We used to train by hiking in the mountains with sixty pounds of gear. This is nothing."

I focused on the road in front of me. The last thing I wanted to do was trip and fall on my ass. Especially while Noah was over here doing a Navy Seal workout.

As we got to the end of Main Street, he shifted into a jog, opening up his stride and looking completely at ease.

Tess giggled happily and waved at passing cars.

"Plus, this is a good way to show the town we're dating."

Daphne Elliot

He saluted to Ricky, who was out on his mail route. "Figured it was best to get in front of it."

He wasn't wrong. Dozens of people had already seen us, including a school bus full of kids. I had no doubt the news would spread.

There were bound to be plenty of awkward conversations, but at least I didn't have to figure out how to casually mention that I was now dating Noah Hebert. Since the decision in the car yesterday, he and I hadn't spoken of it. We hadn't laid out rules or parameters or even discussed the details. He'd just agreed to be my fake boyfriend, like a knight in a backward baseball cap and a baby carrier.

As grateful as I was for his easy agreement, we couldn't wing it. We had to have a plan if we wanted it to be believable. But the whole thing made me cringe. Aunt Lou was right when she said this was childish. Me, a professional woman in her thirties, needed a fake boyfriend? I had a 401(k) and a nighttime skincare routine. I was supposed to be past all this juvenile shit.

But the thought of facing my family without him by my side made me ill. So I'd figure out how to embrace the reality that I was a hot mess and play along.

We jogged past neighborhoods and Baxter Park, then crossed over the footbridge toward Lake Millinocket. Noah smiled and chatted with Tess and made me feel at ease.

Graham loved running too. He had tried to guilt me into training for marathons on several occasions. These conversations usually dovetailed with his "concern" about the amount of chocolate I consumed or the state of my hips. The man had a whole boatload of concerns. If only I could go back and tell him to shove them up his ass.

Axe Backwards

As much as he loved it, he never ran with me. I was far too average to be caught dead exercising with. He was mister super serious, wearing five-hundred-dollar training shoes and a fancy GPS watch.

So, post-divorce, I'd sworn it off. Who needed that kind of psychological torture in their lives? This morning, though, with the sun shining and a light breeze? I felt great. We were moving at a snail's pace, but Noah seemed happy and content.

And I didn't feel as awful as I'd expected. In fact, I was filled with a powerful sensation I wasn't sure I'd ever experienced. The muscles rippling in my running partner's arms were a welcome distraction. It was unfair how good he looked jogging. How good he looked doing anything, really. The broad shoulders, the dark stubble, and the tattoos were unfairly attractive.

Throw in a baby stroller, and it was a good thing I'd sworn off men.

A *very* good thing.

We went up the junction at Route 45 before turning back toward town.

"Can I ask you something?" he said after several minutes of silence.

I nodded. How he could have complex conversations while exercising confounded me.

"Do you still have feelings for Graham?"

I winced. Our friendship had blossomed so naturally, and there weren't many topics that were off limits. But as with every other conversation I had about my marriage, this one made me feel even worse.

"No." I practically spat the word. "Not at all."

I took a deep breath and focused on my steps to keep from stumbling.

"He fucked me up, for sure, but no, I don't love him." I panted for a moment. I was not in good enough shape to carry on an entire conversation while running. "In fact, I'm disappointed in myself for marrying him in the first place and then for so blindly trusting him. I learned that lesson. Zero out of ten, do not recommend."

He laughed up at the sky. "Okay. I didn't mean to pry, but I figured that since I'm your fake boyfriend, I should make sure you're not secretly pining over your ex."

Pining? Not even close. My stomach roiled at the thought.

"Trust me." I stifled a laugh. "Getting rid of that gaslighting, cheating prick allowed me to find freedom and peace. I'm never going back."

His smile stretched across his face, his dimples causing me to lose focus. "Excellent."

"I love my freedom and my autonomy. I'll never get married again. Hell," I said, emboldened by the endorphins and the dimples, "I'll probably never have another romantic relationship again. A real one, at least. So far I like having a fake boyfriend."

For the space of a heartbeat, his face fell. Or maybe I was imagining it, because in the time it took for me to check that I wasn't veering off the road, the smile returned.

"Huh. You're done with the entire male species?"

"Not because I think all men are terrible. Sure, a good percentage of them are, but there are absolutely good ones." I peeked over at him. "Great ones. But I'm not interested."

He was one of them. He was selfless and loyal and the

Axe Backwards

most caring parent I'd ever seen. As a friend, he was respectful and supportive. With any luck, he'd one day find his perfect woman and live happily ever after. He and Tess both deserved that.

The thought was slightly unsettling, but I ignored the sensation.

"On behalf of men everywhere." In a ridiculously coordinated way, he put one hand over his heart, still steering the stroller with the other. "That's a damn shame, but, having met your ex-husband, I get it."

He gave me a wink, and I almost tripped over my feet.

We ran the rest of the way back in silence, waving to folks as we passed.

By the time we stopped outside the building, I was red-faced, sweaty, and smiling.

I'd woken up so out of sorts and exhausted from the wedding fiasco. But now? The world seemed right again. All because of Noah.

"Thank you," I said, catching my breath. "I needed that."

He unlatched Tess, scooped her up, and kissed her cheek. "Yeah, I could feel your pent-up rage all the way from upstairs. I'm always down to help you work it out physically. All you have to do is ask."

His eyes widened at the moment my core clenched. We stood frozen, staring at each other. My brain instantly went to a very dirty place, and by the way his nostrils flared, I was certain his did too.

He blew out a loud breath and adjusted Tess in his arms. "Sorry. I made it weird, didn't I?"

"No," I lied, tucking my chin and inspecting my shoes.

My face was hot, and it hit me then, just how sweaty I was. God, I needed a shower.

"I did. Sorry. I wasn't trying to make you uncomfortable. Sometimes, when I'm nervous around a pretty girl, I default to flirting."

My stomach flipped. Pretty? I had to exit this conversation before it got even more cringey.

"I gotta get to work." I scurried to the door, digging my key out of the small zipper pocket at the back of my athletic shorts.

"See you tonight?"

I nodded, then gave Tess a big wave goodbye. Once I was inside my apartment with the door shut behind me, I fell against it and heaved in a deep breath.

Chapter 14
Victoria

Since I'd gotten nowhere with the Huxleys so far, I focused all my energy on planning the summer fundraiser. Last year, we'd done a wood chopping competition where I'd pitted the Gagnons against the Heberts. In a town that was home to two large timber companies, a town where a large percentage of the citizens worked in the timber industry or a related field, we liked to honor our traditions. Gagnon Lumber and Hebert Timber had been business rivals for generations, and the families were just as competitive. The feud between them had been going for as long as either company had been in business, so it made sense to let them duke it out with axes. We'd raised a good chunk of money during the event, and this year I planned to step it up a notch.

Since begging the most well-connected businesspeople in town hadn't been as successful as I'd hoped, I'd have to rely on the power of lumberjacks to push past the fundraising finish line. Despite how much help I had, I was still nervous about the turnout.

Daphne Elliot

When I was a kid, the people of Lovewell hosted festivals every other weekend. Tourists came from all over to sample our blueberry pie, race canoes in our lake, and hike to the myriad of hidden jewels in our mountains.

But the past decade had been hard on the town, and when the inn closed, the rest of the tourism businesses had folded.

Last year, our outlook had begun to improve. RiverFest, a fun fall-themed event that brought people from the entire region together, had been revived. Several new businesses had opened in the past couple of years. The salon was newer, as was the coffee shop, and the pizzeria would be open any day now.

The inn had recently been sold at auction. With any luck, the new owners would remodel and reopen. That property was exquisite. A facility like that could change things for this town.

We'd all worked hard to boost the local economy, and I was doing my part by providing opportunities to ogle muscular men with axes. All for a good cause, of course.

As I walked into the diner, Denis Huxley, dressed in a sky-blue polo and sharply pressed chinos, stood and waved. I had to suppress a shiver. For hours, I'd been reminding myself that I needed his help. A big grant from the Huxleys would go a long way. They hadn't explicitly said no, so there was a chance. But it felt as though they weren't taking me seriously. Denis was like a bored cat, tossing me around like a toy.

He'd called me in twice for meetings and asked me for data, only to admit that he hadn't even looked at my prospectus. Now he was demanding we meet for lunch. I had actual

Axe Backwards

work to do, and these bozos were only causing me to fall behind.

Still, I couldn't alienate the richest people in town. I pasted a smile on my face and forced myself to think of the folks who were currently waiting for the Monday produce delivery to arrive. Our clients were mostly seniors, single parents, and babies who needed formula. I couldn't let them down.

So I swallowed my pride and slid into the booth.

Bernice greeted me immediately, handing me a menu and pouring coffee into the mug on the table. "Here you are, sweetie. Heard about you and the mystery Hebert. So exciting. He's quite handsome."

The smile that spread across my face this time was genuine. Our morning run had done the trick. News of Noah and I had spread through the town quickly, along with details of our romantic weekend getaway to Kennebunkport. The knitting club was already taking bets on when we'd be engaged.

My phone had been going off all morning, lighting up with texts, which I studiously ignored. I wouldn't set the record straight. Not when, for once, the town rumor mill was working in my favor.

As Bernice shuffled away, Denis rubbed his hands together. "I'm so pleased about our partnership."

Partnership? What was he yammering on about?

With a flourish, he produced a spiral-bound packet. The front page was laminated and said "Huxley Industries and Lovewell Food Pantry Partnership proposal."

I flipped it open and thumbed through it, finding page upon page of charts and tables. What the hell was this?

Daphne Elliot

He was talking, likely explaining the details, but all that registered were buzzwords here and there. Terms like "Collaboration" and "synergy" He went on for a few minutes, a corporate word salad, each phrase making a bigger jumble of my thoughts.

"Sorry," I said, stirring the milk into my coffee. "I'm confused about what you're proposing. We're a nonprofit. A partnership with us wouldn't be beneficial for your business." The Huxleys owned a construction company and controlled a ton of real estate. They were the kind of shady rich people who had offshore accounts. I wasn't sure how they made their millions, and I probably didn't want to know.

"My accountant pulled your 990s so we could see the tax records, and between that and the fact sheets you sent over, it seems the food pantry generates a great deal of waste."

I sat up straighter, my hackles raising. He was pulling our tax records? Yes, they were public, but what the fuck was he playing at?

"The reporting available from the IRS is from two years ago." I did my best to keep my tone even, though I was flush with anger. "So the records you reviewed were from before I took over. Furthermore, we've met multiple times. You've had ample opportunity to ask me questions, yet you're relying on documentation you've dug up? I could have provided you with up-to-date numbers."

Unbothered by my annoyance, he took a large bite of his club sandwich.

My food sat untouched. I'd lost my appetite. This was nothing but a game to him.

Axe Backwards

"Turn to page seven," he said through a mouthful of food. "I went through your filings and made some improvements."

Improvements? He had no idea how a food pantry operated. I highly doubted he could so easily come up with ways to optimize our use of funding.

If this wasn't the definition of the audacity of a spoiled rich kid, I didn't know what was.

Teeth gritted, I squinted at the pages, trying to make sense of what he was proposing.

"Tell me, how is it possible that you receive so much donated food, yet you still struggle to meet demand?"

I pinched the bridge of my nose. "Since the pandemic, food insecurity is at an all-time high." My pitch was a little too high, my tone a little too sharp, but there was no helping it now. I was far too close to the edge. "And while the state food bank provides us with nonperishables and some additional items, our produce, meat, eggs, and milk come from local farms and grocery stores. Most of which are products that cannot be sold. In turn, that means a large percentage of it is unusable."

The first time I volunteered with Aunt Lou at the food pantry when I was probably ten or eleven was a memorable experience, mostly because while I went through crates of apples, bagging them for clients, I pulled out one that was so rotten it exploded in my hand, covering my face and arm in moldy mush.

Every week we unloaded crates of produce that farmers wouldn't even feed their animals. How could we consider passing it out to human beings?

"I refuse to serve rotten food to my clients." I clenched

my hands together in my lap, willing myself to control my anger. "We all deserve nutritious food, and every person we interact with deserves to be treated with dignity. We compost with the co-op in Heartsborough, and a pig farm in Belfast takes some of the other stuff. Nothing is going to waste."

He looked down his nose at me, his lips turned down, clearly unsatisfied with my explanation.

"I've been seeking corporate partnerships for long-term giving," I continued, ignoring his haughty expression, "in the hopes of obtaining more buying power. With more donations coming in monthly, I can buy fresh meat, cheese, and eggs from suppliers. Diapers and formulas are gold in my world. With an influx of cash, I could even provide turkeys for Thanksgiving."

Though I wasn't the least bit happy, I gave him a big smile. Maybe, if I was lucky, he'd jump at the chance to be the official Thanksgiving sponsor. That would be a huge step.

"We're committed to our charitable profile," he said distractedly while he tapped at his phone as if he'd barely heard a word I'd said. "And I think our resources can assist with the improvements."

A knot formed in my stomach. "Improvements?"

"Yes. My father and I would be open to using some of our construction resources to help make some capital improvements to the food pantry. We'll charge you a reduced rate, of course."

A wave of confusion hit me. What in the ever-loving fuck was he talking about? "We replaced our roof last year and rebuilt the garage to support all our refrigeration." Owen

Axe Backwards

Hebert had made most of that happen, and my lumberjack competition had done the rest.

Reaching across the table, he opened the proposal and pointed to a list of figures.

"We'll make regular donations," he said, suddenly wearing a too-bright smile. "For tax purposes. And come up with a project schedule."

"So you'll donate and get a big tax break. Then I'm supposed to use that money to hire your construction company to do work I don't need?"

He tapped the portfolio. "Read it. You'll see. What else would you do with this kind of money anyway?"

"Buy food," I quipped, frowning.

"How much do people really need?"

My eye twitched, but I kept my mouth shut.

"What about food stamps?"

I held back a sigh. "Food stamps are great, but they don't cover everything. And more importantly, a lot of people in need don't qualify for food stamps. They may make too much to qualify, yet still struggle to afford regular access to nutritious food."

He pressed his lips together, his brows lifting, as if he was vaguely amused.

My blood heated, and not in a good way. "Other people go through rough patches or get sick and can't work. Government benefits, while great, require a lot of paperwork and take months to kick in. And that's not accounting for those who have transportation challenges, language gaps, or health challenges. We're a stopgap," I explained. "A necessary and essential service that keeps people healthy and fed."

Sure, our facility could use some updates, but it wasn't in

dire need of any repairs at the moment, thank God. I needed cash and supplies. Mrs. Miller was anemic, and Laurie's baby was growing rapidly. It was impossible not to feel personally responsible for helping every person I could. That was why, despite the mandate from Aunt Lou and the urging of our accountant, I still wasn't paying myself a salary.

"I think starting with rewiring would be best." He stroked his weak chin, clearly not listening to a single word I'd said. "Maybe an addition. Surely you could use more space."

My blood was boiling now. Of course, we could use more space. Who couldn't? But we could get by with what we had for a long, long while.

"New windows," he went on. "We could repave the driveway and add some landscaping. Rip out the kitchen and bring in top-of-the-line appliances."

It sounded like he was trying to sell me a used car.

Not only was I vibrating with anger, but my head was spinning with thoughts of all the things I could be doing instead of listening to him drone on about things that were nowhere close to relevant to our needs.

"Rewiring the building would mean shutting down." I pulled my shoulders back. "We can't do that. Too many people need us. Our windows and wiring are fine. We need food and supplies." Forcing myself to take several steadying breaths, I looked down at the page in front of me and assessed the figures. "I'm not going to pay you six thousand dollars for landscaping services. We're a nonprofit trying to keep families from going hungry. We don't need landscaping."

Axe Backwards

"Good landscaping is essential," he said, "and only part of what I'm offering. Keep reading."

I didn't keep reading. Instead, I stared at him, at a loss for words. This man was ridiculous, and every one of his suggestions was disgusting.

"We could write up proposals." He broke into a creepy smile. "Generate some invoices. Maybe delay the work for a more"—he leaned back, lacing his fingers on over this abdomen—"convenient time."

In moments like this, I wished I possessed a poker face. I had no doubt that a big *what the fuck* was written all over mine. He was talking in circles and ignoring the needs of the organization we were here to discuss. Instead of listening, he was trying to use his money to influence me to do useless construction projects.

I scoffed. "This is a waste of time." It wasn't until the words had left my mouth that I realized how loud they were.

Several heads turned in our direction.

Eyes narrowed, Denis leaned forward in the booth. "I'm proposing a synergistic relationship, Ms. Randolph." He sneered. "And may I remind you that you came to us begging for money?"

His predatory tone made the hair on the back of my neck stand up. What was he trying to do and how on earth did I fit into his plan? This was absolutely some kind of corporate bullshit scenario he was concocting so that he could avoid paying taxes or God knew what else. His aggressive response set off every alarm in my brain.

So I stood and tossed a twenty-dollar bill onto the table to cover the salad I'd refused to eat. Then I picked up the bound prospectus and shoved it into my purse. "I came to you asking for donations to help food-insecure people in our community. Instead, you've jerked me around and are proposing unnecessary construction projects."

His voice, when he responded, was low and controlled, almost like a sinister whisper. "You'll come around," he said. "Or you won't. And if that's the case, you'll be very sorry."

Chapter 15
Victoria

I stayed late, breaking down boxes for recycling pickup on Tuesday, inventorying the meat in the freezers, and applying for a grant that would allow us to become a designated regional diaper bank. It was a long shot, but if we received it, I could buy diapers from the federal government at reduced rates.

I was no stranger to applications, spinning things, and marketing what we did and how we did it in order to present the strongest case possible.

It was after seven before I made it home. I bypassed my own door and headed straight up to Noah's. I wasn't sure what I was looking for, but I knew I wouldn't find it in my empty apartment.

"Come in," he called, and I opened the unlocked door.

He was on the couch, watching something on his phone. Tess, dressed in green footie pajamas, was stacking rubber blocks on the floor.

He greeted me with a sheepish grin, quickly putting his phone down.

"What are you watching?"

"Okay, this probably sounds weird, but I'm watching girl hair tutorials on YouTube."

"Seriously?" I put my purse on the table and toed off my sneakers, then padded over to investigate.

"Ick," Tess said, surrounded by her mess of toys.

I leaned down and gave her a kiss.

Noah held up his phone. "Yes. There's this guy, Jeff." He held up the phone so I could see the screen. Sure enough, there was a middle-aged guy braiding a girl's hair. "He's a single dad and started a channel so other single dads could learn how to do their daughters' hair."

I straightened, frozen for a moment, processing how stupidly adorable the concept was.

"Tess's hair is growing." He ducked his head. "I've mastered pigtails. You should have seen my first few attempts. My hands are so big." With his hands held up, he gave me a sheepish grin.

Yep, they definitely resembled bear paws. Wide and strong but with long, graceful fingers.

"And the elastics are so small. It took forever to figure out how to get them in the right spots."

"You're doing great." Tess's hair was currently in two tiny, perfectly symmetrical pigtails. He had nothing to worry about.

"For now. But her favorite movie is *Frozen*. How long until she's requesting an Elsa braid?"

I shrugged. I didn't have a clue, but my gut told me not long, given how opinionated the little diva was about most things.

Axe Backwards

"So I'm training." He gave me a big, crinkle-eyed smile. "Being a girl dad is serious business."

Dropping to the vacant cushion, I snatched up the remote. "I have no doubt."

"I even got a doll." He leaned over the arm of his side of the couch and plucked a plastic doll off the floor. Her bright yellow polyester hair was twisted into a wonky braid. "For practice."

The scene was too sweet for words. It was so Noah, to worry he wouldn't be good at doing hair and to train himself.

"Now that you've got pigtails down, you're working on braids?"

With his lips pressed together, he dipped his chin, gesturing to the doll. "Clearly, I need more practice."

"You can practice on me," I said, taking out my scrunchie and letting my hair down.

His eyes went wide. "Seriously?"

"Yeah. I'm eating your snacks and watching your TV." I settled on the floor in front of him and hit the Power button on the remote. "Braid away."

He hesitated, but eventually he slid over and bracketed my shoulders with his legs. I hadn't thought about the, um, intimacy of this position until we were in it, but it was too late to get up now.

"You sure?" he asked, his tone low, as he loosely gathered my hair.

I nodded, though I was already regretting the offer.

At the warmth of his fingers lightly trailing along my neck, up around the shell of my ear, I shuddered.

It was more physical contact than I'd had in a long time.

"Did I hurt you??"

I turned gently, taking in his panicked face.

"Totally fine. Sorry. Just getting comfortable." I shifted, took a sip from my water bottle and gave him a thumbs-up.

For a moment, he seemed frozen behind me, but I didn't dare turn around again. Eventually, he ran a brush through my hair, gently tugging it to the ends. The sensation was foreign—I couldn't remember the last time someone brushed my hair for me—but with each stroke, I relaxed a bit. It wasn't all that different from going to Becca's salon for a trim.

Or maybe it was. Becca was professional and fast, and Noah was slowly brushing each strand with care, gathering the hair, sectioning it, and gently braiding it.

"Can I try a few smaller braids?" he asked.

I nodded and inhaled sharply. I was doing my best to distract myself by stacking blocks for Tess to violently knock over, but it wasn't helping.

His hands were clumsy, but he was so focused and gentle. The tenderness made my heart ache.

"You're a really good dad."

"Doesn't feel that way."

Tess crawled into my lap now, getting snuggly and staring at the TV, where Moira Rose was wearing a platinum blond wig and a fur hat.

Contentment bloomed in my chest. It was accompanied by a hint of unease, due to the hot guy braiding my hair and leaning in so closely I could feel his breath on the back of my neck. Unease or not, it felt like I was in the right place with the right people.

This type of tranquility had been rare in my life. I'd always felt like an outsider in my own family and then I'd been isolated in an unhappy marriage.

Axe Backwards

But with every passing moment, anxiety about today's meeting crept back in.

I couldn't lose focus. I'd come too far to have everything derailed by Denis Huxley.

"Okay. I think I'm done," Noah said proudly.

I patted the back of my head with my free hand. My hair had been divided into three sections, each braided separately. They seemed normal enough. Walking around with three braids may be a bit unorthodox, but I didn't care.

"Not bad," I said, handing him a sleepy Tess and standing up to stretch.

It was only then I noticed the circles under his eyes and his disheveled hair. Caregiving, even for the most perfect baby ever, was a big job.

I reached for Tess and pulled her back into my arms.

"I'll take the first shift." Swaying, I rubbed circles on her tiny back. "Go sleep in my bed. You look wiped."

He opened his mouth, but the noise that echoed through the small space came from behind me.

The eerie voice said, "I like warm hugs."

I spun around.

"It's Olaf," Noah said, his tone was rough and full of exhaustion.

Tess lifted her little head from my shoulder and whimpered. "Laf."

Noah retrieved the snowman stuffy from the couch and brought it over. She practically lunged for it, and when she had it in her arms, she cuddled it close, tucking it beneath her chin. There it repeated several unsettling phrases.

With a step back, Noah put his hands on his hips. "I have my mom to thank for that one."

"The voice," I whispered as Tess got comfortable. "It's unnerving."

He nodded. "Yup. It was driving me insane, so I hid it. But Tess screamed for an hour. She's obsessed with the damn thing."

Eventually she settled, and while I wandered the apartment, soothing her, Noah made a cup of tea for me.

"You gonna tell me what's bothering you?" he asked as he set the mug on the end table.

I settled on the couch and shifted Tess so I could hold her with one arm. No, I did not. The thought of rehashing the Denis debacle made me want to vomit, so I pivoted.

"Think we should talk about..." I inhaled, looking into those deep blue eyes, garnering my nerve. "This fake dating arrangement?"

"Sure, what's up?" He arched a brow. "Like I said, I'm all in, whatever you need. Tess and I are on the case."

I shifted so I was facing him. Why did this feel so strange? Noah was my friend. I could be honest with him. I'd just let the guy braid my hair, for God's sake.

"Don't you think we need rules?"

"If you want 'em, sure. Let's make 'em. But I'll warn you. I'm not great with rules. Reminds me too much of school. I prefer to feel things out."

God, he was exasperating sometimes. I tensed, causing Tess to stir. "You can't feel me out."

He raised one brow and burst into laughter.

"Perfect example. Rule number one," I said. "Don't flirt with me. You do it all the time."

He shuffled to the doorframe and stretched lazily, like this wasn't the world's most painful conversation.

Axe Backwards

"There's baby drool on my shirt and probably in my hair," he said. "I can't flirt."

"Bullshit. You could flirt covered in moose shit. You're doing it right now. Are you flexing?"

"Yes," he admitted easily.

This man. He was shameless. Normally I enjoyed a bit of light flirting, but if this was going to work, we had to create clear boundaries.

Despite the way my body temperature rose, I affected a chastising expression. "Stop it."

"I can't." He shrugged, still gripping the top of the doorframe. The move caused his T-shirt to ride up and expose a strip of taut abdomen. "It's involuntary. Like a muscle spasm. It's my natural reaction when a hot woman yells at me. You're lucky I don't have a boner."

"Ugh, stop it." I slumped against the couch, silently praying he couldn't make out the way my cheeks were flushing. "Never say boner in my presence again. What is wrong with you?"

He chuckled. "Sass is a big turn-on for me."

"Stop talking about turn-ons." I wanted to rip my hair out.

"You're my friend. I thought we promised to be honest with each other."

"Yes." I sighed. "But let's stick to normal stuff. I don't care about your dick."

"It's an important part of me, Vic." He was grinning from ear to ear.

He was lucky I was holding a sleeping baby and a creepy Olaf doll. Otherwise, I'd slap him.

"As my fake girlfriend, you should care."

"Spoiler alert, I don't."

"Okay, then." He resumed his stretching, wearing a smirk that made it clear he was annoying me on purpose.

"You're flexing again." I was sweating now. Dammit. I forced a scowl to my face and huffed. "You look like you're posing for a body-building competition."

He feigned innocence, clearly enjoying learning how to push my buttons. "I have no clue what you're talking about. I'm stretching. I can't help it that I'm very strong and tall." He tipped back, and his T-shirt rode up again, this time exposing several inches of toned stomach muscles and dark hair. "And manly," he added, releasing his hold on the doorframe and striking a pose that emphasized the size of his biceps.

The man was ridiculous. But as he turned to one side and flexed again, the dam burst. All the frustration eating away at me after my shitty meeting and the exhaustion weighing me down flooded out of me in one big wave, and I started to laugh.

He joined in, his chuckles making me feel lighter.

It was all so absurd. At what point had my life taken such an insane turn?

Noah collapsed on the couch, a hand on his abdomen as he continued to laugh. I fell into a fit of giggles, tears streaming down my face.

He handed me a box of tissues, and I dabbed at my wet cheeks, even as the laughter and tears continued. Eventually, I'd exorcised all my demons, and I slumped back in exhaustion.

I'd never experienced a moment like this. I'd never understood how laughing could be stress relief. But Noah had known what I needed the moment I walked through the door.

He got up and did a silly dance, his arms flailing.

I scoffed. "What are you doing now?"

"A victory celebration." He pumped his fist dramatically. "I made you laugh. Usually, when you laugh, it's at *Schitt's Creek* or Tess. But today it was me. Even if I had to act like a complete idiot to pull it off, I feel like I accomplished something significant."

Significant? This man was so invested in making me laugh that he'd gone through all of that? My stomach flipped as I assessed him.

"You make me work for it. It takes effort to earn your smiles and your laughter."

The stomach flip quickly turned into a lurch. This was another prime example of why I was difficult. Why I was too much.

"Yeah." I sighed, settling back again. "I know. I'm too serious. Too intense."

Frowning, he dropped to his knees in front of me. "You misunderstand me." He wrapped his hands around my calves. "You may not be easy, but that doesn't mean you're not worth the work."

Chapter 16
Noah

"This is so strange."

It had been decades since I'd stepped through the doors of my old school. Not much had changed. Though it was more colorful and the fixtures had been updated, it still held the same sense of foreboding.

My entire childhood, I struggled to sit still long enough to learn anything. I swore the only reason I learned to read at eight years old was because my mother, who worked long shifts as a nurse, sat with me every night for over a year and gave me the one-on-one instruction I needed.

The taunting and teasing of classmates still haunted me, along with the annual threats that I would be held back. Kissing Tess's forehead, I prayed she'd have an easier time than I did. That she'd have tons of friends and that schoolwork would come naturally to her.

"Da," she said, smacking at my face, annoyed that I was blocking her view of the crowd.

I shifted the diaper bag on my shoulder, exhaling with

relief. My girl was already a genius. I had nothing to worry about.

"This way." Vic clutched my elbow and dragged me into the gym. "We need good seats."

She looked extra pretty tonight. I couldn't have turned her down when she asked me to come to the town meeting with her if I'd tried. Her hair was down, and she was wearing a summery dress with little flowers on it that swished around her legs. If I wasn't mistaken, she was even wearing a little makeup.

She snagged seats at the end of the second row, marking them with the diaper bag.

"Go grab snacks," she said, pointing to the back of the gym.

Frowning, I glanced over my shoulder. "They sell snacks?"

"Yup, it's a fundraiser for the school. There was a motion last year to sell alcohol, but, shockingly," she teased, "an elementary school isn't eligible for a liquor license. After that, there was talk of parking a beer truck in the lot next to the playground. But then the zoning board got involved, and it was a whole mess."

Tess squirmed in my arms while I gaped at my friend. Between all that information and the hum of the growing crowd, my mind was beginning to scatter.

"Seriously. Give me Tess and go get the snacks. I'll save the seats."

I complied, saying hello to several people on the way and getting completely fleeced by elementary schoolers in the process.

Upon my return, I found Jude sitting beside my empty

Axe Backwards

seat. The large room was filled with chairs aligned in neat rows, and a large projection screen had been set up at the front of the room. The basketball hoops had been folded up to the ceiling, and the buzzing lights highlighted the fraying pennants that hung from the rafters.

Tess, who was happily munching on yogurt melts, waved at every person she saw.

I sat, and Vic leaned in, taking the lemonade from me. As she whispered in my ear, it was impossible not to breathe in her honeyed scent. "I'll catch you up on the basics," she murmured as Tess plucked another yogurt melt from her cupped hand. "Mrs. Dupont is feuding with Mrs. Blakely because she stole her parking spot at church bingo and then spread a rumor that she wears a wig."

I fought back a snort. That was far more information than I needed.

"When Mrs. Blakely reads the agenda, Mrs. Dupont heckles her."

"Heckles?"

"Oh, yes."

When Mayor Lambert walked up to the podium and tested the microphone, Vic straightened, taking her warmth with her, and the crowd quieted in anticipation. "Good evening," he began, "We've got a packed agenda for the night, so if you could please take your seats, we'll get started."

All over the room, people were shuffling into seats. I wasn't sure I'd ever seen a school gym this packed before.

Gus stood in the back, arms folded. Beside him, Finn was smiling and chatting with one of the Gagnon brothers. Our families had been adversaries for years, and though I

Daphne Elliot

wouldn't say we were on the best terms, tensions had eased since Finn and Adele Gagnon had gotten together.

From the look of things, every single resident of Lovewell, and a few from neighboring towns, was here.

"Where the hell am I?" I whispered.

Vic patted my thigh, the contact sending a bolt of electricity through me. "Lovewell, Maine. Buckle up, hotshot. This is gonna be wild."

"Before we get to the more exciting town business," Mayor Lambert said, his voice echoing off the high ceilings. "I need to address the current policing situation."

Several people around the room inhaled sharply.

"As many of you know, Chief Souza has been placed on administrative leave pending an investigation."

Many people nodded, and others wore surprised expressions. I'd known the police chief since I was a kid. He'd coached my little league team and had been fishing buddies with my dad. But earlier this year, he'd drugged my brother Cole and attempted to frame him for destroying the hockey rink.

Thank God for Cole's wife. Without Willa's quick thinking, it might have been impossible to prove. She'd shown up on the scene and had quickly taken a blood sample that showed without question that he had been drugged.

According to my mother, the chief was found in possession of the drug that had been discovered in his system. Now Souza was facing charges and all kinds of trouble.

For years, I'd been out of the loop with my family. As disorienting as it was to jump back in and be involved, I needed to. Even if it included accepting the ripple effect my father's actions had on this town and our family.

Axe Backwards

He'd been locked up for a couple of years now, but unanswered questions and suspicions still abounded.

"With the generous help of the state," Lambert said, "we're doing an audit of police activity. It will take approximately six months, and during this time, we will digitize records, retrain all officers, and appoint an interim chief. I want to assure you all that the safety of our town and our citizens is our top priority."

I craned my neck and found Cole. He was such a tall motherfucker, it was impossible to miss him. He stood next to the bleachers where Willa was sitting with her parents. Her dad had been the town doctor for decades before she took over and had given me stitches more times than I could count. It was yet another reminder of how long it had been since I'd been back here.

And how much had changed. My father was in prison, our family business had been sold, and our town was struggling far more than when I'd left.

But while I was untethered, floating around and scrambling to find my place in this world, my brothers seemed to have fared much better. Perhaps they'd worked through the fallout of my father's crimes while I was fighting fires and living in a bubble of ignorance. But they were thriving members of this community with families and careers.

Even Jude was happy and fulfilled these days, playing music, hiking with his dog, and continuing to work for the family company now owned by Chloe, Gus's ex-wife-turned-girlfriend.

As the meeting continued, several people spoke. The water commissioner droned on about lawn watering restrictions, the cub scouts updated us on their flower fundraiser, and Mrs. Blakely, with a steady stream of boos from Mrs. Dupont, outlined the schedule for the Fourth of July festivities.

When it was Vic's turn, she passed Tess to me, and strode to the podium, her dark hair down her back and her eyes shining.

Shit, I couldn't help but be entranced by her.

With a broad smile, she adjusted the microphone. Speaking in front of hundreds of people would scare the shit out of me, but she looked completely at ease.

After expressing gratitude for the recent donation drive, she launched into her plans for the summer fundraiser. Last week, she'd made a PowerPoint between episodes of *Schitt's Creek* and a box of Annie's Mac & Cheese we split for dinner.

"As you know, last year's wood chopping was a big success." A series of whistles and whoops rang out around the room, the majority distinctly female.

Tess clapped and shouted, "Ick-Ick."

With a smile, Vic waved at her.

"This year, we hope to include even more activities."

"Bachelor auction!" a woman shouted.

Vic gripped the edges of the podium and glared.

Lucy Myers, who had been our lunch lady in school, stood with a huff. "I was told there would be a lumberjack bachelor auction this year."

Several other older ladies hooted and hollered.

Vic's shoulders stiffened, and she rolled her head to one side, then the other like she was tamping down her annoyance. Next to me, Jude slid lower in his seat. He was the most eligible lumberjack in town, after all. I plopped Tess in his lap to distract him, and she immediately buried her hands in his beard and tugged.

"While I appreciate your letters, phone calls, and emails on the subject." She narrowed her eyes. "We will not be auctioning off any lumberjacks this year."

A chorus of boos went up around the room, and Jude's shoulders relaxed.

"Instead, we will be hosting an expanded lumberjack competition with multiple events, including a children's competition."

The applause in response to that was subdued.

"The heritage and history of Lovewell are tied to timber. Leaning into the lumberjack branding could bring in more tourists and give us an economic boost."

That statement had several people perking up.

"We'll have a professional demo, and Remy Gagnon—"

The room erupted in applause for the hometown athletic hero.

Vic broke into a relieved smile. "Remy will be there, and we've invited other athletes from the New England area to participate. Cole Hebert has volunteered to handle permits for local businesses to participate, so for any of you interested, email either of us."

Dozens of hands went up at once.

"Can I do a yodeling demonstration?"

"Where can I submit my petition that the lumberjacks be shirtless?"

"How many tourists?"

"Will there be a senior division?"

Vic patiently answered each question and went through her slides. As she explained her projections and how vendor fees and ticket sales would benefit the food pantry, people grew more and more excited.

The longer the presentation went on, the brighter her expression got. It made her that much more gorgeous. The passion she had for helping people shone through every day. No matter how exhausted and sleep-deprived, no matter how many pallets she'd unloaded that day, she loved what she did.

The mayor eventually had to step in to urge citizens to hold their questions. If the meeting didn't move on, then we'd never get out of here.

It was impressive, the way she got the room buzzing. This town had been down and out for so long that new events and the promise of tourism dollars motivated everyone to get involved.

Vic dropped into the seat beside me, and instantly, Tess squirmed in Jude's arms, reaching over me. When my daughter was in the arms of the woman who was quickly becoming her favorite person and mine, she gave her a big, wet kiss on the cheek.

I leaned over and did the same. Maybe it was over-the-top, but I couldn't contain my pride.

This felt right. Being here with my girls and my town.

I paused. My girls.

Turning my head, I stole a glance at Vic, who was snuggling Tess on her lap while the next people droned on about some boring municipal issue. Tess had her head on Vic's chest and had a lock of her dark hair tangled in her chubby fingers. Vic was listening while slowly rubbing gentle circles on my baby girl's back.

It was so natural, so maternal. It made my stomach flip.

Axe Backwards

After the zoning committee gave its report, Earl launched into an impassioned speech on behalf of a motion to ban motorboats on the lake on Sundays. The public debate got quite heated, and it was voted down.

There were lots of hugs and goodbyes as we made our way to the parking lot. People kept pulling Vic aside to ask questions, some of which she deferred to Cole, who I was learning had recently become the town's expert on all things festivals and events.

The night air was chilly and clear, but by the time we got to the car, Vic's face was flushed. As I buckled Tess into her car seat, an overwhelming rush of affection for my fake girlfriend washed over me.

I'd been floating along on a sea of grief and ambivalence for months, but every minute spent with Vic pulled me closer to shore, forcing me to see the vast opportunities in front of me.

She never called me out, but her example alone had my mind spinning. What could I do to help? How could I apply my skills in a way that would benefit the community?

My heart clenched. She was so fucking awesome and didn't even realize it.

Once I was settled in the driver's seat, I inhaled deeply and blew the breath out, attempting to compose myself.

Snagging her hand, I gave it a squeeze. "You were incredible in there," I said softly. "Thanks for letting Tess and me see that side of you."

She gave me a confused frown. "It's nothing."

I shook my head. "It's not nothing. You are passionate and articulate, and you're fucking trying to create change in this world."

"It's what I do, hotshot. My job is to raise money for the food pantry."

"Yes, but don't you see that you're doing that while lifting up, inspiring, and helping the whole town? Everyone walked out of there buzzing. You just got an entire community to put together a whole weekend's worth of events in less than a month."

Grimacing, she shifted in her seat and gave a little shrug. "That's the power of Lovewell."

"No," I said, giving her hand another squeeze. "It's the power of Victoria Randolph."

Chapter 17
Victoria

With one more sip of my latte, I shouldered my bag. I had a meeting with Ronnie, the bank manager, to talk about extending the food pantry's line of credit. As a nonprofit, I didn't qualify for most small business loans, but I could borrow against the property itself, and at this point, I was researching every option.

It was what Aunt Lou had taught me. Never depend on anything or anyone. Always have backup plans. And backups for your backups. It was the only way to survive in this world.

So while I was chasing the Huxleys, planning the lumberjack competition, trying to recruit more volunteers, and applying for every possible grant, I was also hitting up the bank. Because I was nothing if not determined.

Noah, Tess, and I had gone on a short run today. He'd dropped me off at home to shower, then he'd gone out for a few more miles while Tess snuggled her stuffed Olaf in the jogging stroller and babbled encouragement at him. By the time I'd showered, changed, and mentally prepared, they were at the Caffeinated Moose, with my regular latte waiting for me.

It felt good, having a routine, having people to come home to. Yes, I was working harder than ever, but I was also laughing more, spending more time outside, and having a hell of a lot more fun.

But I had to get going. So I gave Tess a kiss on the head and took a step back before she could smear blueberries on my top. She was halfway through her second muffin, though she was wearing almost as much as she'd eaten.

As I stepped outside, Cole Hebert appeared on the opposite sidewalk and waved.

"I've been meaning to text you," he said as he jogged across the road, a big smile on his face. "Figured you'd want to hear the good news. We've had more vendor applications than expected."

I clapped, cognizant of my half-full coffee. We needed those vendor fees to pay for the setup. The stage and bleachers we were building were not cheap.

"Mayor Lambert was a bit shocked, but I'll get him to sign off on the additional parking."

I nodded, overwhelmed with gratitude. I needed this event to be a success.

"You're really doing this." Cole's voice was soft, genuine.

I looked up at him, way up—the guy was at least six and a half feet tall—and smiled. "I owe you. Thank you for doing this."

He shook his head. "I'm happy to help. Maybe this kind of stuff is boring to most, but I actually like doing it. And city hall owes me some favors."

Axe Backwards

"You gonna compete?" I lifted my brows, hopeful. He was a former professional hockey player, after all.

"Willa is forcing me." He sighed. "Said she married a lumberjack, so I better get up there and make her proud." He rolled his eyes, but his grin was wide. He was so in love with his wife.

"I knew I liked her."

Chuckling, he looked at his watch. "I gotta run, but I'll email you all the details later, okay?" With that, he was off, jogging down the road toward the diner.

I tipped my head up, soaking in the sun's warm rays. Instantly, though, my stomach clenched. I wasn't used to things going right. I wasn't used to feeling this good. At any minute, I was sure the other shoe would drop.

And when I lowered my face, ready to move on, I saw him.

The other shoe.

Graham.

Headed straight for the Caffeinated Moose. His eyes were on his phone, so I ducked into a small alcove next to the building, hoping he wouldn't notice me as he walked by. Sure, hiding from my ex-husband was juvenile, but given that a single interaction with him had the power to derail my week, I chose to believe it was actually a mature decision.

It would only take a second for him to walk by—

"Hello." That voice, that tone, was imperious as always, and maybe a bit surprised. From where I stood, he couldn't see me. So I peered around the edge of the brick wall.

Noah stood just outside the door to the coffee shop, hat backward, smile on his face, and Tess turned forward in her carrier. He'd cleaned up the blueberry mess from her face, but her shirt was likely ruined.

She was babbling happily.

"Hey," he replied.

The two men stood a couple of feet apart, watching one another. It was a study in contrasts.

Graham was all pretense and superiority. His frame thin, his clothes perfectly pressed, and his watch worth more than my car.

Compared to him, Noah looked carefree and casual, friendly and approachable. And tall. Very tall. And built. And tattooed.

Okay, now my hormones were going wild again. But seeing my fake boyfriend in proximity to my ex-husband wasn't helping my growing attraction to the man.

It's just physical, I reminded myself. *Hormones. Evolution. It's not real.*

"Since you're dating Victoria..." Graham said my name as if it tasted bad in his mouth.

"Ick." Tess giggled.

My bastard of an ex ignored her. "And since I'm her ex-husband, it's my duty to, you know, talk to you. Man to man."

Suddenly, Noah's easy, casual air vanished. He pulled himself up to his full height and his smile morphed into a glare.

Graham, clearly not reading the signals, continued. "She's barren."

"I'm not sure we use that word anymore," Noah said flatly.

The arrogant fucker across from him shook his head.

Axe Backwards

"Infertile. Whatever. I don't know you or your circumstances, but you should know. She kept that from me. Deceived me."

My body went hot, my limbs shaky. Bile rose up my throat. *Deceived him?* Was that what he thought?

I leaned against the wall, concerned my legs wouldn't hold my weight. How could he say these things? To Noah, of all people?

I couldn't see Noah's face and I didn't want to. I considered hopping over the chain-link fence next to the dumpster and making a run for it, but my damn feet wouldn't move.

Instead, a hot vortex of shame pulled me in, weighed me down. I hadn't been enough for Graham. I would never be enough for Noah.

"Dude. I'm holding my daughter right now," Noah said. "So I am not going to punch you."

My heart lurched. *Huh?*

I peered back around.

Noah's face was pure fury, and Graham was eyeing him like he thought he might take a swing after all.

Tess whimpered, clearly upset. My heart clenched at the sound. It killed me that Graham was scaring her.

"But I want to make sure you understand that you deserve to lose a few teeth. Vic told me you were a cruel prick, but this is even worse than I could imagine. Don't you ever, ever speak of her again. And if I ever hear the word barren come out of your mouth again, you'll be drinking your meals through a straw."

Graham took a step back and held up his hands. "I was trying to give you a heads-up. You seem like a family man. Don't you think you should know that she can't have kids?

That she shouldn't be around them?" He squinted at Tess, who glared right back at him. "She's not maternal. Not mom material."

Noah clenched his fists. "Victoria Randolph is the kindest, most generous person I've ever met. Every day, I watch her interact with my child, and love her the way she deserves to be loved. I know in my bones that she has the biggest, most beautiful heart. There is no one I trust more, and my daughter is damn lucky to have her in her life."

"I'd watch out," Graham said, chin lifted and defiant. "She's paranoid and a bit crazy."

My head spun. Of course he was calling me crazy. If he discredited me, made me look like I was unstable, then people couldn't blame him for ending our marriage. That was his thought process. And everyone, including my parents, had bought it.

Noah took a step forward, raising a fist.

Graham brought an arm up to shield his face, but before Noah could speak again or throw a punch, Tess cried out.

And promptly projectile-vomited.

She spewed chunky blue bile directly onto Graham's chest.

And not just once. When I thought she couldn't possibly have anything left in her stomach, she did it again.

"What the fuck?" Graham screamed.

Several people stopped to gawk. One or two even stepped out of the coffee shop. Ricky, who was delivering mail to the businesses on Main Street, paused, and Becca stood in the doorway of her salon. Kara Mosely, who was pushing her baby in a stroller, cackled. Soon Noah was laughing too.

Axe Backwards

"That baby is a demon." Graham spun and stormed down the street toward his car. "You and Victoria deserve each other," he shouted over his shoulder.

The onlookers either gaped or laughed or tried to hide their smiles as he stomped off like a toddler.

I wasn't sure whether to laugh or cry. The humiliation ran deep, but seeing Graham covered with blueberry baby vomit did help soothe the sting a bit.

Noah, who had switched back into cuddly dad mode, was softly rocking Tess and wiping her mouth with a baby wipe.

"You're not a demon," he said, with a kiss to the top of her head. "You're a little hero." He tossed the wipe into a nearby trashcan, then headed toward our building. "We're going home to get you cleaned up. Then Daddy's giving you extra treats for being such a super baby and defeating the bad guy."

Chapter 18
Victoria

I threw open Noah's door. We were past knocking at this point, and I could hear Tess screaming from downstairs. Tossing my bag onto the table, I shuffled into the living room. Noah was rocking her softly back and forth, but her little face was beet red and sweaty.

"Poor baby." I caressed her cheek, and when the heat radiating from her registered, I pulled back.

"Ear Infection," Noah said, over her wails. "Willa checked her out a couple of hours ago. We got antibiotics, but it will take a day for them to kick in. She woke up this morning with a fever of 102."

Tess pushed her face into her dad's chest and sobbed.

The painful sound broke my heart. I wanted to scoop her up and tickle her and make silly faces until she laughed. All the thoughts of the confusing day and a half I'd had disappeared when I looked at the two of them. They needed me.

"Okay." I pulled my sleeves up and tied my hair back into a ponytail. "What can I do?"

"She needs fluids. I've got a bottle with Pedialyte over

there." He nodded to the counter where the bright orange liquid sat.

I snagged it off the Formica and frowned. "This is room temp?"

He raised one eyebrow.

"I drank this stuff in college."

His face scrunched up in disgust. "Why?"

"Prevents hangovers." I shrugged. "It's so much better cold. Hold on."

Rounding the counter, I headed for the fridge. I deposited the warm bottle and picked up a cold one.

"Here." I twisted the cap and held it out. "Try this."

Tess took a few tentative sips before pushing it away and squirming again.

"I've been alternating Tylenol and Motrin. It's helped lower her temperature, but she's still miserable."

His eyes were blue pools of panic, and the muscles in his arms were clenched. On top of that, he looked so damn weary. I wanted to hug him as desperately as I wanted to hug Tess. This big bear of a man was in pain because his daughter was sick.

I never grew tired of seeing his devotion to her. If I knew him, he'd been so busy taking care of Tess that he'd forgotten to take care of himself.

"Have you eaten?"

Head lowered and attention fixed on his baby girl, he shook his head.

"I can fix that." I hustled downstairs and threw together a sandwich.

When I returned, I set it on the table and took the

fussing baby from him. "Sit down, eat, drink a glass of water."

Nodding dazedly, he dropped into a chair.

I kissed Tess's forehead and smoothed down her unruly hair. "Sweet girl, I'm so sorry you're sick."

"Ick," she said, her cheeks red and little face forlorn.

"I'm happy to see you too." Tears welled in my eyes. I would do anything to help her feel better, especially after what she'd done for me yesterday. I loved this kid, and no matter what Graham said, I was devoted to her.

Noah watched me intently with those icy blue eyes. "Thank you."

I shrugged. "It's a sandwich on a paper plate. But I did get the good sliced turkey breast when I went to Heartsborough yesterday."

"Not only for the sandwich. Though this is really good." He held up the second half. He'd already inhaled the first. "But for being here."

"I want to be here," I said softly.

He caught my eye, the gratitude in his expression so potent it made my breath catch.

It was true. I looked forward to coming over. I loved Tess, and Noah was quickly becoming my best friend. Plus we had appearances to maintain. Though that seemed less and less important lately.

My desire to spend time with him was beginning to feel far more urgent than my need to prove myself to my family.

Alexandra and Mom had been spotted at the coffee shop and a few other places over the last few days, but they had mostly kept to themselves. I'd seen them on the sidewalk outside the grocery store, and we'd had a polite, if stilted chat, where Mom insisted I must come over and see the new house but offered no specific date or time.

With every day that passed, I found that I cared less about their opinions. The panic and shame I'd felt at the wedding only a couple of weeks ago was already beginning to fade.

But then Graham had to show up and badmouth me on the street. Declare to the world that I was a failure as a wife and as a woman. And crazy to boot. I walked around, rubbing Tess's back and trying to calm myself down. It didn't matter. He didn't matter. It had taken years, but my nervous system was finally getting the message. He couldn't hurt me anymore. I had to stop giving him that power.

Tess nuzzled into me, and I held her tight, knowing that this little person believed in me. That she and her dad were part of the reason why I was starting to heal.

"When was the last dose?" I asked, pressing my cheek to her heated forehead.

"Only an hour ago."

I walked the room, making my usual loop, murmuring and stroking her little back as I told her about the big moose I'd seen by the side of the road today.

After slamming the sandwich, an apple, and a glass of water, Noah was looking more like himself.

He leaned in, putting his arm around my waist and kissing Tess's forehead while she was cradled up against my chest. The feel of his hand on me and the warmth of his body, even for that brief moment, almost knocked me off balance.

Hormones. They were totally normal. Sick baby,

concerned dad. How could I not be a little rattled in such close proximity to these two?

Evolution. In the end, I was no better than a cavewoman.

I handed her back to him, needing space and a moment to compose myself.

"She's still warm. I should take her temp again."

Nodding, I picked the ear thermometer up off the kitchen counter and held it out to him.

He put the tip of it in her ear, and when it beeped, he checked the reading and shook his head.

Then he put it in the other ear.

"Fuck. It's 103."

He dropped the thermometer onto the couch and paced, tugging on his hair with his free hand.

"Should I take her to the ER? Fuck. Her temperature has never been this high."

My pulse pounded in my ears. God, did she have a serious illness?

"She probably has something horrible, like meningitis, and I'm the dumbass who didn't notice." He was spiraling now, his pacing growing faster.

His panicked self-loathing stopped my own racing thoughts. He needed me to be the calm presence here.

I grabbed his shoulder and gave it a hard squeeze. "Breathe. Your sister-in-law is the town doctor. Call her."

He handed Tess back to me and frantically patted his pockets for his phone before finally locating it on the couch.

On speakerphone, Willa was calm and authoritative, assuring us that nothing was gravely wrong. Since Tess was breathing normally and had no troubling rashes, it really looked as though it was a standard, if not severe, ear infection.

"Cool her down," Willa instructed. "Take off her clothes, turn the heat down, that sort of thing."

I immediately laid her on the couch and unsnapped her pajamas, wincing as she cried out.

"Can I give her more medicine?" Noah asked.

"No. Stick to the schedule I gave you. Between doses, keep her cool and comfortable and make sure she's drinking liquids."

Once I was cuddling her again, she continued to cry. I paced like we did every night, rubbing circles on her back. Her little body felt so hot.

"A cool bath or shower can help bring her fever down. Not cold, just slightly cooler than normal. Do you want me to come over?"

Willa was a few years younger than me, and I didn't know her well, but it was obvious she was devoted to her patients and this town. I didn't know many doctors these days who would make a middle-of-the-night house call for an ear infection.

"Nah. It's okay. Vic is here. We'll manage."

"Keep me posted."

We spent the next hour trying to keep Tess comfortable, counting down the minutes until we could give her another dose of Tylenol. But as time went on and she fussed, Noah got continuously more restless.

"Here, hold her." He held the diaper-clad baby out to me.

Gently, I took her. The moment I made contact with her

bare skin, my stomach sank. Her body was on fire and the lines on her tiny face were etched with discomfort.

With a grunt, he stripped off his shirt.

"What are you doing?"

"You heard Willa. A shower. Cool, not cold."

I froze, entranced by his large, masculine torso. The sleeve of ink on his left arm snaked up his bicep and continued over his shoulder, meeting the designs on his chest and back. I could spend days decoding each one, studying how they wrapped around his thick muscles.

He was stripping. Right in front of me. Alarm bells rang in my head, startling me back to reality, and I averted my eyes.

He spun and strode away without another word. Still holding the feverish baby, I followed him into the tiny, pink-tiled bathroom, so much like my own downstairs.

Maybe it was the tight quarters, or maybe I was coming down with an illness as well, but either way, I was suddenly feeling hot.

Sweaty and twitchy too. Unsure of where to look or how to act.

Where did Noah leave that thermometer? Did I have a fever?

Noah's bare chest was too close. He was muscular and strong, with dark chest hair that tapered down to the waistband of the jeans he was now unbuttoning.

My heart stuttered. Christ on a cracker. *Was he getting completely naked? Should I leave?*

I peeked over at the door, ready to dart through it, only to remember that I was holding the baby. I couldn't leave.

Tess cried out, and I patted her back, swaying from side

to side while Noah, who was now only wearing a pair of black boxer briefs, adjusted the temperature of the water.

Unable to tear my eyes away, I studied his tattoos more closely. There was a fireman's helmet, an axe, and a copse of trees, all woven together with intricate script and symbols I didn't recognize. Interspersed throughout it all were tiny reddish-purple flowers.

"You okay?" he asked, reaching into the shower to check the water.

"Mm-hmm." I forced a smile, pretending I wasn't captivated by the sight of his bare chest and back.

In reality, my mouth had gone dry and my palms had begun to sweat.

I focused my attention on Tess. On keeping her comfortable. Yes, that was the responsible thing to do.

"Hold her up so I can take her diaper off."

Once she was naked and cradled in his arms, he stepped into the cool shower and swayed under the spray, talking to her softly.

She clung to him, whimpering, her little arms wrapped around his neck.

I stood there, mesmerized as he ran a soothing hand over her head and down her back.

The tender concern on his face and the way that, even bone tired, he would do anything for this child cracked my heart in two.

This man, a wall of muscle, ink, and chest hair, held this tiny baby like she was the most precious thing to ever exist.

Her distress was causing him physical pain.

As I watched the two of them, an ache formed low in my belly, a sensation I hadn't experienced in years.

Axe Backwards

Breathing became difficult. My breasts felt heavy. My legs didn't seem to want to walk away. With every second that passed, emotions shifted, thoughts realigned, and feelings grew. Like a complicated Tetris game inside me opening up a sensation that felt suspiciously like want.

And Noah Hebert was not something I could afford to want.

Chapter 19
Noah

"I can't believe she's sleeping in her crib." Smiling, Vic gave me a double thumbs-up.

After a long, cool shower, we changed Tess, fed her, and got her to the next dose of medicine. Shortly after that, she finally drifted off.

Since the only ceiling fan in the apartment was in her room, we figured we'd see how long she'd sleep in there. When I laid her down, she instantly rolled over and burrowed her face into the mattress.

She seemed comfortable, and her temperature had come down a bit. Perhaps she only liked the crib when sick? Because she usually acted like it was made of thorns and fire.

After leaving her door open a few inches, I leaned back against the wall in the hallway and let my body deflate.

It was after two, and I was dead on my feet.

As a first responder, I had extensive training and experience in handling crises and life-and-death situations. But all that training and my ability to keep cool in the face of danger were completely lost the minute my daughter was sick.

"Thank you," I whispered as we dragged ourselves into the living area.

Vic looked wiped too. Her ponytail was disheveled, and she'd changed out of her jeans and top, trading them for a pair of my athletic shorts and a Yosemite T-shirt. The sight of her in my clothes lit up a part of my brain I wasn't sure had ever been active before. And I didn't hate it.

"No thanks necessary."

My chest tightened. "I was spiraling, and you were here for me. And for Tess. You are a damn good friend."

It was dark, and I was dangerously close to slipping into unconsciousness, but I swore her face fell at that last word.

And suddenly, I was overcome with the urge to be near her. So I stalked to where she stood by the window.

After the chaos of the evening, my brain had quieted, as if it had worn itself out. For once, the racing thoughts, endless distractions, and nonstop noise had ceased.

My only focus was Vic.

Her soft skin, illuminated by the *Bluey* nightlight and the streetlights outside.

The rapid rise and fall of her chest.

Every time I looked at her, that persistent ache inside me intensified. Tonight, it was all-consuming.

The need to be close overwhelmed me.

The desire to touch her was impossible to resist.

We stood together in the quiet.

Quiet was scary. Quiet was dangerous.

Yet it was strangely exhilarating with this woman at my side. Like I was standing at the edge of a cliff, ready to jump off into oblivion.

"Thank you," I rasped. I'd said it before, but it was

impossible to put into words how grateful I was. She'd been by my side for hours, helping and encouraging, even making me a damn sandwich.

"You already said that."

It was two a.m., and we were both deliriously tired.

But yet.

I ran my fingers along the edge of her jawline, testing the boundaries of the new territory we'd entered.

Leaning into my touch, she peered up at me. Vulnerable and beautiful. Did she feel this too?

Gently, I tucked a strand of hair behind her ear, unable to take my hands off her.

To my shock, she responded in the most unexpected and incredible way. She moved in close, and when our chests were mere inches away from one another, she bit her lip.

As she regarded me, there wasn't an ounce of self-doubt. No hesitation.

The last of my resolve crumbled.

Cupping her jaw, I angled in, eager to savor the sensation of our lips touching.

She gripped the front of my T-shirt, her breathing picking up.

God, I'd never wanted anything more than I wanted to kiss this woman.

Slowly, I tilted my head and brushed my lips against hers. Breathing her in, I—

"I like warm hugs."

I jumped back.

Vic did too, a small squeak escaping her.

"Do you want to build a snowman?"

"I like warm hugs."

She gasped and whipped around, zeroing in on where the noise was coming from. "Is that... Olaf?"

Eyes closed, I vowed to smash that fucking toy with a hammer. When I opened them again, I found the possessed stuffed snowman. It was lying on the floor next to the Pack 'n Play.

Motherfucking Olaf.

"Some people are worth melting for. I like warm hugs."

"*Warm* hugs."

Vic was shaking with silent laughter. "Is it malfunctioning?"

"I have no idea." Though disappointment was like a heavy weight pressed against my chest, I couldn't help but laugh along with her.

He spoke again, his words coming more quickly, the creepy phrases slurring together. "Do you want to build a snowman I like warm hugs do you want to—"

With a shudder, I snatched him up off the floor. Then I quickly and efficiently flipped him over, unzipped the pocket at his back, and pulled out the AA batteries.

As I tossed them onto the coffee table, Vic cackled. "That thing is creepy." She slapped her thigh. "And your face." She guffawed. "I thought you'd smash it."

I was laughing again too. Hell yeah, I wanted to smash it. Actually, I wanted to twist Olaf's stupid snowman head until it popped right off his body. But that was neither here nor there.

I sobered quickly, remembering what we were doing before Olaf had ruined the moment.

The spell we'd been under had passed. She was smiling

and laughing and yawning now. Not biting her bottom lip and watching me with heated eyes.

It was probably for the best. I had a feeling that if I kissed Vic once more, it would only make it harder to resist doing it again. It would only lead to disappointment. Vic had been clear about her lack of interest. Not only in me, but in anyone. As her friend, I had to respect that. She was too precious to me, too important to Tess. My attraction to her was growing by the day, but I would learn to control it.

I had to.

She squinted at the toy, suspicious. "Do you think he's done now?"

I shook my head. "Nah, he'll rise again to annoy me. I know it."

She gave me a weak smile, and suddenly, a thread of awkwardness wove around us.

"I should go," she said. "Call me if you need anything."

I nodded. Shushing the symphony of thoughts in my brain. The quiet, the focus I'd felt when touching her, was long gone. I'd have to drop and do at least one hundred pushups to turn down the volume. Running would be better, but with Tess sleeping, that wasn't an option.

"Well, Okay." She hesitated, giving me a forced smile. The situation had gone from hot to funny to awkward in the span of two minutes.

As she headed toward the door, my brain screamed at me to say something. To ask her to stay. To pin her up against the wall and kiss her until she couldn't stand up straight.

Because the emotions inside me were raging. A jumbled mess of them.

Instead, I silently watched her slip her shoes on and grab

her bag from the table before she stepped out into the hall and closed the door carefully behind her.

The moment the lock clicked, I collapsed on the couch and put my head in my hands.

I needed to get a hold of myself. A lifetime of impulsivity and snap decisions had done me absolutely no favors when it came to the superhuman self-control it would take to not kiss her.

The moment had been so perfect.

And also, did I just get cock-blocked by a fucking stuffed snowman?

Chapter 20
Noah

"You showed up a month ago with a surprise child, and you've already landed yourself a girlfriend?" With a shake of his head, Jude scratched Ripley's ears.

I smirked. "We're faking."

His eyes went wide with shock.

I hated lying, and when it came to Jude, there was no point. The twin connection meant he could read me, sometimes better than I could read myself, and I wasn't nearly a good enough actor to fool him. The thought of even trying was exhausting, and right now, I couldn't spare the energy. Plus, he was a vault.

He dropped the six-pack onto the counter with a loud thud. "Not you too. What the fuck?"

"Me too?"

He shook his head, muttering to himself.

I scrutinized him, trying to employ that twin telepathy, but he was much better at it than I was. "Do you have a fake girlfriend too?"

He pinned me with a glare.

I only shrugged. It was worth asking, given his reaction.

He took off his glasses, cleaned them on his shirt, and then put them back on. It was a classic Jude tell. He had a secret, and he wouldn't share it with me. "Next, are you gonna tell me you're secretly in love with her and ask for advice about how to win her over?"

"Weirdly specific question, but no." Although a tiny voice in my head was screaming that my statement was not entirely factual.

"Good. Don't. Rule number one of a fake relationship: Don't fall in love."

Huffing a laugh at how bothered he was, I crossed my arms. "How are you the expert on fake relationships?" There had to be a story here.

He ducked his head, avoiding eye contact as he pulled two beers out. "I read," he said. "And people tell me things."

"I'm only telling you—"

He held up a hand. "I won't say a word. So what do you need from me? Advice? Absolution? Since I'm basically the family priest these days, lay it on me."

"I'm here for the pizza and beer." I twisted the cap off mine and took a quick sip. "You know I can't lie to you, so I figured I'd get it out of the way."

Lips pressed together, he nodded.

"You sure I can't help?"

He shook his head, slicing mushrooms so paper thin they were practically transparent.

It was such a Jude thing to do. He'd clearly mastered the art of the homemade pizza. He was like that, focused and fastidious. The total opposite of me.

Axe Backwards

I wouldn't be surprised if he was studying the Italian language in order to make the experience more authentic.

He might have been a bachelor, but he was anything but stereotypical. His house was a small cape north of town, near the mountains. It was pristine and looked nothing like one would expect the bachelor pad of a professional lumberjack to.

His refinished hardwood floors gleamed, and every window was adorned with a flower box overflowing with color.

His furniture was tasteful, and his walls were decorated with artwork. The spare bedroom housed several musical instruments, and his graphic novel collection took up one entire wall of his living room.

Jude had always been this way. He paid attention, and regardless of what he was doing, he gave it his all. It was why he was such a talented musician. As a kid, he'd stay up all night learning new chords on the battered acoustic guitar my mom had bought him at the pawnshop.

In many ways, I was jealous of him. He knew where he fit in this life. He did his job, and he had his hobbies, dog, and home. He was settled.

In contrast, I was deeply unsettled. I was the one who had a child to care for, yet I had no plan, no career, and no idea how I'd make it through the next few years, let alone a solid eighteen with Tess. The thirty-four years I'd been on this earth had been spent chasing the next adventure, the next opportunity to be a hero. I'd trained and drilled and traveled, chasing fires and good times.

I collected scars as I went, both physical and emotional. Being home, spending time with Jude, though he was my twin and my best friend, had made me realize that I would never fit the way he did. I'd never settle.

My brain wouldn't quiet down enough to let me.

I'd always be itchy and chasing the next thing.

For the first time in my life, that terrified me.

Because I had more than myself to think about now. I had Tess.

Jude was pulling dough now. Rather than a rolling pin, he was using his hands.

"You look like a professional."

He ignored the observation. "Why are you and Vic faking?"

With a long exhale, I dove into the details, though I kept it as brief as I could.

"Victoria is beloved around here. This town would rise up and chase her family off with pitchforks and torches if she asked them to."

My chest tightened with affection for this place. If the people here had her back, then that elevated my opinion of the town where I was raised.

"That ex-husband of hers?" Jude laughed. "He should know better not to show his face in Lovewell. If the knitting ladies got wind he was here, shit." He shook his head, scoffing. "His life would be in danger."

I raised one eyebrow. "The knitting ladies?"

"Dude, you have no idea. Ask Cole. He'll be here soon."

"You should have seen her at her sister's wedding. She was so jumpy and anxious. Like she was a completely different person. These people get under her skin. I gotta help her."

Axe Backwards

Jude pinned me with a weary look. He'd lectured me many times about my hero complex.

"What would you have done?" I asked. "She helps with Tess. I care about her. And she asked me to be her fake boyfriend."

"I would have agreed," Jude said without hesitation. "Doesn't mean it's a good idea, though."

A whoosh of air escaped me. "See?"

"But," he said, peering at me over his glasses. "Victoria is beautiful, kind, and generous. I can also see how easy it would be to fall in love with her."

A thread of anger wound through me as he continued to speak about her.

"She's fun and down-to-earth..."

My fists clenched of their own accord.

"And a bright spot in this town."

My vision went red around the edges. "Are *you* in love with her?"

Jude tilted his head and gave me a look of sheer pity. "No," he said slowly, "but you may want to consider whether you are."

My stomach twisted into a knot. I'd do no such thing. She was my friend, and I loved spending time with her. But I didn't get attached. I didn't develop deep feelings. It wasn't who I was.

She deserved someone steady, someone grounded. Like Jude.

And now my fists were clenched again.

Before I could tell him to take his suggestion and fuck off, Ripley scurried toward the door, barking.

Gus stepped inside, talking to the dog as he did, followed by Cole, who was holding a Tupperware container.

"Are those what I think they are?" I asked, my mouth already watering. Damn, it had been a long time since I'd had one of my mom's salty-sweet, crumbly cookies.

He nodded. "Debbie taught me the secret recipe."

Jude, who was hand-tearing mozzarella, nodded. "His are good."

I reached out to grab the container, but Cole slapped my hand away. "Don't be an animal."

A laugh rumbled out of me. "What, you got married and magically acquired manners?"

He gave me an eye roll and bent down to scratch Ripley's ears. Cole's marriage had been about as big a surprise as my return to Lovewell with a baby. As big as discovering that Gus had an ex-wife. A woman who came back after twenty years as his enemy and was now the mother of his child.

It was still hard to believe. Cole, our wilder, reckless half brother, had married responsible, upstanding Doctor Willa Savard.

I'd missed so much. Luckily, Mom had insisted on babysitting tonight so I could catch up with my brothers.

Cole leaned over, his reach half the length of this house, and stole a slice of bell pepper.

Jude glared at him.

He shrugged. "I'm hungry."

"You know I have a process," my twin grumbled.

Gus cracked a beer and handed it to me, then opened a second and set it on the counter near Jude. But for reasons unknown to me, he skipped over Cole.

"You hit nine hundred yet?" he asked.

Axe Backwards

Jude didn't look up from the dough. "Check."

Gus sauntered over to the sliding glass door that led to a small patio and a tidy yard surrounded by dense pine forest.

I followed, curious about what he was checking. When I saw it, I was pretty sure my jaw dropped. "Holy shit. That pizza oven is massive. Where did it come from?"

The outdoor oven was dome-shaped and beautiful, with colorful blue tiles and storage for wood underneath.

Cole snorted as he filled a glass with water. "Owen."

I looked at Gus. Cole was married to Owen's fiancée's best friend, and yet the two men did not get along.

"You know Owen. He gets obsessed." Gus shrugged. "Lila's got celiac disease, so Owen made it his mission to make the best gluten-free pizza on earth. During his search for the best pizza oven, he bought several. He gave the rejects away. I have a small one in my garage somewhere."

"He'd bought half a dozen of them before he decided these models weren't good enough," Jude said, still expertly stretching the dough. "So he flew some Italian artisan in to build an oven at his place in Boston. State-of-the-art, mosaic tiles from Tuscany. This guy is in his seventies and has been doing it since he was a kid."

"Had to get a special permit from the city for the exhaust." Cole rolled his eyes.

Gus let out a low, quiet chuckle. "Totally over-the-top. As usual."

"The guy, Pasquale, stayed a month. He was great. He mentioned that he wanted to visit Maine, so Owen sent him up here. I showed him around, and we drove down the coast. Before he went home to Italy, he built this in my backyard as a thank-you."

Daphne Elliot

It was so Jude. He *would* befriend an elderly Italian stone mason. Just like Owen would fly in a senior citizen with decades of experience so he could make fancy pizza for his girlfriend.

Gus, our practical brother and the oldest, would surely think it was all absurd. He'd probably chop down a couple of trees and roast a whole cow over a fire for Chloe. And the woman would probably think that was romantic.

I'd missed them. They'd grown and evolved into men I didn't really know. Even my twin was now a semi-professional pizza chef and hadn't bothered to tell me.

Finn showed up at the exact moment the first pizza came out of the oven. Which was a minute after it went in, considering Jude had that thing cranking at nine hundred degrees and Gus tended to the fire, keeping it replenished with fresh hardwood.

Finn's hair was pulled back into a messy bun, his beard needed a trim, and his T-shirt had a hole in the back, but his smile lit up the tiny house. His first order of business was to pull me into a hug, complete with a firm back slap. The second was to whip out his phone so we could compare photos of our kids. Thor was a couple of months older than Tess and already walking and causing chaos wherever he went.

Finn was gearing up for a busy season. His relatively new flight tourism business had exploded when a celebrity featured him in a magazine spread. He was booked for years in advance and had hired staff to keep up with the demand.

We settled into the Adirondak chairs on the patio, the air warm from the pizza oven. Ripley patrolled our surroundings, ready to snatch up any fallen pieces of crust as we demolished pie after pie.

Fig and prosciutto.

Mushroom and fontina.

Sopresetta and artichoke heart.

My stomach groaned.

"You're all animals." Jude reclined in his chair, beer in hand.

"And you're amazing," Finn said, raising his bottle. "How many fancy pizzas did we eat?"

My twin huffed a laugh. "Nine."

Finn lifted one shoulder lazily. "Next time we'll hit double digits. That fancy cheese was incredible. How far did you have to drive to get that?"

"Mom picked it up at the Trader Joes in Bangor."

That made sense. We had decent produce up here, and there was a natural food store in Heartsborough, but imported Italian cheese was a delicacy in these parts. One I'd overindulged in tonight.

I'd be running tomorrow. And I'd have to add more weight to my vest.

The thought of running brought an image of Vic to mind. She looked so damn cute, with her face red and her hair disheveled. She'd been doing well and seemed to enjoy herself.

"I brought you something." Cole held out a gift bag. "It's for Tess."

I wiped my hands on my napkin again for good measure before digging into it. "Wow." A rush of warmth hit me as I pulled a beautiful yellow blanket out. The buttery softness of the yarn against my fingertips lit up comforting instincts in my brain. Or it could be the pizza coma.

"I knit it."

A scoff escaped me before I could stop it. "You knit?"

Cole was practically a giant. He was by far the biggest of all of us, had been the wildest, and was a former pro hockey player. The vision of him fussing with knitting needles that floated into my mind was comical.

"Thor loves his," Finn piped up. "And it washes well. He's barfed on it at least a dozen times already." He raised his beer and shot me a grin, leaving no doubt in my mind that he was delighted by everything his son did.

"Thank you," I said, clutching it a little tighter. "This is so thoughtful."

Cole shrugged. "Knitting is good for my anxiety."

My chest pinched at the idea. I was taken aback by the way he'd laid that out. What was even more surprising was how the rest of my brothers nodded, as if discussing one's feelings and emotional challenges was normal.

"And my sobriety."

Huh. The lack of beer for him made sense now.

To be honest, our dad came from the toxic masculinity school of fatherhood, where screaming was required and all vulnerabilities were suppressed. It was heartening to see my brothers doing things differently.

It was also more than a bit jarring.

I had a lot to catch up on.

While the conversation shifted from Tess to Thor to Gus's newborn daughter Simone, then to machinery he and Jude used regularly on logging sites, I sat back and enjoyed the night air and the feeling of being back home.

Axe Backwards

For years, I would have argued that Lovewell was not home. That it was the place I'd grown up and nothing more. But this town was just what Tess and I needed.

It hadn't taken me long to realize I needed to return. After the order had been extended and I'd parted ways with the guardian ad litem and my lawyer at the courthouse, I was finally free to plan for the future. To map out the legal plan and try to figure out how to shape my life around being a parent.

Within days, I was homesick. After years of moving, then moving again, and jumping from one adventure to another, I missed my mom. I missed my brothers.

I needed this place. And Tess needed this place.

"That's what Parker thinks. We all need to be aware of what could happen next." Gus was standing now, arms crossed and looming over us, looking like the eldest brother he was.

"We can't move on what Cole found yet?" Finn asked. "And what about Huxley?"

Gus shook his head. "Working on it. Legal channels, blah, blah, Fourth Amendment."

I sat, studying each brother, piecing together what I could from this conversation. For a decade and a half, I'd been worlds away from the business and my father's dealings, which meant I didn't even have most of the basics.

Most of what they said went over my head.

"Back up for a minute," I said. "What did you say about Charles Huxley?"

The guy gave off a weird vibe, and his son was a super creep. And with the financial state of the food pantry and the need of the community, Vic was constantly being forced to meet with them. She seemed to think they were going to make a big donation, but I was dubious.

"He's dirty," Cole declared.

My lungs seized up. Wasn't he the richest guy in town? The former lieutenant governor? Didn't he cut ribbons and make donations?

"We're working on it," Jude assured me.

"Cole connected some of the dots," Gus said, slapping our baby brother on the shoulder. "Got us our best lead so far. And we know he was mixed up with Chief Souza."

"I caught the chief wearing one of Dad's watches," Cole explained from where he sat on the floor. He had one leg stretched out, and he was massaging the muscle.

My father collected rare and expensive watches. I knew nothing about them—hell, I knew next to nothing about the man himself; he'd taken no interest in me whatsoever—but apparently Cole did.

"When the police seized his collection, one was missing. I recognized it when I met with him one day, and he knew I knew."

"What does it mean?" None of these pieces were coming together to create an image I could decipher.

Gus sighed. "Dad was the tip of the iceberg. There is a whole network of people involved in the drug trafficking and fuck knows what else. They're still under the radar. We've partially exposed Chief Souza, and we know Huxley and his son are mixed up too."

"Owen and Lila found evidence of potential money laundering," Jude explained. "Chloe had some strange encounters. Cole got mixed up with the police when he was

Axe Backwards

asking questions about shell companies owned by the Huxleys."

I shook my head, my heart rate picking up. What the fuck?

"And no one has been arrested yet? You said the FBI has been all over town for months."

Cole grimaced. "They're working on it."

"But we've hired Parker Gagnon," Gus said, finally sitting again. "She's an excellent PI. She's made more progress in the past couple of months than the FBI has in the past year."

I took off my hat and scratched my head, realizing that I wasn't only out of the loop. It was like I'd lived on another fucking planet for years. "Our sleepy little town has a PI?"

Cole nodded. "She's ex-state police, married to Pascal Gagnon, and it's very likely she'll be named the new police chief."

"How do you know that?"

"He's got all the connections at city hall," Finn explained.

"And knitting club." Jude chuckled.

Cole's smirk was smug. "You do not mess with the knitting club ladies."

"We keep telling him to run for mayor." Gus's chest puffed out a little as he made that statement.

Cole's cheeks went pink above the scruff on his face. He'd certainly turned his life around and found a place for himself in this town. Less than a year ago, according to Jude's updates, he'd been a washed-up former hockey pro who was self-sabotaging and spiraling.

If he could build a life here, maybe I could too.

After the rest of the guys left, I took Ripley out for a walk, then helped Jude clean up. He taught me how to rake the ash out of the pizza oven and check the chimney for blockages.

"So..." he said once everything was back in its rightful place and the dishwasher was loaded.

My chest tightened. The way he dragged out that word made me concerned that he was winding up for a hard conversation, and I really needed to get home. Tess needed her nightly pacing around the apartment to sleep. She'd done well at Mom's while we were at the wedding, but I couldn't chance it. My mom was so generous, but I refused to allow her to be up all night.

"I'm glad you're finally home."

I blew out a breath, half relieved, half defeated. "Lovewell hasn't been home for a very long time."

"That's the thing about home, don't you think? It's always there for you when you need it. You should stay."

That was the million-dollar question. Would we stay? Could we stay?

"I need a job." I went with what felt like the easiest way to sidestep the emotional landmines of settling down in Lovewell.

"Do you? You have your share from the sale of the business."

I nodded. "And Owen set up some investments and a trust for Tess. And—" I swallowed past the lump that had suddenly formed in my throat and lowered my attention to the floor between us. "And Jack and Emily had life insurance. Tess is covered. College, all of it."

Jude nodded. "I'm glad she's provided for. But how are you doing with all this? You want to talk about it?"

I shook my head. The emotions were still so raw. And watching my girl grow and change every day, knowing Jack and Emily would miss every milestone, only compounded my guilt. "No, I really don't."

"Okay, then." With a shrug, he closed the dishwasher. "I'm here when you're ready."

Chapter 21
Noah

Being Vic's fake boyfriend was the easiest job I'd ever had. Mostly, it consisted of hanging out like we had been and going about our lives normally. Most mornings, Tess and I would walk to the Caffeinated Moose. We'd pick up a latte for Vic or wait for her to meet us after she'd gotten cleaned up after our run, and I'd inevitably be trapped for at least five minutes while people gushed about us.

One thing was clear: everyone I encountered adored Vic. They respected how hard she worked for the community. I'd never thought to stop and appreciate the way Lovewell valued character and hard work before.

I'd lived in many remote places, but nothing compared to the unforgiving terrain up here. The harsh winters, steamy summers, endless mosquitos, and wild storms that made the people here band together and take care of one another.

Now I saw it clearly. Day in and day out. The way people helped one another. Leaned on each other. And Vic was an important piece of this community puzzle.

Tess and I let ourselves into Vic's apartment to deliver her coffee. It had become our tradition on the mornings we didn't run together.

"Ick-Ick," Tess called out happily, squirming in my arm.

The moment I set her on the floor, she dropped to her knees and crawled at a high rate of speed toward Vic's bedroom door.

When it opened, I almost fainted.

My fake girlfriend stood in the doorway wearing nothing but a bathing suit.

And not a normal bathing suit.

This one had all kinds of cutouts in the torso. Technically it was probably considered a one-piece, but it covered less skin than a bikini. The sides were cut up high, exposing her hips and just barely covering her ass.

I shuffled sideways and splayed a hand on the table to steady myself.

In the suit that left nothing to the imagination and her hair down like that, she looked like a goddess. The scrap of fabric was a deep chocolate brown and dipped low in front, barely covering each of her round breasts.

My mouth went dry, and I lost the ability to form a sentence.

Then she leaned down to scoop up Tess, and all blood flow to my brain ceased.

She sauntered over, mostly naked, with my kid on her hip, and took the coffee cup off the table. With a small smile, she brought it to her lips and took a long sip.

"Thanks. I need this today."

Words.

I should speak words.

Axe Backwards

Yes, brain. Good plan.

"Wow."

Fuck. It was like I'd never seen a pretty girl in a bathing suit before.

Scratch that. I'd seen lots of pretty girls.

But I'd never seen a woman so sexy. Her proximity made it hard to breathe.

"It's gonna be hot today," I said. "You should turn the AC on."

The month of June in Maine was like one extreme mood swing after another. The temperature could be anywhere between thirty and ninety degrees. We'd had a frost a couple of weeks ago, but today was already stifling.

Though it could be because there wasn't enough oxygen in this apartment.

With a nod, she took another sip of coffee.

"You look..."

Words. Need words.

Good words.

"Very beachy."

Beachy? I wanted to slam my head into the wall.

"My parents are hosting a party at their lake house today." She sighed, holding her cup to one side so Tess couldn't reach it. "Or compound, as my mother insists on calling it." Hip jutted out, she rolled her eyes. "I didn't plan on going, but then I remembered that I bought this cute swimsuit when my annual bout of winter depression was at its peak."

She put Tess on the rug and dragged over the basket of toys she'd collected.

Sweet mercy. I could tell the suit cut high on her backside, but the sight of her full ass on display was enough to cause a guy to stroke out. The ass I'd always thought was quite nice, I suddenly discovered, was so much greater than that.

"What do you think? Too much? I'm probably way too old to pull this off."

"It's sexy," I blurted out, sweat suddenly beading at my temples. "You look confident and beautiful." I tore my hat from my head and wiped at my brow with the back of my wrist.

Her neck and chest flushed. Damn. I'd never get tired of seeing her skin go pink in response to my compliments.

"Thanks." She lowered her head and focused on her feet, as if she could hide the reaction from me. "So," she said, her shoulders deflating. "I wasn't going to ask. But..." She covered her face with her hands. "Can you come with me? You know, as my doting boyfriend?"

"Yes," I rushed out without a moment to think it through. "I'd love to."

I'd do anything she asked if it meant seeing her in that bathing suit again.

I may need to take a very long shower first.

"It's okay if you—"

"No." I held up a hand. "We planned to swing by my mom's for a play date with Thor. I'll text her. I'm sure she'd love to hang out with Tess for a few hours."

She nodded. "It was a last-minute invite. It will probably be awful, so I'll apologize in advance."

I took a step toward her, eliminating the space between us. With my chest so close to hers they'd probably touch if either of us inhaled deeply, I put my hand on her bare shoulder. For a moment, I got lost in the sweep of her neck and the idea of kissing my way across her collarbones.

"I told you I'd do whatever you needed. As your boyfriend, I have to be there."

Her chest rose and fell rapidly, her ragged breaths caressing the skin of my neck and her heat radiating through me.

"Fake boyfriend," she whispered.

"Right." My heart pounded in my ears. Fuck, she smelled so good. "Fake boyfriend."

"But my real friend."

That word was a bucket of cold water over my head. I took a step back and sucked in air that didn't smell like her.

Friend. Just friends. Friend zone. Zone of friendship.

This interaction had fried my synapses. I'd momentarily lost my sanity. This was Vic. The best person I knew. And she'd been very clear that she was not interested.

Day after day, as she became a bigger part of my life and Tess's, my resolve to do whatever it took to keep her around grew.

I couldn't lose her. Tess couldn't lose her.

No matter how badly I ached to touch her and kiss her, it couldn't happen.

"When do we have to be there?"

"Noon."

With surprising ease, I shifted into dad mode and scooped my little girl up. "Okay. Let me feed Tess, call my mom, and get organized." I kissed her on the nose, eliciting a baby giggle. "Wanna go play at Grandma's today?"

She vigorously rubbed her chest, signing "please" over and over, the giggling turning into a delighted squeal.

"I guess we've got a plan."

VIC'S MOM HAD BEEN RIGHT. THIS PLACE WAS A compound.

The mile-long driveway wound through dense forest. Along the way, we passed a handful of small buildings, and when we reached a perfectly manicured field, what looked like a horse stable sat on the far side of it.

The main house had a massive circular drive with a fountain in the middle.

A fucking fountain.

The white-brick structure with massive columns was totally out of place in Northern Maine. It looked like it belonged on the French Riviera.

Champagne and flowers in hand, we made our way past several cars and headed to the front entrance. "How many people did they invite?"

Vic shrugged. "With my mother, you never know."

The home hugged the shoreline, with large wings extending on each side.

"Shit," Vic hissed as we stepped into the massive foyer. "I didn't realize houses like this existed in Lovewell."

Head tipped back, I blinked at the cavernous space. I'd known there were a few big estates on the lakefront, but nothing like this. Everything, from the massive crystal chandeliers to the large ornate vases, screamed money.

My flip-flops slapped on the marble floor as we headed for the back of the house.

Miranda, looking only mildly annoyed to see us, greeted

Axe Backwards

us near the floor-to-ceiling windows that lined the back of the house. The view of the lake was incredible.

"The pool is over there." She gestured to the elevated area surrounding the massive swimming pool and hot tub. It was dotted with blue-and-white-striped umbrellas and stark white reclining chairs. "We've got two bars. The caterers are setting up now."

She wore a floral caftan and a large diamond necklace that glinted in the sun as she surveyed the patio and her guests. I wasn't sure it was wise to tempt fate by wearing several carats' worth of diamonds so close to the deep lake, but she didn't seem concerned.

With the warmest expression I could muster, I held out the bouquet. "Your home is beautiful."

She gave me a forced smile. "Thank you. It was a steal. We'd been looking on the coast, but everything up here in the sticks is so cheap. It was hard to pass up."

Vic winced next to me, as if she, like me, was steeling herself for a painful afternoon.

Outside, a somewhat snoozy party was in full swing. Kids were splashing in the pool while adults chatted over cocktails.

Miranda, the trained hostess she was, I was certain, showed us around, introducing us to various guests. Several people I knew from town were here, while others, including some of Vic's aunt and uncles, had come to visit from Downeast.

"This is Victoria's boyfriend. She married a bond trader, but now she's dating a firefighter." She infused so much disgust in the word *firefighter*, one would think I was a petty criminal or cleaned port-a-potties for a living.

"Don't worry, Mommy." Alexandra, clad in a ruffled bikini, sidled up next to her mom. "I married the bond trader."

The circle of older ladies sipping prosecco laughed like it was the funniest joke they'd ever heard while Miranda beamed at Alexandra, who was rubbing her belly. It had grown a little since the wedding, though now it looked like she'd eaten one too many cheeseburgers. Though I doubted the woman would deign to eat such pedestrian food.

My gut sank. Were these people for real? Beside me, Vic had pasted on a strange smile. I wanted to shake her, to scream at everyone here, and then, with my hand in hers, jump into the lake and make a swim for our freedom.

Instead, I steered her over to a pair of lounge chairs. My timing was impeccable too. The moment our backs were turned, Alexandra had pulled up ultrasound photos of the baby she and Graham—her sister's asshole *ex-husband*—had created.

I guided Vic to sit, then snagged two bottles of water from a server passing by before I joined her.

For a moment, I let her sit in the quiet. But when she hadn't moved an inch for more than a minute, I scooted my chair closer to hers and squeezed her hand.

Sunglasses lowered, she looked at me, her eyes rimmed red.

"Thank you," she mouthed. With that, she slid them back up and rested against the back of her chair, never letting go of my hand.

I squeezed her hand three times and looked out at the water. The lake was pristine and the forest surrounding it thick. The only signs of civilization were a few mansions and the town marina on the far end. The rest of the expanse appeared untouched, wild. Katahdin and the Appalachian Trail created a serene backdrop. It was the perfect reminder that no matter how fancy the house, we were still in Maine.

We'd spent our childhoods in this lake, jumping off tree limbs, skinny dipping, and all kinds of other stupid stuff. It made me strangely happy to be here with Vic.

Elizabeth wandered over, along with a little boy wearing *Bluey* swim trunks who darted straight to Vic and looped his arms around her waist.

"Look how grown up you are," she said as she stood and ruffled his hair.

Head tipped back, he launched into a monologue about what he was learning in kindergarten, bouncing on his toes the whole time.

While I watched, not even bothering to hide a chuckle at his excitement, I felt a pair of eyes on me. I inhaled and stood as well, bracing myself for a conversation I wasn't sure I was ready for.

Instead of being met with scrutiny, I found Elizabeth smiling widely. "So good of you to come."

"It's a lovely home," I replied, letting my shoulders fall a fraction.

"Can I get you anything?"

I shook my head.

She stood there smiling at me, the moment getting more awkward by the second. Eventually, blessedly, her son led her away.

Vic sat and adjusted her chair so she was reclined fully, giving me an eyeful of her swimsuit.

The lake view was amazing, but nothing compared to the sight of my fake girlfriend.

Thank fuck I'd worn sunglasses. It meant I could ogle Vic without looking like a total perv. Though now that I was studying her, I could see the tension radiating off her.

I flagged down a server and took two more bottles of water before I sat. With the backs of my knuckles, I brushed her jawline, then used my thumb and forefinger to tip her chin up so she met my eye.

Vic leaned over, sliding her sunglasses down her nose. "I'm sorry."

I laced my fingers behind my head and leaned back in the chair. "Don't be. I'm having fun. It's not every day I get to hang out in a fancy mansion with a gorgeous date. The rest of the company may be lacking, but I could happily sit and talk to you for days."

She huffed, lowering her focus to where she was wringing her hands. "My mother is such a snob. What she said about firefighters?" Another huff, her shoulders drooping. "Then there's Elizabeth. I have no idea what's come over her. She keeps awkwardly staring at you like a piece of meat. I'm so sorry."

"Hey."

I cupped her jaw, noticing then that her sister, who was now across the pool, was watching intently. Since we had an audience, I figured I'd put on a show, so I pulled Vic into a lingering kiss. It was chaste enough for public, but possessive enough to ensure everyone here knew who she belonged to.

I pulled back slowly, and the smile that spread across her face lit me up inside. I wanted to properly kiss her. To take my time savoring the taste of her and the feel of her curves under my hands.

"I'm not a piece of meat." I brushed a kiss against her knuckles. "I'm your piece of meat."

She giggled, her cheeks going pink. "They're just jealous because you're so hot."

I shook my head, relishing the way my lips ghosted over her fingers while I kept them close. "Nah, they're jealous because you're so hot."

She propped herself up on her elbow and glared. At least I thought she glared. It was hard to tell when she wore sunglasses. "Don't do that. I don't need you to lie to me to make me feel better. I'm a cow compared to them." She looked down. "My hips are huge, I've got cellulite, I—"

I squeezed her hand firmly to shut her up. "Are you drunk? You are the most gorgeous creature in this county, maybe the state."

She sat up and crossed her arms, which made her breasts press against the skimpy fabric.

"That"—I nodded, allowing myself the briefest of peeks at her cleavage—"is not helping your case."

"Elizabeth is a former ballerina". She said it as though the title was some kind of indication of her worth.

Sure, Elizabeth was tall and was so thin that in the skimpy bikini she wore, anyone within twenty feet count every one of her vertebrae. The task was only made easier by her perfect posture. She had been civil to me and seemed like an engaged parent, so I couldn't fault her.

Compared to her sisters, Vic looked like a Renaissance painting. All creamy skin and delicious curves. Long legs, curvy waist, and pouty smile.

I would never understand why women were always comparing themselves and finding so many faults in their own bodies. Beauty came in many forms. So did desirability.

Standing, I pulled her up with me. Then I placed my hands on her shoulders and angled in until my lips skated over her earlobe.

"When I saw you in that bathing suit this morning, I was dangerously close to popping a boner while holding my child. You're a goddess, Victoria."

She let out a little gasp, and the sound went straight to my dick. I wanted to unleash a tirade of every filthy fantasy I'd ever had about her, but I'd already crossed the line. I couldn't light the match and watch it burn.

Instead, I pulled her close and gently kissed her forehead.

"And more importantly, you're my friend. I won't let you talk shit about my friend."

Chapter 22
Victoria

"I like your laugh."

I froze with a chip halfway to my mouth.

Another episode of *Schitt's Creek* played while we sat side by side on Noah's couch. Slowly, he was learning to sit still. He didn't pace as much as he used to, and when he didn't have Tess strapped to his chest, he still dropped to the floor to do pushups or sit-ups, but only between episodes. During season one, he'd do it every ten minutes or so, to get his excess energy out.

Now he insisted on braiding my hair when I walked in the door. He had mastered the regular braid and was now learning to French braid. Or "Elsa braid" as he liked to call it.

I was sitting on the floor, his strong legs on each side of me. If I turned my head too much, I got an eyeful of muscular hamstring.

At the moment, he had his hands threaded through my hair. Keeping the strands separate and adding was giving him a lot of trouble.

He dropped the hair with a huff and tapped my shoulder. I turned and looked up at him.

"Why are you making that face?" His eyes softened. The man was so damn perceptive. He could sense small shifts in my mood, sometimes even before I did.

"It's nothing."

He stole the bag of chips and held them out of my reach. "It's not. Talk."

Lips pressed together, I exhaled through my nose and stood, retrieving the bag and sitting next to him. "My ex always said I had an annoying laugh."

He stiffened. "Are you fucking kidding me?"

"Nope." I emphasized the *p*, my lips making a popping sound. "He said it was too much."

He had that opinion when it came to a lot of my qualities, really. I was too loud, too excitable. My hips were too wide, my ears too big, and my taste was terrible.

"You know how wild my hand motions get when I'm talking, and yeah, I am loud, but he was so offended by it."

He arched an unimpressed brow. "And you were okay with that?"

I winced. Every time I talked about Graham, I was surprised by how bad things sounded out loud. While I was wading through the thick of things, it all seemed normal. I'd always figured that he loved me and wanted what was best for me. That he was only telling me so I could work on reining in my flaws. So maybe my laugh was weird. Maybe I should have been quiet and serious.

"We'd go to charity events or out to dinner with his clients, and afterward, in the car on the way home, he'd scold me for what I said or how I behaved."

Axe Backwards

Noah scooted forward, narrowing his eyes. "He scolded you?"

I examined the tortilla chip I was still holding, deliberately avoiding his eyes. "Yeah. He'd pick apart everything I said and point out all my wrongdoings. I was too loud. I'd said something that embarrassed him. I should have passed the pepper to the right. That kind of stuff."

Sighing, Noah kissed Tess's head. She was nestled in one of his many wraps, snoozing on his chest. It was stupidly adorable. This big, strong man dressed in sweats and a tight T-shirt, all his ink on display, with a purple baby swaddle thing wrapped around him and those sweet blond curls peeking out.

Thank God I wasn't attracted to men anymore. If I was, it would be a problem.

A serious problem.

"Vic, I say this with total respect. But why did you allow this man to live?"

I grasped the throw pillow beside me and considered tossing it at him. In the end, not wanting to wake Tess, I settled for flipping him the bird while shoving a chip into my mouth.

It started when I was a child. The feeling that I was too much. I'd always had a tendency to get overly excited about things. At school, I sat in the front row and raised my hand each time the teacher asked a question.

I cared.

I tried hard.

Yet, for some reason, that was bad.

"My mother was always horrified by me." I picked at the fringe along the edge of the throw pillow, pushing down the defeat that always plagued me when I talked about the way my mom treated me when I was a child. "My crooked ponytail, my loud voice. She called me a loudmouth. Sometimes I interrupt people. I know it's rude, but it's not intentional. I just get so excited."

"It's okay." He squeezed my knee and stood. From the way he eyed the floor, then his sleeping daughter, it was clear he wished he could drop and do a set of pushups, but he settled for lunges instead. I didn't mind. In fact, I liked it. This meant he was comfortable around me. That he didn't feel as though he had to force himself to sit still when the urge to move hit him.

"No, it's not. It even affected my career. I've never mastered the ability to be cool and impersonal. Looking stone-faced in meetings? Forget it. I'd feel things, and you know me."

He turned back toward me, one leg out, hands on his hips. "Yeah. You have no poker face."

"Long ago I made peace with the knowledge that I'd never be one of the cool girls. You know, all aloof and disinterested and quiet."

"Can I offer something?" He stepped, lunged, and stepped again, then turned.

I picked up my water bottle, appreciating the view of his very round, very muscular ass in those mesh shorts as he squeezed his glutes.

"Have you ever thought that maybe it's not that you're too much? Could it be that the people you surrounded yourself with weren't good enough? Graham wasn't good enough for you. He wasn't smart enough, passionate enough, kind enough."

Axe Backwards

I blanched.

He spun and straightened, adjusting his hat. "And instead of realizing that and pushing himself to be better, he convinced you that you were the problem and made you feel small, which made it easier for him to control you."

His words hit me like a punch to the face. *Holy fucking shit.* "We've been friends for a matter of weeks, and already, you're cutting to the heart of it. I spent eight months in therapy, and it took at least half that for me to get there. I'm still learning to embrace my big feelings."

He shrugged. "Maybe big feelings are your superpower."

That was truly laughable. "Oh, please. You're a man. You can get away with saying that shit, but women? Can't have feelings, lest we make the menfolk uncomfortable." Out of habit, I waved my arms wildly.

"Feelings don't make me uncomfortable." He sat on the floor in front of me, patting Tess's back. "For my entire adult life, I've compartmentalized and suppressed feelings. They had no place in my job or in my life." With a soft smile, he dropped a kiss to her head. "Now? I'm all feelings, and it's okay. There are days they pile up on my chest like bricks and I worry I won't be able to breathe—"

"Noah."

"For years and years, I pushed it all down. I didn't feel connected to myself, let alone anyone else. I learned in childhood to channel my manic energy into physical stuff."

"Hence all the injuries."

He nodded. "If not for Jude, I'd be dead. He talked me out of so much stupid shit and dragged my ass home every time I broke a bone. But that mindset fucked me up."

"I'm sure."

"By the time I hit high school, I was itching to get away from my family, to get away from everyone. Because I was crazy and wild and untethered. Every woman I ever dated told me I was best in small doses."

My heart panged for him. Scooting back, I pulled my legs up under me. "What the fuck does that mean?"

"It means I had no depth. No points of connection. I was the wild, fun guy. Nothing more."

With a frown, I studied his serious expression. "I don't believe that."

"I chased the lifestyle that reinforced my beliefs. I was constantly on the move, constantly looking for excitement and danger. It made sense for me. I was that guy."

I slid onto the floor next to him and put my arm around his broad shoulders. "You are not that guy. You're a hell of a lot more than that guy."

"And you're fucking perfect."

His words hung in the air between us, making it hard to breathe. Normally I'd brush off a comment like that, but the sincerity in his eyes was like a blow to the solar plexus.

His focus dipped to my lips, like maybe he was considering kissing me again. We hadn't spoken of the almost kiss that was interrupted by psychotic Olaf or the one we'd shared by the pool, the one for show, but I'd thought about both almost constantly.

But I was drawn to him. I was both comfortable in his presence and challenged by it.

Could it happen again?

I leaned in almost imperceptibly, watching his face.

Before I found the courage to move in closer, he looked away.

Okay, then.

In one quick move, he was on his feet and patting Tess's back again, headed for her room.

I scrambled back up onto the couch and focused on my breathing, embarrassed by what I'd almost done and hoping like hell he hadn't noticed.

When he emerged a few moments later, he gave me a big thumbs-up. I still couldn't quite believe Tess was sleeping in her crib. It felt like this massive accomplishment.

I thought we'd watch TV and ignore the tension that had been building.

But no.

Instead, he sat right next to me and put his arm around my shoulders. I was hit with a wave of warmth from his strong body and the desire to burrow into his chest.

"I meant what I said." His voice was soft yet urgent. "You are perfect. You are so good at what you do. Your passion is inspiring."

I clutched my hands in my lap and fixed my focus on them.

"It's clear by the conviction you possess when you talk about food insecurity that you want to help every single client who walks through that door."

My chest tightened. "I do."

"Exactly. Superhero. Don't let your toxic mother and ex-husband convince you otherwise."

Tears pricked at the backs of my eyes. This man was so good to me.

"When I came back, it meant escaping them and all the stories I'd told myself over the years. I can be myself in Lovewell."

"Of course you can. The town loves you for who you really are."

"I ran away from my life and took the job to help Aunt Lou. I wasn't sure I'd stick with the food pantry, but it didn't take long to realize it was my calling. And the more time I spend here, the more I feel like my old self. I wear the clothes I want to wear. I can grow out my hair."

With a smile, he tugged on the ends of my hair. "I like your ponytails. And you love running the food pantry."

I really, really did. I didn't notice it at first. In the beginning, I did it to help Aunt Lou and to keep myself busy. Now? It was a part of me.

"Most days it feels like I'm pushing a rock up a hill. But it gives me purpose and allows me to use my energy for good. The headaches are endless. Handling suppliers and grants and managing clogged sinks and broken freezers and deliveries is exhausting. There are days I dream of going back to the corporate world."

He sat beside me, his blue eyes darker. The intensity of his stare made my stomach drop.

"Then I'll send a family home with groceries and know kids are being fed because of my efforts, and it's all worth it."

He broke out in a slow smile, those dimples taunting me.

"Good. I'm glad you can acknowledge how amazing you are."

I snorted. "What about you? Do you miss the fires?"

In an instant, the joy in his expression was gone.

"Honestly?" He took off his hat and ran his hand through his hair. "Yes. I do." A sharp burst of air left him. "It's a shitty thing to say. I know that. Fire is terrible. It destroys lives and homes. But when we'd load up to deploy to a fire, the buzz, the focus, would take over. Knowing that even if I didn't come back, I was doing something good. That my life would be meaningful."

My stomach plummeted. I'd never left for work wondering if I'd come home alive.

"I miss that version of myself. The man who can home in on what needs to be done rather than the kid with ADHD who didn't read until third grade. When I'm coordinating a response, I'm sharp, and all the noise disappears. The world gets clear. And I'm good at it. Or at least I was."

I grasped his hand. "You're a great dad. And you have so much potential. Yes, your life has changed, but it's far from over. Trust me. I started over in Lovewell, and I'm better than ever."

He pulled me close and wrapped his arms around me.

I did the same, putting my head on his shoulder.

"I'm scared," he said softly. "What if I can't do it? What if I can't build a good life for my baby girl or be the dad she needs?"

"It's okay to be scared." I held him a little tighter. "But don't you dare think you're not enough. You, Noah Hebert, are amazing. And your little girl is lucky to have you."

He lowered his head, and we stayed like that, supporting one another for a long moment.

"And," I said, "I'm lucky to have you too."

Chapter 23
Noah

Mom's house was not large but had a spacious yard that was perfect for a party.

It was a breezy summer day, but she had a fire pit if the air turned chilly and plenty of space inside to congregate.

I'd been against the gathering at first, but she'd insisted. Hosting her granddaughter's first birthday was a privilege, she'd argued. I'd given in pretty easily after that. Even though she wouldn't remember it, I wanted to make a huge fuss over Tess's birthday.

It was how I'd grown up. We'd have cake for breakfast, and Mom would shower us with all our favorite things. She'd plan themed parties for our classmates on a shoestring budget, staying up late to make *Ninja Turtle* or *Blue's Clues* decorations.

I wanted my girl to experience that kind of joy. Life was about making memories, about taking photos to reminisce over later. I wanted her to have the gifts, the excitement, the cake all over her face. Given all she'd lost, I'd work doubly hard to give her all the special moments I could.

The birthday girl was passed from family member to family member, smiling and soaking up all the attention.

Vic and my mom had come up with the theme. "Tess in One-derland" had become a massive Mad Hatter tea party.

Mom had gone overboard with streamers, garland, and twinkle lights. There was a giant outdoor chess set, where Jude and Adele were locked in a very intense game. She'd even bought Tess a frilly blue dress and a black headband.

Kids ran wild wearing giant cardboard hats while adults drank out of mismatched teacups and ate cookies decorated to look like playing cards.

My brothers were all here. Even Owen and Lila had come up from Boston. I'd barely spoken to him over the years, but it was good to see him, even if I was still getting used to the idea that he was engaged to Cole's ex-girlfriend.

Not that Cole minded. He was happily married to Willa. That was a whole dynamic I would never understand.

Everyone who loved Tess was here, and while guilt still gnawed at my gut regarding the people who were no longer here to love her the way she deserved, I wouldn't regret giving her this special day.

Vic approached me, bottle of water in hand. "I need to hydrate. The knitting ladies have been talking to me nonstop for twenty minutes, and I need a break."

I turned, using my body to shield her from the crowd.

"Happy to protect you, milady," I said with a tip of my hat.

She bit her lip and smiled at me. She'd been gracing me with that beautiful expression more and more lately. I wasn't

Axe Backwards

complaining, but the way her teeth sunk into her plush bottom lip made it difficult to maintain control of my hands and my lips.

No matter how often my brain blared the "just friends" alarm, my body wasn't listening. All day, my eyes had been on her. The way she lit up while she chatted. How the sundress she wore swished around her knees when she walked.

Vic had been a constant presence in my life and in my mind. She'd jumped right into planning this party with my mom and genuinely enjoyed creating a special day for Tess.

I loved the way she talked with her hands when she was excited. She'd been telling me a story about putting too much hot sauce on a taco a couple of days ago, and in the process, she'd knocked over a coffee cup. The more time we spent together, the more the mask came off. She laughed and joked and yelled and gesticulated wildly. I loved every word, every sound, every movement.

Vic, the real Vic, was ballsy and hilarious. She was nothing like the silent, terrified woman I'd taken to a wedding a month ago.

"Thank you for doing all this. You are an amazing fake girlfriend."

Angling closer, she peered around to make sure we weren't overheard. "I'm not here as your fake girlfriend. I'm here as Tess's number one fan and favorite person."

With a chuckle, I arched a brow. "Oh, really?"

"Yes, card-carrying member of the fan club. Trust me, I earned it. Though others may try to best me. I'm watching your mom. She fights dirty."

A laugh rumbled out of me. Damn. This woman was

incredible. Her eyes were bright and her smile was wide. The smile I used to have to coax out of her was present more and more every day.

"You look pretty in that dress."

She rolled her eyes. "Don't flirt."

"Just a friendly compliment," I replied, affecting an innocent expression. "The color brings out your eyes."

She put one hand on her hip. "Really? Pink compliments my brown eyes?"

I winked. "I think so."

"Watch yourself, hotshot." She may have grumbled the phrase, but she was smiling as she walked away.

That attempt at flirting was tame, especially considering the thoughts I'd had recently.

I was getting swept up in the magic of this day. It was sunny and joyful and all about my sweet baby girl. But I had to be careful not to let myself want things I couldn't have. Things I wasn't cut out for. Things I didn't deserve. Otherwise I'd end up flat on my ass and having to dig myself out of a deep hole of self-pity.

What scrambled my brain further, making it even trickier to stay the course of friendship, was seeing my brothers settling down. They'd all become so... domesticated.

Finn had been in the Navy, and he'd had his daughter Merry young, so I wasn't surprised that he was eyeball deep in dad life and loving every minute of it. He and Adele were well matched, and their son was fast becoming Tess's best friend. Given how fast he could run already and how good he was at scamming treats from my mom, I knew he'd be the best kind of bad influence.

But Owen? He was an uptight accountant who loved his

custom-tailored suits and exotic travel. Yet he was engaged and totally smitten. Gus? The world's grumpiest workaholic? The man was cradling his baby and cooing at her incessantly. And Cole was happily married and following his wife around like a lovesick puppy. That last fact alone made me feel like I'd found myself in an alternate universe.

While some parts of Lovewell had remained comfortingly the same in the years I'd been gone, many had changed, and they were constantly throwing me for a loop.

Though I tried to ignore the sensation, it stung, seeing how they all interacted and connected in various ways. Owen, who I'd assumed had similar feelings to mine and wanted nothing to do with this place, had bonded with Gus when he'd spent a few months here getting the family business sold. He fit in seamlessly, save for some subtle tension with Cole.

They were all so happy, working and building successful, fulfilling lives. My father had done so much damage. I'd spent much of my adulthood assuming there was no successful path out of the mess he'd created. But my brothers were proving me wrong.

The party was lively, with kids and dogs darting between the adults. My mom was in heaven, snapping photos with her six boys and all four of her grandkids.

My brothers had all grown. They had overcome.

It gave me hope that maybe Tess and I could too. Maybe we could find a place for ourselves, a fulfilling life.

With a stack of serving platters in hand, I shuffled into the kitchen, where my mom stood in front of a sink full of soapy water.

I gently hip checked her. "I'll do it."

She shook her head. "Just getting ahead before it's time for cake. It turned out nicely, didn't it?"

I put my arm around her and pulled her close. "It's amazing. Thank you."

Snagging a dry towel, she wiped her hands and beamed up at me. This close, I got a sense of how small and delicate she was. She'd amassed many wrinkles in the time I was gone, and her hair was now silver. The contrast between this woman and the woman who'd raised me—the larger-than-life force, raising five, sometimes six, boys and working and volunteering—was stark, but the kindness she'd always possessed was there too, shining through.

I'd kept my distance for so long, but suddenly, I couldn't remember why. Right now, being so close to her, was healing parts of me I didn't know had been hurt.

My dad had been an asshole extraordinaire, cheating on her with his secretary. Not only that, but impregnating the woman when Jude and I were barely more than toddlers. Unsurprisingly, he had the nerve to then leave her to raise five boys mostly on her own.

She never complained, and she never spoke ill of him. The woman was a saint who eventually welcomed Cole, my half brother and the product of my dad's affair, into our lives as if he were one of her own.

Heart heavy, I bowed my head. "I'm sorry."

"For what?" Washing dishes once more, she handed me a

serving platter and looked pointedly at the towel on the counter.

Obediently, I picked up the towel and took the platter from her. "For going so far away and not staying in touch. For making you worry. For not realizing how grateful I should have been for all you've done for me."

She sniffled. "You're going to make me cry."

"I mean it. You are spectacular. I'm sorry it took me thirty-four years to realize it."

A rush of emotion was threatening to overtake me. I had been so damn selfish. For years, I'd mostly ignored her calls. I'd never once flown home for the holidays, always insisting I was too busy. I'd been a shitty son. And yet she was here, loving me anyway.

"Oh, Noah. I love you so much. You always were the one who needed to fly free. You had to chase your adventures and find your way." She patted my chest. "And look at you now. Back home and the most devoted father."

I continued to dry as she washed. "I'm barely getting by. I have no idea what I'm doing."

"No parent does, hun." The corner of her mouth curled up. "That's the secret. We're all making it up as we go along. No one's got all the answers. Now go back to the party. I'll finish up here. It's almost time for cake."

Chapter 24
Victoria

Noah and I, trash bags in hand, picked up paper plates and cups, doing our best to put Debbie's house back together.

She'd long since disappeared with Tess. Probably to rock her to sleep. She seemed to have a fully stocked grandma pad here and reveled in time with her granddaughter.

"You don't have to stay and clean up," he said, tying his already full bag.

I scoffed. "It's the least I can do after the epic party your mom threw."

He grasped my forearm, and a flush of awareness shot through me. "I mean it. You've done so much."

I turned to face him fully, eyes locked with his, silently willing him to understand that I needed this. I needed to tidy up and take out the trash and wash the platters and vacuum. Because I was processing.

My brain was in overdrive and swamped with affection for my fake boyfriend and love for his daughter. Then there were the creeping feelings of loss and sadness that loomed in the periphery of all the positive emotions. The voice in my head was loud today, reminding me of my inability to get pregnant. Of the birthday parties I'd never get to plan.

With a deep inhale, I pulled my shoulders back resolutely. "Noah, I need this right now."

Nodding, he backed away. Without a word, we worked for several more minutes. By the furrow of his brow, it seemed like he needed some quiet time too.

After breaking down the folding tables and chairs, stowing them in the garage, cleaning the guest bathroom, and dealing with the leftovers, Noah retrieved a sleeping Tess from the nursery upstairs and we headed home.

His energy was off. He'd been so happy all afternoon, but some unnamed concern was eating at him.

I was feeling similarly, I guessed, though I had no trouble labeling the weight pulling me down.

Inside our apartment building, I headed straight for my door. "Good night."

With a low murmur, he shuffled to the stairs leading to his place.

I stood there in the hall watching him go, thinking he might ask me to come up. When he disappeared without another word, I let myself in. With the door shut behind me, I sank to the floor and dropped my head back. I wanted to be upstairs, eating microwave popcorn and watching *Schitt's Creek* while Noah paced and did pushups. I wanted to rock Tess and watch her sleepy eyes slowly close.

But I didn't belong up there. I belonged here, in my home. Alone.

Slipping into comfy jammies and applying a Korean face mask did nothing to tame the restlessness inside me. I thought about calling Alice, but it was late, and she'd taken her kids to Massachusetts to visit her sisters.

So I paced. With every pass I made, I stopped in front of the window and looked out at downtown Lovewell. I rearranged the books on my shelves by color and fluffed the throw pillows. I was about to give up and go to bed when Tess's cry interrupted the quiet night.

My heart lurched.

I could hear Noah's footsteps and his muffled attempt to soothe her. Rather than settle like she always did in his arms, she screamed even louder.

Before I could think better of it, I had my slippers on and my phone in my hand and was halfway up the stairs.

When he opened the door, holding a crying Tess, his eyes were red, as if he'd been crying too, and his shoulders were slumped.

My chest pinched tightly. "You okay?"

Nodding, he pulled the door open all the way. He walked with Tess, gently rubbing her back, but she wasn't having it. His movements weren't as fluid as normal, and he looked as though he was far away.

Stepping into the living room, I waited for him to turn to pace back in my direction. "Noah, what's going on?"

"Nothing." His voice was low and shaky, his head down and his focus fixed on Tess.

"Bullshit." I put my hands on my hips, my breaths coming a little too quickly. "If I did something..."

He stopped a couple of feet away and raked his hand through his hair. It was a habit, a gesture he did multiple times a day, but it felt especially telling at this moment.

"No. You were perfect. You are perfect." He sniffed and

wiped at his face with the back of his wrist. "It's me. On days like this, the grief is overwhelming."

"Let me put her down." I stepped in close and held my arms out to take the fussing baby. "Today was a lot. So many people and so much happiness. Give yourself a minute."

Wordlessly, he let me take her.

Once she and I were in her room, I flipped on the small lamp on the dresser and laid her on the changing table. After a clean diaper and a fresh set of pajamas, I cuddled her and sank into the rocking chair.

While we rocked, I sang "Let it Go"—her favorite Disney song—off key. After several repeats of the chorus, which was about all I knew, her little eyelids became heavy and she drifted off.

I eased her into her crib, holding my breath and hoping she'd stay asleep. Then I switched on the fan and the white noise machine.

For a moment, all I could do was watch her sleep. One year old. I'd known this sweet baby for less than two months, but I was astounded at how much she'd grown and developed. Every single day was an adventure. I was so grateful to be along for the ride.

Carefully. I tiptoed out and closed the door behind me. In the hall, I breathed deeply again. Since that night she was sick, Tess had been mostly okay with sleeping in her crib. I was grateful that she'd settled in enough here to feel safe, but I missed the nights where Noah and I would take turns pacing. The nights I'd go to bed with the smell of him on my pillow.

In the living room, Noah sat on the couch, his head hanging.

Axe Backwards

I sat next to him and gathered his hands in mine. "Talk to me," I pleaded. "Please let me in."

He turned to me, his teary eyes holding mine. For a moment, he didn't speak. Rather than pushing, I sat and waited. The best thing I could do for him was be here.

Finally, he cleared his throat. "I would give her anything. I would do anything. I love her so much." He was so overcome he could barely get the words out.

I squeezed his hands harder. "I know you do."

"But the one thing she needs, the one thing she deserves, I can't give her. I can't bring them back. Jack and Emily. She deserves her parents. They should be the ones planning birthday parties and cutting her strawberries the right way."

"They chose you," I said softly, emotion clogging in my throat. "They looked at that perfect baby and knew you'd take care of her. And you are doing an incredible job."

With a sigh, he sat back.

He stared into the distance for a long time. Then, finally, he shook his head. "It's my fault," he whispered. "It should have been me. Tess should have her parents."

I didn't know much about how Jack and Emily had died. I assumed Noah would tell me when he was ready. Though I did know there was a fire.

"Fire is unpredictable. You told me that. You fought it and were injured yourself. It is *not* your fault. It's no one's fault. You can't carry that guilt."

As he met my eye, a tear crested his lashes.

"It was."

I wrapped my arms around him and squeezed him hard. He was a large man, but I did my best to shelter him, and I prayed that it would be enough to anchor him as the grief took over.

He cried quietly into my neck, his tears dampening my shirt.

"For so long, I just kept moving. Always running. Always chasing the next rush, never worrying about the consequences. I'd push and push so I didn't have to think." He sniffled. "And now? Now I'm stuck with the quiet. With my thoughts. With the guilt that keeps pulling me down. They should be here. They should be celebrating her birthday."

I stroked his hair and kissed his forehead, murmuring words of truth. I told him he was a good man, a great man, and a wonderful father. That it was okay to feel the way he did.

Day after day, minute after minute, he gave everything he had to his child. It broke my heart to know he was carrying the weight of this crushing guilt and grief. I wanted to take it away, to make it better. To give him joy.

But all I could do was be here to weather the storm alongside him. So as I held him, I cried too. For Tess, whose life began with tragedy, and Noah, who was plagued by a culpability that wasn't his to bear. And I cried for myself. We were all broken people. We got up every day and worked to fill in the cracks, but no matter how much we toiled, they got deeper.

I'd never cried with a man before. I typically saved my tears for when I was alone, but there was no way I could control the tidal wave of emotions crashing over me.

After a while, he pulled back and snagged the box of tissues off the end table. As I took one from him, I couldn't help but be grateful I'd taken my makeup off already. Otherwise, I'd look like a rabid raccoon.

He put his arm around me and squeezed. "Thank you."

"Anytime."

His thick swallow was audible. "I'm embarrassed."

I pushed him away, wiping my runny nose in a very unladylike way. "Why? Because you expressed emotion?"

He shrugged, his lips pressed into a line.

"Please, that is the opposite of embarrassing. You're expressing your feelings and processing your trauma. You're working to be better for your child. Fuck, if we put you on a billboard, every woman on planet earth would line up to date you."

He froze, his gaze darkening. "I don't need a billboard. I already have a girlfriend."

Slowly, he used his thumb to wipe an errant tear from my cheek.

Electricity sparked under my skin, and an awareness took over.

Suddenly, I realized how intertwined we were. His arms were still looped around me, and I was almost on his lap. Our faces were only inches apart.

And I felt more alive than I ever had.

I should have defused the situation. Put some distance.

Instead, I leaned into him, letting myself enjoy his warmth and his strength.

"I know it's fake. I know you're not interested. You don't feel..." He swallowed thickly, the column of his throat far too close. There was no avoiding the sexy way his Adam's apple bobbed as he trailed off.

It wasn't true. Not entirely.

Though I denied it, though I refused to let myself admit to feeling anything for him, the pull was strong, and it was harder to ignore every day. The desire to see him and hear him and smell him was all-encompassing sometimes.

I craved the warmth and comfort that came with sitting on this very couch with him and Tess.

I'd lain in my bed, smelling the pillow he'd slept on only minutes before, thinking about what his scruff would feel like against my skin. How those strong, calloused hands would hold me.

And his lips. I couldn't stop staring at them.

"I feel it." I held my breath, anxious for his response.

His eyes widened in surprise, and his body tensed, but he didn't let go.

I expected him to respond with a quip, to make light of the situation. To brush it off. If he didn't, what happened next could change everything.

He didn't speak. Instead, he cupped my face and kissed me.

Hard. Insistent and hungry.

It wasn't like any kiss I'd ever experienced. There was no tentative testing of the waters.

No, Noah dove right in.

I threw my arms around his neck, and in one fluid movement, he pulled me into his lap and held me so close our chests were pressed together.

He deepened the kiss, taking all I had to offer.

In the space of two heartbeats, my body went into overdrive. My pulse pounded in my ears and all the way down to my toes. The feel of his lips on mine sent tingles coursing through me.

Axe Backwards

When he slid his hands down my back, cupping my ass in my sleep shorts and pressing me against his body so I could feel him, hard and needy, my vision went spotty.

This.

This is what I had been missing.

The desperation and the pure want.

Squeezing my ass, he pulled me impossibly closer.

Moaning, I nipped at his lips. God. I needed more friction. More contact. More of him. All of him.

I was more achy, more desperate than I'd ever been before. Than I ever knew was possible.

"Fuck, Vic." He pulled back, panting and wide-eyed, tangling one hand in my hair. "Did I hurt you? Are you okay? I lost control."

If this was him out of control, I wanted it all the time.

"No." I shifted, rubbing my center against his erection again to show him just how unhurt I was. "I like you wild."

"Oh, sweetheart, you have no idea how wild you make me. But we should stop before things get out of hand."

I arched my back and dropped kiss after kiss along his jawline, reveling in the feel of him under me, his hands on me. "I want this."

He tensed beneath me, and when he spoke, his tone was soft, uncertain. "Me?"

"Yes, hotshot. I want you. All of you."

Between one breath and the next, he was standing, and I was in his arms. As he effortless carried me to his bedroom, he buried his face in my neck.

"Then I'm taking you to bed," he said, his tone low and husky. "Sadly, it's a twin, but I'll make it work."

Chapter 25
Noah

Shedding our clothes was a bit of a challenge. The room was so tiny that I banged my funny bone trying to get my T-shirt off.
I barely felt it.
Because Vic wanted me.
She'd said it. *With words.*
For weeks, I'd been convinced that it was one-sided, that the attraction would never be reciprocated. She'd told me outright she wasn't interested. I didn't understand how her feelings had changed so quickly. But knowing she felt the chemistry between us too made my heart feel like it was exploding in my chest.
Vic. In my bed.
Yes, it was a shitty twin in a closet-size bedroom in a sad little apartment, but none of that mattered when she looked up at me through those dark lashes, her eyes filled with lust.
This would no doubt produce some challenges, but I was more than up for it. The first challenge, getting her naked, wasn't hard, despite the confined space, since she was

wearing pajamas. I traced my fingers under the collar of her soft, loose-fitting shirt. She giggled as I ghosted over her collarbones.

I wanted to touch every inch of her, and then lick every inch of her.

My brain buzzed. Strategy, plan, focus. Where to start? What to do?

She pulled me down on top of her, kissing me deeply and making my mission clear. I'd make this woman mine. I'd claim her and savor her and worship her.

I'd make tonight count because I wasn't sure I'd get another shot.

She mapped out the muscles of my back and my triceps, her hands eventually finding her way into my hair. When she tugged, a bolt of lightning hit the base of my spine. Fuck. Having her pinned beneath me was better than any fantasy.

I took my time, kissing her neck, touching every part of her I could, reminding myself that this was real. My dream girl was in my bed.

She gave as good as she got, nipping and biting, trailing her hands down my chest to grip my throbbing cock.

"Slow down," I said. "I'm barely holding on and want to take my time."

"Slow is overrated." She bucked her hips against mine. "I want to feel you inside me."

Hands splayed on the mattress, I straightened my arms and peered down at her.

She hit me with that gorgeous smile, undoing all my carefully laid plans with one bite of her lip.

The smart thing would be to talk first, to decide what this meant. But there was very little blood flowing to my brain, and currently, I was happy to agree to do anything she wanted.

Propping myself up with one arm, I fiddled with a button on her pajama top. "You want this?"

"Yes." She whimpered, bucking her hips up against me.

"Then," I said, popping the button, then worked on the next. "I need to see you."

"You want...?" Her voice quivered with need and maybe a little fear.

I pushed one side of her shirt away, then the other, licking my lips at the sight of her perfect breasts. "Yes, Vic. I want you on top. You're going to ride me, and you're going to feel every inch as I sink into you."

I got off the bed so we could change positions. Fuck, I would kill for a king-size mattress right now.

"Are you sure?" Her eyes were wide and her cheeks were flushed.

I hauled her up, then sat on the bed and peeled off her pajama shorts, kissing her hip bones and trailing my fingertips along the outsides of her thighs.

She hovered above me, her hands in my hair again, naked and glowing in the dim light.

"Do you have any idea how much time I've spent fantasizing about your body? You're incredible."

Yanking her closer, I kissed her belly button.

"Vic, please. You have no idea how badly I need to see you on my cock."

Eyes flashing, she hit me with a seductive smile and pulled the elastic from her hair and shook it out, letting it fall wildly down her back. "When you ask so nicely," she purred, "how can I refuse? Condom?"

With a yank, I forced the drawer of the old bedside table open. I sheathed myself, then lay back and watched as she climbed up my body, kissing and teasing me along the way. Heart pounding, I reveled in the way her breasts hung heavily between us. Her lips were perfection. Everything about her was better than I ever could have imagined.

Once she was straddling me, her hips lined up with mine, she teased me, rubbing the tip of my cock over her slick entrance.

"You're torturing me." I lifted my chin and pinched my eyes shut with a huff, staving off the need to thrust up into her.

She twitched one shoulder, a tiny shrug. "You said you wanted to see me take every inch of you, hotshot." She stuck her tongue out at me. "And damn, there are a lot of inches here to work with. I'll take my time."

It was the most perfect misery, the teasing sensation of her wet heat. I thought I might pass out from the anticipation.

Finally, she lowered her hips and sank down slowly. I grabbed handfuls of her glorious ass, guiding her lower. She wasn't done taunting me, though. She'd lower a fraction, give me an inch more, then take it away.

It was a slow, torturous tease.

And fuck, was it sexy.

Heart pounding, I heaved in a breath. "That's a good girl. Take what you want."

"What if I want all of you?"

"Then take it," I growled.

With her hands anchored on my chest, she dropped

down and bottomed out. The blissful violence of the sensation made my eyes roll into the back of my head.

"Hotshot," she cried out, her head tossed back. "I'm. So. Full."

A fire ignited inside me, licking up my spine. "Yes, gorgeous. Move."

She ground against me in response.

Fuck. I had to squeeze my eyes shut and force my body not to react so acutely. If I didn't gain control now, I'd embarrass myself. It was as if I'd reverted back to the teenage boy I had once been, giddy with lust and affection for this incredible woman.

She was a goddess, riding my cock with abandon and giving me the most incredible view of her tits.

With my attention fixed on her gorgeous, flushed face, I slid my thumb down to where our bodies were joined and found her clit.

Her eyes widened and her core tightened around me.

"You like that, don't you?"

Chest heaving and with her lip caught between her teeth, she nodded.

"Tell me," I commanded, running slow circles around it.

"I love it." She breathed heavily. "Everything feels so intense."

"Play with your tits." I wished I'd spent more time worshipping them alone, but this would have to do until next time. Everything had been so rushed, but I'd been waiting so long for this moment; there was no way I could be methodical about exploring her body.

Without hesitation, she cupped them, rolling her nipples between her fingers.

The blaze inside me flared, engulfing me in an inferno of need for this woman. "You have no idea what you do to me. Fuck. You drive me crazy in all the best ways."

Back arched, she whimpered. Her pussy pulsed around me, signaling she was close.

I narrowed my focus. Bringing her to orgasm was my sole mission. I needed to watch her come more than I needed my next breath.

With my thumb still on her clit, I arched up and met her thrusts. "That's a good girl. You're almost there, aren't you?"

She nodded, her movements jerky, her body clenching in rhythmic waves.

Crying out, she came apart around me. But she didn't slow. No, she rode me harder, her hands on my shoulders as she shook and shuddered.

It was too much. I couldn't hold out any longer, so I followed her into the abyss. As I let go, I wrapped my arms around her and pulled her close, wondering how the hell I'd ever recover from this night.

Chapter 26
Victoria

"There's nothing better than summer in Maine." Alice closed her eyes and took a deep breath of mountain air.

Becca and I murmured in agreement. The three of us were sitting on the fieldstone patio behind Alice's house, enjoying a much-needed moment of peace.

I loved these long summer days, when the sunlight lingered and all my burdens felt a little bit lighter. I'd been working nonstop, unloading trucks, making deliveries, and meeting with Cole Hebert to finalize the layout for vendors for the lumberjack competition.

He'd connected me with a company out of Portland that would build a competition platform and bleacher-style seats for spectators at a discount. The event was growing in a way that terrified me. The cost of setup and logistics was already far too high for my comfort. We already had over sixty competitors signed up, and the children's events were proving to be extremely popular. All I could do was hope that we could pull this off.

When Alice texted, suggesting an impromptu girls' night, I jumped at the chance. I was still sorting out all my thoughts and feelings about Noah and the incredible sex we'd had the other night. Every time I stopped moving, I could feel his hands on my body, the way he tasted and the way he groaned when he saw me naked for the first time. I'd spent so long denying my desire for him, and once I opened the floodgates, it knocked me right on my ass.

I needed to sort this out, be rational.

"How are things at work?"

I deflated. "Still hustling to bring in more donations," I admitted. "And frustrated that I can't do more."

They both nodded thoughtfully. They knew how far we had to stretch to get folks what they needed. Both Alice and Becca volunteered frequently and even brought their kids along.

It was personal to Alice. Her children had been clients of the food pantry back when they were in foster care. Kids like Tucker and Goldie were the reason I knew I had to do better. But I didn't know what else I could do. Most days it truly felt as if I'd tapped every possible resource.

"I could always sell photos of my feet," I mused.

Becca spit out a mouthful of rosé. "Sorry?"

"I have nice feet." I slipped off my sandals and wiggled my toes at her, teasingly defensive. My nail polish was chipped, but otherwise they were fine.

Alice laughed, but Becca inspected my feet carefully.

"They seem ... nice." She trailed off.

"Not fetish-worthy?" Straightening, I crossed my arms.

"Sorry to disappoint you, but I'm not familiar with what constitutes fetish-worthy feet."

Axe Backwards

"Can we circle back for a moment?" Alice asked. "Are you okay financially? What's going on? Why have we jumped right to foot fetish photos?"

I shrugged. "Graham kept our condo and bought me out, and I do get a bit of alimony, so I'm getting by. I can't imagine ever stepping away from the food pantry, but I need to supplement my income and come up with a long-term financial strategy."

"You could pay yourself a salary. People who work for nonprofits don't work for free. You know that, right?"

I winced. Every time I considered it, I'd take a look at our financials and be reminded of why I couldn't. "I'd be taking money away from operations, and we need every penny right now." I couldn't imagine standing face to face with someone in need and not have food for them. How could I speak to a mom with a baby on her hip and tell her we were out of diapers or formula? I couldn't. That was why I was purchasing some of those necessities. To supplement our donations.

"You can't work yourself to the bone and then not even pay yourself a wage."

"I know. I know. It won't be forever. I'm still trying to get things running smoothly and stabilize the finances. I'd love to take on other work and earn an income, but there's not a lot of need for corporate PR up here."

"Nonsense. First of all, we're living in a global world. You can do remote work."

Becca held her glass up. "And you have tons of useful skills."

I gave her a dubious look.

"You write one hell of a grant proposal." Alice was a

former English teacher turned school principal, so naturally, I had her proofread all my grant applications.

I tipped my invisible cap. "Thank you."

"And you're great at organizing fundraisers and events," Becca said. "Like the lumberjack competition. You threw it together on a whim last summer, and now it's a major town event."

"Ooh. The wood chopping?" Alice kissed her fingertips. "Perfection."

Becca cackled. "You're only saying that because your husband was one of the hunks up there swinging an axe."

"Girl, he chops wood for me all the time. The competition was strictly a bonus." She smirked. "You've got talent and inspiring ideas, and you're incredible at motivating people. Don't sell yourself short. Get through the lumberjack competition, and then we'll brainstorm. I promise there are opportunities out there."

Henri and the kids stepped out, along with their two dogs, Rochester and Heathcliff, ready for an evening walk. Goldie hugged Becca, then me, while Tucker gave us a wave.

They were gone as quickly as they came, Henri hoisting Goldie onto his broad lumberjack shoulders and Tucker beside him, his too-big feet and too-long legs making him lope.

"Is there anything hotter than a good dad?" Alice tipped her sunglasses down to check out her husband.

A laugh escaped me. "Silly question. There is nothing hotter than a great dad."

Becca raised her wineglass again. "Agreed. And you?" She pointed a finger at me. "Since we're talking about hot dads. Noah Hebert walked by the salon yesterday, backward hat, arms covered in tats, wearing this damn cute baby." She fanned her face. "I almost fainted."

There was no stopping the wide grin spreading across my face. Yes. It was a lethal combination. I had a front-row seat to the baby snuggles and all the sweet murmuring he did while he loved on her. He gave her everything he had twenty-four hours a day. It might have been the most irresistible thing I'd ever encountered.

"I'm so happy for you," Alice gushed.

My cheeks heated. Every time I thought about Noah, it happened. The rest of my body warmed too. The feelings, the flashbacks. I couldn't keep my brain from reliving every glorious, naked moment with him.

Becca set her empty glass on the end table next to her seat. "Graham can go fuck off. Thank God you didn't have a baby with him."

It still stung, thinking about it. My inability to get pregnant, even though I rationally knew it wasn't the right path. "I always wanted to be a mother, but I guess I spent too much time focused on the goal of getting pregnant and not nearly enough on whether Graham would be a good father."

"He'd be a dogshit father," Becca quipped.

"Don't say that," Alice hissed. "Alex is pregnant."

I shook my head, still unable to wrap my mind around it. "I sincerely hope my new niece or nephew has the most beautiful life. But I know now that having a baby with him would have been a huge mistake, no matter how much I wanted to be a mom."

Alice put her head on my shoulder. "You'll get there, sweetie."

I nodded. Once I put my shitty marriage in the rearview

mirror, I began working on making peace with my fertility struggles. But the sadness, the feeling that my body was broken, still crept up on me from time to time.

"She's right. You can have a family in one of a million different ways. Look at us," Becca said. "We're not poster children for the typical *get a degree, get a job, get married, buy a house, have 2.5 kids and a dog, and go to Disney every year* path."

Alice raised her glass. "Truth. We all took different routes to get here, and that's okay. The journey is the fun part. The part where you grow and become who you were meant to be."

My eyes welled, making my vision go blurry. God, my friends were the most incredible people. "I love you both so much."

"Yeah, yeah," Becca grumbled, her eyes going a little misty. "We're amazing and supportive, I know." She pulled her shoulders back and arched one pierced brow. "Now let's get to the good stuff. Did he fix your broken vag?"

"Becca!" Alice huffed, her cheeks flushing. "It wasn't broken. Just hibernating."

My lungs seized, and I could only imagine the color of my cheeks was closer to purple than the adorable pink of my blond friend's.

"Not anymore." Becca barked out a laugh. "Look at how red her face is."

"I take it all back. You two are the worst." My stupid cheeks had been giving me away since I was a kid.

"No more hibernation. Someone is awake!" Alice kicked her feet and squealed. "I'm so happy you're getting some."

Becca tapped her chin. "We've been telling you for

months to get back on the horse, and let me just say, that is one fine thoroughbred."

"*Stop.*" These ridiculous women were delighting in my embarrassment.

"He defends you to your shitty family." Alice held up one finger, then another. "He's got a cute baby whom he's adores."

"And," Becca interrupted, "he's hot and looks at you like you're a delicious snack."

"He's an amazing friend." The smile was back. It was impossible not to feel like I was floating when I thought about Noah.

"That's the dream. A guy you can have a conversation with."

"Don't overthink this. Enjoy it."

Ha. As if that were remotely possible. I was the queen of overthinking. And right now I was bogged down by an array of complex feelings. Noah started out as a friend, a great friend. Then he was my fake boyfriend, the kind soul who helped my pathetic ass with my terrible family. Then he was just more.

I still couldn't pinpoint the moment it happened. It wasn't the night we finally gave in and slept together. It had happened before then, a small shift that gave way to a massive change. The physical stuff was confirmation of what had been growing between us.

He'd claimed me. And I'd claimed him right back.

Oh God. My face was heating again.

"Look at her," Becca said. "She's having a sex flashback. I'm calling it right now—wedding in a year."

I frowned and my stomach sank a little. "You know I

hate the institution of marriage. I'm having a lot of fun. But this isn't serious. He's got a lot on his plate and a lot of plans to work out. And since my divorce, I'm far too broken to be a good partner to anyone."

Both my friends leveled me with glares.

"Broken?"

"Da fuck?"

Becca shook her head. "No. Alice, please tell her how fucking wrong she is before I slap her."

Alice pinched the bridge of her nose and closed her eyes. When she opened them again, they were sharp. "You are not broken. Sure, maybe you have a few dents. We all do, but you're stronger for it. And I'm telling you right now, we won't let you self-sabotage."

As much as I wanted to argue with her, I couldn't help but feel a rush of affection.

"This is all part of the magic," she explained. "Helping to repair the cracks in one another. Healing is a hell of a lot more fun with a supportive partner by your side."

"You're rocking his baby in the middle of the night," Becca added. "Think about how special that is. The kind of bond you have. It's the kind that transcends friendship."

"There is no rush," Alice said. "Go slow, enjoy yourself, but don't write this off or sabotage it because of all the shit Graham put you through."

"Guys." As much as I wanted to give in and gush with them, dread had seeped into me and was slowly rising like a flood. "I can't do it again. I can't take the risk and live with the fallout."

"You already have," Alice said gently. "You're falling in

love with him. Rather than fight it, accept the risk and do it anyway."

Shit. Was she right? Was I falling in love with Noah? My heart ached at the idea.

"I'm scared." My words were barely a whisper. I was already in so deep. Noah and Tess had carved out a place for themselves in my heart. Losing them would hurt so much more than Graham's betrayal.

Tears pricked at my eyes, and before the first could escape, I was crushed by hugs.

"You'll find a way." Alice held me tight. "It's gonna look different from what you expected, but isn't that the whole point?"

Becca stroked my hair. "Life is full of surprises. Good things are coming."

I closed my eyes and let the tears fall. Maybe my friends were right. Maybe I was capable of more than I gave myself credit for.

Chapter 27
Noah

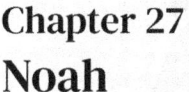

I was in trouble. Huge trouble. So I went to the one person I could trust with this information. The one person I could trust to give me the hard truth.

Jude answered the door, Ripley at his heels, and sighed. "Here for confession?" Before I could respond, he took Tess from me and hugged her close. "Hello, beautiful," he said in a singsongy voice. "What did your daddy do now?"

With a grunt, I stepped inside. Ripley sat at my feet, tongue out and panting, so I crouched and gave her some love. By the time I stood, Jude and Tess had already disappeared.

"I brought scones and coffee," I said, holding up the tray from the Caffeinated Moose.

He ignored me. He'd put on a record and was dancing around the living room to Prince with my daughter. That was so Jude, using music to avoid having a conversation.

My avoidance mechanisms tended more toward bungee jumping or backcountry treks, but I understood the urge to steer clear of uncomfortable feelings.

Daphne Elliot

I sipped my coffee, admiring how organized every aspect of Jude's house was. Eventually, Tess wiggled her way out of his arms and scooted into the kitchen, then pulled the pots and pans out of his cabinets and banged them together, which freed Jude up to listen to me.

"What's with the grin?" Eyes narrowed, he took a tentative bite of a maple walnut scone.

I tried to rein in the look, but there was no helping it. "Something happened."

He tilted his head back and looked up to the heavens as if asking for strength. "Let me guess. Now you're in love with her, but you're not sure if she loves you back. If you want to ensure that she'll fall in love with you, I'll tell you what I told Cole: chop some wood."

A scoff escaped me. "No. You misunderstand."

With one brow raised, he took another bite of his scone.

"I'm not in love with her."

He coughed, sending crumbs flying.

"Gross." I took a step back. "Fine, maybe a little." There was no use lying. "But right now, I'm spinning. We were friends, good friends, and now we're..."

"More?"

I nodded. "It's not fake anymore."

"Does it feel real for her too?"

"I'm not sure. We didn't exactly talk things through the other night, and she's been working on the lumberjack competition."

Jude smacked his forehead. "It must be genetic. Why not have a conversation? It would clear up a lot of questions."

"I will. But I'm all mixed up. I don't know what to say or

how to say it." I gave him a pleading look. Jude didn't talk much, but when he did, he said the right things. He was smart and thoughtful, and I was... not those things. I was impulsive. A jump first, ask questions later type.

My brain was a mess. I was a snow globe in a paint shaker. Every smile, every kiss, every night spent wrapped around each other. Visions and memories swirled around in my mind, clouding my thoughts and judgment and leaving me in a lovesick haze.

"I'm used to the chaos in my head, but this is so much more severe than the everyday scatter," I admitted. "I'm consumed by her. I want to be with her all the time."

He nodded, lips in a straight line, letting me talk it out.

"And when I'm with her? I'm a better version of myself."

That made his mouth tip a fraction.

My heart stumbled. "You're not surprised?"

"Not in the least. I called this a month ago."

"Yes..." My pulse pounded in my ears. "But..."

"But what? You like the girl, she likes you. Lock it down. Also, I'm your only single brother. I should not be your first stop for love advice. Call Finn or Gus. Even Cole. Willa is smitten with him; there must be some magic involved."

I snagged a scone. "Nah. You're my twin. The yin to my yang. The others wouldn't understand. Not many people play fake boyfriends for their platonic neighbor friend."

Jude shook his head, apparently finding this sentiment amusing. "These wild scenarios are more common than you think." He pulled a wooden spoon from the utensil holder on the counter and handed it to Tess so she could make even more noise. Once she was banging away happily, the sound so loud I couldn't help but wince, he rested his forearms on the kitchen island and angled forward. "So talk to me. What's holding you back?"

I looked at my little girl. She was on cloud nine, causing chaos.

"Where do I even start?" Defeat wormed its way back through me. "I've got no career and no permanent home. I'm a single dad with no idea what I'm doing. I've never had a successful serious relationship." I tore off a piece of my scone with my teeth. "Should I keep going?"

Jude sipped his coffee and pushed his glasses up his nose. "If you want this, then not one of those things is enough to stop you. They're all manageable. I'm not saying it's easy to overcome obstacles, but come on, man. You just came back. You've got time."

It didn't feel that way. Tess had already turned one and I'd yet to even catch my breath since taking custody of her. I lived every day making sure her needs were met, and when I was done, I had nothing left to give to anything or anyone else.

As if she could sense I was thinking about her, Tess crawled over to me. When she used the cabinet knobs to pull herself up to stand, the look of pride on her face made my heart clench.

"Dada," she shrieked.

I picked her up and peppered her face with kisses. "Good job."

"She's walking?"

I shook my head. "Not yet. She's standing and starting to cruise a bit, but we've still got time, thank God."

Once we'd picked up the pots and pans, we took Ripley

out for a walk so we could enjoy the warm sunshine. Tess's jogging stroller was set up for roads rather than the trails behind Jude's house, but she was delighted by the bumpy off-roading experience. For the first thirty minutes, she squealed and shrieked and incessantly signed for "more." The excitement soon caught up with her, and she conked out, her head slumped to one side and her mouth open.

"You want a job at the company? I can make it happen." Although our family timber company had been sold, Jude still worked there and had recently been promoted to director of operations. In a strange twist of fate, Chloe had purchased the business and kept on Jude and Gus and the rest of the employees. It was flourishing, and Jude always talked proudly of his crew.

I shook my head. "I know nothing about timber, and I have no heavy machinery certifications. I'm hoping to find something that feels like me."

As we continued along the path, I found myself more at ease. It took a while, but I finally got Jude chatting about what was going on with him.

"It's the most dreaded time of the year."

"You barely have to work in the summer. How is that dreadful?"

"We don't cut in the summer, but that doesn't mean there aren't a hundred other things that have to be done." He grunted. "And now that I'm the director of operations, I have to deal with the Department of Fish and Wildlife."

I frowned at him, confused.

"The bats." He let out a beleaguered sigh. "The bats determine whether we'll have a good year or not."

Fuck. I was still lost.

Reading my mind, he went on. "The northern long-eared bat. They're critically endangered and essential to the ecosystem. And their primary habitat encompasses a big chunk of our land. Every year, the DFW sends out their consultant to chart bat colonies, determine which caves and tree systems they're nesting in, and designate the areas where we're not allowed to work."

"You can't work at all?"

Jude shook his head. "We can't even drive in the area. I get it. Bats are important. They eat their body weight in mosquitos every day."

That was impressive. Given the massive number of mosquitos in Maine, I could see the necessity of preserving them.

"But they're a wildcard. We can't make solid plans until we know where they're nesting. So it's a mad scramble once we do, working on which routes and roads we can use and how to be most efficient and productive with what we've got.

"Between the bats and the FBI and Parker's investigation, I can see the appeal of taking off. Gus got a job out west last year. He was ready to start over before Chloe came back. And now I'm thinking that might be my next step."

"Where?"

"Oregon."

I'd spent a lot of time there. Beautiful mountains, rivers, and many, many trees. Jude would be happy. It was basically Maine on the Pacific Ocean.

I nodded. No one understood the allure of picking up and getting out of Dodge like I did.

"But I'm stuck here, at least until we make some decent progress on the investigation."

Axe Backwards

He dove into explaining a series of seemingly unconnected incidents. A fire in the machine shop, small thefts and break-ins over the course of a year, vandalism, missing financial records, and a brutal attack.

"What happened to Cole, that's not related, is it?" My mind was spinning and sick with guilt. My family had been dealing with far more than most would be equipped to handle, and all the while, I'd been thousands of miles away, completely oblivious.

Cole being framed was deeply messed up, but how did that connect to timber and narcotics and my father's criminal enterprise?

"Absolutely connected. FBI is still investigating." He whistled for Ripley, who'd gotten a little too far ahead. "He was sniffing around city hall, making connections between the Huxleys and some shady corporations. He found the chief out at a construction site in a blizzard with Denis Huxley and noticed he was wearing one of Dad's watches, and boom, he ended up being a target."

"Denis Huxley?" my stomach clenched.

Vic was working with them. She'd complained several times about how difficult they were and how they made her jump through hoops.

"Yeah, and his dad. They're rich and well-connected. They know how to cover their tracks, but they're definitely tied up in all kinds of shit. We haven't connected all the dots yet. Parker is an incredible investigator. She's worked her ass off, but the feds aren't all that motivated to figure shit out."

I snorted. "Of course, they're not. That guy was the governor."

Daphne Elliot

"Lieutenant governor," Jude corrected. He snapped, and Ripley immediately kept pace beside him. "But yes."

"I gotta talk to Vic. The Huxleys have been stringing her along, promising donations, then being evasive. They've also asked for all kinds of information about the food pantry."

Jude pulled up short. Ripley did the same, mirroring his motions. It was eerie.

"She needs to talk to Parker." His tone was serious, his blue eyes dark. "We may not have all the pieces yet, but all signs point to some shady shit."

Nausea swept through me. Vic, who wanted to feed the entire world, whose heart was so big it could barely fit in her chest, could be mixed up with potential criminals?

"They're not dangerous," Jude said, sensing my concern the way only a twin can. "At least as far as we know. Parker has been digging for months, but we all still have a lot of questions."

I nodded. I may only have a basic understanding of the drug trafficking Dad was involved with, but it was clear this went way beyond his crimes. He was in prison now, but there were others out there carrying on in his absence.

Another wave of guilt hit me. "I had no idea. I'm so sorry. I've been—"

Jude clapped my shoulder. "You had your own stuff going on. And it's okay. We've lived in Dad's shadow for so long. We've all had to find our way out of it, and we each took a different path."

I nodded, but I still felt like shit. My family had been going through hell, and I was living for myself and no one else.

"You're here now," he said. "And you brought the best

Axe Backwards

gift with you." He looked down at a sleeping Tess, who now had her arm wrapped around that stupid Olaf toy. "We're gonna be okay."

I nodded.

"But keep Vic away from the Huxleys."

Chapter 28
Victoria

"I don't want to get anyone in trouble. I swear I was just trying to get donations." I scanned the official-looking conference room, feeling like I'd been brought into the principal's office.

Parker Gagnon stood at the head of the table. She was a study of contradictions. She was athletic, with her brown hair pulled into a perky ponytail, yet the energy that radiated from her was all business. There was no hiding her background in law enforcement. It was her posture, her stance, and the pen behind her ear. She was not someone to be fucked with.

I smoothed my own hair over my ears.

"You're not in trouble." Expression softening, she surveyed the people in the room.

Noah sat next to me. His brother Gus was here too, along with his girlfriend Chloe, who now owned the timber company. I didn't know them well, but they'd been nice enough.

"We've been digging for the better part of a year. We've

collected all kinds of pieces—random strings and theories and tidbits of information," she explained. "The connections are tenuous, but most of them lead back to Charles Huxley and his corporate holdings."

She focused on me again, brows raised in anticipation.

So I dove in. I told them everything I knew, hoping I could help them push the investigation to the finish line so the Hebert family could finally rest. And after months of back and forth, I had plenty to share.

"I approached them the same way I approach any potential corporate partner. Opportunities to donate, to set up recurring giving, that sort of thing. Most people are interested in the tax breaks alone." I uncapped the bottle of water Gus had set in front of me and took a small sip. "They made it seem like they were on board, which would be a game changer for the food pantry."

My stomach twisted at the memory of how eager and excited I'd been. How naïve.

"I usually provide a prospectus with a financial overview, but they wanted more. They requested information and records that should have no effect on their ability to donate or use those donations as write-offs. Then Denis wanted to inspect the premises. I allowed it, since he's in the construction business." I shrugged. He'd taken photos and asked a million questions. "We made some significant structural upgrades last year. Owen helped us out."

"Did they propose anything to you?" Parker asked. "Give you anything?"

"Yes." That meeting had been disastrous. "Denis gave me a proposal. It mostly involved work on the building. Endless construction projects with massive price tags." I shuddered at the thought of shutting the whole operation down so the building and the garage could be rewired.

"Construction projects? And there were prices?"

"Price ranges, yes." I closed my eyes, trying to visualize the proposal I hadn't looked at in weeks. "And a schedule that lined up with the donations they'd make."

"So they weren't offering the work as a donation? Or pro bono?"

I shook my head. "It was strange. He was condescending and offensive, so I got out of there as quickly as I could. Sorry," I said, already feeling stupid. "I should have asked more questions."

Noah squeezed my hand. "Don't apologize."

I swallowed, the lump in my throat making the task difficult. "The numbers and proposals were off. The whole thing was weird. I've been in the nonprofit world for less than two years and still have a lot to learn, but it seemed unorthodox."

Parker nodded, still taking notes. "Yeah. From what I've seen during my investigation, I wouldn't be surprised if they were attempting to use the food pantry to launder money."

Heart dropping, I gasped. "Money laundering? Does that actually happen in real life?"

Gus and Chloe nodded, clearly not all that shocked.

My mind spun.

"Thank you," Parker said, bringing me back to the moment. "This insight is incredibly helpful."

"Doesn't this seem far-fetched?" I couldn't keep the defensiveness out of my tone. I didn't like the Huxleys either. They flaunted their wealth and rubbed me the wrong way. But Charles Huxley didn't exactly seem like a crime kingpin.

"We have some insight into their activities and corporate filings," Parker explained. "It's not as far-fetched as you think."

Bile rose in my throat. Had I been courting donations from criminals? Surely I wasn't that stupid.

"Should Victoria worry that any of this could come back to her?" Chloe asked. The woman was authoritative and businesslike and scared me shitless. But I had the feeling that she was the kind of person I'd really want in my corner.

Parker shook her head. "No. She's done nothing wrong."

Thank God. I was just trying to buy diapers and eggs for my clients.

God, I was such an idiot.

"Are you okay?" Noah whispered, reaching out to squeeze my hand.

"I feel so stupid. I was so obsessed with getting a big donation that I handed over vital information that probably helped them without question. No wonder they picked me as a mark. I'm a dumbass."

"You are not," Noah said, his tone gruff.

"You've done nothing wrong," Parker said again, her tone kinder this time. "And if our theories are correct, a lot of other people have trusted them too. You're not alone."

That did nothing to make me feel like less of an idiot. I still couldn't trust my own judgment. God, I'd worked so hard to make things better, yet I'd inadvertently made them worse.

"Should I speak to the police?" I asked, my heart thumping against my breastbone. "The FBI?"

"We're still piecing things together. So far, the feds haven't shown much interest in this lead."

"Why?" Noah asked, his hand on my knee, imbuing me with his comforting warmth.

"Officially, we only have anecdotal evidence. Records that tell only part of the story."

"And unofficially?" Noah asked.

Parker sighed. "You know how this world works. This guy is a politician. He knows everyone. He appointed half the judges in the state. He's friends with powerful people and donates strategically.

"Anything we come up with has got to be rock solid. We have no eyewitnesses or whistleblowers and only one side of some complex business records."

The bile threatening to make an appearance churned in my stomach.

Story of my fucking life. Yet another shitty man has taken advantage of my excitement and passion to further his own agenda. More manipulation.

I was a tool to be used. Nothing more.

The shame was palpable. Maybe my mother had been right. Graham too.

I wasn't good enough.

I was reactive and excitable. Not cool and calculated.

I trusted too easily and allowed myself to be led astray.

With my head in my hands, I willed myself not to cry. I could do that when I was alone in my car.

"You've done nothing wrong." This was the third time she'd assured me of that. "And you could be the person to help us."

I sucked in a breath and looked up. "What do you need? I'll do anything." I had to fix this. God, I'd been so stupid.

"You don't have to." Noah put his hand on mine and

straightened in his chair, his focus fixed on Parker. "You can't put her in danger."

"We have no reason to believe they're dangerous," she said. "And Vic could be a huge help. Can you play along? Keep taking meetings and learn what you can? Keep them spinning their wheels while I investigate?"

I nodded. Easily. "Denis is all ego. It probably won't take much encouragement to get him to reveal things."

"Yes. Go through the proposal. Ask a million questions. Take notes."

"I can play dumb."

She nodded and gave me a grateful smile. This woman was whip-smart, but something told me she'd had to play dumb to get ahead a few times herself.

"If you see or hear anything suspicious, call me. Ask him about the construction proposals. Make him walk you through them, line by line."

The dread receded, and a little spark of excitement ignited. I smirked. "I'll ask him to mansplain construction to me."

Parker grinned. "We won't ask you to do anything that makes you uncomfortable."

I barked out a laugh. "Trust me. I have plenty of experience as a people pleaser seeking approval. I can make it work."

"You should come over to our place for dinner soon," Chloe said, leaning forward with a smile. "I'll beat all those pleasing instincts right out of you."

I had no doubt she would. She was pocket-sized, but I did not want to get on her bad side.

"You don't have to do anything." Noah regarded me, his lips turned down and his eyes swimming with concern.

"It's fine. All I have to do is attend more boring meetings and talk about roofing materials and electrical wiring. It's hardly international espionage."

That didn't lighten his mood. His only response was a long exhale.

"I'm fine. You know me. I like to be useful." They may not have hard evidence yet, but if the Huxleys were really responsible for hurting this town and putting people in danger? Then I was all in.

No one hurt Lovewell. This place was my home.

And if I could help Noah's family and take the obnoxious Denis Huxley down a peg or two in the process, how could I resist?

Chapter 29
Victoria

Even as I gave Henri a big thumbs-up, my head was spinning. This had to be a dream. The weirdest dream ever. I pinched myself again, certain I'd wake up this time. Wrong. While I stood in the wide driveway, still trying to find my bearings, Henri was unloading his truck. Pallets of wood, wire fencing, and roofing materials. It was a big ask, but I didn't have a choice.

The humane society had called me two days ago. They had seized them from a hoarding situation, and the girls were in need of an immediate placement. They were healthy, vaccinated, and laying eggs. I couldn't say no. I'd take all the free eggs I could get.

Noah was helping Tucker carry some of the larger pieces. He was wearing a very tight T-shirt that showed off every muscle. I had the strange urge to lick every one of them. The sight of him like this was borderline obscene.

In the space of a few days, I'd become a horny teenager all over again. After years of little sex that wasn't any good, then not even a sexual urge, I had become insatiable. I didn't want to scare him off by being a perv, but holy shit.

Noah, I'd discovered, was a sweet single dad in the streets and a domineering, bossy stallion in the sheets.

Stop it, Vic. Stop fantasizing about your fake boyfriend, real friend, maybe fling. Get focused. Be professional.

Alice sidled up beside me and looped her arms around me, interrupting my thoughts. "So. Forty chickens?"

"Thirty-eight." I grimaced. "And technically, they're hens."

She shook her head, but her smile was bright. "You're lucky I love you."

"I'm ruining your weekend. I'm so sorry."

"Not at all. We Gagnons love to help. I owe you about a million favors. Plus, I get to watch my husband build stuff." She elbowed me and lifted her chin, gesturing to where the men were stacking wood.

"Also, there may be a condition—"

"Miss Vic!" Goldie Gagnon ran at me at full speed, cutoff overalls swishing and wild blond curls bouncing. She was a hurricane in eight-year-old girl form.

"Mom said you need our help and we have to follow directions and work together." The words spilled out of her. "But." She put her hands on her hips. "I wanna name a chicken."

"Sure. Just one?" I assumed Goldie and Kali would claim naming rights to the entire flock.

"Mom said it would be rude to ask for more."

Alice adjusted her daughter's pigtails, tightening one, then the other. "Go help your dad."

With that, Goldie was off, running at full speed again.

Axe Backwards

Alice surveyed the mountain of supplies. "We're gonna do this." Her eyes sparkled.

Her eagerness didn't surprise me one bit. Not much got in Alice's way.

She was a transplant, so I'd never met her until I came back to town. We hit it off quickly, and she persisted, badgering me into girls' nights when I was drowning in work.

Her warmth and insistence on constantly bringing me food had done the trick.

Then she started volunteering at the food pantry.

And brought her kids.

And her husband.

Since Henri was part owner and the CEO of a timber company, he was a useful friend to have.

Hence all the free wood being used to build a mansion for my rescue chickens.

Noah approached, dusting his hands off on his jeans. He pulled me close and kissed my forehead. "Don't stress. We got this."

I was doing my best not to. But it was virtually impossible knowing that I had two days to build a coop with proper ventilation, laying boxes, perches, and a door I could access for egg collection and cleaning.

Not to mention a predator-proof fenced run with a roof.

"I should have said no."

"Nope." He squeezed my side. "You did the right thing."

"Henri made some modifications to the plans you found online. I'd be shocked if it's not a luxury chicken penthouse when he's done."

"It's a big ask..." I hedged.

My friends were giving up an entire weekend to help me.

"Ignore her," Noah said. "Her first instinct is always to people-please. But we still love her."

My stomach did a weird swoop in response to that word. *Love*. He hadn't meant it in a deep, heartfelt way, but I couldn't help but read more into it. Especially since we hadn't defined our current situation.

I shook off the thought and focused on the chickens. On what having them here could mean for the food pantry. I started to do the mental math.

"Guys," I said, bouncing on the balls of my feet. My mood had done a total one-eighty in a matter of seconds. "Each of these chickens will lay four to five eggs per week. That means I'm looking at adding more than one hundred and fifty to what I can give out every single week."

Noah beamed at me as I did my chicken math.

Henri waved Alice over, but before she went, she poked Noah in the chest. "We haven't had a chance to get to know each other, but I've got this one's back." She thumbed over at me. "She's incredible. Don't fuck it up."

As she walked away, Noah broke into a grin. "She's awesome."

I swatted at his chest. "Get back to work."

We spent the morning measuring, cutting, laying out the foundation, and planning.

Mid-morning, a giant truck rolled up, and Henri's sister and Finn's wife, Adele, hopped out.

"Someone order a backhoe?" she asked, her blond ponytail swishing.

Axe Backwards

"Just in time." Alice waved at a patch of grass. "We've taped off the area."

A backhoe? For what? With a frown, I looked between Henri and Alice.

"We've got to bury wire mesh," Henri explained. "So predators can't burrow in."

Burrow? Shit. I hadn't even considered that. God, I was already a terrible chicken owner.

"Henri did all the research when he built my coop." Alice beamed at him. "Though we only have six. Plus you know Adele. That girl has never met a piece of heavy machinery she didn't want to play with."

The woman herself strode over, wearing a bright smile. Goldie rushed toward her. Tucker followed, moving quicker than any thirteen-year-old boy typically would, but according to Alice, he was Adele's biggest fan. She often let him come into her shop and work on equipment with her.

Within minutes, she was in the cab and digging while Henri directed her and Goldie cheered.

"You've got quite a team," Noah said, surveying them.

I bit my lip, suddenly overcome with emotion. These people, my friends, were giving up their weekend to help me. That thought hit me hard. For so long, I had felt alone. I assumed it would always be that way. That I'd be on my own.

But at this moment, I knew that wasn't true. I just hadn't found my people until moving back to Maine.

And for better or worse, the citizens of Lovewell were my people.

Henri, Noah, and Tucker stretched the wire and anchored it, then Adele covered it with a layer of dirt and drove over it in a zig-zag pattern to pack it down. I marveled at their efficiency.

Then the whole lot of us held the posts as Henri nailed the frame together. It was hard to hold still. I'd been dreaming of chickens for so long, and with every minute that passed, my excitement grew, making it hard to contain.

I was in charge of measuring and double-checking the plans as we went. Alice was surprisingly good with a hammer, and the kids were great at finding the right pieces of wood.

Occasionally, Noah's T-shirt bunched around his shoulder muscles, showing off his bulging biceps and distracting me. I was only human, after all. He handled the huge beams easily, lining them up while joking good-naturedly with Henri.

Henri, who only ever smiled at his wife and kids, joked back. My heart panged as I watched the two men interact. Noah thought so little of himself. He always brushed off how special he was. I wished he could see how much value he added to the lives of the people around him.

In the afternoon, Jude arrived, hat pulled down over his eyes, with his toolbox and a circular saw in tow. He gave Noah a hug and shook Henri's hand warmly.

While the rest of us were pouring concrete for the fence posts and framing the roof, Jude took Henri's plans and whipped up six nesting boxes in rapid succession. The guy was a machine.

"You should call Gus," he said while carefully showing Tucker how to use his circular saw. "He's an electrician."

Noah pumped his fist. "I forgot about that. Good call. He could do lights, heating, cameras, whatever you want."

Axe Backwards

He yanked his phone out of his pocket and tapped at the screen.

"Yes," Tucker said. "You need cameras. Probably motion sensor lights too. They'll scare off the raccoons." He was a gangly teen with kind, dark eyes. He looked nothing like his mountain of a father, but they had the same posture and identical mannerisms. In Lovewell, he'd made a name for himself as the resident tech guru. He single-handedly kept the library computers operational and was constantly helping the town's seniors understand their phones.

"Yeah," Goldie said. "Raccoons are nasty buggers." Stepping closer to me, she tipped her head back and put her hands on her hips. "Have you thought about paint colors? Could we do glitter? The chickens need something jazzy."

I shook my head. This project was moving quickly, and it was growing in scope by the minute.

By evening, we were fully framed and the fence was up. Every person here was brimming with ideas, and Henri and Noah had been discussing where I should put a greenhouse. Apparently, it was time to think about growing my own vegetables.

My stomach was beginning to growl when Becca and Kali showed up with pizza.

"Brought dinner!" Becca said, her arms laden with several slim cardboard boxes. She let out a whistle. "Damn, you guys have been productive. I felt bad that I couldn't be here to help, but it looks like you didn't need me."

Alice dusted off the old picnic table and waved Becca over. "Where did you get pizza?"

Lovewell did not have pizza. It was one of life's great

tragedies. But we survived. Heartsborough had an okay pizza place that would do if one was really craving it.

"The pizzeria," Becca replied.

"It's not open yet." I opened the top box and took a big whiff of the greasy, cheesy deliciousness. "The windows are still covered with cardboard." Rumors had been swirling since the empty storefront had been leased earlier this year. A sign had been erected and a construction crew had been there working, but the guys were from out of town, and they'd all been tight-lipped about it. Even the town gossips were in the dark.

Becca smiled. "Marco is my neighbor. He's been firing up the oven and experimenting with recipes."

Alice turned, her eyes widening. "Marco?"

Becca ignored her look. "Yes. As you all know, his shop is next to my salon. I met him a few weeks ago, and he makes incredible pizza."

"You've tasted his pizza?"

"Yes. He brings his experiments over for Kali and me. He trained in Italy. This pizza is the real deal."

I eyed Alice, who was already giving me a knowing look. This conversation was not over, but the kids had descended, cheering for pizza and grabbing slices from the box, so it would have to wait.

Becca procured a stack of paper plates, and Henri ran up to the gas station for a couple of six-packs of beer and nonalcoholic drinks for the kids, who ran through the yard and shrieked with glee as the air cooled and evening set in.

As I surveyed the people who'd gathered to help, I was struck with wonderment. These were my friends, the people I cared about the most. And they'd shown up. Not for me, but for this community. So we could build something that would help our neighbors.

"To the chickens." Noah raised his beer. "May they lay a million eggs."

"I think I'll feature them on our Instagram and website. Make them the food pantry's mascots," I mused. "Try to work in some marketing and fundraising in addition to the million eggs."

"You could offer naming rights," Alice suggested

Becca perked up. "In exchange for donations."

That was brilliant. I could use what we raised to pay for feed and upkeep. We needed every single dollar we could scrape together right now.

We ran lean and relied on volunteers and the generosity of the state and federal governments. As Alice and Becca had pointed out, I was the director and I was allowed a salary. But after I maintained our facility, paid all the bills, and provided as much food as I could to those who needed it, I only had enough left over to pay for my own health insurance.

I couldn't keep this up forever, but day in and day out, I talked to people who needed help. Children, mothers, the elderly. It felt wrong to even consider paying myself.

So far, I was doing fine living off the money Graham had given me for the condo and my alimony. I hadn't asked for a lot, and thankfully, he hadn't really put up a fight. Mainly because he'd been fucking half of Boston.

Eventually, I'd need to figure out my finances, but tonight, I didn't want to taint this feeling by allowing anxiety to creep in.

No, tonight I'd relish in the love and support this community possessed.

I'd eat my pizza, joke with my friends, and enjoy Noah's comforting embrace. And the warm fuzzies I got every time he kissed the side of my head. Which, by my count, was seven times today.

"Can I take you home?" Noah asked once our friends all packed up and headed for their cars with promises to return to finish up tomorrow.

He pulled me to my feet and kept his hands locked with mine once I was steady. God, he was sexy. Even sweaty and dirty and wearing a ratty old ball cap. My legs felt like jelly as I looked up into his heated gaze.

"Yes, hotshot. Take me home."

Chapter 30
Noah

Side by side, we collapsed on the couch. Mom had brought Tess over to the food pantry today to see how the chicken coop had turned out. Then we'd gone out to celebrate the successful weekend build. We headed for celebratory burgers at the Moose with Alice and Becca and their kids.

My little girl was off her schedule and fussy, so it took several rounds to get her to sleep in her crib, but we did it.

I needed a shower and eight hours of sleep, but when I was in such close proximity to the exhausted, beautiful woman next to me, I wanted something else so much more.

"Thank you," Vic said, her voice raspy. "I'm amazed by how it all came together." She sat up, her dark eyes shining. "Truly. You worked so hard."

I let out a quiet laugh. "Of course. You've got me wrapped around your finger. You know that, don't you? I'm in too deep now. And that means I'll build you all the chicken coops you want."

Daphne Elliot

I leaned over, gently tickling her ribs. Which drove her crazy.

"Or a pigpen."

"Or a goat barn."

She writhed beneath me, and suddenly I felt a hell of a lot less exhausted.

"How do you feel about alpacas?"

She giggled as I pulled her into my lap.

"Or a greenhouse? Whatever you need, I'll be there."

I leaned down and kissed her softly.

"I really thought the Gagnons were gonna dunk on you Heberts," she teased, wearing a big grin.

"But I got Jude," I protested. He'd been quiet but frighteningly efficient.

She tilted her head and squinted at me, skeptical. "Jude's great, but Adele showed up with heavy machinery on a trailer. That was pretty badass."

Okay, fine. It really was. And she was my sister-in-law, so I supposed I had to tip my hat.

She took off my hat and ran her hands through my hair, lighting up every nerve ending in my body. "But then you brought Gus. Next-level."

She mimed her mind exploding.

I nodded, proud of my oldest brother. "He's talented."

"The man set up chicken surveillance cameras. And put an app on my phone." She shook her head. "I owe you."

"You do not. I told you, whatever you need, I'll be there to help. But." I pulled her hips back so she was lying on the couch and pinned her beneath me. "I wouldn't argue if you wanted to show me your appreciation."

She kissed me deeply, running her hands down my back

and squeezing my ass hard. "What did you have in mind, hotshot?"

I pressed my mouth to the column of her throat, enjoying the taste of her and the soft moan that escaped.

"Many, many things. Dirty things. Filthy things. A long list." I toyed with the hem of her shorts as I bit her earlobe gently.

"Then we better get to work. You know I love a to-do list. What's first?"

"First..." I pushed up onto my knees and drank her in. She was fucking gorgeous, spread out below me. "I'm going to eat your pussy until you're begging for my cock."

I inched her shorts down slowly, watching her face, relishing the way her eyes grew dark with lust.

"Then." I lifted her hips and pulled the fabric off. Shorts tossed onto the floor, I spread her knees wide. "I'm going to bend you over my couch and fuck you senseless."

I bent down, ghosting my lips over her pussy, teasing her as badly as I teased myself. Fuck, I was desperate to taste her.

"Yes please," she breathed, grasping at the couch cushion.

Obediently, I lowered my head farther, taking a gentle taste and making her squirm. Rather than dive right in, I adjusted her so she sat upright with her legs spread wide. Then I kneeled in front of her, paying respect to my queen, and feasted.

I licked and sucked ravenously, savoring her taste and the electricity that arced through me when she tugged on my hair.

Sex with Vic was hot as fuck. And it was fun. We

laughed and smiled the entire time. I was still getting to know her body, so every day felt like a glorious exploration.

"Noah," she hissed. "You can stop. I'm warmed up."

I scowled up at her. "No fucking way. You're going to come on my tongue before you come on my cock."

"But—"

I pushed her thighs wider, giving myself better access. I was going to make her regret even asking me to stop. Clearly, I had to teach her a valuable lesson: if she was in my bed, or my couch, in this instance, then she would come multiple times before I was through with her.

I eased my fingers inside her, enjoying her gasp, and got back to work.

Sure enough, moments later, she exploded on my tongue, riding my face and screaming my name. As she collapsed in a heap, her chest heaving, pride surged through me. We still hadn't defined what we were doing, but my heart was galloping at full speed. There was no way to stop it. I was gone for her.

She peered up at me, her eyes hooded. "You mentioned something about bending me over the couch. Is that today, or..."

"Smart-ass." I shot up and pulled her with me, then kissed her hard. "I was just giving you a moment to recover."

"I don't need a moment," she panted. "I need your cock." With that, she spun and bent over the arm of the couch, wiggling that perfect ass in the air.

The sight knocked the air from my lungs. My brain was screaming *mine*, and my cock surged.

On instinct, I spanked her.

With a gasp, she whipped her head around, eyes wide, peeking over her shoulder at me.

"Sorry," I said, flexing my hands in hopes that I could gain some control over my caveman instincts. "Is that okay?"

She licked her lips. "It's very okay."

With a grunt, I spanked her again. This time on the other cheek. My hand stung from where I'd made contact.

I gripped my dick through my pants, needing a little relief, as I watched her creamy skin turn pink. Out of my mind with need but not ready to end the torture, I spread her ass cheeks wide and ran my fingers up her seam, collecting her arousal.

God damn. "You're soaked. You really do want to get fucked, don't you?"

With a whimper, she nodded against the couch. "Please."

I couldn't deny her any longer. I tore the condom wrapper with my teeth and sheathed myself quickly. Gripping her hips hard, I surged into her, desperate to be as close as I could get.

"Noah," she cried as I bottomed out inside her. She arched her back, her neck elongating in a way that made me want to sink my teeth into it.

I was ravenous. Desperate for her. My movements erratic and wild. It took all my strength to cling to the few remaining threads of control I still had.

This woman had the ability to make me go full caveman without even trying. I couldn't help myself. Every moment with her was incredible. Not just the fucking, but sleeping beside her, talking about anything, sitting on the floor side by side and playing with my daughter. She was everything I'd ever wanted, wrapped up in the sexiest, sweetest package.

"Harder," she cried.

I trailed my fingers up her spine and wrapped her hair around my hand. When I gave it a little tug, her knees wobbled.

"Yes, Noah."

Oh God, I'd never get used to how good that sounded.

Draping myself over her, I brought my lips to her ear. "You like it when I'm rough?"

"*Yes*. Fuck yes. Be rough, hotshot. Take whatever you want."

As if I could control myself after that.

I straightened and tugged her hair again. "Rub your clit."

She gave me a saucy smile over her shoulder. "What if I say no?"

She really was trying to kill me.

Without letting go of her hair, I spanked her hard. "Then you get punished."

Chest heaving, she snaked her hand down and brushed against where we were joined. The sensation made my vision blur.

Fuck. "That's it. Rub that clit. I can feel you getting tighter." I thrust harder, the violence of the action making the couch move a few inches. I didn't give a shit. If we put a hole in the wall, I wouldn't care. Not when I felt this incredible.

We fucked like that. I slammed into her, pulling her hair and slapping her ass occasionally. She pushed her ass back into me, still rubbing her clit and making the most provocative noises.

Axe Backwards

I released my hold on her ponytail and trailed my fingers down her ass crack. When I came to that ring of muscle, I pressed my thumb against it to add to the pressure.

Instantly, she screamed in pleasure and bucked wildly. Teeth gritted, I focused on holding back my release and riding it out with her, giving her everything I had while she came apart beneath me. Every pulse of her orgasm was perfect torture. I felt like a fucking king as I finally allowed myself to follow her over the edge, my own orgasm ripping through me and leaving me spent and breathless.

Chapter 31
Victoria

I dug through the freezer, the move exposing my ass. Rather than tug at the hem of Noah's T-shirt, I peeked over my shoulder to see his reaction. It didn't disappoint. His pupils were huge and his expression hungry.

We'd worked up an appetite. The man was an absolute stallion, and when he touched me back there, I'd gone off like a rocket. This was still so new, and I was just getting used to the constant lust, but now my brain wondered. What other sexy tricks was he hiding up those tattooed sleeves? Because I wasn't sure my vagina would survive many more.

Noah had installed a window AC unit in Tess's room, but the rest of the apartment was not exactly cool, especially after our naked activities.

"Vanilla?" I pulled out the carton of ice cream with a frown.

"There's a container of the kind you like in there too. Chocolate chunk, peanut butter, cookie dough, pretzel everything," he said. "It's in the back."

Grinning, I pulled the Ben & Jerry's out. I liked my ice cream crammed with as much stuff as possible, thank you very much.

We stood in the dark, the moonlight shining through the bay window, eating ice cream and laughing. Revisiting our busy weekend and how sore my arms were from hauling so much plywood. I would head to Greenville tomorrow with the food pantry van to pick up our flock of hens.

We were joking about the logistics of transporting thirty-eight chickens when he suddenly went serious.

"You okay?" I gave him a gentle hip check.

He set his ice cream on the counter and stabbed the spoon into it, his expression troubled. "I need to say something."

"Okay." I braced myself, heart sinking. Was he asking me to leave? Had we gone too far tonight? Was he ready to end things?

"We're friends first, and friends are honest with one another, right?"

With a nod, I swallowed past the lump in my throat.

He dipped his chin resolutely and blew out a breath. "I've fallen for you a little more every day since I rescued you from the coffee shop bathroom. You've become my best friend. And I don't want to lose you."

I gasped.

"I'm tired of lying to myself. I care about you. So much. You've seen me at my worst, yet you keep showing up. And I trust you with my life. I trust you with my daughter's life."

My mind whirled. I cared about him too. So much it frightened me. The feelings I had for him were growing bigger and more unmanageable every day. He was Noah. My neighbor. The sweet goofball who did pushups during TV shows. Tess's doting dad, who owned seven baby carriers because he never wanted to put her down.

The risk was so great. I couldn't lose him. For two years, I'd worked to put myself back together, piece by tiny piece. I couldn't jump into a relationship. It would be reckless.

But our connection was strong. We were tethered. It was impossible to fight the pull to be with him all the time.

I cleared my throat. "What are you saying?"

"I'm saying I want to do this right. Date for real. See where it goes."

My throat tightened, making it hard to breathe. I should be elated. I was crazy about him. But the pressure was too much. What if I wasn't good enough? What if I screwed everything up?

I froze, and after an excruciating moment of silence, I forced myself to be honest with him. "I need more time."

His eyes went wide like he'd been slapped.

"That came out wrong," I scrambled to say. "I want to see where things go too, but I'm all fucked up. Between my divorce and work, I worry I can't be what you need."

Shoulders relaxing, he stepped in close. "You don't have to be anything other than Vic, the beautiful, smart, kind woman who lives downstairs and took pity on me when I couldn't get my baby to sleep." He gently kissed my forehead. "I have no idea what the future holds, or even if Tess and I will stay in Lovewell long term, but I want to be with you while I can."

I nodded, chest aching. I wanted so many things. But did

I deserve them? Did I deserve the man who was standing in front of me in nothing but a pair of boxer briefs, declaring his feelings for me?

"Will you dance with me?"

My heart stuttered. *Dance?* "Here?"

He nodded. "Our dance at your sister's wedding was tense and forced. I need to collect my thoughts. And the only time my mind is clear and focused is when you're in my arms."

He held out a hand.

How could I possibly resist? I nodded.

He pulled me into his chest with one hand and tapped at his phone screen with the other.

As the music began to play softly, I wrapped my arms around his neck.

"Wait," I said, pulling back so I could look at him. "Is this...?"

"'Love is Like a Butterfly'? Yup," he said. "Lou told me it was your favorite."

"It is. I have always loved Dolly. I wanted to dance to it at my wedding. Graham laughed and said it was a ridiculous choice."

"Then I'm honored to dance to it with you."

With a sigh, I put my head on his chest and swayed to the music, my body melding to his.

These lyrics sank deep into my bones. In all my vulnerable moments, as a teen, a lonely newlywed, and after the devastation of my divorce. But now, hope seeped in along with the ache Dolly's voice incited.

When it came to an end, he pulled the phone out of his back pocket and started it again.

"One more time. Once wasn't enough." He put his lips to my forehead and lingered there for a moment.

My heart melted. If only I could bottle up this feeling and save it forever. Even if I was still confused by my emotions, they were weighty and significant.

"Sometimes I don't know how to let myself have good things." I admitted, my head tucked against his chest. "Growing up, I was never good enough, and my family..." I trailed off.

"You deserve all the best things. I want to crush anyone who ever made you feel otherwise. But..." He tucked an errant strand of hair behind my ear. "Sometimes I think the person you need to convince is yourself."

That hit deep. And he wasn't wrong. He was pulling back the curtain on all my insecurities, but it was my job to heal them.

Noah didn't care that I always wore my hair pulled back. He didn't mind my big ears. He didn't care that I talked with my hands and sometimes got so excited I shouted.

He didn't mind that I snored when I slept on my back or that I had cellulite on my thighs.

With him, I felt totally accepted. It was a heady sensation. One that brought with it a sense of safety as well as terror.

Because Noah wasn't my friend anymore.

He wasn't just the sweet single dad.

He wasn't my fake boyfriend.

He was the man I was falling for. It was dangerous and ill advised, but it was inevitable.

We stayed like that, dancing through the song four times. In his arms, I was wrapped in a comfort I'd never found anywhere else. I'd never before been the kind of person who needed physical comfort and affection. But here we were, wrapped around one another, swaying along to my favorite song. Making a lifetime's worth of promises without a single word.

Chapter 32
Victoria

"I heard you like the maple latte." I plastered a smile to my face and held up a to-go cup from the Caffeinated Moose.

Denis took it from me. "Thank you, Victoria. You're so kind."

"I wanted to apologize," I said, my voice dripping with forced sincerity. This was the hardest part. "I was very..." I cleared my throat. "My emotions got the best of me at the diner. I shouldn't have been so rude. I know you're trying to help."

I'd needed to gargle with bleach when I got home to erase the taste of those words, but by the satisfied smile creeping up his face, it was worth it. He was buying it. Looked like it wouldn't be too difficult to convince him that I was dumb and desperate for money.

I'd asked for a meeting at their office. Then I'd dressed up and put on my game face. I was a woman on a mission. If he really was trying to rope me into some money laundering scheme, then I would make sure he was sorry. No one messed with the food pantry. It was too damn important to too many people. I'd do anything to defend it.

Sadly, a lot of people messed with me. I'd let it happen for far too long and had a lot of work to do to stop it. But this was bigger than me. This was our community, the neediest among us, the kids and the seniors and the single parents.

Standing in his office, I realized the old Victoria would barely recognize me anymore. I hadn't anticipated that my life would take this direction. Between my infertility struggles, Graham's cheating, and constant put-downs from not only him but my family, I had been so down on myself, so lost.

So I'd come back to Lovewell. At first, it was to help Aunt Lou. She'd been diagnosed with MS and was struggling. I took a week off, drove up here, and spent as much time as I could with her. We took walks, played chess, and talked.

While I was visiting, it all came back to me: How much I'd loved growing up here. How good the mountain air felt.

I felt more like myself. More like the person I wanted to be.

So I went back home, finalized the divorce, quit my soul-sucking corporate job, packed up the car, and moved to Maine.

Lovewell was not for everyone. Small-town life could be challenging. But I had a purpose, and that was enough for me. I dove into taking over the food pantry and I reconnected with nature. The town took me in and kept me busy. I met Alice and Becca, and everything clicked.

So I'd be damned if the Huxleys destroyed this place. It was bad enough that our region had been ravaged by the opioid epidemic. The promises of economic relief rarely became reality in rural communities like ours. We struggled and we fought for everything we had. And slowly, this town was rebuilding.

People had jumped in to help with the lumberjack competition, which was now a two-day event and had sponsors, vendors, and a police detail to manage traffic. This place stood up for itself.

So I was here, doing my damndest, to stand up for my town.

Denis settled at his desk again. Then he slipped a thin blue thumb drive out of his computer and put it in his breast pocket, giving it a single pat.

A thrill zipped through me. Keeping a thumb drive close like that? There was likely something worthy of interest there.

"Let's get to it. I am a very busy man, but I'm happy to explain it all to you."

Eye twitching, I pressed my lips together tightly and opened up the booklet he'd given me, as well as a notebook.

"I have so many questions," I gushed, a little over-the-top, I supposed. "Can you walk me through page three? The schedule?"

I let him explain every detail, biting my tongue as he criticized my financial management and ordering schedule and bemoaned the terrible state of my wiring. How he'd assessed the wires, I didn't know. Though I was vibrating with annoyance, I nodded along and took notes carefully, as if he was sharing hot stock tips.

I tapped my chin, doing my best impression of an

airhead. "Couldn't you send your construction guys over to do it for free? These proposed invoices are so confusing."

He gave me a condescending, pitying look. "I can see how you'd be confused. We run a complex business empire comprised of many subsidiaries. Our main outfit is here, but we've got our hands in lots of things. Phobos, which does construction and Alkaios, which does the real estate investment and development. And Kratos manages the properties and collects rents." He smirked, loving the feel of bragging about his family's business. "Then there are Deimos and Hyperion, which manage our less traditional businesses." He chuckled to himself. "But you don't need to worry about that."

Nodding, I wrote down each name. Parker would have a field day with these.

"For sophisticated business entities like ours, it's very normal to move money around, especially for tax purposes."

Internally, I scoffed, but externally, I gave him an encouraging smile.

"So when someone contracts with Huxley Construction, they're buying materials through Phobos and funneling payroll to Kratos." He laced his fingers on top of his desk. "It gets complicated, but it's necessary for tax purposes. Not that you would understand. And we really want to help you out."

Was he admitting to tax fraud? I didn't have a good grasp on what tax fraud really entailed, but this definitely sounded like it. Was this how the rich got richer? Moving money around to avoid taxes? *Motherfuckers.*

"How does the food pantry figure in?"

"Let me take this spreadsheet and make it into a graph."

He picked up his laptop, then rounded his desk and hovered beside me. He didn't sit. Instead he stood a little too close and set the laptop on the desk so I could see the screen. "It may be easier for you to understand this way."

He pulled the thumb drive out of his pocket and plugged it into the USB port. Why a thumb drive? Why couldn't he store his work in the cloud like a normal person? He was definitely hiding something.

When he double-clicked on the thumb drive tab, a window with hundreds of folders appeared. Each was labeled, but one jumped out at me.

Hebert.

Why would he have a Hebert file? What was in it? I kept my face neutral as he toggled around in front of me, not even bothering to be discreet, though I scanned the files and committed as many names to memory as I could. Lots of Greek names, the last names of several people in town, including Souza, our former police chief, Lambert, our current mayor. What were they doing?

"Here we go." He opened up an Excel spreadsheet and quickly converted it to a graph.

"These are your expenses. These are the proposed upgrades. Invoices, materials, labor."

Head tilted, I studied each piece of the graph he pointed out.

"Our donation schedule is here."

My heart lurched. The donation amounts had doubled. This would be more than enough to keep every person we serviced fed and every baby diapered. It was more money than I'd ever even considered asking for. And way more than his initial offer a few weeks back.

He turned to me and smiled. He was entirely too close for comfort. "See what I'm talking about? Everyone wins. We help you financially, you hire us to work on the property."

Holding my breath, I nodded. His body heat soaked into me, making my stomach roil.

"We see this as a long-term beneficial relationship." He licked his lips, his eyes dipping to my mouth. "And I'm prepared to be very generous."

For a moment, I considered screaming. But I kept my wits about me. I promised Parker that I would get all the information I could.

"I know all about the diaper bank designation." He smirked. "And your application to the Feeding America grant program."

I nodded, though the move was disjointed, jerky. How the hell did he know about all of this?

"And the others too. You've been busy, applying for every penny, every scrap."

"How do you know about the grants?" I asked, my voice weaker than I'd like. "And the diaper bank designation?"

His beady eyes narrowed further. "Do you know who my father is?"

I dipped my chin, my throat tightening.

"He's well-connected. He can make these grants happen or…" He trailed off. He didn't have to finish the sentence. The message was loud and clear. He could easily ensure I didn't receive any of the grants the food pantry so desperately needed.

All that hard work potentially down the drain. I wanted

to punch this smug little turd in the face. Instead, I forced myself to speak calmly. "I understand."

He took a step back and crossed his arms.

"Great. I had my secretary draw up the initial contract." He pulled out the thumb drive and once again deposited it in his pocket, then snapped the laptop shut. "I'll grab those, and you can sign. We've got a notary on staff so—"

I stood, hitting my knee on the desk in the process. "I-I'm sorry. Do you mind if I take them to review with Aunt Lou first? She still likes to be involved and is so excited about this partnership."

He frowned, assessing me dubiously.

"You've been so kind explaining it all to me," I said, mustering all the faux enthusiasm I could. I had to get the hell out of here. "I'm so excited."

With a nod, he picked up a tan folder and held it out to me. "We need to get started soon." He warned. "Come in next week, and we'll sign everything."

I snatched the folder, then picked up my purse and backed toward the door. I needed to get to Parker and info dump everything I'd observed.

"Sure thing. Thanks so much for all your help."

As I scurried down Main Street, recording voice memos on my phone so as not to forget any details, my confidence surged. Not only had I gone in there and pretended to eat my humble pie, but I'd seen some potentially damaging evidence.

I just hoped it would be enough.

Chapter 33
Noah

Thor threw a blueberry, then tossed his head back and laughed hysterically.

"I thought Merry was coming." I was hurt. I missed my niece.

Finn chuckled. "And get up this early? She's a teenager now. She doesn't function before noon on summer vacation. She did, however, wake up long enough to give me a to-go order."

He handed Thor a sippy cup, which he banged on the table before chugging.

"I don't know how Mom did it. Five boys." He shook his head. "I've only got two kids, and we're run ragged. This one is straight-up feral. We had to put him in a toddler bed because he kept hurtling himself out of his crib. Walked into our bedroom in the middle of the night. Scared Adele half to death."

I eyed Thor, who was now smearing blueberry into his hair. "He stays in it all night?"

My next oldest brother dropped his head, his shoulders

shaking. "God no. Escapes constantly. Most mornings, we find him passed out on his bedroom floor, surrounded by toys. We put a baby gate up in the doorway, but it's only a matter of time before he figures out how to scale it."

Bernice stopped by and topped off our coffee. Thank God. I hadn't had enough to run on all cylinders yet.

"I'm too sleep-deprived to be tactful, so I'm just gonna come out with it." Finn rubbed his temples. "Are you staying? What's your plan?"

I choked, and coffee dribbled down my chin. "Dude."

"We're getting attached to you two." He smiled at Tess. "You can stay. You can build a life here."

Over the past two months, we'd gotten comfortable here, but I was still treading water. I was still trying to figure out what the future would look like. What I'd do now that fighting wildfires was out of the question. My life had changed in almost every way.

But Lovewell was growing on me. Being near my family, watching Tess interact with her cousins and aunts and uncles and her doting grandma.

Not to mention Vic. Last night was a dream come true. It felt like an acknowledgment that we were doing something substantial. Special. Although she wasn't ready to commit to a serious relationship, I couldn't help but think it could become that. Once she had time to get used to it. And if I could get my shit together.

"I need a job." It was the easiest nonanswer I could come up with. "And the prospects here aren't great."

"I've got lots of ideas." He sat back and rubbed his hands together. "In fact, I've got a buddy in emergency response."

That piqued my interest a little. "What's that?"

Axe Backwards

"The Maine Emergency Management Agency. They handle natural disasters and nuclear emergencies. That kind of thing. Everyday stuff too. It's the government agency that keeps people safe."

With a sigh, I shook my head. "I'm probably not qualified."

He straightened in his seat and sipped his coffee, unfazed by my dismissal of the idea. "It's coordinating a response, setting strategies, and implementing them. That's your thing."

My stomach flipped over. Okay, he wasn't exactly wrong.

"Last time I checked, your resume is stocked with certifications and training. And"—he looked up and to one side with a stupid smirk on his face—"oh yeah, years of field experience."

Head tilted, I frowned at him. These days I wasn't qualified to coordinate much of anything. And keeping people safe? That was the most essential part of the job I'd left behind, and I'd failed at it. Miserably.

He put his elbows on the table and leaned in. "Can I give you a tip? As your older brother?"

I shrugged, weighed down by a sense of defeat.

"You gotta grow. You gotta evolve. You're a dad now, sure, and you're putting your kid first, like you should. But that doesn't mean you have to give up every part of yourself. You've got to set an example for Tess. Stretch, learn some new things."

As I unrolled the napkin from around my silverware, I considered his words. I needed to do something. And at the very least, this sounded interesting.

"They're looking for a regional director. Someone who can coordinate responses up here. Mountain search and rescue reports to them as well."

I couldn't help it. I sat up a little straighter.

Finn handed Thor another piece of bacon, and the little guy snagged it with ferocity. "I understand the need to be useful, to help and have a purpose. After I left the Navy, I spiraled hard."

That was only a small part of it. I'd been on my own since the day I graduated from high school. As a kid, it always felt as though my skin was a size too small. I never fit in here in Lovewell the way my brothers did.

School was a challenge. It was a struggle to remain a solid C student. I'd hoped to go to the technical school in Heartsborough after I graduated, but my father had forbidden it. He was obsessed with the idea of his sons attending a four-year college. Maybe because he didn't. Gus was the only one who wasn't expected to follow that path. He had attended the technical school so he could quickly be Dad's right-hand man at Hebert Timber.

But I knew I'd never make it. The thought of sitting in a classroom for hours every day for four more years made me itchy.

So I worked my ass off for Dad every summer and during the school year. Between the money I earned and the cash people had given me for graduation, I had enough to buy an old pickup. The week after school was out, I got in my truck and never looked back.

"Think back." Finn leaned over and picked up the sippy cup Thor had dropped. "Why did you want to be a hotshot in the first place?"

Axe Backwards

Excitement, danger. A bunch of stupid reasons, really. Before I responded, I took a minute to really remember that first summer on my own. I drove west and camped all over. Visited a bunch of national parks and spent time considering what I wanted out of my life.

"I wanted to be outside." My throat was tight with emotion. The memories that I'd stirred up were more powerful than I'd expected. "No, it wasn't a want. It was a need. I knew I couldn't work indoors."

He lowered his chin slowly. "I can see that."

I nodded. "Mountains, rivers, trees. Unforgiving terrain away from the hustle and bustle. It's what I needed. It's still what I need. I love sharing it with Tess. I want her to have the kind of childhood we had. Running in the woods, swimming in the lake, and being surrounded by community."

He raised an impressed brow. I was making his arguments for him at this point. "What else?"

I got to work cutting up Tess's pancakes, keeping the plate far enough away that she couldn't reach. "I want to be useful and help."

Growing up, all five of my brothers were impressive. Capable, ambitious, and smart. I was the wild one, the stupid one who got in trouble because I couldn't sit still. I kept that part to myself.

"I earned an associate's degree in fire science. Then got into the US Forest Service training program. That was a three-thousand-hour ordeal. I went to Idaho, Oregon, Wyoming. Fought all kinds of fires and helped with hundreds of rescues."

Those were wild days. We trained nonstop. The requirements were insane, like running up mountains wearing a weighted vest for hours, but I had a blast.

"I excelled at the chainsaw training."

"Course you did. You're a fourth-generation lumberjack."

"Because of that, I was sent to earn a certification in engineering firebreaks, and that led to more strategy."

"You loved it." It was a statement, not a question.

I took a bite of my eggs Benedict. Fuck, it was good. "I used to love it. But once I hit thirty, things changed. Fire season keeps getting longer. For months, we'd travel and train with our crew, then we'd be deployed all over the Northwest. We pushed hard. Every day felt significant. We were saving people and homes and national parks. Preserving and battling mother nature."

My brother hummed in acknowledgment. "She's quite a fucking opponent."

"But after what happened to Jack and Emily?" I looked down at my hands, guilt sweeping through me. "I lost my edge. I can't do it anymore. I can't be brave. I can't step up and save lives."

Finn inhaled deeply, then let the breath out in a slow, heavy whoosh. "Respectfully, there are a lot of ways to be brave. The way you've stepped up for this little cutie." He reached over and bopped Tess's nose, making her giggle. "And fighting Jack's shitty family for custody. Then moving across the country. That's brave."

Untrue. I did what I had to do for my friends. It was a vain attempt to make up for my mistakes.

"Hear me out," he said. "I hated this place. Coming back here after my Navy career ended felt like a personal failure.

But." He chomped on a piece of bacon. "It turned out to be a blessing. I was forced to confront my demons. And deal with my shit. It's made me a better father, a better person, in the process.

"I never thought I'd fit here. But Lovewell has a way of forcing you to confront and make peace with the things you've tried to avoid. I promise, if you give yourself a chance, give this town a chance, you'll be pleasantly surprised."

His words gave me pause. Finn loved this town. The guy was deliriously happy all the time, flying planes and building his business, spending his free time with Adele, Thor, and Merry. I had a hard time imagining him being miserable, especially here.

"It's true," he admitted, clearly reading my mind. "I was so set on being unhappy, on being stuck. It took a while, but eventually, I stopped punishing myself and got to work. You'll get there too. Give yourself permission to be happy. I know you miss Jack and Emily, but you do not have to suffer. You're not required to pay a penance for what happened. You and your baby girl can have a good life."

My nose stung and my eyes got hot. Fuck. If I wasn't careful, I'd break into tears right here. Finn had never been the serious, thoughtful one, but his words hit me deeply. Wasn't that what I was doing? Forcing myself to be stuck and sad all the time?

I opened my mouth to thank him, but before I could, the bell over the door jangled violently, snagging my attention.

When my gaze landed on the person who'd just stepped in, a wave of anger washed over me.

Graham. In our diner.

"Is that...?" Finn asked.

Daphne Elliot

I nodded. Or at least I thought I did. All my focus was fixed on the bozo at the door. He had on shorts that had pink palm trees all over them and a shiny aqua-colored polo shirt. Bright white shoes and socks pulled up to his shins completed the look.

He was probably headed out for a round of golf. There was no course in Lovewell, but there was a beautiful country club near the university about thirty minutes east of here.

There was no other excuse to be dressed the way he was.

I wasn't even sure golf was an excuse.

Every eye on the place was on him. For good reason. He would have looked less out of place in a tutu.

Tess reached over my carefully cut pieces and clutched an entire chocolate chip pancake, then smashed it against her wide-open mouth.

"She's got a Hebert appetite." Finn laughed.

I rolled my eyes. Thor was on his fourth slice of bacon. If he was anything like his dad and uncles, there probably wasn't enough food in the county to feed him.

Graham scanned the diner with his lip curled up on one side, as if he was afraid he'd catch some kind of infectious disease from the place. Thoughts like that were high treason in Lovewell. The diner was sacred.

Yes, it was the quintessential small-town diner, and yes, the menus were plastic the booths were vinyl and there was a beautiful pie case on the countertop featuring the daily specials, but Bernice and Louis kept the place in tip-top shape.

When Bernice appeared with a coffee carafe in hand, the smarmy fucker glared up at her over his menu. "I'll have the eggs Benedict."

Axe Backwards

Bernice took his menu with a grimace. Oh shit, she was not pleased. The guy was fucked. Everyone knew not to get on Bernice's bad side.

"Sorry, hun. That's not available today." Her tone was so friendly, only someone who'd grown up here would know how much trouble they were in.

He huffed, his brows pulled down. "Eggs Benedict." He spoke loudly, enunciating each syllable, as if she was hard of hearing.

"Not available," she replied slowly, mimicking his tone. "How about an omelet? We make great omelets."

"I don't want an omelet."

The omelets really were good, but Louis's eggs Benedict was next-level. Comparing the two was unfair. Finn and I exchanged a glance. This guy had no idea how thin the ice beneath him was.

"Have you run out?" he asked.

She shook her head and gave him a polite smile. "No. Benedict's not available."

"If you have the ingredients, go and make it. What kind of place is this?" He scoffed.

"Sir, this is Lovewell, Maine," she said, pulling her shoulders back. "And I know you'll love your omelet."

I almost laughed. Beside me, my brother's face was split in a grin.

Graham stood and surveyed the surrounding tables. He pointed to Father Renee, who was almost finished with his breakfast. "That guy has it."

Looking offended, Father Renee speared the last piece of his Benedict and shoved the massive chunk into his mouth, thus hiding the evidence.

"Is there a problem here?" Mayor Lambert, wearing his patented smile, approached the table.

"Who are you?" Graham hissed, looking around as every person in the diner blatantly stared.

"I'm the mayor, and I've been frequenting this fine establishment since before you were born, so how about you calm down and enjoy an omelet? The eggs are farm fresh and the coffee is excellent."

Looking chastened, Graham sat back down and took a sip of his coffee.

He grimaced, his cheeks puffing out, and when he swallowed, it looked painful. "Ugh. This coffee tastes like swamp water."

Finn leaned forward, his face lit up with glee. "Bernice gave him the out-of-towner coffee."

"Out-of-towner?" I didn't follow.

"The coffee here is good," he said. "Not excellent like Lambert promised, but good enough."

I nodded.

"But if someone shows up and rubs Bernice the wrong way—usually an out-of-towner, especially if they're some rich prick from Boston in golf clothes..." He peered over at Graham who was red-faced and holding his paper napkin like it was a live grenade. "She breaks out the gross stuff. I doubt the machine they use for it has been cleaned in a decade. It's really bad. Like prison quality. It's the perfect way to fuck with people she's not thrilled to be serving."

I chuckled, the sound rumbling deep in my chest. "That's savage."

"She's protective of Victoria. We all are. She's one of us.

Axe Backwards

She busts her ass every day to make the town better for everyone, despite all the shit she's been through."

Graham stuck his tongue out and wiped at it with a napkin as he yanked more from the chrome dispenser on the tabletop.

"Ready to order that omelet?" Bernice gave him her fakest smile.

"That's it." He tossed the pile of napkins onto the table. "You've lost my business."

"Oh no." Grinning, Bernice slipped her pencil behind her ear. "Now I'll lose my Michelin star."

Graham glared. "Looks like I'm headed to the fancy new coffee shop instead." With a grunt, he picked up his Louis Vuitton man bag and stomped to the door.

"Good luck." Bernice gave him a finger wave.

All around us, people were pulling phones out of pockets and purses, no doubt to warn Raeanna and her staff at the Caffeinated Moose that he was on his way in.

"Bernice," Finn hissed. The sound was all tease. "Are you colluding with the other small-business owners?"

She nodded, though she didn't look up from her device as she tapped one long nail on the screen. "He's lucky I let him walk in here after what he did to poor Victoria." She shook her head. "Shoulda put ex-lax in his coffee."

Finn shot up straight. "*Bernice.*"

She glared at him. "Finn Hebert, don't you dare sass me. I'll call your wife."

"Yes, ma'am." His shoulders fell, and without another word, he picked up his fork and went back to eating his breakfast. Like the rest of us, he wouldn't risk pissing off

Bernice. She knew everyone and everything in this town. Not to mention the eggs Benedict were that good.

"And you." She pointed at me. For a moment, her face softened. "You've got the cutest baby and the best girlfriend, but"—that stern look returned—"if you hurt her—"

I put my hands up. "I would never."

"Noah is a good egg," Finn said. "He knows he stumbled upon a winning lottery ticket when he moved into the apartment above Victoria Randolph. I swear on Marge that he wouldn't."

Damn, if my brother was swearing on his plane, he meant it. I wasn't sure I really deserved that kind of loyalty.

Her shoulders relaxed. "Okay, let me go get the good coffee. You need a refill."

Chapter 34
Victoria

The energy in the apartment had shifted overnight, and in turn, my anxiety spiked. I couldn't for the life of me figure out the cause. Was it something I'd done? Something I'd said?

I should have gone back down to my own apartment last night. Instead, we'd slept in his twin bed, intertwined. I'd wanted to be close to him, and at the time, he'd seemed just as eager. Now, though, he was distant.

Dammit. I was screwing this all up.

Leaning in to catch his eye, I pointed toward the door. "I should go. I have errands to run."

He looked up from where he was feeding Tess in her highchair, his face stricken. "Oh. Okay."

I turned, eager to put some space between myself and this strange tension. But halfway to the door, I thought better of it.

This wasn't who I was anymore. I wouldn't bury my head in the sand. The last thing I needed was to spend my day beating myself up over all the things I could have potentially done wrong. It was time to put on my big girl pants.

"Noah. It seems like something is bothering you." I did my best to keep my terror in check, but my voice quavered anyway. "I'd like to help if I can."

Holding my breath, I waited for him to kick me out. To yell at me. To criticize me for being needy.

Instead, he rose and shuffled over to where I was awkwardly lingering in the middle of the living area.

With a sigh, he pulled me into a hug. "This day," he said into my hair. "I'm struggling with it."

I hugged him back, silently praising myself for having the courage to ask.

"Today is the one-year anniversary. Of the fire."

I pulled back and examined his face. His cheeks were hollow and his skin was pale. He was completely wiped out. He hadn't divulged many details about Tess's parents' deaths, but I knew they were related to a big wildfire Noah had fought.

"I'm so sorry." I put my head on his chest, hoping to imbue some of my strength. "What can I do?"

"I need to get out of my head for a while."

Pulling back, I patted his chest. I knew exactly what he needed. "I've got an idea."

"WE'RE ALMOST THERE," I SAID AS I LED THE WAY TO one of my favorite places. The trail headed past the lake and up toward Baxter State Park. About two miles in, there was a turnoff where the Millinocket River cut through the woods.

Axe Backwards

Over time, the river had carved out a wide bank, leaving a pretty clearing dotted with giant rocks. I'd come here many times to watch the water flow and think. It was a great spot for a picnic.

When I came upon the small path off the trail, I signaled for him to follow. He was carrying Tess, who was in her hiking backpack with her floppy sun hat on, happily grabbing leaves off trees and throwing them in Noah's face. It was hilarious.

We carefully climbed down the bank, using exposed roots for balance as we navigated through the trees and rocks, until we finally came to my secret patch of paradise. Big, smooth rocks that had once been cleaved off the mountains dotted the edge of the river.

Noah smiled as he approached. "Look at that view."

I followed his line of sight and took a moment to admire the peaks in the distance. They looked majestic in the cloudless blue summer sky.

"We can hang here. I'll spread the picnic blanket, and I brought a few toys for Tess."

He nodded, hands on his hips, still cataloging the scenery. He'd regained some of his color, and a few miles of quiet hiking had helped him settle. But I could only imagine how crushing the guilt and grief must be for him.

I had pulled out the picnic blanket when a strange moaning sound echoed around the clearing. I turned and scanned the riverbank, cupping a hand over my eyes to block out the sun.

A small brown animal was wedged between two rocks, and every time a burst of water washed over it, its head went under.

My heart plummeted. "Is that a baby moose?"

Knees wobbling, I followed Noah down to the riverbank. Sure enough, a moose calf was struggling in the water. The river wasn't deep, and it did move quickly in some spots, but the calf looked like it might be stuck.

"Here. Take Tess." Noah unbuckled his hiking backpack and slowly lowered it.

Tess fussed, confused, when he didn't immediately take her out of it.

Speaking in a hushed voice, hoping I could keep her calm, I unlatched her and picked her up.

Noah rifled through the front compartment of the pack, tossing out water bottles, protein bars, and a first aid kit. Eventually, he found a thick knot of paracord, a ratchet, and a handful of carabiners.

He jogged to a large tree close to the riverbank and looped the thin rope around it. He locked it into place with the rachet, then looped the other end around his waist.

"Noah, you can't go in there. It's not safe."

He shook his head. "I'm trained in swift water rescue, and this water barely qualifies as swift. I'm not going to let it die."

The moose was maybe thirty feet from the riverbank, but the slippery rocks and current were dangerous. Yes, he was qualified. Yes, he was trained. But that didn't make me any less scared.

But then I looked at that poor animal, watched how hard it struggled to keep its head above the water, and I got it. Noah couldn't leave the creature there to suffer. At his core, he was a fixer, a helper.

"What can I do?"

Axe Backwards

"Hold Tess. Keep her away from the water. Climb up on the bank. This thing may kick or freak out when I pull it to shore."

With a nod, I held Tess closer and scurried up toward the trees.

When I turned around again, Noah was wading into the river. Though it was August, the water was frigid. The current was strong. Even from here, I could see his body fighting it. He walked carefully, slowly putting one foot in front of the other on the slippery rocks, fallen trees, and God knew what else.

"You're almost there," I yelled.

Nodding, he carefully approached the animal, coming up next to it to avoid spooking it.

It didn't have antlers, and it was clearly a baby, but moose were deadly, no matter the size.

A deep, loud braying sound ricocheted off the treetops.

Tess shrieked and pointed a tiny finger down the riverbank.

Heart in my throat, I clutched her tight and searched for the source of the noise. I swore my soul left me when I caught sight of the massive bull wading into the water, letting out pained wails.

Noah ignored the giant creature, remaining focused on keeping the calf's head above the surface.

Crouching until his head and back were the only parts of his body visible, he tried to pick it up, but the animal didn't budge. From far away, it looked tiny, but next to Noah, it looked like a mini horse.

Shit, how the hell was he going to get it out?

"Its leg is stuck," he hollered over his shoulder. Head

held high, he inhaled deeply, his chest expanding. Then, without warning, he ducked under the water.

My stomach lurched, and I squeezed Tess a little too tight. "Noah."

He came up quickly, took a breath, and then dove back under again.

By the time he surfaced again, I was shaking in terror. This time, he looped a second rope around the calf's neck. Once he'd situated it the way he wanted, he slid his arms under the moose's body and lifted.

The calf bucked and squirmed as Noah hugged it close to his chest and turned. The fear coursing through me lessened a fraction when he started back toward shore with the now free moose.

The water was up to his waist and every muscle in his arms and torso rippled and strained under the weight of the calf and against the current. If the situation weren't so dire, I might have taken a moment to appreciate the way his wet T-shirt clung to his sculpted frame.

The bull on the bank brayed, louder this time. The menacing tone made me worry that he'd charge.

"Noah," I yelled, pointing at it. "Careful."

At the sound of my voice, the creature turned slightly. The move gave me a better view of his body and the distinct puckered scar along his right flank.

It was Clive.

Oh shit. A normal bull moose was unpredictable and dangerous. But Clive? He was a menace.

He'd been known to crash weddings and destroy cakes. He'd broken up town parties and damaged sporting equipment. I wanted to scare him off, but I was holding Tess, and I wouldn't put her at risk.

As Noah climbed around rocks along the bank, I held my breath. He kept the moose, which had to have been over one hundred pounds already, close to his chest as he took one careful step after another.

I held Tess just as close when Noah stumbled onto the riverbank, and my shoulders slumped as he set the calf on the ground and dropped to his knees to catch his breath.

My pulse pounded in my ears. I wanted to rush to him, to help him, but I wouldn't go anywhere near either moose with this little girl in my arms.

He looked up, water dripping down his face and neck and arms, and gave me a big smile. "Stay there," he mouthed, holding up a hand.

Clive lumbered toward the calf, yet Noah didn't move.

He looked my way again. *I'm fine.* His lips formed the words, but he made no sound.

When Clive approached the calf where it lay on the ground, he nudged it gently with his muzzle. The much smaller creature tipped its head up, then clambered to its feet, stumbling and collapsing again.

I winced, scared that Noah would be trampled or worse if Clive got mad or felt threatened.

He remained perfectly still, his body language unthreatening, just kneeling on the rocky shore, waiting for the wildlife.

Clive nudged the baby again. This time, it pushed itself up on its front legs, and when it stood, it wobbled but didn't fall. It took several slow steps, then stopped.

Keep walking. Just keep going. Go back into the woods now.

It took a few more tentative steps, looking more and more steady with each one, heading toward the tree line. Clive followed behind, but before he could disappear into the forest, he stopped and turned. Looking at him head-on like this, I had no doubt his rack was the width of a car.

The beast froze like that, looking straight at Noah.

Oh shit, was he gonna charge?

Before terror could overtake me completely, Clive turned and lumbered into the forest.

Body shaking, I hugged Tess tight. She pulled at my hair and squirmed in my arms, her little feet banging against my hips.

Once they'd disappeared completely, I eased back down the large rocks to where Noah still sat, soaked and out of breath.

"You idiot." I looped my free arm around him and squeezed. "You could have gotten yourself killed."

He gave me a cocky smile. "You were worried about me."

Rearing back, I punched him in the arm. "Of course I was worried about you, hotshot."

I had a quick dry towel in my pack, and the spare T-shirt I had on hand was comically small on him, but he wore it and his boxer briefs while he put his own shirt and cargo shorts on a rock positioned in the perfect spot to get the best of the sun's rays to dry.

We sat on the riverbank, willing our hearts to settle and the adrenaline rush to abate, eating snacks while Tess threw rocks into the river and made piles of small sticks I'd gathered for her to play with.

Axe Backwards

"You scared me."

"I'm sorry. But I saw the moose, and my training kicked it. My brain was clear and focused, and a plan formed so perfectly." He sighed and took a long drink from his water bottle. "I'm not..." His throat worked and his shoulders slumped as he turned away, looking over at Tess. "I'm not in a good place today."

I squeezed his hand. "You can be sorry you scared me," I said, kissing his knuckles. "But don't be sorry for being a hero. Don't be sorry for being so good at what you do. You literally save lives."

Head lowered, he gave it a shake. "I'm not good at it."

"You are." I peeked over at Tess, who was sitting with her sticks, poking at the ground. "You may have lost your confidence, but if today showed you anything, it's that you still have a lot of gifts to share with the world."

He glanced over his shoulder to check on his little girl, then angled in and kissed me softly.

I tangled my fingers in his damp hair and kissed him back. The connection was exactly what I needed after so much adrenaline.

"Thank you," he whispered against my lips. "For bringing me out here. For getting me out of my head for a bit."

There was nothing I wouldn't do for him or his sweet little girl. Until this moment, I hadn't been ready to admit that to myself, let alone say it out loud. But after what I'd witnessed, it felt crucial that I tell him the truth, no matter how terrifying it was.

I opened my mouth, but before I could get the words out, Tess stood all on her own.

Daphne Elliot

"*Oh my God,*" I whispered, my heart soaring.

Noah whipped his head around, his body going rigid.

"Is she—"

"Walking?" he finished.

We were both frozen, terrified to move, lest we startle her or discourage her.

Tess was still standing, swaying a little and looking at the ground as if contemplating her next move.

Between one blink and the next, she did it. She took a small, shaky step.

When she wobbled, Noah jumped up, arms out and ready to catch her. As if sensing that Dad was going to end her fun, she took another two steps in quick succession before plopping onto her butt.

Beaming, she peeked up at Noah. "Da. Da."

He scooped her up and spun her around, covering her little face with kisses.

"You walked, baby girl. You walked."

Holding her to his chest, he looked at me, his expression filled with pride.

My heart clenched. There was no denying it. I was wildly in love with this man.

Chapter 35
Noah

Once Tess had had a bath and dinner, I put her to bed, more than ready for a shower and some time to process.

When I'd discovered that moose calf and realized it was in danger, a switch had flipped in my brain. I was overcome by a sense of total clarity. Every step I needed to take came to me. So I did it.

I had not bargained on the giant bull confronting me on the riverbed, but he seemed... grateful?

It was as if the deadly thousand-pound animal had stared into my soul. And though I was still reeling, I thought it might have changed me forever.

It must be his calf. Though that didn't make sense. Moose calves stayed with their mothers. But Clive—according to Vic, he was well-known—had been braying and crying as if he was concerned for the little creature.

While I'd given Tess a bath, Vic had called in a favor. The pizzeria still hadn't opened, but after Becca showed up with pizza the night we built the chicken coop, Vic had befriended Marco, the owner. She'd gushed over the pizza and marveled at the beautiful oven in his new storefront, and voilà, we had become recipients of his "test" batches.

When I left California, I had no idea what was in store for me. In my wildest dreams, I could never have imagined a woman like Vic coming into my life and turning it upside down.

"You were incredible today, hotshot," she said, wiping tomato sauce from the corner of her lip.

I wanted to brush off the compliment, but I knew she wouldn't let me get away with that. So I nodded and left it at that.

"I'm here for you. I hope you know that. If you need to talk, I'll listen. I want to help." Her dark eyes were brimming with concern and affection.

It hurt to see the genuine emotion so close to the surface like that. I'd relived that day a year ago over and over in my mind. The last thing I wanted to do was talk about it.

What I did want, more than anything in this moment, was to be close to Vic. I wanted to share my life with her. She deserved to know who I was, deep down. And she should know what had happened to Tess's parents.

How could I expect her to feel about me the way I felt about her if I wasn't completely honest? If I didn't give her the full history?

It wasn't possible. So I swallowed past the trepidation rising up my esophagus and forced the words out.

"Jack and Emily were my best friends." I set my slice of pizza down and wiped my hands on a napkin. "Jack and I trained together, then we served on the same crew for a few years. He and Emily had been together forever. The three of us lived in Tahoe for a while, in this shitty old apartment above a laundromat."

She put her plate down on the coffee table and snuggled up next to me.

"When they got pregnant with Tess, they bought a little house on a few acres outside of town, toward the national forest. They were building the family they'd always dreamed of. I was so happy for them. Jack had always wanted kids, and Emily had finally been promoted at the hospital."

Emotion welled up inside me, making it hard to speak.

She squeezed my hand, gently urging me to keep going.

"We were so close. Always spent holidays together. The day they made it legal, I stood beside them as their witness at the courthouse. After, we went to our favorite dive bar and had the best burgers ever. Emily craved them nonstop while she was pregnant. While we were there, they said they had something to ask me."

I closed my eyes and breathed. I could smell the stale beer and I could hear the country music playing on the jukebox in the corner.

"They asked me to be their baby's guardian if something happened to them." My stomach had sunk at first. I wasn't qualified to be anyone's parent. I tried to convince them to pick someone else, but they'd insisted.

"In our line of work, you have to plan ahead. Wills, medical proxy, life insurance. We joked around about it on the crew, but Emily, being a nurse, saw what could happen."

"Did they have other family?"

I shook my head. "Emily's mom died a few years ago. Jack came from a toxic, abusive home. He wanted to make sure they wouldn't have access to his kid. Eventually, I said yes. How could I not? Maybe I wouldn't have if I really thought anything would come of it."

I sipped from my bottle of water and cleared my throat.

"We toasted and laughed, and I put it out of my mind. The guys on our crew all used this attorney who gave discounts to first responders. We met at her office, and I signed the paperwork the week before Tess was born."

My eyes stung with tears at the memory of Jack hugging me after, thanking me so sincerely for what I was doing. To me, it was a small thing. Nothing more than signing a few documents. To him, it meant far more. I just didn't realize it at the time.

Vic curled up against me, her head on my chest.

"What happened with the fire?"

"I fucked up." My pulse fluttered and picked up pace as I forced the words out. "We usually deployed out to fires, but this one was close to home. Right outside Tahoe. Jack was technically on paternity leave and at home."

A familiar ache settled in my stomach as I stroked Vic's hair. Running my fingers through the silky strands always helped settle me.

"I was given command of the west front of the fire. It was weak then, but it gained significant strength as the day went on.

"Jack could have stayed home." I bit back a sob. Fuck, he should have. "But he chose to suit up and join us. A fire close to home like that one? It was personal. There was no way he was going to sit out."

I ran my tongue over my teeth, collecting my thoughts. I hadn't spoken aloud about this in almost a year.

"He was on the east side, doing analytics and taking out

Axe Backwards

potential brush. The plan was to build up the firewall to keep it away from the town center. Tahoe City is small, but the area around the lake is densely populated. We calculated the wind speed and direction, the terrain, and fuel density.

"But..." I swallowed past the lump in my throat. "But it turned. Bay laurel goes up fast. A whole crop of them caught fire, and the blaze moved farther south than we'd anticipated. We issued evacuation orders, but by the time I realized it was heading toward Jack and Emily's house, it was moving too fast. The terrain was pure tinder."

With a gasp, Vic clutched my T-shirt.

"We sent a crew over there, then I jumped in a truck and went myself, panicking and spiraling. When we'd come in the day before, we'd anticipated northern movement."

My heart pounded so hard I could feel it in my toenails and blood whooshed in my ears. I'd broken out in a cold sweat, and my tongue felt too big for my mouth.

"Emily had tried to drive out but couldn't get around some downed trees. She walked out toward the main road with Tess. She'd put a respirator on the baby and secured it to her tiny face with tape. But she only had the one. When we found her, she was staggering. I don't know how she was still on her feet. She was wheezing and coughed the whole way to the hospital."

A wave of grief swept through me as images of my friend hit me one after another. Eyes closed, I took a deep breath and steeled my spine. I'd made it this far. I had to get through the rest.

"But the damage to her lungs was too severe." This time, a sob made its way out of me before I could stop it. It felt like I'd returned to that day. To the time I spent sitting with Tess.

I cradled her tiny body while I sat beside Emily, who'd been put on a ventilator, praying for her to be okay.

I was shaking now, the fear and pain taking over.

Sitting up, Vic snaked her arms around me and held me close. She didn't speak. Just comforted me silently. It was all so fucking unfair. I'd lived with this reality for a fucking year, and I still couldn't accept it. It still felt like a nightmare I was desperate to wake up from.

"It's my fault." My heart cracked in two as I voiced my greatest shame.

She stiffened, but she didn't release me. "No it's not. You were doing your job. You've told me so many times how unpredictable fire is, how human intervention can only do so much."

It *was* my fault. It should have been me. I lived my life ready for the inevitable. My family could have handled it.

Instead, a perfect, helpless infant lost her parents.

"What happened to Jack?"

"He tried to get home to get them. Got caught behind the firebreak." I trailed off. "Fuck." I buried my face in Vic's neck. "I just hope he knew. I hope he knew I did everything in my power to keep them safe."

I couldn't hold it back any longer. All the pain and regret and guilt I'd been carrying for the last year rushed to the surface. Combined with the adrenaline and joy of the day, I broke down.

Vic held me, her head on my chest, as I cried. My tears fell right into her hair and she didn't care. I'd never felt this before. The kind of support that held me up when I was ready to crumble.

Axe Backwards

"Let's go to bed," she said gently after we'd sat, wrapped around one another, for close to an hour.

We changed in silence and brushed our teeth. I hated that she'd have to squeeze onto the twin bed with me, but she didn't seem to mind.

In the dark, she draped her body over mine, holding me tight and nuzzling into my neck. "You're not ready to hear this yet, but you will be someday. So I'll repeat it as often as I can until it sinks in."

She took a deep breath and let it out, her warm breath tickling the skin at my collarbone.

"This was not your fault. It was a senseless tragedy, plain and simple. You are not responsible. You did nothing wrong."

She clasped my hand and squeezed it tight.

"You're doing exactly what they asked you to do. They knew if they had to leave her, she'd be loved by the best man they knew. They trusted you with the most precious thing they had."

My eyes welled. I was too tired to fight back tears, so I silently let them fall.

"They live every day through her. She is how they exist in this world. I promise you, they know how devoted you are to her, and because of that, they are at peace."

She didn't look up, but she cupped my cheek and swiped at my tears with her thumb.

"So please, please, stop blaming yourself. Stop punishing yourself. Because that child needs you at your best. And she deserves it."

Chapter 36
Victoria

My hands shook as I made my way to the office of Huxley Construction. I was due to sign the contract today. I'd have to come up with a believable excuse for why I couldn't. And I needed to get more information out of Denis.

But how?

I'd reviewed everything with Parker and given her copies of the presentation and contracts. She'd laughed out loud at his tables. According to her, this was the textbook definition of money laundering.

I guess he really thought I was that stupid.

"Or he's the world's biggest dumbass," Parker had mused.

That was probably closer to the truth. Either way, she needed more time, and I couldn't sign any documents or piss off Denis in the process.

I had no plan, no strategy. Only a growing hatred for this guy and everything he stood for. I wanted to protect Noah and Tess and the entire town. This wasn't only about me anymore. It was about my home, my people, and doing the right thing.

So I showed up. Being in his presence made me sick, but I was in a unique position to help, so I'd fight to bring the guy down.

"Victoria." Charles was coming out of the office as I approached the door. He was impeccably dressed, looking like he was headed for the country club. "I'm afraid I'm running out to a meeting. Denis mentioned you were signing your contract today."

I smiled serenely. "So thrilled to work with you," I said, not quite confirming or denying.

"That's great. We'll take good care of you." With that, he strode away.

After I waited for several minutes, I was shuttled into Denis's office. He sat at his desk, laptop open in front of him. The thumb drive had been inserted into the side. If only I could get it. The damn thing probably contained enough information to end all of this and put the Huxleys away for good. But I wasn't a spy. I wasn't even particularly stealthy.

But I was a woman on a mission. I had people to protect, so I'd figure it out.

"Ready to sign? I can call the notary over."

"Not yet," I hedged, putting my coffee cup on the edge of the desk. "I have a few more questions, and you know Aunt Lou. She wants to be here too, for the 'historic moment.'" I used finger quotes and a little eye roll to make it appear as though I didn't agree. In fact, Lou knew nothing about this. She'd beat me with her cane if she thought I was getting mixed up in anything illegal. She loathed Charles Huxley.

Axe Backwards

Denis's face fell. "We really can't afford more delays, Victoria."

I swallowed, scrambling for an explanation that would placate him. "I know. But the food pantry means so much to her. I promise I'll bring her over this week to get everything sorted."

He looked at me with disdain. *Shit.*

My pulse quickened, and I broke into a sweat. But by some miracle, an idea struck.

"I actually have a question about this clause." I spread the contract across the desk and leaned over it to point out the language.

As expected, the slimy fucker lowered his attention to my cleavage and held it there for a beat too long before he stood to look at what I was referring to.

Once he was angled close, I brought my arm up to point out a random line on the document. I swung wide, clipping the paper cup I'd set on the edge of the desk.

"That's standard procedu—oh fuck." He shouted as hot coffee sloshed across the desk, soaking the papers.

"Oh no. I'm so sorry."

Panicking, he plucked his phone off the desk before it could get wet and lifted a fancy clock as well. Muttering about paper towels, he ran out of the room.

I took the opportunity to move things around, making it look like I was cleaning up. I stacked papers that hadn't been damaged by the coffee and set them on top of his laptop. As I did, I discreetly slipped the thumb drive out. Then I stuck it in the side of my bra cup.

Denis plowed into the room with a stack of paper towels. "What are you doing?"

"Cleaning up." With a chipper smile, I took them from him. "I made this mess; I'll clean it."

I wiped up the coffee, being sure to continue to move things around to create more chaos. With any luck, he wouldn't notice the thumb drive was gone.

After thoroughly cleaning the surface of the desk—and moving his laptop around three times, eventually burying it under a newspaper and a folder full of receipts—I left, promising to return with Aunt Lou to sign the contracts.

By the time I made it to Noah's, it was late.

"I was worried." He pressed a kiss to my temple. "Hard day at work? Is Mrs. Dupont giving you trouble about the proposed traffic flow for the lumberjack competition?"

I shook my head. "I had to see Parker."

He stiffened, squeezing my arms and frowning. "You didn't sign the contract, did you?"

"No. I managed to stall, but I got this." I held up the thumb drive.

"Did you give it to Parker?"

My stomach twisted into a knot. "I tried. She wouldn't take it. She said she's close to being named interim police chief, so she can't risk accepting illegally obtained evidence."

With his lips pressed together, he nodded slowly. "Okay."

"She asked me to hold on to it until she can look into a legal way to search it."

Frowning, he scanned the room, his brain working. "Are you sure you're not putting yourself in danger?"

Axe Backwards

It took effort not to laugh. "No way. This is Denis Huxley we're talking about. Trust me when I say there is nothing remotely dangerous about this guy." I draped my arms around his neck and popped up onto my toes to kiss him.

He kissed me back, his lips urgent, and I sank into his embrace. This was what I'd been craving all day. He grabbed my ass and dragged my body against him and—

"I like warm hugs."

Startled, I jumped back and spun around.

Tess sat on the living room floor, clutching her Olaf and laughing hysterically.

"You rascal." I picked her up and swung her around. After I'd kissed her cheek and blown a raspberry into her neck, eliciting more baby giggles, I turned to Noah and gave him a mock glare. "You put the batteries back in."

Hands up, he took a step back. "I'm weak. She was so sad he didn't talk anymore. You should have seen her face."

I nuzzled Tess, and she leaned into me. "One year old and already manipulating your dad. I don't know whether to fear you or worship you as my queen."

Dinner was a simple affair. The three of us sat at the tiny table while Olaf remained in the living area, occasionally piping up, unprovoked. The thing was a demon, I was certain.

"I had a call today," Noah said. "With that friend of Finn's from Emergency Management."

I perked up. "How did it go?"

He broke into a wide grin. "It was interesting. I think I'm going to apply."

My heart surged. "That's amazing." I was tempted to get

up and do a happy dance but reined in my excitement. I was known for going too far, but that was too much even for me.

"I think." He lowered his head and cleared his throat. "I think we're going to stay for a while." With a long exhale, he studied me. "I want Tess to grow up here, running in the woods with her cousins. And knowing my brothers, there will probably be more cousins soon."

"She's got family and friends here. And she can go to Alice's school." It was getting harder not to jump out of my seat.

He smiled. "You okay with that?"

I stood, but instead of making a fool out of myself, I climbed into his lap and threaded my fingers through his hair. "My two favorite people staying in Lovewell? Yeah, I'm okay with that."

Giddy, I kissed him.

"I want to be with you too," he said against my lips. "I know we promised to go slow, and we will. But I want you in my life. I want you in Tess's life."

I squeezed him tight. "I want to be here too."

Once Tess was down for the night, we curled up on the couch. Instead of watching *Schitt's Creek*—we'd finally started Season three—we chatted.

I took my hair down and ran my fingers through it.

"Don't do that." He frowned. "Don't put your hair down over your ears."

My chest tightened as he studied me. "But..."

He tucked a strand behind my ear and cupped my cheek. "Do what makes you feel comfortable. Your ears are beautiful, just like the rest of you."

Face heating, I put my hair back up. The whole time, I

watched him, scrutinizing his expression and finding nothing but affection and honesty.

"It's a habit," I said. "I do it when I'm nervous."

"I know, and I'm going to break you of that habit." He angled in closer. "I'm so happy you asked me to be your fake boyfriend."

The raspy quality of his tone made my heart stutter.

"I'm happy you accepted."

"It's wild to think this all started because I didn't want you to go to your sister's wedding alone. It seems so long ago."

It did feel like ages ago, and I was so happy to have put that whole experience behind me. Cheeks warming, I hung my head. "I still can't believe I had to bring a fake date to my sister's wedding to my ex-husband. I should be on a Bravo show."

He brought a finger to the underside of my chin and forced me to look at him. "There is nothing I won't do for you. If you need me to fake being your boyfriend, your husband, anything, I'll do it without hesitation. Hell, I'll fake being an astronaut for you."

"Aw." I tilted close and brought my lips to his.

With a groan, he pulled me into his lap, situating me so I could feel every inch of him.

Tongues tangling, we relished one another. I soaked in his warmth and his scent, dragging my nails up his back, loving the feel of his muscles beneath my fingers.

His touch was intoxicating. For so long, I'd lived without physical intimacy. With him, I was constantly aching for more.

He pulled back. "Did you hear that?"

I held my breath and listened. After a beat, I heard it. It sounded like a chair scuffing against the floor.

Unease threaded through me. "Dylan is away for the summer."

The third tenant in our building, the one who lived on the third floor, taught science at the middle school and was teaching at a summer program in Vermont. He'd been gone a few weeks and wouldn't return for at least a couple more.

Noah tilted his head and looked up at the ceiling. "Maybe he's home early?"

I stood from the couch and held still, waiting. It wasn't long before I heard it again.

"It's coming from downstairs."

My stomach sank. My friends didn't have keys to my place, and I wasn't close with my family like that. The only person who would let themselves into my apartment was Noah.

I tiptoed over to the door, straining to hear what was going on beneath us. This building had little insulation, hence the reason Tess and Noah used to keep me up at night.

There was a scraping sound, like a drawer being pulled open. A moment later, it happened again.

Someone was downstairs, in my apartment.

My body seized up and fear trickled into my veins. Noah moved across the room without a sound and dead-bolted the door. He spun around and held his phone out.

"Go into Tess's room and call the police," he whispered. "I'll walk around and make noise so whoever is downstairs doesn't hear you calling."

Nodding, I headed to Tess's room, where the whir of the

Axe Backwards

AC unit would hopefully drown out my voice. Once I finished giving my information to the dispatcher, Noah appeared.

"Stay here," he instructed. "With Tess."

My heart thudded with dread. "Don't go downstairs," I begged. "The police will be here in a few minutes. Please stay here."

His face was a mask of panic as he pulled me into his arms. "Okay." He kissed the top of my head. "We can wait."

The police arrived in a matter of minutes. This was a small town, after all. But they found no evidence of a break in.

Officer Fielder accompanied me as I walked through my apartment, looking for items that had been disturbed, but everything looked the way it should. The door had been unlocked, but there was a good chance I'd left it that way when I went upstairs, in a rush to see Noah and Tess.

After Officer Fielder instructed me to lock my doors and call if I discovered anything was amiss, the police left.

And I felt like an idiot.

"I heard it," I insisted. To myself and to Noah.

"I heard it too." He held me tight. "Someone was in your apartment. The good news is they didn't take anything or do any damage. You'll sleep up here tonight, and tomorrow, we'll get new locks, okay?"

We stood like that, locked in one another's embrace, for a moment. This entire day had been unsettling.

As we lay in bed, his body wrapped around mine, I whispered, "Do you think it was Denis? Do you think he came back for his thumb drive?"

Noah didn't respond at first, his breathing remaining

steady. "I don't know," he admitted eventually. "And I hate to think something like this happened because of my family."

"No one made me take it."

He hugged me closer. "I know, but it all leads back to my father. I worry we'll be haunted by what he did forever."

I rolled so I was facing him, squished between his thick chest and the wall, and cupped his face. "You are not your father. You are your own man. A wonderful man. And more importantly." I pecked his lips. "You're my man."

Brows arched, he smirked. "You're claiming me?" As he asked, he ground his hips against mine.

With his hard cock pressing insistently against my stomach, I suddenly wasn't tired anymore. Words weren't enough to express how much he meant to me. I'd have to show him. And I needed to feel him inside me.

I kissed him gently on the lips, relishing his scent and his heat and his hands on my body. "Yes. Noah. You're mine."

Chapter 37
Victoria

With a growl, he rolled me over and pinned me to the bed. "If you're claiming me, then I get to claim you right back."

He lowered himself and kissed the hollow of my throat.

"This?" he said, his fingers gently caressing my pulse point. "Mine."

In one swift move, he whipped my oversized T-shirt off. Then his lips were on my skin, leaving a trail of feathery kisses along my clavicle.

"And these." He squeezed one breast, then gently bit each of my nipples. "Also mine."

Core tightening, I arched off the bed.

He pulled back, his blue eyes burning like flames. "You think I'm done? I have so much of you left to claim."

I could lie back and let him have his way with me, but where would be the fun in that? So with all the strength I had, I flipped him over and pinned him to the wall, since the bed was so small, then pushed up onto my knees.

"This is unfair," I teased. "I'm naked and you're still clothed."

It took a few tugs on his shorts and a little awkward maneuvering in the tight space, but eventually, his cock sprang free.

"That's what I'm talking about." Eyes locked with his, I lowered myself and ghosted my lips over his tip.

His leg muscles involuntarily clenched, and my core responded by doing the same.

"If we're claiming body parts," I said, trailing my fingers up his length. "Then I'm gonna go for it."

Lips parted, I took him into my mouth until he hit the back of my throat.

I pulled back, running my tongue along him, and when I reached the crown, I smacked my lips and savored the taste of the salty bead forming there. "Mine."

"All yours," he gritted out. "Anything you want." He nodded, the movement jerky, the sheets clenched in his fists.

God, he was gorgeous like this, all needy and wound up.

Slowly, I licked up his shaft. I cupped his balls, then grazed my teeth gently over the head.

Every groan, every growl, heated my core. I teased him, taking a bit more every time, working slowly and deliberately as he struggled to maintain control.

"Your mouth," he gritted out. "Fuck, Vic. You're gonna kill me."

I smiled against the smooth skin of his dick. "Nah, you're tough, hotshot. I'll just maim you."

With one hand wrapped tightly around him, I relaxed my throat and took him as deep as I could. He pulsed and let out a string of curses. I was the one giving him pleasure, but the sensation was incredible. I clenched my thighs together, desperate to quell the ache building inside me.

After two years of celibacy, my desire had come back with a vengeance. With Noah, sex was playful and fun. He made me feel safe and comfortable.

I could tease him and try new things without fear. I didn't panic at the idea of being naked in front of him. Most importantly, I'd never laughed so much while in bed with a man. Until him, I didn't know this kind of intimacy existed.

"God," he groaned. "That's so good."

I kept at it, using my hands and mouth, ensuring no part of him was neglected.

"But I won't last if you keep at it."

I looked up, dislodging the tip of his cock with a pop. "I don't mind."

"I do." He gripped me under the arms and dragged me up until I was sprawled over him. With a moan, he kissed me roughly. "How can I claim your sweet pussy if I'm unconscious from the world's greatest blowjob?"

My face warmed, though not as thoroughly as my body.

His fingers teased at my entrance. "You can finish that job anytime. Right now I need to be inside you."

Stomach fluttering, I pushed up so his erection was pinned between us. "How do you want me, hotshot?"

Searching me, he bit his fist. "I want you every fucking way. For now, I want to look into those gorgeous eyes as I fuck you."

He hauled himself up, then flipped us around so I was flat on my back. Looming over me, he tore his shirt off and pulled a condom from the drawer.

"Spread wide for me." He pushed my thighs open, then dove in, licking up my seam.

"Soaking wet and fucking delicious, as always." He brought one knee up, then the other. Then he gripped the headboard and lined himself up at my entrance.

As he pushed inside me, I cried out. The friction and delicious fullness were too much to bear. I looped my arms around his neck and pulled him close. As I devoured his mouth, I raked my nails over the skin of his back.

His thrusts were controlled but deep, hitting me in spots I never knew existed.

"God, you were made for me," he said.

I arched up, the sensations making me dizzy, my vision going spotty.

"You are mine," he said between kisses. "And I'm all yours. Anything you want. Take it. Everything I am, everything I have. Please, Vic. Let me be yours."

"Yes," I cried, chasing my release. "I want it all."

"Good girl, because you're getting it."

He pinned my arms above my head and pounded into me. Normally, a loss of control like this made me panic. But with Noah, I was filled with empowerment. A surge of lust rushed through me as he teased my nipples with his mouth and fucked me hard. Was there anything this man could not do?

I wiggled, and he tightened his grasp. "Oh no, I'm not letting go until you come on my cock. I want to watch you come undone."

It wouldn't take much. His dirty words had pushed me close to the edge.

Head thrown back, I gasped for air. "I'm close."

Axe Backwards

"Good girl. Your pussy is tightening around me. I love watching you like this. So beautiful. So sexy."

As he pressed his lips to mine, I felt the first flutters of my orgasm. In the next heartbeat, it was barreling through me at high speed. I was clenching and screaming and thrashing as wave after wave washed over me.

Noah remained steady through it all, keeping my arms pinned above my head and telling me how beautiful I was. I was still gasping and crying when he shuddered and collapsed on top of me.

I held him tight as he panted into the curve of my neck. We lay like that, still joined, our sweat and breaths mingling, for a long time.

"You're mine, hotshot."

Chapter 38
Noah

I was impressed. The Lovewell Lumberjack Festival was a lot bigger and grander than I'd imagined. I knew Vic had been working for months, but she'd seriously downplayed the magnitude of this event.

The town common had been transformed. It had been decorated with balloon arches and plaid signs, all bearing the food pantry's logo. A massive stage had been erected, and the periphery was lined with vendor booths and food trucks. The morning air was cool, but dozens of people rushed around, already sweating, furiously setting things up.

Vic was wearing cutoff jean shorts that showed off her legs, and her plaid shirt was knotted at the waist. She looked like the Maine version of a pinup girl. Fuck. I couldn't help but grab her as she passed and plant a kiss on her lips.

Next to me, Jude cleared his throat.

I ignored him. Like it was possible to control myself around this woman.

"Hey, guys." Vic talked a mile a minute, her cheeks flushed and her eyes sparkling. "So happy you're here. We're almost finished. Jude, could you find Alice? She needs help with a few event setups."

With a silent nod, he headed off in search of Vic's friend.

"And you." She threw her arms around my neck and kissed me again.

I grasped her hips and squeezed, relishing the way my fingers dented the exposed flesh there. "I'm here. Put me to work."

"You're going to help Henri set up the food pantry booth, but first, I have a favor to ask."

She batted her long, dark lashes at me. If she'd asked for a kidney like that, there was no way I'd say no.

"Anything."

"So, your brothers are competing..."

I nodded. Of course they were. They did this stuff all the time. People up here didn't play golf or tennis. They chopped wood for sport. It was our culture.

"I was thinking you should do the boom race." She trailed her fingers up my chest and bit her bottom lip. God, she was so pretty.

But I couldn't. "Running along spinning logs? In the lake?" I shook my head, my chest pinching.

"Noah." Her shoulders slumped. "You're a super athlete. You'd be so good at it."

I looked at her in shock. Not possible.

"You run up mountains with a weighted vest while pushing a jogging stroller. You are more than capable of a little log race." She batted her eyelashes at me, and I was ready to cave.

Noah from fifteen months ago would have signed right

Axe Backwards

up for all of it, but I had to think about Tess, if I fell and got a concussion, who would take care of her?

She patted my cheek. "It's perfectly safe." It was like she could read my mind. "And..." She peered over her shoulder. "There may be another reason I'm asking."

Frowning, I scanned the crowd. "What's that?"

"Because Graham signed up to do it."

My stomach dropped. "He's still here?"

I'd gotten used to seeing Vic's mother and sisters around town. They were cold but weren't rude. But I figured Graham would have hightailed it out of here after he couldn't secure a decent cup of coffee within town limits.

"He was always so obnoxious about running his marathons." Vic wrung her hands. "It would kill me if he won." With a thick swallow, she shook her head. "I'm sorry. I'm being petty and ridiculous. Forget I even asked."

"I'm in." I fisted my hands at my sides. "I'll run, chop, climb. Anything you need, gorgeous. Just promise me I can go up against him."

Lips parted, she bounced on the balls of her feet. Then, between one breath and the next, her expression changed, and she gave me a saucy wink. "Oh, hotshot, you are so getting laid later." She patted my chest. "Now go build that booth."

With a salute, I headed off in the direction of Henri.

I guess I was a lumberjack now.

THE DAY'S FESTIVITIES KICKED OFF WITH A KIDS' competition. They were adorable and frighteningly good.

Tucker, Henri and Alice's son, could chop wood like a professional. For a gangly teen, he was shockingly strong.

After that, Merry won the teen axe-throwing competition.

Finn and Thor and Tess and I all cheered while Merry hit bullseye after bullseye.

Chest puffed with pride, Finn draped an arm over his wife's shoulders. "Adele taught her the technique."

Thor squirmed in his dad's arms, waving at his big sister.

"Just think, in a few years, these two will be out there."

I looked at the chubby babies who were morphing into toddlers more every day. I could see it. Summer festivals and days on the lake, waterfall hikes and family cookouts.

And axe-throwing, I guessed. Though I never would have considered it a childhood hobby.

"You want to go out there like your big cousin?" I asked Tess.

She shrieked and kicked her pudgy little legs.

"See?" Finn said. "She's already a Mainer."

Everywhere I looked, kids dressed in plaid darted about, their faces smeared with ice cream, having the time of their lives.

As I took in my surroundings, a peace settled over me. This place wasn't only my hometown anymore. No, with each day I spent here, it was becoming a part of me.

Vic was the perfect emcee. She spent the weekend smiling and laughing, and each time she took to the stage to announce the next event, the entire crowd quieted down to listen. She was truly the most captivating person I'd ever met, and I was certain I wasn't the only one who felt that way.

Axe Backwards

I did my shift at the food pantry booth, distributing information and accepting donations. The fees vendors paid to participate had covered setup costs, but we were banking on the cost of admission and good old-fashioned donations to get the funds necessary for the food pantry to thrive for the next year.

The silent auction held an impressive number of items, and the game booths were slammed with kids and adults alike. The Lovewell Lumberjack Festival–branded merchandise was well designed and selling quickly.

We were all praying it would be enough.

Vic found me late in the afternoon and gave me a quick kiss. Then she was off to judge the chainsaw art contest. It was epic.

Gus's carving of Clive won. The whole town had gone wild for it. He'd suggested Vic auction it off, and I had no doubt many people in town would want a five-foot-tall wood carving of a moose. It was Maine, after all.

The crowds were large, especially when Remy Gagnon got up on the main stage and competed against his brothers in the standing block chop. If the crowd was excited about Gus's carving, they were all-out feral for the guys on the stage.

After handily beating his brothers, Remy took the microphone and thanked Vic.

"Also, my wife and I, along with my sponsor, Racine Trading Company, will be making a donation of twenty thousand dollars to the Lovewell Food Pantry."

All around me, gasps and cheers sounded. But on stage, Vic lit up like a Christmas tree.

"I hope you'll join us in donating," Remy challenged his

audience. "My wife Hazel grew up relying on food assistance, so this is a cause very close to our hearts."

Hazel joined him on stage, smiling and waving. She was younger than me, and I didn't know her well, but her brilliance was widely known and respected in Lovewell, and so was the work she was doing to better the rural areas of Maine.

"And," she said, pushing her glasses up, "Remy and I will be at the food pantry booth for the next two hours. We'll be available for photos and autographs for those of you who donate."

Vic hugged them both and thanked them and the rest of the Gagnons before she announced the next event. Happiness radiated from her. Her ponytail bounced, and her eyes were bright.

She belonged here. This was her place and her purpose. The way she'd put all this together, then spent the weekend running around, fixing every issue with a smile on her face, further convinced me she was a superhero.

And the people of this town had shown up for her. They loved her just as much as she loved them. Would I ever feel that kind of connection?

I'd never belonged anywhere. I went where I was needed and did my job. I was the guy who could rappel out of a helicopter to help a person in need.

But it wasn't bravery that allowed me to do it. It was the ability to compartmentalize. To turn off parts of my brain that experienced fear.

And that was only possible because, until recently, I'd no attachments.

There hadn't been a person waiting for me at home who

Axe Backwards

would be heartbroken if I never returned. Sure, Jude and my mom would be devastated. My other brothers too. Maybe. But I'd kept my distance for a reason.

I'd built my life around the idea that no one depended on me.

That fact—and the freedom it allowed—was the foundation on which I'd built my career. It's what enabled me to do the job.

But everything had changed when Jack and Emily died. And in the time since, I'd changed too.

These days, I wanted attachments. I wanted to belong to Tess and to Vic and even to this weird little town.

I wanted to go to work, where I could help people, then come home to my family each night. I longed to spend time with my brothers on the weekends. Maybe I'd even pick up wood chopping as a hobby. The life I'd run away from, the life I'd worked so hard to avoid, now felt like the one thing that could save Tess and me.

But even if I could obtain it, how could I avoid screwing it up?

Chapter 39
Noah

"I can't believe I agreed to this."

Vic patted my cheek. "You're going to do so well."

It was after midnight before we fell into bed last night. The festivities had gone late, and there were events to prep and arrangements to be made before the second day of the festival.

Vic had been going nonstop, but she handled it all with ease and a smile.

We stood side by side, nursing coffees, while the chained logs were set up for the boom races. There was a smaller, shallower course for kids, but this was the main event.

There were eight logs, each around twenty feet long, chained together between the dock and a floating swim platform. We'd run across them and back without falling into the water as they dipped and spun beneath our feet.

It looked like fun, but if I fell ass over teakettle into the lake, my brothers would never let me live it down.

Vic rested her head on my shoulder.

Daphne Elliot

"I still can't believe how well yesterday went. It still feels like a dream."

I hummed. "The number of donations was wild."

She buried her face in my neck and inhaled. "Never in my wildest dreams did I think we could raise this kind of money. Remy Gagnon signed autographs for hours. People were practically throwing money at me. First thing Monday morning, I'm placing a huge order of diapers, vitamins, and meat. All the good stuff."

With a smile, I dropped a kiss to the top of her head. "I'm proud of you."

She shrugged. "It wasn't my doing, really. Be proud of the town. And thank freaking Remy Gagnon."

I grasped her upper arms and pulled her back so she was forced to look at me. "Don't do that. Don't minimize your accomplishments. You're creative and passionate and you work so damn hard."

A slow smile spread across her face. "Want to know what's sad? Yes, I am proud. But I still want my mom to see this. I want my parents to see what I've done and be proud of me too."

My heart cracked wide open for her. I'd only been a parent for a year, but I couldn't imagine turning my back on Tess or belittling her the way Vic's parents did.

Every comment, every snub, hurt Vic. The worst part was that it would only take the smallest, blandest compliment to appease her. She wanted so badly to share her passion with her family.

"They are coming, right?"

"I think so. Graham signed up to compete, and you know how much they adore their son-in-law." She rolled her eyes.

Axe Backwards

"Then they'll see all this"—I held out an arm and swept it from one side to the other—"and be blown away. You are a superhero, Vic. I'm incredibly proud of you."

"Thank you." She clutched the front of my shirt tight. "And thank you for signing up to do the silly race."

I raised one eyebrow. "One thing you need to know about the Heberts: we are dangerously competitive. Trust me when I say I can't wait."

"I can see that. Gus's chainsaw art? And Finn with the long saw? You Hebert boys came to play."

I straightened my shoulders. "Our family legacy might be a bit tarnished, but I'm a fourth-generation lumberjack, baby. Don't worry about me."

THE DAY STARTED WITH SPEED CHOPPING. THE LARGE number of competitors meant it had to be broken into heats. The crowd was even bigger the second day, and the line for blueberry pie at Bernice's booth was dozens of people deep.

Every person here was smiling. The whole town and many people from neighboring areas loved the lumberjack festival. All day, I'd overheard conversations about how this should be a yearly event. My cheeks hurt from all the beaming I'd done. The word *proud* couldn't possibly encompass the depth of what I felt for Vic. I only wished she'd wake up and see how incredible she was.

Tess, my mom, Adele, and Thor sat with me in the front row while Finn and Jude chopped wood. Fuck, were they good at it. I made a vow then and there to give in to Jude's assertion that he should teach me. At the very least, it would be a great workout.

Jude was on a roll, his rhythm perfect until, mid-swing, he looked up into the crowd and froze. A strange sense of dread flooded me. Something was wrong. Was he okay? Had he injured his back or something?

He stared, his jaw hanging. It was only for a moment, but in that time, the axe slid out of his grip.

Fuck.

Startled back to the moment, he instinctively grabbed it, trying to regain control.

His hand caught part of the blade.

And then there was blood.

Wordlessly, I shoved Tess into my mom's arms, then darted onto the stage. I was already grasping his arm when Finn appeared on his other side, his axe no longer in hand.

Jude blinked at me several times, his face pale.

Blood whooshed in my ears. "Are you okay? What happened?"

Willa, who was the official medical volunteer for the competition, jogged up to us and immediately applied pressure to his hand. "Doesn't look deep. Let's get the bleeding under control, and we can see if you need stitches."

She led him to the stairs, and I followed. He lifted a hand to the silent crowd, signaling that he was okay, and they erupted into cheers.

"Jude." My heart was still beating too quickly.

Willa sat in front of him and cleaned and bandaged the gash. She was right: it stretched all the way across the back of his hand, but it wasn't deep.

"What happened?"

Axe Backwards

He stared at me. "Nothing. Sorry. I thought I saw someone. Got distracted."

I huffed in disbelief. Jude? Distracted? This guy had been chopping wood since he was in diapers. Who the hell would have the power to make him lose his grip on his axe like that?

"You can tell me. It's okay."

Mom rushed in then, fussing and asking Willa questions, but I didn't take my eyes off my twin.

He shook his head, his expression shuttering.

Something was up with him. And my twin spidey senses were tingling.

Hands on my hips, I exhaled deeply. "We can talk later."

He nodded. "Don't you have to go run logs soon?"

I checked my watch, and my stomach twisted. Shit, I needed to get over to the lake. With a peck to Tess's cheek, I took off, hoping I hadn't missed the warmup.

It turned out that I should have been more worried about boom running. We were given a few practice runs to get a feel for the logs, and every time, my ass went straight into the lake. I was fast and I was agile from all my training, but I was missing something.

Graham, the asshole, had special spiked shoes. Of course he did, fucker. He was running the logs like a gymnast on a balance beam. I was shocked he hadn't done a cartwheel to show off.

Fuck, I was going to embarrass myself and Vic by losing to this popped-collar finance bro. Vic's whole family was here watching too. Alexandra wore a full-length dress that looked like it belonged on a runway in Europe as opposed to a town festival in rural Maine, but she gave me a friendly wave, which I reciprocated.

They would all bear witness to me making a fool of myself. And the asshole who had cheated on Vic—the kindest, most selfless person I'd ever met—would come out victorious.

No. I wouldn't allow it.

As I dried off, I caught sight of Gus. He stood by the edge of the lake, arms folded over his chest, surveying the scene.

"What am I doing wrong?" I asked my oldest brother as I approached him.

"Is that the guy?" He nodded toward Graham.

"Vic's ex, who cheated on her and married her little sister? Yes."

He grunted. "You gotta beat him."

"Fuck. I know, but I don't know how. He's got special shoes and weighs like a hundred pounds. I'm a moose compared to him."

Gus shook his head. "Your mechanics are wrong. You gotta angle your feet and lean forward while you run, create forward momentum and try to take fewer steps. This isn't about speed. It's about strength."

I squinted at him, dubious. "It's a sprint."

"Yes. But it's nothing like running on the ground. Trust me. Angle the feet. Focus on moving and leaning forward. He's fast, but he's got skinny legs. Once things start to really move, he won't be able to work against the momentum of the logs."

I did two more practice runs, keeping Gus's tips in mind.

Axe Backwards

Both times, I stayed upright, but I was still painfully slow.

"You're getting it. Now keep your focus on the finish. Do not look down. You'll get there." Gus surveyed the competition as he coached me.

Since there were only four sets of linked logs, we'd be doing this in heats.

In my first race, I made it down and back in one piece. I wobbled a bit, but the forward lean kept me upright. And in the end, I won.

Gus clapped me on the back, his lips quirking in a half smile.

Tess sat with my mom, shouting "da, da, da" over and over.

The sound of her voice bolstered me. So did the wink Vic gave me as I lined up for the next race.

This time I was faster. The practice had helped me to anticipate the roll of the log so I could compensate with my footing. I stepped the wrong way on the last one and stumbled forward, but I managed to get my feet under me and launch myself onto the platform. It wasn't pretty, but I finished in first place.

While the next group of guys ran, I chugged water and said a prayer of thanks that I hadn't yet ended up injured, concussed, or embarrassed.

"And now for the final race. This one will determine our boom race champion," Vic said, her voice blaring from the speakers set up around the area.

A decent-sized crowd had gathered. Damn, the pressure was starting to get to me.

The remaining four of us lined up.

Daphne Elliot

I was on one end, with fucking Graham next to me.

One of Chloe's brothers shook out his arms in preparation on the other side of him. Jack Mosely, a friend of Jude's who worked as a crane operator, stood at the other end.

With a friendly nod to Jack and Chloe's brother—I could never remember which was Calvin and which was Cedric—I bounced a little, bending my knees, trying to psyche myself up.

Gus clapped me on the shoulder. "You did good. one race left." He narrowed his eyes on Graham, then gave me a stiff nod. That was Gus speak for *beat the cheating city-boy asshole.*

I nodded in response. That was the power of Gus. He didn't need words to get his message across.

"Get out there and impress your girl. And don't disgrace the family name. Dad already did that."

The moment the starting gun sounded, I was off. The first log was the easiest. It was chained to the dock, so it moved the least. The logs in the middle were the trickiest. Dangerous too. They bobbed and spun pretty freely, especially with the others close by disturbing the water.

Keeping my breathing steady, I slowed down, focused on my foot placement, and pushed forward through the middle.

Behind me, the crowd roared, and several people screamed my name.

Focus, Noah. Lock it down.

I made it to the floating platform, turned around, and zeroed in on the finish line, pushing out all other thoughts as I took off.

Halfway across, Gus's voice rang out above the din. At

Axe Backwards

the same time, movement in my periphery snagged my attention. Fucking Graham.

No fucking way was he going to pass me. Not in my town.

Hands balled into fists, I picked up the pace, willing my burning legs to move faster as I navigated the treacherous middle. I sprinted at full speed over the last two logs and dove onto the platform.

Flat on my back, I stared up at the sky, panting.

My pulse had just stopped thumping in my ears when she appeared above me like a beautiful angel in plaid.

"You won, hotshot." Her face broke into the brightest smile.

As the fans cheered, I hauled myself up. Standing face to face with her, I not only realized that I was madly in love with her, but I was in love with this whole damn town too.

Chapter 40
Victoria

We'd done it. It still felt like a dream. Two days, thousands of visitors, and more donations to the food pantry than I thought possible. I would have to sit down tomorrow and do the math, but I was confident we'd be close to six figures when it was all said and done. The number of volunteers we recruited was unbelievable too. Chip, who ran the retiree crowd, had new folks to train, and since Alice was on summer break, she had offered to take on the rest and show them the ropes.

This town had shown up in the biggest way. The town common had overflowed with competitors, and every event for the kids hit its capacity. I never would have imagined that letting toddlers climb trees would be so popular. Thankfully, Alicia, Finn's ex-girlfriend and Merry's mom, was a lawyer and had drafted the wavers for me pro bono.

"I know what you're doing." Noah sidled up beside me and held out a cold beer. "I can see the wheels turning in your mind. Tonight, we're celebrating."

I nodded, my head bobbing a little too forcefully. When

was the last time I really had the chance to blow off steam? I was brimming with affection for this town. We'd come together and achieved something amazing. The number of people who would benefit was huge.

"Victoria." Alexandra approached, with Graham in tow, a large smile plastered across her face. "So much fun!"

My parents lingered behind them, looking out of place in their far too-fancy outfits. My dad gave me an awkward thumbs-up. My mom only stared.

"Great job out there," I said to Graham. It was the truth. I'd figured he'd be in the water after the first step, but he'd placed second.

"It was fun." He scanned the Moose, taking in the chaotic atmosphere. He held out a hand to Noah, who took it. "Well done, man. That was pretty wild."

"Thanks." Noah dipped his chin. "Hope you all enjoyed yourselves. Vic worked around the clock on the event for months, and it shows. It was a huge success. Mr. and Mrs. Randolph, did you ever imagine Victoria would be such a trailblazer?"

My cheeks heated. I appreciated Noah sticking up for me, but my family wouldn't buy it. Or they wouldn't care.

Though as that thought crossed my mind, my sister shocked the hell out of me. Alex raised her bottle of water and toasted me. Graham raised his glass of wine as well and gave me an almost genuine smile.

"She is a very capable young woman," my mother replied, her chin lifted and her nose in the air.

My heart stuttered. Holy shit. For her, that was a ringing endorsement. It was probably the nicest thing she'd said to me in twenty years. I was putting this one in the win column.

Axe Backwards

Noah nodded at them, then he put his hand on my lower back.

Taking the hint, I gave my family a tiny wave. "Enjoy the party."

Side by side, we wandered to the dart boards, where his brothers had all set up.

"That was uncharacteristically nice," I said, still trying to wrap my brain around the encounter.

I'd expected Alex to criticize my outfit, and I figured Graham would complain about the lack of proper vintages of wine. Instead, they seemed to be having a nice time. It was truly baffling.

Noah shrugged, eyes twinkling. "Or you're uncharacteristically amazing and they got tired of denying it."

With a huff of a laugh, I slapped his shoulder and headed over to the dartboard.

We drank beer, ate waffle fries, and played multiple rounds of darts. For so long, I'd been only going through the motions, doing the things I was supposed to do. I pretended to be happy in my marriage. I pretended to care about my soulless corporate job. And I pretended to enjoy living in the loud, bustling city. Every day I woke up on autopilot and did what was expected of me.

Now? Now I was fucking living. This weekend had been so much work and had taken months of planning. The number of stomachaches this festival had given me was probably in the triple digits. But it had all been worth it. Bringing the community together to benefit the food pantry was a dream come true.

I never wanted to pretend again. I wanted real and

messy and challenging. I wanted Noah and Tess and the rest of this zany town.

"I'll get the next round," I announced as Adele was tallying up the score. It was unnecessary, given the massive margin of her victory, but she insisted, nonetheless. Weaving through the dense crowd, I made it to the bar and waved at Jim, the cranky owner of the Moose, who was bartending tonight. He routinely dropped off supplies at the food pantry. He claimed they were "extra," but I saw right through him.

With five beer bottles in hand, I turned away from the bar and ran right smack into Denis Huxley.

His beady eyes narrowed, his lips curling into a smile. "Just who I wanted to see."

"Hi, Denis," I said weakly, stepping to his left so I could walk around him.

He stepped that way too, moving forward as he did, forcing me back against the hard edge of the bar top.

"Parker Gagnon filed freedom of information requests about some of our businesses," he said. "You know anything about that?"

"Sorry, I don't," I said with a forced smile.

He put his arms on either side of me, pinning me against the bar, his breath heavy with alcohol. "I know what you took," he hissed. "And I warned you about crossing—"

His body was yanked back, and then Noah was there, one hand clenched into a fist like he was going to throw a punch.

"Do not put your hands on her."

Jude appeared beside him, then Cole, Gus, and Finn. Apparently, the entire Hebert cavalry had arrived.

Axe Backwards

Denis put his hands up. "I'm just having a conversation with my business associate."

Those words nauseated me.

"We have no business to discuss," I said, pulling my shoulders back. I didn't need the Huxleys or their dirty money. This weekend had been a success, and I was more confident than ever that I could scrape together anything the food pantry still needed.

Denis scowled. "Warned you." With that, he turned and stalked away.

"You okay?" Noah took the beer bottles from me. The concern on his face instantly melted the anger building inside me.

"I'm fine. Thank you for coming to my rescue." Tilting to one side, I surveyed his brothers, who were all standing behind him, still puffed up and ready for a fight. "All of you. But I'm good. We can go back to celebrating now. Gus, you still owe me a game of darts."

Eventually, the jukebox started spitting out tunes we couldn't help but dance to. Alice and Becca twirled me around for ages, taking selfies and gushing over me in the most ridiculous way.

"Certifiable badass." Becca spun me as Britney Spears played on the speakers.

"So proud of you, sweetie," Alice said, clearly tipsy. She was the group lightweight. "I gotta find my hunky husband. He owes me a dance."

As Becca and I chugged waters and caught our breath, a firm feminine hand landed on my arm.

I peered over my shoulder, finding a striking woman

Daphne Elliot

standing behind me. "Oh. Hello, Magnolia," I said as I turned.

"Victoria." She pulled me in for a double-cheek kiss. "Congratulations. What an event. It was fun for all ages and will probably go down in town history for its success. Bravo."

Magnolia Stephens-Thomas was a tall, glamorous force of nature. I hadn't met her, but I knew who she was. Everyone did. She was a summer person who owned one of the lakefront mansions near my parents.

She lived in New York City and visited often, swanning around town in her designer clothes and trendy haircuts. Though her social status was likely more elite than my parents, she was beloved by the town of Lovewell. She happily spent her money in the local shops and went out of her way to help out. From what I'd heard, she owned a glamorous event planning company in New York and threw wild parties.

"Here." She held out a thick embossed business card. "I want to talk."

I blinked at her, my tongue suddenly too big for my mouth. Magnolia wanted to talk to me?

"I recently bought the Lovewell Inn," she explained. "I plan to renovate and reopen. I was hoping you could consult on some events for me. I need someone in Lovewell who can help get things moving."

I stood in shock, unsure what she was asking.

"I understand you're devoted to the food pantry and respect your dedication. I'd only enlist your help for the occasional project and understand you'd have to work around your existing commitments. But you're good at this, and I want to employ as many locals as I can."

Axe Backwards

I nodded, at a loss for words.

"If you've got too much on your plate already, I understand. But from what I've seen, you're creative and motivated. I need help from someone like you in order to pull off the big plans I have for the inn."

"S-sounds great," I said, finally finding my voice.

"Call me next week. We can have lunch and chat. I have so many fun ideas." With a squeeze of my arm, she turned and strutted back toward Willa and Cole.

I stared at the fuchsia business card in my hand, breaths shaky. It may not lead to anything, but the thought of the inn reopening made my heart swell. Lovewell had become more of a tourist destination in the last couple of years, and this would increase that number significantly.

Giddy and practically walking on air, I headed back over to Noah, who was standing with Finn and Adele. When I told him what Magnolia had offered, he picked me up and twirled me around. "See? I told you. Everyone in town knows how talented you are."

This man was my biggest cheerleader. There was no way I could ever repay him for what he'd done for me. I was still learning to trust myself, but with Noah by my side, I'd learned that I was capable of so much more than I'd ever given myself credit for.

He slid his hand down my arm and laced our fingers. "Let's dance. Your friends have been hogging you. I want you in my arms."

Swoon. I melted into a puddle right there.

"Okay, hotshot. I'll give you a dance."

He pulled me onto the floor and signaled Jude, who was standing guard at the jukebox.

Noah tucked me in close when the opening notes of "Love Is Like A Butterfly" played.

My heart stumbled over itself.

"Our song," he declared, pulling me closer.

We swayed together while the people in the crowded bar chattered and laughed and hollered. Like this, in the arms of the man I loved, my heart was full.

I was musing about how perfect life was at that very moment when the music stopped.

"Excuse me." Denis Huxley stood on the small stage, holding a microphone. "Hello, I wanted to congratulate Victoria and the town on a wonderful festival." He swayed slightly, his words slurring. "But there's something you should all know." He hiccupped. "Or hear, I mean."

He fumbled with his phone, each tiny movement echoing through the speakers. Then he held it up to the microphone.

At the sound of Noah's voice, I frowned in confusion. Then a wave of dread washed over me.

"*I'M SO HAPPY YOU ASKED ME TO BE YOUR FAKE boyfriend.*"

"*I'm happy you accepted.*"

"*It's wild to think this all started because I didn't want you to go to your sister's wedding alone.*"

"*I had to bring a fake date to my sister's wedding to my ex-husband.*"

"*If you need me to fake being your boyfriend, your husband, anything, I'll do it without hesitation.*"

. . .

Axe Backwards

It was us. Noah and me. The conversation he'd recorded was a private one. One we'd had while we were alone in his apartment. And it had been edited. Like this, what we were saying sounded insane. Like we were two kids coming up with some kind of elaborate prank.

As a collective gasp rang out, Denis broke into a menacing grin.

Several people turned and gaped at me. My head spun and my world imploded. I sounded pathetic. I sounded dishonest.

My heart pounded wildly and my vision went spotty.

Alice appeared at my elbow, her concerned expression only adding to my panic.

Bile rose in my throat and shame washed over me. Victoria, the pathetic spinster who'd had to bring a fake date for her sister's wedding. The pitiful single woman whose husband cheated on her with half of Boston.

All those old emotions I'd fought for months, the ones that had finally died down and become manageable, came roaring back to life. My knees wobbled, and for a moment, I was sure I'd crumple to the floor.

But Noah gripped my arm, holding me tight, even as he wore his own look of shock and confusion.

"Let's get out of here," he said, giving me a gentle tug.

I let him lead me to the exit. Every eye in the place was fixed on us, every mouth agape.

As we approached the door, I saw them. My family.

Mom and Dad stood with their arms crossed, and Alexandra's face was red, her expression murderous.

"You brought a fake date to my wedding?" she hissed.

Daphne Elliot

Noah stepped closer, his body angled in front of mine protectively. "Let me explain—"

"You are so pathetic," she spat. "Get it through your head. He chose me. I'm having his baby." With that, she took Graham's arm and stomped out the door. My parents followed silently, my mother looking positively mortified.

My knees gave out, but Noah caught me before I could hit the ground. I wanted the floor to open up and swallow me whole. I was pathetic. An utter failure. How could I delude myself into thinking I was finally worthy of respect and maybe a little admiration? God, I was an embarrassment.

"Vic. Talk to me." Noah put his arm around me, shielding me from prying eyes.

"I want to go home," I said softly. "Alone."

Chapter 41
Noah

I couldn't fucking sleep. So I paced and fought the urge to punch through the walls.

Thank God Tess was at Mom's for a sleepover. I was in no position to care for her tonight.

I dropped and did a set of pushups, then another, trying to exhaust myself. When that didn't work, I yanked headphones over my ears and tried to focus on a parenting podcast.

But I could not shake the feeling that something had broken tonight.

Her face.

The memory of her expression crushed me.

The way Vic went from triumph to utter shame in an instant. How her loud, buoyant personality was turned off in the blink of an eye.

I lay on the couch and attempted to close my eyes. I didn't have the mental energy to walk the ten steps to my bed. The bed we'd squeezed into together so many summer nights. A bed that had started as penance and had become a haven.

Sleep. Just fucking sleep.

I focused on my breathing, working to shut out my racing thoughts. But as they quieted, a strange sensation crept over me.

It was... eerie.

Pulling a pillow over my face, I resisted the compulsion to run downstairs and pull her into my arms.

Where the fuck did Denis get that recording?

My brothers had held me back from crushing his skull, and then my concern for Vic had taken over.

She powered down.

The light behind her eyes went out. In the truck on the way home, she was nothing but a shell of herself.

She stared out the window silently. Once we'd made it into the building, she'd gone into her apartment and locked the door.

Leaving me alone in the dreary hallway, desperate to help her, but utterly helpless.

The looks, the whispers. All of it.

And her sister's face.

God, those terrible people thought they'd won.

I feared they were right.

Vic had been blossoming for months, and this weekend, she'd triumphed. The town stuck up for her. She'd become such a vital part of this place, and she'd accomplished so much for our community.

Fuck.

It was too muggy to sleep.

I stood with a grunt. I'd get a glass of water, then I'd pace

Axe Backwards

and finish this podcast. Toddler brain development was fascinating. I may as well get ahead on things. I was too keyed up to even think about sleeping.

I was bringing my glass to my lips when I felt it again.

The hair on the back of my neck stood up.

Fuck. Something was wrong.

I went into Tess's room to turn on the AC unit, desperate to cut the oppressive heat.

As I stepped over the threshold, I smelled smoke.

Between one heartbeat and the next, my brain had cleared.

In the next instant, the smoke detector began to screech.

I ran into the main area of the apartment, searching for telltale signs of fire.

The stove wasn't on. There were no candles. What the fuck?

My heart seized.

Downstairs.

I stuffed my feet into my boots, then I threw the door open, leaped over the banister, and ran down the stairs. The closer I got to Vic's apartment, the denser the smoke was. It was coming from her apartment. Why hadn't her smoke detectors gone off? The building was old, but I'd replaced the batteries in hers when I'd checked mine a month or two ago.

The first floor was dark and smoky. With the neckline of my shirt pulled up over my nose and mouth, I splayed my hand on her door. It was warm but not hot to the touch, so I grasped the knob and pulled. The door wouldn't budge. It had been dead-bolted.

I twisted the knob again and pushed as hard as I could.

When that did nothing, I threw my shoulder into it. I let the calm settle over me. I could get her out.

Heart racing, I ran outside and darted to my truck. I yanked on the tailgate and popped the toolbox open. Axe and respirator in hand, I ran back into the building. I barely had my respirator in place before I was swinging.

I had no idea how the door had been jammed or tampered with, and I didn't care. I swung with everything I had and was halfway through the solid wood when I heard her cries.

"Vic," I shouted as I cleared away shards of wood. It was too dark and smoky to see anything inside the apartment. "I'm coming."

I hacked at the barrier between us, my movements methodical.

"The windows won't open," she shouted, her voice high-pitched and panicked.

I swung a final time, then kicked, sending wood and debris flying. When I stepped through the gaping hole, I finally laid eyes on her. She stood on the other side of the kitchen, arms wrapped around her torso, her face a mask of horror in the light of the flames that devoured the ancient linoleum floor.

"It's okay. I'm here."

She wore a T-shirt and cotton shorts, her feet bare, her body trembling violently.

Adrenaline coursed through my veins as I devised a plan. I was in control. I knew what to do. I'd save my girl.

"Stand on that chair," I said, inspecting her past the line of flames that was clearly caused by an accelerant. "Then jump. I'll catch you."

Axe Backwards

She nodded, her movements jerky.

The heat was overwhelming, the flames so close they singed the hair on my legs. I ignored it all. Vic needed me.

She climbed onto the chair, unsteady, and coughed. At the sound, I spiraled for a moment. Had she inhaled smoke? How much?

I pushed the thought from my mind. I couldn't worry about that now.

"Jump." I stepped forward, arms outstretched, ignoring the searing pain licking at my skin.

Without hesitation, she obeyed. As I caught her, a blistering sensation on my forearms forced me to back away from the fire quickly.

Holding her to me, I turned and pushed through the debris. In the hall, I set her down.

"Go outside and call 911," I instructed, yelling so she could hear me through my respirator. "I gotta check the third floor."

"Dylan is gone for the summer." She clung to me, her fingers digging into my burned skin. "He's not home."

I cupped her sooty cheeks. "I have to check."

With a nod, she turned. As she stepped outside, I spun and darted up the two flights of steps to Dylan's apartment. I banged on the door, and when no one answered, I kicked it in. Quickly, I flipped on the lights and swept the place. Empty except for the screaming smoke detector.

Now that no one was in immediate danger, my thoughts shifted to Tess.

I adjusted my mask and headed back to my place. In her bedroom, I snagged the large box off the top shelf of her closet and the framed photo of her with her parents that hung above her crib.

With these precious memories in hand, I raced out of the apartment. The heat was increasing rapidly. I needed to get out of here.

As I hustled down the steps, my mind was filled with thoughts of Jack and Emily.

I promise.

I promise I'll be okay. I promise Tess will be loved and cared for forever.

Sirens blared from nearby as I burst out into the night air and collapsed on the sidewalk.

My skin prickled in a way that told me I had relatively serious burns. I ripped off my respirator and took in our building. Our home. It was consumed in flames, so far gone there was no saving anything inside. A sharp pain cut through my chest. It had only been a few months, but this place had given Tess and me what we needed.

"Are you okay?"

Vic was kneeling next to me, shaking and pale and crying, hands cupping my face.

I pulled her into my arms.

"You saved me," she whimpered. "I was so scared."

"I'm here. You're here. That's all that matters."

We remained there on the ground as the engine and ladder trucks pulled up and firefighters clambered out.

When Chief Mitchell stepped out of his truck, I hopped up and ran to him.

"Started on the ground floor. There was definitely accelerant. Place went up quick. No one inside. I swept the top unit."

Axe Backwards

With a nod to me, he pressed the button on his radio and barked orders.

"The primary power is on the south side," I said, my whole body trembling from adrenaline. "There may be risk to the neighboring buildings."

Behind him, a firefighter in turnout gear was working to remove the cap from the nearest hydrant. I ran to help him and held the hose to the coupling so he could focus on using his wrench to open it up.

The police pulled up just as we got the hoses running.

The crews got to work, and, not wanting to interrupt their flow, I stepped out of the way.

As the EMTs approached, I ran back to Vic and picked her up. "She inhaled smoke," I shouted.

"I'm okay." She wiggled in my hold.

"No. She needs to go to the hospital."

Her body stiffened. "I do not."

With a grunt, I set her on her feet. But I didn't let go. Grasping her arms, I shot her a glare. "She's experienced trauma," I said, keeping my tone even. "She inhaled smoke and needs proper treatment."

The EMT eyed Vic, as if waiting for permission.

"Camden," she said. "I'm okay. Just shaken up."

"How about I get you some oxygen and take your vitals?" The EMT who Vic was apparently on a first-name basis with said.

Shoulders slumping, I gave in. It was better than nothing.

"Both of you," he insisted.

Chapter 42
Vic

Camden and the other EMT on scene gently got me settled with a blanket and an oxygen mask.

Aside from being a bit lightheaded, I was fine. But Noah was fussing over me. He was far more concerned with my well-being than his home and belongings, which had literally gone up in flames.

He wouldn't leave my side. He sat on the back bumper of the ambulance with me, wearing a matching oxygen mask and draped in a blanket like mine. His care included some bandaging on his arms and legs for the burns he sustained while rescuing me and sweeping the rest of the building. Every minute or so, he'd squeeze my hand, as if to remind himself that I was still here.

The blaze had spread to the post office next door before the firefighters could get it under control. My heart cracked wide open as I watched them battle the flames. This was all my fault.

I'd never been as terrified as I was when I woke to find flames licking across the floor of my apartment.

Daphne Elliot

After the absolute humiliation at the bar, I'd put on my pj's, taken a melatonin, and gone to bed. It was only when I heard a cracking sound that I woke up.

Drowsy and disoriented, I'd stumbled into the living area. With no clear path to the door, I'd pushed the table against the kitchen window so I could climb out, but it wouldn't budge.

I'd opened it the other day, desperate for a bit of a breeze when I was making pasta, so there was no reasonable explanation for why it was jammed.

As a crowd of neighbors gathered, shame washed through me. Between the incident tonight and the fire, I wasn't sure the citizens of Lovewell would be interested in having me around.

Noah sat next to me, a steady, silent presence. Thank God Tess was at his mother's. Just the thought that she could have been in danger made me sick with panic.

Officer Fielder, who was talking to Chief Mitchell, turned and strode our way. He had basic questions for us. Thankfully, Noah took the helm and answered most of them. He went through the details of being up listening to a podcast and smelling smoke, then rushing down to my apartment. With each word, my heart raced faster and my stomach roiled more violently. How could this have happened?

"The door was barricaded when you came down the stairs?" Officer Fielder asked again.

"Not barricaded." Noah sighed. "Someone had jammed it. I couldn't tell with all the smoke, so I went in with an axe."

The police officer raised his brows.

"Someone was trying to hurt Victoria," he gritted out, his

Axe Backwards

free hand balled into a fist on his lap. "You need to find this motherfucker."

Officer Fielder held up his pen. "Once I have the details, son, we can take the next steps."

"She was trapped in her apartment. Someone deliberately set a fire," Noah shouted, his chest heaving.

I put my hand on his arm and lowered my oxygen mask. "My windows wouldn't open, either. And the fire ripped right through the kitchen. Someone set it deliberately."

My stomach sank as details started coming together. Could Denis have been responsible? He was an entitled jerk, but he didn't have it in him to hurt someone like this, did he? I easily could have been killed. Noah too.

"Ma'am, have you been the recipient of any threats lately?"

"Yes," I said softly.

Noah put his arm around me, giving me his strength.

"I received several threats from Denis Huxley."

Officer Fielder's eyes bulged.

"He threatened me earlier tonight. At the Moose."

Jaw flexed, he scribbled in his notepad. "Why?"

"Business conflicts." I left it at that for now, not knowing how much I should reveal. I needed Parker to help navigate this. I'd been trying to help, trying to do the right thing, and I'd almost lost my life.

"He has been harassing Victoria for a while," Noah growled. "I have no doubt he's the one who did this."

The police officer hummed noncommittally, his attention fixed on his notebook.

Noah went rigid and stood, towering over him. "Denis Huxley tried to kill people tonight. It's a miracle my infant daughter wasn't home. If she had been..." He clenched his fists, his whole body vibrating. "This isn't a joke, and it's not a mystery. We know exactly who did this and why. So do your fucking job."

Officer Fielder looked up, his brows lowered. "No need to talk to me like that. I know you're shaken up."

"I'm completely in control." Noah's voice was stony. "The citizens of this town are in danger. Get your officers, investigate the scene, call the state police, call the FBI, for all I care. But go do your job and lock that motherfucker up."

Officer Fielder, looking far from rankled by the events of tonight or Noah's demands, calmly continued to jot down notes. "The fire inspector will make a report. Then we'll take photos and collect evidence. I know you've had a terrible scare and you've lost your homes. I'm truly sorry for that. I'll walk the perimeter, take some photos. Please remain here so I know where you are if I have further questions."

When Noah was seated again, his whole body heaving with angry breaths, I leaned my head on his shoulder.

"I won't let anyone hurt you," he said.

My stomach twisted painfully. Denis hadn't just hurt me. He'd hurt Noah too. The single dad who loved his baby so much he never wanted to put her down. The man working so hard to overcome the terrible trauma he'd experienced.

And I'd put him and Tess at risk with my recklessness.

"I'm so sorry." I buried my face in his shoulder. "This is my fault. I shouldn't have taken that stupid thumb drive."

He straightened, his muscles tensing. "Shit, the drive. Where is it?"

Axe Backwards

"At the food pantry," I whispered. "In a locked file cabinet."

I hadn't wanted it in my apartment after Parker had told me to hold on to it. I knew it was valuable. But I didn't think it was worth burning a building down over.

A second fire engine pulled up, this one with *Heartsborough* emblazoned across the side. My stomach sank. If they were calling in reinforcements from other towns, then the fire was *bad*.

"It's okay," Noah said, as if sensing my shock. "It's just an apartment."

My apartment. The home I'd created for myself. The cozy, peaceful space that had welcomed me when I arrived, hurting and alone. Gone in an instant.

And Noah. God, the way he'd busted down the door to save me, then insisted on making sure no one was in Dylan's place.

I wanted to hug him and slap him and make him promise never to take a risk like that again.

I'd gone to bed feeling worthless and pathetic. Now, after coming so dangerously close to losing my life, it all seemed so ridiculous. I'd been so afraid of facing my family, of facing my failed marriage, that I'd made Noah pretend to be my boyfriend.

And worse, I'd gone ahead and fallen in love with him and his daughter.

Like a pathetic pick-me woman who was so desperate for affection, I forced my way into their lives.

I'd come to Lovewell to start over. To become a version of myself I could be proud of. But lying to the town, dragging

Noah and Tess into all my baggage? That was far from the best version of me.

And now I'd destroyed his home. I'd destroyed Tess's crib and all her clothing and toys. All the memories the two of them had made here.

Noah pulled me closer. "This is not your fault." The man had become a mind reader. "All that matters is that we're safe."

It didn't feel that way. I always felt safe in his arms, but right now, with a blanket draped over my shoulders and an oxygen mask in my hand, while our homes burned in front of us, I felt more vulnerable than ever.

After we'd been cleared by the EMTs and Willa, who'd come over to do her own examination, we headed for Noah's truck. The only thing either of us wanted right now was to set eyes on Tess.

Matt, one of the full-time firefighters, walked over with his helmet under his arm.

"I found this." He held out Tess's plush Olaf. He was a bit sooty, but otherwise intact. "Strangest thing." He shook his head. "So much destruction, but this toy was fine."

He held the snowman out to Noah, and as if on cue, it said, "I like warm hugs," his creepy voice even more disturbing after he'd survived the fire.

The hair on the back of my neck stood up. "How did Olaf survive?"

"He's possessed by demons," Noah said, tossing the snowman into the back seat.

Chapter 43
Noah

It had been more than twenty-four hours since I'd slept, and I was jittery. With Tess in her carrier, I brought the tea that Alice had made me to my lips. I could only tolerate a couple of drops at a time.

She was so kind, the way she whisked us to her house, offering food and showers and anything else we might need. She fussed endlessly, wiping tears from her eyes every time the fire was mentioned.

Thankfully, she didn't mention the scene at the bar or the whole fake date to the wedding thing. While it seemed like years ago, it had happened only last night.

I smoothed Tess's hair and studied her beautiful face as she slept, so damn grateful to have her in my arms.

It had taken a few hours to get the fire out, and the building was severely damaged. The first-floor apartment was completely destroyed, and everything Vic owned was gone.

We weren't sure about my unit. I couldn't go in yet, and the fire inspectors, building inspectors, and insurance folks were all due in the next couple of days. For now, we'd lie low and wait.

But we were okay and we were together. That was all that mattered.

When we left the apartment, Vic went straight to the police station to answer more questions. I'd wanted to go with her, but she'd convinced me to get Tess and meet her at Alice's house. I wanted to be by her side to support her, and it was hard not to worry that she was pushing me away.

"We want you to stay at the cabin." Henri put his arm around Alice and pulled her in close. "It's fully furnished, so you'll have everything you need."

Vic, who had been curled up at the end of the massive couch, sat up and shook her head. "That's too much—"

"No," Alice said, using a stern tone I imagined she typically reserved for students who were sent to her office. "You need a place to stay, and it's empty at the moment."

"We have cameras," Henri said. "And loud, noisy dogs." He cleared his throat. "You'll be safe here until the police work everything out."

"I can stay with my mom," I said, focus fixed on Tess. Her rhythmic breathing helped keep me from crawling out of my skin. "She's got a crib and everything."

Vic exhaled. "I can ask my parents—"

"Absolutely not," Alice said. "You're not going to compound this trauma by forcing yourself to be anywhere near your parents. The three of you are a family. You need to be together."

I reached out, resting my hand on the cushion between us, and Vic took it, giving me a squeeze. There was no way I'd let her go to her parents' place.

"You're right." I gripped Vic's hand tighter. "We are a family. Thank you."

Alice broke into a wide smile and checked her watch, then looked over at Henri. "Should be about time, yes?"

He gave her a single nod.

"Let's take a walk."

With Tess in her carrier and strapped to my chest, Vic's hand in mine, and their two big dogs on our heels, we headed down the hill from their large timber frame house. With each step we took, Alice's smile grew and her steps quickened.

The small log cabin was charming. Between the green metal roof, the wraparound porch, and the spectacular mountain backdrop, it looked like it belonged on a postcard of Maine.

My mom's car was in the driveway. So was Jude's. And a couple others were pulled along the side of the longer driveway leading to Henri and Alice's house.

Grinning and practically vibrating with excitement, Alice threw open the door and stepped away.

My heart leaped in my chest. "How?"

The cabin was just as charming inside as outside. But what struck me was the highchair. And the pickler triangle, and the foam playmats.

"Where did you get this stuff?" I stumbled inside, keeping one hand on Tess's back.

"Look at the spare bedroom," Jude said, his shoulders pulled back with pride.

With a wave, Henri led us into a small room off the kitchen. "My brother Remy built the bookcases."

One wall was floor-to-ceiling bookcases and on the other

was a beautiful crib. A rocking chair stood in the corner, flanked by baskets overflowing with toys and blankets.

"Mom did some shopping." Jude pulled the closet door open, revealing rows of brand-new baby clothes.

"You didn't have to do all this." My voice was hoarse with emotion. It was incredible how quickly they'd gotten all this set up. We'd only been at Alice's house for a few hours.

Back in the kitchen, Mom was pulling her famous peanut butter cookies out of the oven. "Lovewell moves fast," she said, eyes glinting. "I sent a few texts, and people started showing up. The crib was Thor's. They don't need it since he's already learned to jump out of it. The rocking chair came from Pascal and Parker Gagnon."

Tears welled in my eyes and my heart clenched as she talked about all the people who'd gone out of their way to help.

"The food brigade will start tomorrow. This freezer will be full," Mom joked.

Vic was still marveling at the stocked house as I draped an arm around her shoulders and kissed the top of her head.

"What do you think?"

"I think we're really lucky."

VIC AND I LAY ON THE KING-SIZE BED THAT NIGHT WITH Tess sleeping between us. I couldn't stop staring at the two of them. I wasn't sure I'd ever sleep again. Not when I'd have to watch over my girls and keep them safe.

"Are you okay?" she asked, stroking Tess's cheek. "The fire must have brought up a lot of difficult emotions for you."

Axe Backwards

"Yes and no." I blew out a breath. "Right now I'm still feeling the adrenaline, and the fear won't go until Denis is behind bars."

She worried her lip, her focus fixed on Tess. "I did this," she whispered. "All of it. I poked the bear. He warned me not to mess with him, not to refuse his money."

Sighing, I cupped her face. "He's a violent criminal. You did nothing wrong."

"But you and Tess could have been hurt," she said, tears streaming down her face. "He's done so much damage."

"He tried, but he failed." I swiped at the tracks of moisture on her cheeks. "The fire was scary, yes. But we're okay. That's all that matters. Our things can be replaced. People can't."

She nodded tentatively, her lip trembling.

"I'm proud of you for standing up to him. For being brave enough to collect evidence and help the investigation. You're fucking spectacular."

Her body deflated. "I'm not. I'm a pathetic thirty-five-year-old woman with nothing to show for her life—"

"Stop," I said sharply.

Eyes widening, she snapped her mouth shut.

I admired Vic. Hell, I was in love with her. But I hated how she talked about herself. The way she constantly put herself down. If we were going to move forward, she had to stop.

Words had never been my thing. Expressing myself was practically impossible. Jumping out of a plane was easier than processing and explaining my emotions. But Vic had taught me to be honest with myself and others. She pushed me to be better every day and to keep going even when life felt like too much. Using the strength she and my baby girl gave me, I garnered all my nerve, ready to lay myself bare.

"When I moved back here so I could process my grief and put together a life for Tess, I never imagined I'd find a friend." I grasped her hip and gave it a squeeze. "But to find you? A best friend and the love of my life all rolled into one person? It's unfathomable."

Vic gasped and her eyes went glassy again.

"I'm ready to build forever with you. Slowly. If you're not there yet, I'll wait. But you should know that Tess and I are all-in."

The tears had returned with a vengeance. "I'm a mess," she hiccupped. "I don't deserve it."

"You deserve everything. And I'll spend the rest of my life showing you that. Our happily ever after might not be traditional, but it will be ours."

"I love you too." She smiled, her eyes shining with a mixture of joy and tears. "But I'm scared I'll mess it up. That I won't be enough for you or for Tess."

"You're already perfect." I brought her hand to my lips and kissed her fingers. "I love you. Tess loves you. This whole town loves you. You and I have been through so much, but we can rebuild. Together."

"I want that. To rebuild. But." She sucked in a harsh, stuttering breath. "You know that I can't have a baby of my own, right? I've seen all the specialists and I've been through all the tests. The chances of getting pregnant are virtually nonexistent. If you want more kids, then it's probably better that you move on before we get any more attached."

"I don't care," I said, my chest pinching tight. "Tess is not my biological child, and I love her more than I thought was

Axe Backwards

possible to love anyone. DNA doesn't make a family. Love does. If we want more kids, we'll find a way. If we don't, then we've already got an incredible one."

My own eyes filled with tears as I lay there, holding her and Tess.

Eventually, we pulled the crib Finn and Adele had brought over into the room. I couldn't bear for my baby girl to be so far away.

With Vic in my arms, I looked out at the moonlit mountains. Knowing that Jack and Emily were looking over us, I vowed to make them proud and give everything I had to the people I loved.

Our apartment had been destroyed, but it was nothing more than a place to live. A roof over our heads.

It wasn't my home.

Tess was home.

Vic was home.

And now, despite all odds, Lovewell was my home.

Chapter 44
Victoria

In the two days since the fire, we'd settled into the cabin, though we were still trying to find a sense of normalcy. Already, I missed being in town. I missed chatting with the neighbors and walking wherever I needed to go.

But the mountain was beautiful, and Alice and Henri were the overprotective siblings I'd never had. I'd also gained several brothers and sisters in the form of the Heberts and their significant others, who were constantly checking in and bringing toys and treats for Tess.

Officer Fielder, Parker, and the FBI were working together. With any luck, there would be an arrest any day now. The post office next to our building had a surveillance camera that luckily hadn't been damaged in the fire, and Denis, the pompous asshole he was, hadn't even tried to hide the massive red gas can he carried as he approached not long before I woke to find my apartment on fire. Parker had warned that because his dad had many connections, the arrest warrant had to be perfect.

Though it made sense, that didn't calm my anxiety. I needed this to be over. Only then could I breathe deeply again.

This morning, Noah had dragged me out to the Caffeinated Moose for coffee, scones, and social interaction. We sat at the big table in the window with Debbie, who was bouncing Tess on her knee while feeding her cookies, and Aunt Lou, who was cracking us up with tales of the senior hijinks at the assisted living facility.

Noah sat with his arm around me while we sipped our lattes, and I focused on regulating my senses.

All would be okay. We had each other, and the lumberjack festival had been a huge success. Once we made it through the next couple of days, I had a host of exciting things to look forward to at work.

Whatever happened, we'd navigate it together.

Just as my heart rate was leveling out again, the bell over the door jingled.

On instinct, I looked up. Instantly, I regretted it. The sight of my mother and Alex and Graham was enough to make me feel like I might throw up.

Mom and Alex were fully made up and accessorized, even though it wasn't even nine a.m., and Graham looked dressed for a golf tournament.

I silently prayed for a diversion so I could run out the back door. They were the last people on earth I wanted to see.

My mother marched straight over to us, her expression thunderous.

"What's this I hear about a fire?" She put her hands on

Axe Backwards

her hips. "You couldn't be bothered to pick up the phone and tell your mother you'd been in a fire?"

"My phone didn't make it out of the fire, Mom. And I'm okay. Thanks for asking."

She shook her head, "Great. But we still have to discuss the incident the other night." She lowered her voice. "Your father and I were so embarrassed."

My heart sank. I shouldn't be surprised that my mother cared less about my physical safety than she did about my public humiliation. Maybe one day I'd stop hoping she'd love me the way other mothers loved their children.

Before I could formulate a response, Noah was on his feet.

"Mrs. Randolph, I have no idea what crawled up your ass, but your daughter is an incredible person. The judgmental looks, the snide remarks, and the constant hand-wringing are no longer welcome in her life. You should be ashamed of yourself and of the way you behave toward your daughter."

Eyes bulging, Alex rubbed her rounded belly. "Who do you think you are?"

Noah turned slowly to face her, a slow smile spreading across his face.

"I'm the man who intends to marry her."

My heart lurched and my mouth went dry.

Graham gasped and took a step back.

"Upgrade," Aunt Lou whispered a little too loudly.

"That is, if she'll even consider getting married again. You"—he pointed at Graham—"ruined that institution for her, so thanks for that, you feckless prick."

I was pretty sure my jaw had hit the floor. Noah was

typically easygoing and silly. I'd never seen this take-no-shit version of him. Usually, my family's behavior made me feel small and insignificant. But right now I felt powerful. I was done with their shitty treatment.

Alex huffed. "Don't talk to my husband like that."

"And you? You better hope you're half the mother Vic is. She's done nothing but nurture my daughter and show love, kindness, and devotion to her since the day we met. Caring for others is her superpower. She can't bear the suffering of any child. Did you know that she doesn't pay herself? She's working her ass off for free so she can devote every penny to feeding hungry people. Tell me, what was the last selfless thing you did?"

He cocked a brow. When she didn't respond, he chuckled darkly.

Mom lifted her chin. "This is none of your business."

Noah didn't stop. He acted as though she hadn't spoken. "All she asks for in return is your respect and a little kindness. And you can't even be bothered to give her that."

Alex's face was beet red and her hands were clenched. For a moment, I worried she'd punch him square in the face.

It was about time someone told her off.

Standing beside Noah, I was hit with a rush of bravery.

I put a hand on his shoulder. "Thank you," I said. "But I can fight my own battles."

"Victoria," Mom seethed, her eyes hard. "How can you let this man speak to us this way?"

"Mom, I'm done." I shrugged.

People were staring, but I didn't care. After what I'd been through, the last thing I needed was my mother's bullshit.

Axe Backwards

"I've spent my life trying to impress you, trying to live up to the family name. Trying to be the perfect daughter. I know now that I'll never be what you want me to be. The good news is that you already have two of those daughters. So you can leave me alone."

Mom's face pinched. "You've always been such a disappointment."

Normally, those words would gut me. Today, they didn't even register. I no longer needed her approval.

"You're the disappointment." I breathed deeply and pulled my shoulders back. "After all these years, you're still insecure and superficial. You've pushed me away and you've pushed Alexandra and Elizabeth into miserable marriages. You ignore your grandkids and spend all your energy chasing status. It's a shame all your money can't buy any self-awareness."

My mother scoffed.

"Please leave," I said. "This is my home, my town, and my family."

Behind me, a chair scraped across the floor, then another and another.

Aunt Lou appeared at my side, with her cane ready to strike.

Debbie stood on Noah's other side, holding Tess.

Father Renee joined us, along with Mrs. Dupont, Chip, and Mr. Moran, who'd driven the school bus when I was a kid.

They were all standing with me.

Avoiding eye contact, Graham took Alex by the arm and led her out. My mother sniffed, then followed.

Once the door closed behind them, the whole shop erupted in applause.

Noah looped his arms around my waist and spun me around.

"I'm so proud of you." He pressed a loud kiss to my cheek.

One by one, the people around me patted my back. All I could do was beam up at the man I loved. I felt lighter than ever. I'd pushed through a big barrier today. My mother's voice had lived rent-free in my head my entire life, constantly putting me down and convincing me I wasn't good enough.

But no longer.

"Did you mean what you said?" I whispered. "About getting married."

"Fuck yeah, I did. When you're ready, of course. I want you to be my wife. And I want you to be Tess's mom."

As a tidal wave of emotion hit me, I buried my face in his chest and held on tight.

Falling in love with Noah hadn't been easy or convenient. But it was inevitable. We'd forged a bond that went so much deeper than anything I knew was possible.

In the deepest recesses of my soul, I knew he was my person. My endgame. The life we built together would be messy and imperfect, but it would be full of love.

Epilogue
One Month Later

Noah

"I can teach you axe-throwing," Adele told Vic. "It's excellent for stress relief. Come over. I set up a shipping container for training."

Vic grinned. "I've always wanted to try."

"It's easier than it looks. You just need a good coach."

Finn dropped a kiss to the top of his wife's head. "She's dangerously good with an axe."

Vic shot me a wink. I was still getting used to family dinners and spending so much time with my brothers. Waking up next to Vic every morning had been the easiest adjustment.

We were still staying at the cabin. It had turned into a fun escape for us. Most nights I strapped Tess into the carrier and walked the trails around the property until she conked out. We were considering what to do from here, but one thing was certain: the three of us would be together, as a family.

Daphne Elliot

Tonight we were at Jude's for pizza night. Denis Huxley had finally been arrested this week, so we were celebrating. During an extensive investigation, two sets of video footage and one eyewitness connecting him to the fire were discovered.

The wait had felt endless, but he was finally behind bars. He'd been denied bail, and according to Parker, he'd likely face several other charges. Vic and I could finally breathe, knowing that he would be brought to justice.

Jude had insisted on hosting our celebration. He'd fired up his fancy oven and was wowing everyone with his handmade dough. With glasses of wine in hand, we sat out on his patio, watching the sunset over the mountains while stuffing ourselves silly.

Thor and Tess toddled around the yard with Ripley the wolf-dog anxiously following them, on guard at all times. My daughter and my nephew were becoming best friends. Next week, Tess would join Thor at daycare while I began training for my new position with the Department of Emergency Management.

I'd been out of the game a long time, so I was apprehensive. My skills were rusty and I wasn't in the shape I'd been in before I took custody of Tess. These days it felt like the only thing I was good at was cutting blueberries into tiny pieces and singing the Baby Shark song. But I was excited to try something new and to feel useful again.

Normally, I'd spend my days spiraling and stressed about the process, but with Vic by my side, cheering for me every step of the way, I felt more at ease than I ever had. We'd been through a lot in the short time we'd been together. That alone filled me with hope for the future.

Axe Backwards

I had plenty more work to do on myself, but knowing that Tess and I belonged here, in Lovewell, eased many of my fears. We'd build a future right here, close to our family. I'd always live with guilt relating to Jack's and Emily's deaths, but I could give Tess a beautiful, loving childhood.

Cole was helping me negotiate with Mr. Winters, my former landlord. Since the building had been destroyed, my hope was that he'd be willing to sell the property. Vic loved living in the middle of town. From our old place, we could walk just about anywhere, and if we sat out front for an hour, we'd see half the citizens of Lovewell pass by. Once Mr. Winters had finalized things with his insurance company, I was hoping to buy it and surprise her. We could build our dream house there beside the post office and across from the coffee shop.

Vic stood and scooped Tess into her arms. With a kiss to my cheek, she sauntered inside to change our little girl into her jammies.

"You're so gone." Finn chuckled.

My chest expanded. "Yup." There was no denying it. Every day I spent with her was better than the last.

He tapped his beer bottle against mine. "Welcome to the club, brother."

We moved inside, chatting and sipping drinks. The noise was cut off when Ripley darted for the door and barked. A moment later, a knock sounded from the other side.

It was only eight p.m., but in Lovewell, it might as well have been midnight. People didn't show up unannounced this late around here.

"Got it," I said as I headed to the entryway.

On the porch, I found a tall, lanky woman I'd never seen

before. Her chin-length hair looked almost black in the dim glow of the porch light and her face was heavily bruised.

My stomach knotted at the sight. But before I could formulate a greeting, Jude pushed me aside.

"Amy? What are you doing here?" he asked. "Is that even your real name?"

"Hi Jude," she said, giving him a tiny wave. Her clothes were torn, and there was blood streaked down one arm. The move was far too nonchalant for someone who looked as if she'd just fought off a bear. "My real name's Mila."

"What's going on?" I asked.

Neither acknowledged the question. Instead, they stood, frozen, her on the porch and him inside the door, staring at one another.

"I'm here because I can help you," she said. "And I'm hoping you can help me too. Can I come in?"

Jude threw an arm out and pushed me out of the way, then he ushered her inside. The house had gone silent, and every eye in the room was locked on the stranger.

"Are you okay?" Willa stood and hurried over.

Mila glanced down at her tattered and filthy clothes and brushed her hands down her shirt. "Oh. This is nothing. I'm fine."

"I'm a doctor," Willa said, keeping her tone soft. "Can I at least examine you?"

Mila lifted a shoulder, the move making her wince. "I guess that wouldn't be a bad idea. I think I may have dislocated my shoulder. Can you pop it back in for me?"

Willa gave Cole a look, and without hesitation, he strode out the front door, probably to fetch her med kit from their car.

Axe Backwards

"It's no big deal," Mila said. "It's happened before."

Fuck. Why was she so unbothered by her injuries? We were all gaping. Jude was still frozen in the doorway, his mouth ajar.

"Weren't you reported missing?" Adele asked.

Mila pushed her hair out of her face. "I dunno. I've been in Canada for a few months. What I learned in AP French in high school really came in handy." She looked back at Jude. "Sorry I crashed your party. I wasn't sure where else to go."

"Can someone explain what's going on?" Finn asked. He'd picked Thor up and was holding him tightly. "A strange woman who's speaking in riddles and looks like she just escaped from a *Mad Max* movie appeared out of nowhere."

"Nah," Adele disagreed. "She looks like Uma Thurman in *Pulp Fiction*."

I looked back at Jude, who hadn't moved. Huh. Mia Wallace had been his dream girl when he was a teenager.

"My name is Mila Barrett. Last year my brother was violently attacked outside Hebert Timber. He's still in a coma and I've been chasing the people who did this to him." Head lowered, she blinked rapidly. "I've been tracking down the Deimos Cartel. One of the largest drug trafficking operations between Maine and Quebec. I believe someone affiliated with the cartel attacked my brother."

A hush fell over the room.

"Your father was working for them when he was arrested, and the organization has been terrorizing your business and your town for years."

A pit formed in my stomach. Holy shit. For years, my

brothers, Parker, and the Gagnons have been piecing things together, but I had no idea it was this dangerous. Fuck. My family really had been living under the constant threat of crime and violence.

Mila scanned the room, taking in her captive audience. "And I need your help taking them down."

Are you ready for the last Hebert brother?
See what happens when a mysterious woman from his past shows up and turns Jude's life upside down in
AXE-ING FOR TROUBLE
Releasing Spring 2025

Bonus Chapter

Want more Noah, Victoria & Tess?
Click HERE to read the Bonus Scene!
Warning: it will make you laugh, cry and swoon!

Acknowledgments

Thank you for taking this trip to Lovewell with me! This is my 15th full length novel, and one that is so near and dear to my heart. Like all my books, it would not have been possible without the support of several talented and dedicated people.

This, along with every one of my other books, would not exist without my team.

Morgan Leigh, I asked for help, and you jumped in with both feet, quickly becoming the MVP in my life and the person who keeps me organized and on track. I treasure your friendship and your positive attitude. No one is more willing and more capable of learning new things than you are, and I am pinching myself that I get to call you mine.

Erica Walsh, thank you for being my friend and cheerleader for all these years. From cover design to finding photos and editing blurbs, you are truly in my corner every single day. We have cried and laughed and yelled together over the past four years, and I am a better person and writer because of you.

Beth, thank you for your thorough editing. I am amazed by your patience, professionalism, and kindness. Your careful work has helped bring these characters to life, and I am truly in your debt.

To my oldest friend, the indomitable Caroline, thank you for igniting my love of romance by introducing me to Jane Austen (and Colin Firth in a wet shirt) at the tender age of fifteen. My entire romantic worldview has been shaped by our shared love of happy endings and your friendship for these last twenty-seven (!!!) years is a true gift.

Becca, thank you for your professionalism and excitement about this series. You and the Author Agency have been such wonderful partners throughout this process.

Catherine, getting to know you has been one of the highlights of my year. Thank you for your marketing expertise, your passion for books, and your invaluable TikTok wisdom.

Sue, thank you for the gorgeous cover. You took a simple idea and elevated it with your immense talent. I am so grateful to get to work with you.

To my hype teams, thank you from the bottom of my heart for loving these books and this crazy world I've created. Most days, I pinch myself that I'm surrounded by such an amazing group of positive, kickass people.

Thank you to my mother, who always pushed me to do my best and believed in me even when I did not. I am the kind of person who decides to write books in my nonexistent free time because of you.

Thank you to my family for being hilarious, loving, and silly. To my children, G & T, you push me, challenge me, and surprise me every day. Being your mom is my life's greatest adventure. Thank you for never going easy on me. To G, my mini-me, you are my #1 fan and I can't wait to share my author journey with you as you grow. And T, thank you for kicking ass in Kindergarten, so I had the mental and physical space to write this book.

And finally, I'd like to thank Taylor Alison Swift. For getting me through not only the production of this book, but through all of my life's challenges for the past decade. You have taught me, and countless others, how to harness my creativity and, most importantly, how to invest in my potential. Your work has made me a better mom, writer, entrepreneur, and person. Thank you.

Also by Daphne Elliot

LOVEWELL

The Lovewell Lumberjacks Series

Wood You Be Mine?

Wood You Marry Me?

Wood You Rather?

Wood Riddance

The Maine Lumberjacks Series

Caught in the Axe

Pain in the Axe

Axe-identally Married

Axe Backwards

Axe-ing for Trouble

THE MOM COMS

Mother Hater

Also by Daphne Elliot

HAVENPORT

The Quinn Brothers Series

Trusting You

Finding You

Keeping You

The Rossi Family Series

Resisting You

Holding You

Embracing You

About the Author

In High School, Daphne Elliot was voted "most likely to become a romance novelist." After spending the last decade as a corporate lawyer, she has finally embraced her destiny. Her small town steamy novels are filled with flirty banter, sexy hijinks, and lots and lots of heart.

Where to find Daphne:

daphneelliotauthor@gmail.com

Stay in touch with Daphne:
Subscribe to Daphne's Newsletter
Join Daphne's Reader Group
Follow Daphne on TikTok
Like Daphne on Facebook
Follow Daphne on Instagram
Hang with Daphne on GoodReads
Follow Daphne on Amazon

Hootie

Zeiter eye - medical
sms

NEXXUS Unbreakable
care
for fine + thin Hair

Made in the USA
Las Vegas, NV
25 April 2025